Office Affairs

Qiana Rae
Princess of Erotica Books

Princess of Erotica Books
Copyright © 2016 Qiana Rae
All rights reserved.

Cover Design: SelfPubBookCovers.com/Mystic

This book is a book of fiction. Names, characters, places, and incidents are products of the author's imagination or are used fictitiously. Any resemblance to actual events locales, or persons, living or dead, is entirely coincidental.

ISBN: 978-0-9916187-6-7

I dedicate this book to all the Qiana Rae Fans and Supporters. I love you all!

Love,
Qiana Rae

Table of Contents

Acknowledgments

Hey, y'all! I'm back and they just get better and better each time! I have to first thank my lord and savior Jesus Christ. He's the one who blessed me with this awesome talent in which I possess. Without him, I wouldn't have the creativity to come up with such wild and out of the box ideas, and what I mean by "out of the box" is my last novel, Jordyn: Risqué Behavior. If you have yet to read that one, you need to pick it up like YESTERDAY! Back to giving props to my Father God . . . Without Him, I would not have the strength to sit at my MacBook for hours at a time, writing for my life. I wouldn't have the motivation to keep pushing, even when I have writer's block. I sometimes get frustrated, discouraged, and distracted, but then I remember where my talent came from, and it wasn't given to me to waste. I think of all you fans who are waiting on the next Qiana Rae masterpiece. If it weren't for God, I wouldn't have the energy to be able to make my books a one man, or I should say, a one WOMAN show, writing, editing, and publishing my own work without the help of a middle man. The only help I need is from the man above. Lastly, but definitely not least, if it weren't for God, I wouldn't have such beautiful fans as you. I can't thank you enough for all of your love and support.

I can't leave out my BIGGEST motivator and supporter, my hubby, Devon. When I get off track, he's always there to make sure I do what I need to do to get back on track! I love me some him! Be sure to follow me on Instagram, Facebook, and Twitter – Author Qiana Rae. Much love.

Peace and Many Blessings,
Qiana Rae

Chapter One ~ Keith

My blood pressure rose as I honked my horn at the woman in the silver Camry in front of me who was sitting at a green light, putting her make-up on. Seeing stuff like that always behooved me to wonder how women could try to do a million and one things at a time without being aware of how it might be affecting someone else. My first day on my new job as Senior Editor and I was about to be late because of a woman that was more worried about covering up her flaws to probably impress some cat at her office, instead of having some regard for other people's time. Shit, whoever that man might've been probably wouldn't have noticed if she spent hours on her makeup. What women didn't realize was that men didn't really care about that. Honestly, I preferred my women natural, and what I mean by natural is, I didn't like going to bed with one woman, and waking up to a stranger. I didn't like surprises, and waking up to one was definitely not my cup of tea, especially if it wasn't a pleasant one.

I didn't think anything else could've gone wrong to try to hinder me from getting to work on time. It took everything out of me to convince the Managing Editor who interviewed me that I was capable of handling the job. Her name was Armani and I could tell she was tough and very hard to please. She looked to be a few years younger than me, putting her at around thirty, but her demeanor was all business. All I knew was that I didn't want to prove her right in her thinking she was making a mistake by giving me a chance, and definitely didn't want to start off on the wrong foot with her. I knew from experience that the worse thing to do was anger a woman who had my livelihood in her hands.

I couldn't and wouldn't go back to freelance writing. One of the reasons Armani didn't want to hire me was because I didn't have any supervisory experience. I convinced her by showing her some of my work, which I edited on my own. I kinda sold her on it, but could tell she still had her doubts about me. I was going into this determined to make it work. I had expensive taste, and freelance writing definitely wasn't paying the type of bills that I had incurred. I had women lined up to help a brotha' out, but what real man wants to continue to live off of women? That was just giving women way too much power over my life and that wasn't what I was about.

When I finally pulled up to the building where one of the hottest magazines was produced, I looked at the clock on the dashboard of my black Range Rover and it was already five after eight. I was five minutes late and was not looking forward to the repercussions of my unpunctuality. I grabbed my briefcase, which I purchased just so I could at least look important to go along with the importance of my job title. As a writer, all I ever carried with me was my MacBook carrier, which held my laptop and documents. That's all I ever needed. I also invested in some slacks and dress shirts because I was used to being able to wear Levis and t-shirts for whatever was going on. Armani went over the job description and expectations with me, but I honestly still didn't know what to expect. During the majority of our interview I was gazing into her stern, but sexy eyes. She was a very attractive woman, but I knew she was way above the class of women that I was used to messing with, and was probably mean as hell when it came to relationships.

I quickly walked into the building of *Couture* magazine, and when I made it to the editing department, Armani was standing in the doorway to her office with her arms folded. She had on black-rimmed, rectangular shaped glasses and hair pulled back into a bun, looking like she was going for the naughty school-teacher look, but epically failed. She was dressed way beyond her years in a long plaid skirt and blouse that was buttoned so high it looked as if it was choking her. Armani's actions exuded confidence, but the way she physically represented herself was way off from that of a confident woman. Maybe I was just looking at it the wrong way. Maybe she was extremely confident with her appearance. She had to have been to come out of the house wearing something so awful. Even when I had interviewed with her, I noticed how beautiful she was, but she didn't seem to know what to do with her natural beauty or how to use it to her advantage.

"Keith, can I see you for a moment?" Armani asked before she walked into her office with her arms still folded.

As I walked towards Armani's office, I felt the eyes of the other women who were sitting at their cubicles following me. I had never been afraid of any woman, but the short time that I had known Armani, she had definitely put some type of fear in my heart. When I walked in, she was sitting on the edge of her desk, gazing at me, so I assumed she was waiting on me to explain myself at that moment.

"Armani, I'm sorry I was a few minutes late. I thought I left out in plenty enough time to get here, but there was a woman in front of me trying to put on make-up, then traffic was backed up on the expressway . . ."

As I continued with my array of excuses, Armani's dark eyes squinted and her nose and mouth turned up as if she smelled bullshit. Her light golden skin began to turn a faint reddish color, which was a bit scary. She made me feel so small, that I just decided to shut up. I put my hands in the pockets of my tan slacks and took a deep breath.

Armani stood up and said, "Really? One thing I must've forgotten to go over with you is that we don't do excuses here. Unless you are dying, there is no reason you should be late with anything. When you're late, it makes me look late, and that's never the case."

I didn't think I had given Armani enough credit about how stern she was. She was a bitch, but I had to keep my cool. She probably just wanted a reaction out of me so she could have reason to fire me, but I wasn't gonna give her the satisfaction.

"Again, I apologize, and it won't happen again."

"I'm sure," she said, with a boojie expression on her face like I disgusted her.

"Now that I've wasted valuable time on having to go over with you what I feel is common sense, we can get started with real work."

The more malicious words that came out of Armani's mouth, the angrier I became. If this was the way she initiated newbies, she was real good at it, and I was truly hoping it was just an initiation because if this was how it was going to be everyday, I didn't know how much of it I'd be able to take without snapping. I was a man and it was getting under my skin, so I could just imagine how it was for all of the other women in the office who worked under her management. I knew women pretty well. I'd had enough of them in my life to know they didn't have much tolerance for listening to another woman talk down to or belittle them, let alone, having to listen to them and do what they tell them to do because they're the boss. I wondered how high the turnover rate was in the department, due to Armani not wanting to get up off of her high horse.

The first thing Armani did was introduced me to the rest of the staff. There were several other women who were editors for the magazine and they would be under my supervision. Most of them were attractive in different ways, which made me feel like a kid in a candy store. I could see thirst written on all of their faces when Armani introduced me. I couldn't blame them. They were stuck in an office full of women for the majority of the day, every day, including some weekends. Having a man around was probably something they'd been anticipating for a long time. I just had to make sure I kept myself out of trouble by not taking advantage of that. I had to remember that I worked in supervision now, and I couldn't risk my job for a woman.

After the introductions were over, Armani showed me to my office, where I noticed my desk already had a stack of work waiting for me. She must've seen the look on my face when we walked in because I could've sworn I saw a smirk come across her face.

"We are a little behind because we've been without a Senior Editor for quite some time, but I've taken care of a lot of the work myself. I don't let one man stop the show."

Before I knew it I said, "So, you kinda need me, huh?"

Armani cut her eyes at me and sucked her teeth. "I wouldn't say, "need you" because I've been doing fine getting things done around here."

I glanced over at the stack of papers wanting so badly to tell her it didn't look that way.

She continued, "Anyway, it's not as bad as it looks, but you can handle anything, right?" she asked sarcastically.

"I sure can. I'll get started on it right now."

Armani seemed to be at a loss for words, so she ended the conversation by saying, "Ok. The stack is in order by priority, meaning, everything that I need done first is on top. There's a list of programs you'll need and where to find them on your computer in the top right hand drawer, and also step by step instructions for basically everything you need to know are right there on the desk . . . Sort of like an "Editing for Dummies" tutorial. I also took the initiative of typing out a list of your daily tasks from the beginning of your day to the end. Might I add that some days may be thrown off due to overflow of work, and you are expected to stay as long as necessary to finish the job. Any questions before I go?"

"No, I think you covered everything," I said wondering to myself what the hell I had gotten myself into."

"Good! I was hoping that's what you'd say! You know where I am if you need me."

After Armani walked out of my office with her nose in the air, I said under my breath, "This bitch got me fucked up." She made me believe that she really thought I was stupid by feeling the need to define "priority" for me. Either that or she just enjoyed trying to get under my skin. I began working, constantly being distracted by Armani's sweet smelling perfume that lingered within my office for the rest of the morning. As soon as I would even begin halfway fantasizing about her, her smart ass, sarcastic mouth popped back into my head and got me right back on track.

As I went through the stack of work, I separated stories into piles to assign to my editors. I kept some for myself, just so we could get through them even faster. I was beginning to think I hadn't convinced Armani to hire me at all. She had no choice. This stack of shit was getting bigger and bigger and I was probably the only one who was willing to take the job after she gave her big spill about the job and responsibilities that came along with it. Not only that, but she probably scared off any other prospects with her fucked up attitude.

I stuck my head out of my office and asked the ladies to come see me so that we could have a brief first meeting to get a little more acquainted with each other. Before I could even sit back down at my desk, they were all standing in front of me. My attention was immediately focused on Taryn. When Armani had initially introduced us, Taryn was sitting at her desk, so I noticed she had a very pretty face. She looked a lot younger and had beautiful milk chocolate skin. What I hadn't noticed was her hourglass shape. She had on a skin-tight dress that showed every curve of her delectable body. I really wasn't sure if it was even appropriate attire for work, but I also wasn't sure if it was my place to say so either. As a matter of fact, I might've needed to look at that every now and then to get me through each day while having to deal with Armani, so I wasn't gonna say a word.

Since my eyes were already fixated on Taryn, I stood up and handed her the first stack. I tried to look her in the face, but my eyes seemed to subconsciously drop to her voluptuous cleavage. With her being short, I already couldn't help but to look down.

"What's my deadline?" Taryn asked, batting her long, carefully placed lashes.

"With so much having to be done right now, just get as much as you can get done as fast and as accurately as you can. I'm sure Armani isn't too keen on mistakes, so accuracy is most important."

Taryn nodded, smiled, and walked out with her work. Biting my bottom lip, as I did when I saw something I liked, I watched her as she walked out of my office, until Reagan, who had also caught my attention during the introductions, started clearing her throat, trying to get my attention, and interrupting what had been the best part of my day. I was embarrassed by what had just happened, and knew I was starting off on the wrong foot. Before I could put myself in any more uncomfortable positions, I quickly handed the other girls their work so that I could continue on with my day and try to keep my thoughts clean. Reagan made sure she made it clear that she had noticed my inappropriate behavior by snatching her work from me and shaking her head as she walked out of the office. I instantly knew she would probably be another problem for me. It was always the fine ass women that had the ugliest attitudes.

My first day of work, I found myself in the office until ten that evening, but I had cut my pile down by more than half. Armani had walked past my office several times, peeking in, giving me the indication that she didn't think I was up to the challenge. She just didn't know she had motivated me to show her exactly what I was made of.

<u>Chapter Two ~ Armani</u>

Before I left the office, I peeked in on my new hiree one last time. He seemed to be a hard worker, but he also had a slick mouth on him. I had met men like him before. Just because he was very handsome, sexy, had a nice body, perfectly lined mustache, beard, and goatee, and was beyond charming, he thought he would be able to get away with anything. I wanted him to know that I was a force to be reckoned with, and he would respect me. Yes, I was a woman, and younger than he was, but I worked hard to be where I was in my career, and I expected everyone else to work just as hard if they wanted to be successful and move up within the company. I was pissed that I even had to hire his ass, but for some reason, I was unable to reach every other person that I tried to call back to tell them they had the job. Keith was the only one that answered, and was definitely my last option.

When I finally got home, before even opening up the garage, I noticed all of the lights were off in the house, which meant my live-in boyfriend, Marcus, was working late, and it would be another lonely night of watching missed recorded shows I had saved on my DVR. Marcus and I had been together for five years, and living together for the past three. We met around the same time I was promoted from Senior Editor to Managing Editor. I was out with a few co-workers, celebrating my promotion, when the sexiest man I had ever seen approached our table. He was tall, just like I liked them, had beautiful mocha skin, and a nice, low-tapered haircut. I just knew he wasn't coming to talk to me only because I was always different from most other women. I didn't feel the need to let it all hang out. I was a firm believer in saving something for the imagination and that night was no different.

I remembered it like it was yesterday. The three co-workers I was with, LaDonna, Tara, and Tamia all had on their slinky tops with their cleavages hanging all out and skirts hiked up so high that the black of their asses was showing. I had on a pair of white dress slacks with the matching suit jacket, pink blouse, and pink stilettos.

"Look at what's coming our way!" LaDonna shouted over the loud club music, as she ran her fingers through her long, blonde weave and attempted to push up her breasts that went right back to their original position.

The other two women looked up, also seeing the man coming our way, and hurriedly rummaged through their purses until they finally found their lipstick. I sat there admiring the view, not worried about what I looked like. I was always confident in myself, and if a man decided to choose a half-dressed woman over me, then I felt it was his loss and not mine.

When he finally reached our table, he smiled and said, "How are you ladies this evening?"

"We're fabulous," I said, answering for everyone, looking around the table at my girls who were sitting there smiling and gawking like they had never seen a man before. Before I knew it, this man that I had never seen before grabbed my hand and said, "Come let me talk to you for a minute."

I normally wasn't that easy, but I couldn't resist this one. Maybe it was the way that he instantly took control that turned me on. As I stood up, and followed behind as he held my hand tight, I looked back at my girls and shrugged my shoulders. I was trying to figure out if I had met this man before. He didn't seem familiar in any way, but I also knew I was never any good at remembering faces. I couldn't have forgotten that gorgeous face, though. There was just no way.

We found another table nearby, and he pulled out my chair and asked me to have a seat. Not knowing what this was all about, I slowly sat, keeping my eyes focused on him, squinting them a little, trying to see if maybe he was a man from my past that might've just looked a little different.

I gave him time to sit before I said, "What is this all about?"

"I like what I see and I want you to be mine."

"Well tell me how you really feel!" I said.

"There's no need in beating around the bush, baby. Life is too short."

"You're right about that, but can we at least start by asking each other's names?"

"But I already know yours," he said.

Looking puzzled, I said, "Really?"

"It's Beauty, isn't it?" he replied.

"Really cute," I said, blushing.

"It should be, but what is your name?"

"I'm Armani Blair."

"I love it. Armani, I'm Marcus Atkins. Very nice to meet you," Marcus said as he extended his hand across the table for me to shake.

I extended my hand, taking his into mine, smiled and said, "Nice to meet you, too."

After that night, Marcus and I continued to date and everything seemed to be perfect until he got a promotion on his job as a program director for the local news station. These days, it seemed he was never home and we never got to spend any quality time together. We used to have sex at least six out of the seven days a week, and now we'd be lucky to get it in twice a week. Between my work schedule and his, something was going to have to give before it destroyed our relationship.

When I walked into the house, the first thing I did was turned on some lights. I pulled my glasses off, and snatched the bun out of my hair, letting my jet-black hair hang freely over my shoulders. After I got comfortable, I poured myself a glass of wine and curled up on the couch, hoping my love would be home soon enough for us to at least get some lovin' in before I fell asleep.

The next morning, I woke up to my alarm clock on my cell phone, which was on the verge of dying from me not putting it on the charger the night before. The TV was watching me. I hadn't even tied my hair up like I normally did before I went to sleep. I didn't know if I was just that tired that I passed out, or if the wine had put me out, but I felt like I'd had a long night.

It then dawned on me that normally when I fell asleep on the couch waiting for Marcus, he would pick me up and carry me to the bedroom when he got home. I was hoping that this time he just went straight to bed because he was just so tired. I jumped off the couch and ran up the stairs, straight to my bedroom. The bed hadn't been touched. Marcus was nowhere in sight and I didn't know whether to be pissed or worried. Some nights at the station did run over to the point where he would end up staying the night, but he would at least call to let me know.

I immediately ran back down the stairs, hoping for his sake that I had slept through the call and he had left a message. I looked at my call log and I had no missed calls. I tried calling his cell and it kept going straight to voicemail. As I continued to call, I struggled trying to get ready for work. The day was starting off all wrong and I was hoping it would get better before it got any worse.

In my profession, I had learned to be good at multi-tasking, so I jumped in the shower with my cell phone in my hand, holding it away from the steaming hot water as I kept dialing Marcus. I left a million messages telling him to call me ASAP. My heart was beating rapidly and my emotions were all over the place. I didn't know whether calling the police would be overreacting, but I didn't know what else to do. I would've tried calling the studio, but it was so big, it would've probably taken forever for them to even find him.

After finishing my shower, I went in my bedroom and threw my phone on the bed. Since I hadn't taken the time to get my clothes out the previous night, I had something else that would take extra time out of my morning. I normally had everything together for the next day, and I probably would have if Marcus had come home and woke me up, but since that didn't happen, I had to pull shit together at the last minute, which I didn't like. I pulled out a pair of grey slacks that weren't ironed, so I laid them on by bed and briskly ran my hand across them, trying my best to get the majority of the wrinkles out, and threw them on. I threw on the first top I came across.

When I finished getting dressed, I glanced at my phone once more, and still nothing. I brushed my damp hair back into a ponytail, and finished most of my other morning rituals, having to skip a few, before rushing out the door. The entire way to the office I watched the clock and my phone. I knew I really couldn't afford to be late after the way I had scorned Keith the previous day about his tardiness. I didn't like being a hypocrite and I needed to be a good example.

When I pulled up at work, I tried calling Marcus again, and left him one last voicemail before going into the office. I was already ten minutes late, so a couple of extra minutes weren't going to make a difference. When I walked into the office, everyone looked strangely at me.

"Good morning," I said, trying to act as if everything was ok.

The other ladies looked at each other with question marks on their foreheads and dryly said, "Good morning," in unison, sounding like they weren't sure what they should say. They weren't used to me coming in so late, so I was sure they knew something was up. I walked past Keith's office, peeking in, telling him good morning.

Like the smart ass that he was, he looked at me, then at his watch before he replied, "Good Morning."

I took a deep breath to keep from saying something I'd regret later, went into my office and slammed the door. As I sat at my desk with the huge stack of papers in front of me that I had gotten behind on while I was wearing two hats, I stared at a picture of Marcus and me and shook my head. I put my hands over my face, and suddenly heard a knock at the door.

I took my hands down and said, "Come in," not really feeling like being bothered with whatever nonsense was on the other side of the door.

Keith came walking through the door, looking good enough to eat, and by the arrogant grin on his face, I could tell he knew it. I wouldn't dare give him the satisfaction of knowing I felt he was even the least bit attractive. I was just worried that my eyes would say something totally different.

I was wondering what the hell he wanted. He didn't look like he wanted anything pertaining to work due to the fact he didn't have anything in his hands to show me. As much work as there was that needed to be done, there was absolutely no time for random chitchat.

"Yes?" I said, sounding disinterested, even though I couldn't help but to be just a little curious.

Keith's entire expression changed, so I tried to lighten the mood by asking, "Is something wrong?"

"I just came to make sure you were ok. I know you don't like when people are late, and just yesterday you told me that you're never late, so I figured for you to be late, it had to have been something serious."

"Did you come in here to mock me, or to call me a hypocrite?"

"Maybe it came out wrong. What I'm trying to say is, I was a little worried and the other ladies were, too. You look like you had a rough morning."

I insecurely rubbed my hand over my hair that had begun to frizz from air-drying, and said, "Well, no need to worry. I'm fine. Traffic was just pretty bad from my direction this morning."

"Ok. Well, glad everything is ok," Keith said as he stood in front of me, uncomfortably pounding his fist inside the palm of his other hand."

Before leaving, Keith squinted his eyes and walked closer to my desk. As he got closer to me, I realized how smooth his golden skin was. Much smoother than any man's I had ever seen, and I also noticed how precise his razor lining was. I could tell Keith took a lot of pride in his appearance, which was a good thing, but on the other hand, I couldn't stand a man who thought he was prettier than a woman, and it was very evident that he was one of those who probably spent more time in the mirror than me.

I had no idea what Keith was looking at, but he was making me feel even more self-conscious.

"Is that you and your husband?"

I looked back and realized Keith was looking at a picture of Marcus and me sitting on a shelf behind my desk.

"No, I'm not married," I said defensively. "He's my boyfriend."

"Oh, ok. Nice pic," Keith said before walking out.

As he walked out the door and began walking around the corner, I realized I had been rude, and shouted, "Thank you."

A few minutes later, my phone rang and it was Marcus.

"Where the hell are you?" I exclaimed without even greeting him with a "hello".

"Baby, calm down. I ended up working later than I thought and crashed at the station."

"Ok, and why didn't you call? Do you know how worried I've been? You could've tried to have some consideration for me!" I lowered my voice to almost whispering and said, "I was late for work this morning and everyone knows I'm never late!"

"I'm so sorry. I'll make it up. My cell phone died, and this morning all the phones in the studio were in use. You know it's busy around here. I'm about to head home right now so I can at least freshen up and head back. You can meet me there if you want and I'll have a surprise waiting," he said thinking he was slick.

He thought if he gave me a good quick fuck I would forget about everything and he would be off the hook, but I wasn't dumb and I knew that story just didn't sound right. I didn't have any proof that Keith was doing something he had no business doing, but everything done in the dark always came to light.

"Marcus, now you know I can't leave work. I just got here and I look a mess!" I said. What Keith had said about me looking like I had a rough morning had obviously hit a nerve because I felt like I looked awful.

"Ok. Well suit yourself. You know where I'll be if you change your mind."

"Ok," I said, still pissed about the entire situation.

"I love you," Marcus said.

"Yeah, love you, too," I said as I hung up the phone not caring if Marcus had anything else to say.

After getting off the phone, I grabbed my purse and went into my personal powder room to make some magic happen. Keith had made me feel ashamed that I came in to work in the condition that I did. At that moment I was thanking God that I literally lived out of my purse and was able to come across a brush, comb, gel, hairpins, eyeliner, and lip gloss, which was just enough for me to make myself look presentable. Anything was better than the way I had left the house, and today would be the last day Keith would catch me slipping, as if I really cared anyway.

Chapter Three ~ Keith

I had never known a woman who kept her guards up 24/7. That is, until I met Armani. I figured she had to have either been hurt by someone in the past or she was just absolutely not a people's person. Walking out of her office, I felt like I had been read my rights just by the way she looked at me. I had to think back to make sure she wasn't one of the women I had run through that I had never given a call back to the next day. That would've been tragic! She was always short with me, but today, she seemed like something just wasn't right. Her overall attitude and appearance was completely off. I was never good with reading a woman, and knowing what they needed and wanted, unless it had something to do with sex, which was probably one of the main reasons my relationships never lasted. Armani wasn't my woman to read anyway, and I sure wasn't about to try.

When I opened the door to my office, Taryn was sitting on my desk, with half of her juicy ass hanging off the edge, wearing a tan-colored, tight-fitting jumpsuit that was unbuttoned all the way down to her cleavage.

Trying my best not to stare too hard and act as if her appearance wasn't affecting me, I gave her a casual grin and said, "Taryn, what can I do for you?"

I walked around to the other side of my desk to sit down before how I really felt became quite obvious. Taryn stood up, and bent over my desk, exposing more of her boobage, and allowing her golden brown curls to hang over her shoulders. She popped her minty smelling gum in my face and said in a provocative voice, "I just wanted to know if you had any other work you need me to help catch up on . . . or anything else you'd like me to do before I get started on my column." Taryn grinned, using her sexy dimples to her advantage.

Trying to calm myself down, I took a deep breath and acted as if I was looking around my desk for something else for her to work on.

"It doesn't look like I have anything else for you right now, so go ahead and work on what you need to for now. I'll let you know if I find anything else."

"You sure?" she asked, still smiling.

"Positive," I said, laughing subtly.

"Okaaaaay. Don't say I didn't try," Taryn said as she turned around and slowly walked towards the door.

I couldn't help but to wonder if the same thing that was going through my mind was going through Taryn's. I watched her round ass sway from side to side as thoughts of throwing her across my desk continued to cloud my head.

After I could no longer see Taryn, I still remained in a daze. She was beautiful, with only one flaw that was visible to my eyes. It wasn't really a flaw, but just a preference of mine, which was her height. She was shorter than the women I normally pursued, but everything else on her was pure perfection. I wanted to know if she had a man, but being a boss, there were just some things that would've just seemed too inappropriate for me to ask. I was sure I would eventually think of a way to get around that.

Shortly after Taryn walked out of my office, "Armeany" walked in, surprisingly with a little hint of a smile on her face. The closer she got, I realized that she had improved her appearance from when I'd seen her earlier and she looked like she was in a much better mood.

"Hey, Keith! Just stopping by to see how everything was going," she said as she sat in the chair in front of me.

"Everything's going pretty good," I said with a confused look on my face. "You look like you're feeling better."

"Yeah, I am. I was feeling like I was coming down with something. I took some Airborne and I'm feeling a lot better. So, are the girls taking well to you?" Armani asked.

I didn't know if that was a trick question, so I was very careful in answering it. "Yes, we're all getting along like a happy little family," I said with a phony grin.

"I'm sure," Armani replied under her breath.

Her cell phone went off, and as she sat there in front of me checking her message, I analyzed her face and the gorgeous features she possessed. She was the definition of a naturally beautiful woman, but just needed to turn up her sexy. As I continued to stare while she wasn't paying attention, she suddenly blurted out, "Are you fuckin' kidding me?"

I felt my eyes get big as quarters. I didn't even know what to say. She looked at me and covered her mouth.

"I am so sorry! That slipped," she said, looking ashamed. She then felt the need to explain herself, which I could've cared less as long as it wasn't directed towards me. Maybe if someone else had pissed her off, she would lay off me for a minute. "Sometimes people think I'm more than one person. Don't get me wrong, I can handle it. It just gets old!"

To help the moment feel less embarrassing for her, I said, "Shit happens!" and laughed. By the evil look she gave me, I couldn't do anything but assume that my little gesture didn't help.

"I'm gonna go. You know where to find me if you need anything," she said.

"Thanks, Armani."

After Armani left I couldn't concentrate because I wanted to know what her deal was. I would've loved to be a fly on her wall to see how she acted when none of us were around. I couldn't determine if her coldness was just a front so she could manage to maintain respect in the office or if she didn't have to put any effort whatsoever into being so goddamn evil. As far as I had seen so far, the other ladies in the office didn't seem like the disrespectful type and seemed to be very easy to work with. It would've been nice to hear what they had to say about her. It didn't seem like she got under their skin at all, so either they were used to her ways, or they just had learned to ignore it. Maybe once I got to know her better, I'd get to the point where I would feel the same way. I highly doubted it, but we would definitely see.

Before I went into the office today, I vowed to myself that I wouldn't spend my entire day there and would get out and enjoy some of the nice weather. My normal hours were supposed to be eight to five-thirty, but of course, I was expected to be flexible. When five-thirty hit, I was ready to hit the door. As I was locking up my office, the ladies were at their cubicles shuffling papers, trying to get ready to leave. I walked over to Armani's office to tell her I was leaving for the evening, but she wasn't there. I grabbed one of her fuchsia post-it notes and left a note telling her I'd see her in the morning and to have a good evening. I didn't dare want her to think I left without at least trying to let her know. She was like a ticking time bomb waiting to go off. I walked past Taryn as she stood near the entrance talking with some of the other ladies. I caught her attention and she immediately ended her conversation and began walking with me.

I noticed Reagan walking ahead of us and I had to admit, there was steep competition between her and Taryn. She glanced over her shoulder and saw us coming.

"Have a good evening, Keith," she said, throwing her thick black hair over her shoulder.

"You too!" I replied.

Taryn gave me the side eye, and knowing what that normally meant, I knew I had done something she didn't like, so I said, "You have a good evening too, Taryn."

Taryn then gave me a side grin, and I reciprocated. I wasn't sure whether to take Taryn's behavior as innocent flirtation or as subtle hints that she wanted me to smash. For now I'd just take it as flirtation until I knew for a fact that her actions meant more. I didn't want to confuse or complicate things, and definitely didn't want a sexual harassment case against me. Reagan obviously noticed the interaction between Taryn and me and felt some type of way about it. As we all walked out to the parking lot, Reagan slowed her pace, and waited 'til I was side by side with her before she began walking again. Taryn remained on the other side of me.

"You have any special plans for this evening?" Reagan asked, sounding as if I had said no, she was gonna ask me out on a date. Again, I knew women, and knew they were very vindictive. From the way Reagan had acted towards me the day before, I already knew she didn't really care for me. She was just using that moment as a tactic to get at Taryn because she knew she was interested in me. I just decided to play along with her.

"No. It's been a pretty hectic first couple of days for me, so I'll probably just relax and watch some basketball. How about you?"

Before Reagan could answer, Taryn said, "Well, since I don't have anyone to answer to at home, the possibilities are endless."

Reagan, sucked her teeth, and then acting as if Taryn was no longer walking with us, said, "You know, Keith, I'm a grown woman, but it takes some of us longer to grow up than others. You get what I'm saying?"

I opened my mouth to speak, not knowing exactly what I was about to say, but Taryn beat me to the punch and took my turn. I didn't know whether to be relieved or to get ready to break up a catfight.

"Well, I will give that to you, Reagan. You do have what, ten years on me? So yeah, I would imagine you are very mature."

At that moment, Reagan stopped walking. I knew Taryn had hit a nerve. I had learned a long time ago that one thing you don't do is mention a woman's age. I just knew some blows were about to be thrown. We all stopped in the middle of the parking lot. Reagan stepped in front of Taryn, and all I could think was, *Oh shit.*

"No, I don't have ten years on you, love, but regardless, age doesn't mean a thing. It's all about your mentality, and you still have the mentality of a child! No real man is gonna want you because you're too immature. Grow up!"

Reagan shut Taryn down to the point that she began trying to explain to Reagan what she was "really trying to say."

"Reagan, you're getting all defensive and all I was saying was that I don't have a husband or children, so I can really do what I want to do when I want to do it. You on the other hand . . ."

Reagan put her hand up in the air and said, "You know what Taryn? Forget it. You just don't get it."

Me, feeling very uncomfortable, and literally being in the middle of these two beautiful women, said, "Well, there's my car. Have a safe evening, ladies."

We all went our separate ways, and when I got in my car, all I could do was take a deep breath to regain my composure. I didn't like to boast, but I always had a weird effect on women. They just didn't know how to act.

After stopping at the liquor store to get me a bottle of DeLeon Tequila, I pulled up in front of my house to find clothes and shit all out in my front yard. The neighbors were standing around like they were waiting on a show to start. I grabbed my brown bag with my DeLeon and my briefcase and headed to the front door, which was already open. I heard mumbling and snickering coming from the spectators as I continued to slowly walk towards the door, wondering what the fuck was going on.

Everything, from my clothes to my drawers, was out on the front lawn.

Before I could get to the door, Day'ja, the chick I was living with, came to the door with a basket full of more of my clothes and threw them out on the lawn. Day'ja was extremely light-skinned, so I could easily tell when she was pissed, just by observing her skin tone, which at that moment was becoming redder by the second.

"What the fuck, Day'ja?"

"You know exactly why this is happening!" she said, with her voice and body trembling, which told me to stay as far back as possible before she started swinging.

"No, I don't. If I knew I wouldn't be asking. I just got off work from dealing with bullshit, now I have to come home and deal with it, too?"

"This is not your home! It's mine, and you had the nerve to have a bitch in my house in my bed! Do you really think I'm that fuckin' stupid, and that I wouldn't find out?"

I got nervous because, yes, I did have another bitch in her house in her bed, but my question was, how did she know? Until she showed me proof of her accusations, I wasn't admitting to shit.

"Baby, what are you talking about? Come on now. Are going by what some bitch then told you? You know better than that. These women want what you got, but I ain't goin' nowhere." I sat my briefcase and bag down on the ground and tried to give Day'ja a hug, but she refused by pushing me off.

"Muthafucka, you are going somewhere! You are gonna get the fuck out of my house. Get all of your shit before I blaze it all!"

"You don't have any proof, but gonna put me out over this nonsense?" I looked around and everyone was still staring. "What y'all looking at? This ain't nobody's business but ours!" No one moved, and I couldn't force them to, so I continued to try to plead my case.

"You want proof? I'll give you proof!" Day'ja said and stormed into the house.

I grabbed my bags I'd sat down and followed behind her because I knew for sure she didn't have anything on me. I always covered my tracks and never got caught. She ran up the stairs and I ran after her. As I followed, I felt my cell phone vibrating in my pocket. I quickly pulled it out and glanced at the screen, seeing that it was Armani calling from the office.

"I don't have time for her bullshit either," I mumbled as I hit "ignore" and stuck my phone back in my pocket.

Day'ja went straight to the bedroom and I began getting nervous and started second-guessing myself. Day'ja grabbed her cell phone and quickly began pressing buttons. Her once pale face was now completely red from crying, and eyeliner was running down her cheeks. She brought the phone over to me, showing me what was on her screen. It was a picture of one of the many chicks I had brought over. She gave Day'ja some of the most incriminating evidence she could've given her. She must've taken a picture of herself lying naked in our bed and got Day'ja's phone number out of my phone when I left the room, just so she could have something to blackmail me with, if necessary. She was salty as hell because she got all caught up in her feelings and got to acting stalkerish, so I blocked her ass and never called her again. That had been over a month ago, and she just had to go and do this dumb shit. I guess she got tired of waiting for me to come back around and decided to take matters into her own hands.

As I stared at the picture in the phone, Day'ja stood in front of me, satisfied that she had left me speechless, but at the same time looking like she was hoping I had a logical explanation for what I was looking at. She was a woman that felt hurt and betrayed, but wanted so badly to have a good reason to forgive me because she did love me. She had too much pride to have to explain to her girls, who she had probably already dogged me out to, why she let me stay.

I shut the phone off and handed it to her. She looked me in my eyes, still waiting on me to say something.

After she realized there was nothing for me to say, she folded her arms and said, "And it just had to be a white bitch!"

I shook my head and said, "Day'ja, would you have felt any better if she was Black?"

I should've kept my mouth closed. I could've sworn I saw fire in the pupils of Day'ja's brown eyes as the vein in the middle of her forehead bulged. She pointed her finger in my face and said, "Don't you dare ridicule me! I've been the one here for you helping take care of your black ass while you tried to make something of yourself! I've made sure you had a roof over your head and food to eat and this is what you do to me? Fuck another woman in my bed that I paid for? Was everything I did for you in vain?"

I kinda felt bad at that moment for what I'd done. I was sorry, but wasn't sure if I was sorry for what I'd done, or sorry that I had gotten caught. Truth be told, there had been several women I had brought home and fucked while Day'ja was away, but they stayed in their lane. As I opened my mouth to apologize, which I should've done in the first place, Day'ja cut me off.

"I don't want to hear anything you have to say. I just want you to leave. Get out!" she shouted at the top of her lungs.

I thought about trying to reason with her one more time, but I knew it would be a waste. Day'ja and I had been living together for close to a year. We met at a club, which was where I met most of the women I dealt with. It started off as one of my frequent one-night stands, but she continued to pursue me. I had laid that pipe down on her ass so good, she just couldn't let me go. That was the mistake I often made. Give them the best of my prized possession, and they instantly became addicted. I didn't know how to prevent that from happening besides finding that one person to settle down with, but this was prime example that I wasn't ready for all that. Day'ja had a lot going for herself. She was Marketing Manager for a huge make-up line and was very independent, but she just wasn't the one. I knew that from the beginning, but I decided to use the love she had for me to my advantage until I got myself to where I needed to be. I knew doing what I did to women was basically like playing a dangerous game of Russian Roulette, but I was a man who loved to gamble.

I turned around and walked out the door and down the stairs. I looked around to see if there was anything important I was leaving behind. As I started to walk out of the front door so that I could pick up my things that Day'ja had carelessly thrown out in the yard, I could hear her footsteps rapidly approaching me. I quickly turned around to see that she had pulled her golden brown hair into a ponytail, and was holding my bottle of DeLeon, which I hadn't realized I had set down. She looked like she was ready to bust me upside the head with it, which I'll definitely admit, scared me a little bit. I slowly reached for it and snatched it from her hand. She didn't resist. She just stood there motionless.

"Are you serious? You have no explanation for me and you're just gonna leave without fighting for me?" Day'ja said, sounding more hurt than I'd ever heard her.

What Day'ja didn't understand was, to me, she wasn't worth fighting for. I never developed the type of feelings for her that she had developed for me. Of course I wasn't gonna tell her that. That would've just hurt her more than she was already hurting. I did have a heart.

"Baby, this is one fight I can't win. This is probably for the best. I'm sorry," I said as I walked out the door, leaving her standing in the doorway in tears.

As I stepped off the porch and looked around, everyone had gone inside since there was nothing else to see. I started grabbing all my belongings out of the grass and putting them in the backseat of my car. Day'ja continued to stand in the doorway, fidgeting, with her arms folded. She was a beautiful woman. I never fucked with anyone who wasn't beautiful. I just couldn't understand why she was so weak. She could've probably had any man she wanted, but she decided to get attached to me. I wasn't proud of it, but I also wasn't afraid to admit that I was a man-whore. If I saw a bitch I liked, I fucked.

That was just me, and no woman thus far had been able to change that.

After I finished "packing" my shit, I walked towards the front door with caution. I knew Day'ja was liable to attack at any given moment and I had to be prepared to hold her down. She began wiping the tears from her eyes with the palm of her hand. I stood in arm's length of her waiting to see if she was calm enough for me to express a few words to her. I hated seeing her like this, but I felt like everything happened for a reason in due time, and this was the exact time this needed to happen. I wasn't happy about the way it went down, but it was best to not let this relationship linger on when I knew Day'ja's feelings would just continue to get stronger, while mine went no further than her being a homey lover friend. That's all it would ever be.

"Day'ja, before I go, I just want to say I'm sorry one more time and want you to know I appreciate everything you've done for me. Believe me, you'll thank me later. You deserve better. I'm not good enough for you."

Day'ja looked at me with a confused expression on her face. Her eyes were blood shot red and puffy from crying. I tried to make her feel better so she would know it was nothing that she did that caused me to stray.

I continued, "Some men just aren't ready for what you're looking for, and I'm one of those men. Honestly, I don't know if I'll ever be ready, but only time will tell."

Day'ja stood there, still not saying a word. I stepped closer to her and grabbed her, giving her a consoling hug. She never wrapped her arms around me. She held them to her sides, but I felt her body trembling as I held her. I kissed her on the forehead, and headed back to my car, never looking back.

As I drove through the city, contemplating what my next move would be, I got a text from Day'ja. When I checked it, I was shocked by the words that I saw. "I forgive you," the message said. I didn't know whether she was trying to coerce me into coming back, or if she was just saying she forgave me so it didn't seem like she was going to forever hold a grudge.

Whatever she meant by it, all I knew was it was over and I was never going back. Hopefully one day she would be able to accept that.

Women made things so complicated and I truly wished sometimes they could treat some situations like men treated them. If I found out my woman was messing around on me, there would be no need to discuss anything else, and I definitely wouldn't be crying over the bitch. What was so hard about that? If someone hurt you, why the hell would you want to still be with that person, or even care anything about them? I guess I would never understand. After dealing with all that stress, I needed to see the woman that I was always happy to see because she always knew how to put a smile on my face. My momma. Even though she sometimes said some things I didn't want to hear, she always kept it real with me and made me seriously think about my life. I felt like I definitely needed to hear some realness at that moment, so I headed in the direction of the old neighborhood where I grew up with my momma being there for me as both my mother and my father.

Chapter Four ~ Armani

After my short meeting with my Editor-in-chief, I headed back to my department. When I entered, the first thing I noticed was how empty and quiet it was. I walked towards Keith's office, just knowing he would still be around, trying to keep his head above water, but to my surprise, his desk was clean and he was nowhere in sight. It wasn't a good sign when, on what was only his second day of work, my Senior Editor felt like he was in a position where he could leave the office at a decent hour. Hell, I had been in my position for over five years and still would never be at that level of comfort. Feeling annoyed by the neglect he was already showing to his new position, I felt the need to call Keith and let him know that there was plenty for him to learn and do, and it was unacceptable for him to even think that it was ok for him to leave with his subordinates. He was no longer just a freelance writer and he needed to realize it.

I walked briskly to my office to get to a phone so I could get some things off my chest. Keith was going to understand after I got done with him what type of camp I ran and he wasn't about to come in and try to change that. My department was crucial to the end product of this magazine and no man was going to come in and treat it like a joke and embarrass me in front of my superiors.

When I got to my office, I noticed a post-it note, stuck to my desk with something written on it. It read: **Armani, just letting you know all work is caught up and I'm leaving for the evening. See you in the morning. Keith.**

It was nice of Keith to leave a note letting me know what he was going to do, but what I guess he didn't understand was that he didn't make those decisions on his own. He was to ask me first, and if he had asked me, he would've still been here working on something. There was never "nothing" to do in my department and I needed to let him know that, so there would be no more confusion. I rummaged through my Rolodex until I found Keith's phone number. Once I found it, I sat down and grabbed my phone, quickly dialing his number. It rang twice, and then went straight to voicemail, giving me the indication that he had looked and saw that it was me and hit "ignore." I started to call back, but decided to just save what I had for him and give it to him face to face.

I stayed at the office even later than usual. Even when I felt like I had done enough for the evening, I found something else to work on. I wasn't sure how I was going to approach the situation with Marcus. I felt like going home slapping the shit out of him, but that probably wouldn't have resolved anything, so I continued to work until I felt like I could go home and have a rational conversation with him without swinging.

I worked until I began nodding off in front of my computer screen. I looked at the clock and it was almost nine. Marcus hadn't even called to check on me and I knew exactly why. He knew I was pissed and he for sure wasn't in a hurry for me to come home. It was time for him to face the music and for me to release some of the frustration I had encountered within the past twenty-four hours. I shut down my computer, straightened my desk, and shut off all the lights.

As I walked towards our building's exit, Ben, our night security guard, who was a police officer that did security for us on the side, asked me if I needed for him to walk me out. Me, being the independent woman that I was, of course said, "No, I'll be ok, but thanks."

Ben looked concerned and said, "You sure?" It's late and pretty dark out there in that parking lot. Y'all need to see about getting some more lights out there."

"Yeah, we've already brought the issue to the attention of senior management and the safety committee, but that's at the bottom of their list of priorities."

"Safety always seems to be the least of these big company's concerns, as long as the work gets done," Ben replied.

"You can say that again!" I said.

"Well, I'm not gonna feel right about letting you walk out there alone, so you can be mad at me if you want to, but I'm gonna be your escort."

Ben was always so thoughtful, so I couldn't help but take him up on his offer. If I didn't, he was still going to walk me out anyway.

"Ok," I said hesitantly and smiled. That was probably the first genuine smile I'd had on my face all day.

When I obliged, Ben showed all thirty-one of his perfect white teeth. I say thirty-one because, in my opinion, he had flawed his smile by adding a gold tooth smack-dab in the front of his mouth. I guess women liked it, because every time I looked around, there was a different one waiting around in the parking lot for him. It was true what they said about men in uniform; women loved them. Ben looked to be in his mid-forties and wasn't the most attractive man, but when he was in uniform, I had to admit, his entire swagger changed.

As we walked out of the building, I looked up at the dark sky and noticed the full moon. "Maybe it was best that you walked me out," I said to Ben.

"Why you say that?" he asked looking over at me. He noticed that I was looking up at the sky and he looked up and said, "Yep, the crazies are definitely out tonight."

I felt Ben look over at me as we got closer to my diamond white Benz. I looked at him and said, "Is something wrong?"

"Nah. Nothing's wrong with me. I'm just wondering what's wrong you. You seem like something's on your mind."

"I just have some things I'm dealing with, but I'll be ok."

When we finally made it to my car, Ben opened my car door and told me goodnight before I got in. He stood in the same spot without moving until I pulled out of the parking lot onto the street, and through my rearview mirror I saw him walking back towards the building.

On my way home, I listened to some Goapele to try to calm my nerves some more before I made it home. Ben's soothing spirit had somewhat made me feel a little more in control of my emotions, which was exactly what I needed because going into this without that self-control could've definitely ended badly for Marcus. Maybe for me too, because I would've probably ended up in someone's jail cell.

When I made it home, Marcus' silver Audi was sitting in the driveway. I pulled up next to it and waited about five minutes before I cut the car off. I still sat there, taking one deep breath after another, feeling like each one was still not enough, and it was never going to be enough. I had so many thoughts and emotions going through my mind, I didn't even know where I was going to begin with Marcus. He had definitely pissed me off to the max this time. I couldn't remember a time when he had upset me so much and I knew it was going to take a lot for me to forgive him.

I finally decided to get out of my car and proceeded to walk slowly to the door. I sat my briefcase down on the porch as I found the key to unlock the front door. I pushed the door open and immediately heard Jamie Foxx's "DJ Play a Love Song" playing through the intercom and smelled the wonderful aroma of a home cooked meal. Realizing what Marcus had been doing this evening, my heart began beating rapidly from excitement. My anger was diminishing by the second. I grabbed my briefcase off the porch and walked into the house. The further I made it in, the more potent the aroma became.

I put my things down in the hallway and walked into the kitchen. I heard a noise from behind and looked back to find Marcus standing in the arched entryway leaning against the wall. He was wearing only a white bath towel, exposing his oiled up abs and the print that made it quite evident of just how well-endowed he was. I held back my smile, not wanting him to think I was letting him off that easily. A good meal, good music, and sex wasn't going to be the end of it this time.

"Hey gorgeous. Glad you could join me," Marcus said, showing me his sexy side grin that always instantly got me moist.

"Hey," I said nonchalantly, and walked towards him, still with a frown on my face. As politely as I could, I moved him out of my way, pushing his chest with the palm of my hand.

"Baby!" Marcus said."

It took everything out of me, but I continued to walk without looking back and went up the stairs to take a nice cold shower. After walking in on all that sexiness, I definitely needed to cool down. Surprisingly, Marcus didn't follow after me. My plan didn't go right at all. I planned to go straight in getting a bunch of shit off my chest, but as soon as I opened that front door, everything went left. Marcus knew exactly what he was doing, but I knew the game and knew how to play it even better.

After slipping out of my work clothes, I got in the shower and exhaled, trying to rid myself of all the sexual thoughts that were running through my mind. I felt weak and vulnerable and every time I felt that way, I ended up giving in to Marcus and giving him some. I closed my eyes and let the cool water run over my body. I tried to think about other things, like work. Those thoughts were quickly superseded by the image of Marcus in his towel and what I already knew was underneath that towel. I called it the Powerhouse because of the influence it had over my mind, body, and soul. It was a powerful thing.

My mind knew exactly what it wanted to do, but my body didn't want to listen so I had to give it some type of pleasure before I was back in Marcus' presence. I closed my eyes and lathered up my body with my Caress body wash. I seductively massaged my deceiving "D's". I called them deceiving because I kept them hidden to the point that no one would've even known that they existed unless I took off my shirt. I chose to hide them because I didn't want them to be a distraction from my intellect. I rolled my erect nipples between my fingers until I felt that tingling sensation between my thighs that I was yearning for. I lifted one leg up onto the shower ledge and rubbed my fingertips gently back and forth across my clit. I imagined Marcus' face as I pleased myself, using one, two, then three fingers. My body began to shake. Teasing myself, I stopped and began sucking my fingers, tasting my own delicious juices. I pulled the hood of my already swollen clit back and gently rubbed it with the tip of my finger. With my other hand, I fondled my breasts, quickly losing control of my body. As my body began to feel like it was going to erupt, I suddenly saw Keith's face in my vision, and my volcano erupted with my juices squirting all over the shower walls.

I fell to the shower floor, breathing heavily, trying to fathom what had just happened. I laid there, staring at the stream of water as it hit my limp body, until I was able to regain my composure. I finally reached for the handle of the shower door and pulled myself up. I took another deep breath and grinned, very pleased with what I was able to accomplish on my own, and proceeded to wash off all traces of my self-produced essences.

I smiled at the thought that I was able to pleasure myself so well, and my idea of what female independence meant had just been broadened that much more. I had taken it to an entirely new level. My smile then slowly left my face as my high came down and I realized that I may had just fantasized about Keith. I knew I didn't have any interest in Keith and my mind was obviously playing tricks on me because I was mad with Marcus.

I quickly erased any thoughts of Keith from my mind. When I walked out of the bathroom wrapped in a towel, I still heard music playing, but I walked slowly, hoping Marcus wouldn't sneak up on me. I was hoping he had realized I wasn't trying to be bothered with him and stayed downstairs. Obviously he wasn't done trying because when I pushed open my bedroom door, Marcus was laying there, on top of the covers, naked with his hands behind his head and dick standing at full attention.

"We missed you, baby," he said as he sat up.

"Y'all didn't miss me last night now did you?" I replied, opening up the discussion that Marcus and I needed to have. Before he could answer, I said, "Or maybe the two of you had someone else to keep you company." I carefully studied the expression on Marcus' face to see if I could predict what he was thinking.

"Are you accusing me of cheating?"

I stood there with my arms folded and said, "Are you denying it?"

"I shouldn't have to deny anything. That shouldn't even cross your mind. I'm one hundred percent faithful to you." Marcus stood up and slowly walked towards me. Each of his steps were in perfect rhythm with his words. "Why would I need anyone else when I have a gorgeous, smart, intelligent, sophisticated woman as yourself?"

I was so entranced in Marcus' words that I hadn't even realized he had opened my towel and was kneeling down, sucking on one of my chocolate nipples and fondling the other. I wanted to tell him to stop, and actually I did . . . in my head, which wasn't very helpful. Marcus then picked me up and sat me on the edge of the bed. Realizing I was about to lose my battle, I came out of my subconscious state and managed to push Marcus away from me. As soon as I tried to move, he quickly charged towards me, pushed me back onto the bed and lifted my legs behind my head. Before I had a chance to resist, Marcus' tongue was already exploring every inch of the lips between my thighs, adding to the wetness they had already acquired during our brief, but fulfilling affair in the shower.

Once Marcus' tongue touched my pussy, the battle had been lost. I fucked the shit out of Marcus, or maybe I should say we fucked the shit out of each other, and afterwards, I no longer had any sense of my prior resentment. Our actions substantiated the saying that make-up sex is the best kind of sex.

After making love, Marcus brought me dinner in bed and fed to me the steak and lobster dinner he had slaved over the stove preparing for me. He did so while continuing to plead his case that he had no reason whatsoever to run around on me. He apologized again for not being more considerate and calling me to let me know what was going on. Marcus was overall a good man. I really believed he didn't mean any harm in his actions and he deserved another chance, especially since he did admit he was wrong.

After having dinner and a glass of wine, Marcus and I laughed about how dumb he felt when I walked right past his baby-oiled up ass and went to take a shower. That's what I loved about our relationship. We were able to argue, apologize to each other, then laugh and have a good time like nothing ever happened. We had never had an argument that carried on beyond twenty-four hours. I truly believed he was my soul-mate because no one else would've ever been able to deal with me and my strong personality. I liked to run things and most of the time, Marcus allowed me to do so unless I was just being ridiculous. Even then, he would allow me to think things were going my way before bringing me back to reality.

Realizing what time it was and that we both had to get up in the morning, I turned off my lamp and Marcus reached over to turn off his. Before turning it off, he turned back to face me and grinned.

"What are you grinning about? You look like you're up to no good!"

"I'm always only up to good things when it comes to you. I have to make sure I keep you happy because I can't risk losing you."

I smiled and blushed, basking in the moment.

"Seriously, before we go to sleep, because you've made me do a lot of thinking, I can't help but to ask when we're going to make this official."

I squinted my eyes and said, "Official? What do you mean?"

"When are you going to be Mrs. Atkins?"

"Mrs. Atkins?" I said in shock. I was so shocked because during the entire five years of Marcus and me being together, we never once mentioned marriage to each other. It just had never been a topic of discussion. Not even vaguely. I personally didn't think a piece of paper validated any relationship. I had seen friends of mine get married to who was supposedly the love of their lives and it always seemed that once the papers were set in place, the once almost perfect relationship just completely went awry. That's what I didn't want to happen to Marcus and me.

"Yes, Mrs. Atkins. Armani Atkins. Doesn't that have a nice ring to it?"

I repeated it and said, "Yeah, it does sound pretty good."

"I know it does, and I'm going to make that happen, as long as you'll have me."

Marcus gave me a soft kiss on the lips and said, "Goodnight, baby," as he turned over once again to turn off his lamp.

"Goodnight," I said, and turned to face the other direction, secretly smiling.

I felt Marcus moving closer to me and eventually felt his warm body engulfing mine as we spooned. He made my insides quiver as he gave me a delicate kiss on the back of my neck. The smile that Marcus had put on my face was priceless and wouldn't leave that night until I drifted into a deep sleep.

Chapter Five ~ Keith

I pulled up to my momma's small, two bedroom, brick, ranch home, which was on the corner of the busiest intersection in the city, with my belongings filling the front and back seats of my Rover. I could remember as a kid waking up every night to the sound of police sirens, ambulances, and traffic flying through the streets. We lived in that house my entire life because my momma couldn't afford anything else. My daddy left her for another woman before I even turned one year old and never came back around. The only visual I had of my "daddy" came from pictures I had seen. I probably wouldn't have even known the nigga if I seen him on the streets, and if I did, I would've probably whooped his ass for leaving my momma in the situation that he did.

My moms knew exactly how I felt about my sperm donor because every time I saw her struggling, I made sure my ill feelings concerning him were very evident. She tried to tell me I needed to forgive him because she had. She could forgive him all she wanted, but I would never forgive him because the last thing a child wants to see is their mother struggling, and I saw it all my life. From the time I was old enough to work, I did, so I could try to help support the woman I loved more than anything in the world. I never felt like what I did was enough, but I did what I could.

As I started grabbing some of my things out of the front seat, I heard someone call my name. I looked back and saw it was one of my boys from back in the day across the street standing in front of his mom's house. Sad thing was that after all these years, he had never moved out. I put my stuff back in the car and shut the door, not needing anyone in my business. I sure as hell didn't want him to think I was homeless or some shit.

"Hey, man! What's goin' on with you?" I said, as I stood at the curb, waiting for the cars to pass.

"Nothin' much brotha'. Just been livin' this thing called life. I haven't seen you over this way in a while. I thought you had abandoned Ms. Angie over there," my boy, Troy said.

I finally made it to the other side of the street, and as Troy and I shook hands I said, "Nah, bruh, never that! That's my love over there."

I looked Troy up and down, trying my best not to make it obvious. He didn't look like he had been taking care of himself at all. He had on a dingy wife-beater that looked like someone had dragged it through dirt, and a pair of sweatpants that were rolled up at the bottom and hanging low off of his waist. He had more hair on his face that I had ever seen, which made him look grimy as hell. Grimy was never something Troy came off as. He was always clean cut and one of the best-dressed dudes I had ever seen, outside of myself. I didn't know where Troy's mindset was these days, but I was hoping I had just caught him on a bad day.

"I hear you. That's how I feel about my moms. But for real though, I thought I was gonna have to go over there and keep Ms. Angie company. She still lookin' good!"

"And she always gon' look good, Negro!" I said as I laughed at Troy's little joke.

Since kids, we always joked around about each other's mothers, but I got it the worst of all because all the boys in the neighborhood had a crush on my moms. I even had to beat a couple of dudes down because they just got way too disrespectful with the comments.

"So you still writing?" Troy asked.

"Yeah. I'll never stop. That's my other love. What you doin' these days?"

"I'm just doing little odd jobs here and there. It's rough out here for a nigga'. The struggle is real."

I hadn't seen Troy in a while, but he always had the same sad story every time I saw him. I didn't feel sorry for him because he was able bodied, but just wasn't trying. He was comfortable living up under his momma's roof and had become lazy. I never thought this would be Troy's life. He was so smart in school, always made straight "A's", and his SAT scores were in the top five percentile in the state. He was a good kid and good role model for his younger brother, Tramaine, who was five years younger than us. Troy's daddy wasn't around either, so we lived under very similar circumstances.

Before the end of our senior year, we both received four-year academic scholarships to the University of Miami. We had worked hard to make sure our moms didn't have to struggle trying to pay for us to go to college. We both applied to colleges where we'd be sure to have a good time after all the hard work we had put in academically, and we did just that for our first couple of years.

One night while out partying in South Beach during Spring break, Troy got a phone call just as we were headed on foot to our rooms that we had booked, with a couple of chicks we had planned to have fun with that night. When Troy answered, the girls and I continued to have drunken conversation with each other, laughing for no apparent reason. Troy walked a little bit ahead of us and then suddenly stopped in his tracks, dropping his phone. No matter how drunk I was, brothers always knew when something wasn't right, and I knew this had to be

serious. My smile turned into a look of concern within seconds
and I ran to catch up with Troy. When I caught up to him, his
expression was blank. I didn't know what to think. My first
thought was that something had happened to his mother.

"Troy! What's wrong, man?"

Troy didn't say a word. He began walking again without
picking up his phone. I picked it up trying to find the call log to
see who he had just talked to. The last call was from his mom's
phone. The girls finally caught back up with us and I told them
we'd have to take a rain check due to a family emergency. I
didn't know whether or not it was in fact a family emergency,
but Troy and I were like brothers, so anything that affected him
the way he was being affected was definitely going to have
some type of effect on me.

As I watched the girls walk away in the opposite direction, I
shook my head and took a deep breath only because I didn't
like to turn away pussy, but I had no choice. I continued to
walk with Troy, hoping he'd say something. I was tempted to
call his mom's phone back, but was a little afraid of what I'd
hear.

Troy stopped walking again, but this time tears streamed
down his face. I stood there in front of him, not knowing what
to do because I had never seen my brother like this.

"I should've never left. This would've never happened. It's
my fault," Troy said, with his voice trembling."

"What's your fault? What happened, bruh? Talk to me."

"My little brother is gone."

"Gone where?"

"Gone, nigga'!" Troy said violently.

I was hearing what Troy was saying, but still unable to
comprehend it. I thought I knew what he meant, but I didn't
want to believe it. Tramaine was like my little brother too, so I
became extremely worried. I could feel my heart pounding
through my chest, so I could just imagine how Troy was feeling
inside.

Even though Troy didn't seem like he wanted to say much
else, I said, "Please don't tell me he's dead. He just left the

house right? He ran away?" I said, hoping that's what Troy meant.

Troy looked me in the eyes with his bloodshot eyes and said, "No. Some muthafucka shot him not one time, but ten times! Why?" Troy said as he started hitting himself in the head with both hands and crying uncontrollably.

I tried to stay strong for the both of us, but started crying with my brother, and grabbed and hugged him. I was doing my best to be there for him in his time of grief.

When we made it back to the hotel, we chilled in my room and drank some more until we were numb inside. We couldn't cope with what was really going on and needed something to put us in a different place. We smoked some weed, which we didn't often do, but we did whatever we felt would help us make it through the night without being around other loved ones who shared the same hurt we were experiencing. After we got both drunk and high, we reminisced about the good times we had growing up. We were able to talk about Tramaine and laugh about the times he used to try to hang with the big boys, thinking he was just as old as we were. Tramaine was never any trouble. I couldn't understand why something like this would've happened to him.

The next morning, after passing out the night before, Troy and I got our stuff together that we had brought to the hotel where we had reserved rooms for a few nights with intentions on smashing a different bitch every night. We then headed back to our dorms to pack some luggage so we could get on the plane back to Chicago in a few hours. We didn't say much to each other that morning because the hurt had returned. Our fix was only temporary and now it was time for us to face what was staring us in the face.

The plane ride home seemed longer than usual. Maybe because we were so anxious to get home to find out the full story of what the fuck could've happened. On the plane, I kept glancing over at Troy making sure he was ok. He wore sunglasses the whole time and had his ear buds in his ears. He had the music blasting so loud that I could hear every word of DMX. Whenever Troy listened to DMX, he didn't want anyone bothering him, so l let him have his moment. I completely understood.

When we got off of the plane, I instantly saw my momma standing in the crowd with a look of sadness in her eyes. One that I didn't often see because no matter what my mother was going through, she almost always had a smile on her face. That was why most of her friends called her "Sunshine". Troy finally took off his sunglasses and put his ear buds away.

My momma opened her arms wide, nodding her head, motioning for us to come to her. Troy and I both hugged her simultaneously, swallowing up her petite frame. She held us for a few minutes, saying a prayer for all of us. After she finished and released us, Troy turned his head to wipe the tears from his eyes.

"You don't have to be ashamed to cry, Honey! Let it out. It's ok," my momma said, rubbing Troy's back. She looked over at me as I stood there with my hands in my pockets, trying to keep cool, and said, "Same goes for you!"

On our way home from the airport, my moms told us most of the story of what happened to Tramaine. She didn't want to. She wanted to wait for Troy's mother to talk to him, but he insisted that he wanted her to tell him. She told us that Tramaine had evidently become involved with selling drugs for a big time drug-dealer in our neighborhood who they called Smoke. He was an older cat in his late thirties who had been in the streets for over a decade, and notorious for using young kids to sell for him so he could pay them a little of nothing. My momma said that some of Tramaine's friends had told his mom that Tramaine had gotten robbed about a week ago and whoever did it took all the drug money he had on him, which had been about five grand. When Tramaine came home with a black eye that day, he told his mom that he had gotten in a fight after school and she had no reason to not believe him. He was normally honest with her about everything.

Tramaine's friends said he had been terrified that whole week, trying his best to come up with some money to repay Smoke. He had been dodging him, knowing that there was going to be trouble if he saw Smoke and didn't have his money. Tramaine had finally gotten tired of hiding, so he decided to meet up with Smoke, and hours later was found dead in the back of an abandoned building.

After my mom told us the full story of what supposedly happened, that made Troy feel even worse because Tramaine had been calling him, telling him he needed to talk, but we had been so busy studying for midterms, Troy kept putting off calling him back. My mom kept trying to tell him it wasn't his fault, but he felt like he could've somehow prevented this from happening. He felt like he had failed his little brother. No matter what we said to Troy, he didn't want to hear it. His mind was set on retaliating against Smoke.

After Tramaine's funeral had come and gone, Spring break was over and it was time for Troy and I to return to school. Troy was still having a hard time coping, right along with his mom, so he decided to stay home for a little while longer. A week passed, then two weeks, then three, then a month. I kept trying to call Troy to check on him but he wouldn't return my calls. My mom would keep me updated on his status, which was always, "He's not looking too good." She would tell me all he ever did was sit on the porch looking like he was waiting to kill someone. Troy never returned to school. When his mom finally called and told me he wouldn't be coming back, she asked that I pack up his belongings and ship them back home. It was the least I could do because at that time, I did have sympathy for my brother, but not more than fifteen years later. He'd had more than enough time to recover and get back on his feet.

Smoke was eventually caught and arrested. He was sentenced to life in prison after the police finally talked enough people into testifying against him, which was tough because he had so many people afraid of him. After he was locked up, our neighborhood felt a whole lot safer, but it was too bad that it took losing one of our own for it to happen.

As Troy and I continued our conversation about what he wasn't doing with his life, for the first time ever, he asked me if I knew of anyone that was hiring. It was a start. I told him of a few places and asked him had he thought about going back to school.

"Nah. I don't think that's for me."

"Man, if it was for you once, it still is, and can be. You're a smart man. Don't let that go to waste."

"Ok. I'll think about it. Thanks for the info though, bruh."

I gave Troy a brotherly hug before heading back across the busy street. When I approached my truck, I saw my momma standing in the doorway with a smile on her beautiful face.

Since Troy was still standing outside watching, I decided I'd wait 'til later to get my clothes out of the car. My momma opened the screen door for me as she waved at Troy across the way. I gave her a hug and a kiss on the cheek.

"Hey, Ma," I said, obviously sounding like I had some issues going on.

"Hey, baby. What's wrong?"

"Nothing? Why you ask that?" I asked curiously.

"Now you know I always know when something's not right. You don't look like yourself, in addition to that weak "Hey Ma" you just gave me. Normally you're excited to see me!"

I smiled and said, "I am happy to see you! You just don't know how happy I am!"

My momma folded her arms, shook her head and said, "Woman problems, huh?"

I looked down at the floor in shame and said, "Yep."

"What happened this time? What did you do to that sweet Day'ja?" my momma asked, sounding disappointed in me, as she always did when she found out I did something crazy to a woman who didn't deserve it. She always took the woman's side, which she probably should have, but I felt like she could've sometimes had at least a little compassion for me, with me being her son and one and only child.

She stood there waiting for me to tell her what I had done, and I procrastinated by changing the subject. She wouldn't even join in on the conversation. We sat at the kitchen table across from each other, and as I talked about a bunch of nothing, she held her chin up with her fist, gazing at me. She gave me a look that I was very used to seeing from a whole lot of other women whenever I was full of shit.

My momma finally got tired of hearing it and yelled, "Keith Lamar Sanders! Stop playing with me! I'm your momma. Not one of these naïve women you mess around with! Now what happened?"

I heard moms loud and clear and knew I had better told her something right then. I told her everything that happened between Day'ja and me. As I told her, she shook her head and looked at me with disgust. I knew my momma would be pissed and how she'd react to me and Day'ja splitting because for some reason, she loved the hell out of her. I tried to see what my momma saw just so I'd want to move further with Day'ja, but the chemistry just wasn't there for me.

When I finished telling her, she sat there silent for a minute, still shaking her head. She finally said, "Keith, really? Is this really how I taught you to treat women?"

I opened my mouth to try to plead my case, but before I could speak, she said, "Nope! Don't even try to blame it on how your daddy treated me! You weren't even old enough to know what was going on. All you know is what I told you! You're your own person and make your own decisions."

After my momma rejected my explanation for my behavior before I even got it out, I was stuck. I didn't know what to say. I had nothing else. She had left me speechless once again like she always did.

"So, looks like you have nothing left to say, son, but I got a question for you."

I really didn't feel like answering any of her questions, but I knew if I told her that she was still going to ask anyway, so I looked at her, waiting for her to proceed.

"What are you gonna do now? Live with your mommy until you find another woman to take advantage of for the moment?"

I took a deep breath because I knew I deserved that, but that still didn't mean I wanted to hear that come out the woman's mouth who I had loved unconditionally all my life.

"Ma, please don't do that. I don't mean to take advantage of these women. They offer to help a brother out and I simply accept."

"How about everything I taught you about being self-sufficient and never relying on anyone else?"

Those were things that she strongly believed in and had pounded in my head all my life. Even though she struggled, she would never let anyone know and never asked anyone for anything. She always found a way out of no way. She didn't even like taking money from me when I gave it to her.

"All I can say is I'm a man and I do know right from wrong, but I just haven't gotten to the point in my life where I make all the right decisions."

"You'll never make all the right decisions. Just stop hurting these women. Try to think about a man coming into my life doing the same things you do to them, to me. How would you feel about that?"

I knew I wouldn't like that shit at all. My momma always gave me something to think about.

"I'll try my best momma," I said as I stood up and gave her a hug.

After we hugged, she said, "Now is there something you want ask me?"

I stood there looking at the ceiling, trying to figure out what she was talking about, when it finally clicked.

Laughing, I said, "Can I please stay here until I find some other arrangements?"

"You mean, find yourself a place without moving in with someone?"

I took another deep breath and said, "Yes, Ma."

After having my much needed, but dreaded heart to heart with my momma, I waited 'til the sun went down to start bringing my belongings in the house. I didn't need anyone to know what was going on in my life. It had been a long drama-filled day and I couldn't wait to rest my head in a peaceful environment and start over tomorrow.

<u>Chapter Six ~ Armani</u>

I woke up to the beautiful, bright sun shining through my bedroom window, which was an immediate indication for me that today was going to be a great day no matter what. I heard the shower running in the bathroom and I quickly jumped out of bed to relive, for a brief moment, the encounter Marcus and I had experienced the night before. That was probably the best sex Marcus and I had had in a very long time. It made me feel like we needed to make up a little more often.

I wiggled the knob to the bathroom door and surprisingly, it was locked. I went back in the bedroom to find a hairpin. After rummaging through everything on my dresser and jewelry box until I finally found one, I went back to the bathroom door and picked the lock. I slowly turned the knob and quietly walked into the veil of steam. Marcus' cell phone was sitting on the back of the toilet, as always when he went into the bathroom. Due to the demand his job put on him, he couldn't afford to let his cell phone out of his sight, not even to use the bathroom. I saw that the screen was illuminating, so I picked it up and took a peak as any woman would. On the screen "Text message from work" was displayed, but the phone was locked. I suddenly heard the shrieking sound of the shower curtain being pulled back and I nervously dropped the phone. When it hit the floor, the back cover and battery went sliding across the floor in different directions.

With my heart pounding rapidly, I quickly kneeled to the floor to pick up the phone and its detached parts.

"What did my phone do to you?" Marcus asked, giggling, with his beautiful naked body exposed from behind the curtain.

Briefly looking at him as I attempted to put his phone back together, I embarrassingly said, "I am so sorry. Your phone was going off and I was trying to check it for you in case it was your job."

"So, did you at least see who it was before you dropped it?"

"Yeah, actually I did," I said, as I stood up with Marcus' phone in my hand, back in one perfect piece. "It was your job, but I couldn't check the message. It was locked," I added, just to see what his response would be.

I didn't know that Marcus had put a lock on his phone. We'd had that discussion years ago and we had agreed that since we trusted each other there was no need for either of us to ever have our phones locked, and if we did, we would have each other's passwords. Marcus had evidently reneged on the agreement and I didn't like that very much. I was sure Marcus was able to tell that much by the expression on my face.

"Oh, yeah. I forgot I put the screen lock on my phone because I sit it down a lot at work and I don't want my nosey ass co-workers going through my phone. They might run across one of those provocative pictures you sent me. You know your pictures are all throughout my phone and if somebody got a hold of them I might have to kill somebody."

Marcus did have a very valid point. I did have my moments when the freak in me took over and during random times of the day, no matter where I was or what I was doing, I would send him dirty pictures. I made sure to keep our relationship spicy and I knew that was one way to make sure I stayed on his mind the way he stayed on mine.

"It's no big deal," I told Marcus, lying through my teeth. It was a big deal to me because he knew I didn't like secrets, and a locked phone gave me reason to believe he had something to hide. I never had any valid reason not to trust Marcus. I was just being a typical woman. I waited for Marcus to offer to give me the password to his phone, but he never did. I didn't want to nag him about it because I didn't want him to feel like I didn't trust him.

Marcus smiled and said, "You wanna come in here and finish out this shower with me?"

I smiled back at him, happy that I hadn't spoiled what I had initially come in there to do. I untied my robe, revealing my voluptuous mounds, and my already erect Hershey kisses that I had for nipples. My bald pussy throbbed just from seeing Marcus' dick begin to stand at attention. I stepped into the shower and Marcus immediately grabbed both of my breasts, squeezing them together, and burying his face deep into my cleavage. I held my head back, closed my eyes, let the water run down my chest, and enjoyed Marcus as he worked his way all the way down to my purring kitty. He lifted both of my legs up as I gripped the shower rod, allowing him to devour his breakfast.

After Marcus headed out to work, I looked in the mirror and smiled at myself from ear to ear. I felt like a different woman. I loved a man that loved me as much as I loved him. No other man that I'd been involved with had ever mentioned marriage to me. Part of the reason was because we never made it that far. Before Marcus came into the picture, my longest relationship had only been eight months, and that one only lasted that long because he fed me a bunch of lies from the very beginning.

Damon was a sexy ass man. To go along with his sex appeal, he had the matching personality. Any woman who came in contact with him couldn't help but to fall for his physical attractiveness and charm. He was the definition of a lady's man. He had a certain swag about him that was undeniably appealing. I should've known better than to get involved with him in any way due to the fact that he was already with someone when we met and became intimate. I was the side-chick for a short time. He was partly honest with me when we first met at the grocery store when I only went in to pick up a dozen eggs one evening after work. I was in such a hurry, I was rushing through the store, turned a corner and ran right into Damon, breaking all twelve eggs on his fitted white t-shirt.

He looked like he was going to kill me by the expression on his face, but when he looked up at me and saw the apologetic look on my face, his entire expression changed.

"I am so sorry!" I said looking through my purse for something to wipe the egg yolk from his shirt.

"It's ok. It's just a shirt. Calm down! I have more at home," he said in the most comforting tone I had ever heard from a man. "Where are you in such a hurry to get to?" He asked.

"Nowhere important," I said, knowing the real reason I was in such a hurry was because I had to go home and get caught up on some work that I had to present to the Editor-in-Chief the next morning. I just didn't like for people to think my entire life revolved around work, when in essence, it did.

Just then, I saw one of the store employees mopping the floor and I ran over to him and grabbed a few paper towels from his cart. I ran back over to Damon and wiped as much of the egg off as possible. As I rubbed his chest, his shirt became more and more translucent from the yolk being smeared, and the more turned on I became. I became lost in a fantasy within only seconds, of the complete stranger whose name I didn't even know.

I suddenly felt him grab my wrist and say, "It's ok. I was gonna go home and change anyway. What's your name?"

Still in a semi-daze, I said "Armani."

"Oh! Armani like the designer?"

"Exactly," I replied.

"Well, nice to meet you, Armani. I'm Damon."

It was very ironic that his name was Damon because he reminded me of Boris Kodjoe back in his *Soul Food* days. We stood in the middle of the frozen food aisle for a half hour getting to know a little bit about each other. I normally hated the frozen food aisle because I always nearly froze to death before I could pick up everything I needed, but this particular day it didn't faze me because this perfect man had gotten me so hot I could feel myself beginning to perspire. Throughout the entire conversation, Damon never mentioned a woman in his life. I had already checked his married finger, which did not display a ring, so I was under the impression that he was single.

I looked at my watch and Damon said, "Oh, I'm sorry for holding you. I'm sure you need to be somewhere with those eggs."

"Actually, I have some things to do," I said with secrecy in my voice.

"Ok, well, it was nice talking to you. I would like to talk to or even see you again if that's possible," Damon said, raising his eyebrows, looking as if he was unsure what my response would be.

I didn't want to seem too available or thirsty, so I said, "I might be able to make that happen."

"Do you have a man in your life?" Damon asked.

Is this a trick question? I thought to myself. It seemed like a trick to me because what was going through my mind was, if I said yes, then the man of my dreams might've backed off, and if I said no, he might've wondered what was wrong with me for me not to have a man. It didn't seem like there was any right answer at that moment so I let my mouth make that decision.

"No, I don't," I hesitantly said.

"A woman?" Damon asked.

"Nooo! Why would you say that?" I asked. Then after realizing my reaction, I said, "I don't have anything against lesbians, but I'm not one."

I had to clean that up. I didn't want Damon to think I was homophobic. He might've had a gay sister or gay cousins and I definitely didn't want to offend him in any way.

"I just figured you had to have someone, whether it had been a man or a woman. You're too beautiful of a woman to not have anyone. You don't seem crazy, so why are you single?"

At that moment, I felt so pathetic because I knew that the main reason I didn't have a man was because I didn't have a life. This was during a time in my life when I was trying to make my way up the ladder in my career, so my social life was the last thing on my list of my priorities and I didn't get out much due to my heavy workload. He, however, didn't need to know that.

I reached deep down inside for the perfect answer that screamed, I can have any man I want, I'm single by choice, and you'd be lucky if I choose you.

"I just haven't met the right person who I feel is worth my time. My time is very valuable and I just don't have any to waste."

The answer I had quickly come up with had actually worked.

"Well, that's understandable," Damon said, which I was happy to hear, but the rest was disappointing.

"I'm gonna be upfront with you," he began.

Here we go. It was always too good to be true. This was part of the reason I started putting my career before anything else. That was the only thing that never disappointed me. I waited for Damon to spill whatever it was that he felt he needed to tell me.

"I'm currently in a relationship."

I stood there nodding, waiting on him to explain to me why he had just wasted my time.

"How do you feel about that?" he asked, as if there was nothing wrong with what he had just said.

"What do you mean?"

"Do you feel comfortable with hanging out, knowing I have a woman?"

Is this another trick question? If I told him I was ok with that, he'd think I was a desperate homewrecker who was willing to share. If I told him I wasn't ok with it, it could've been possible that I would be walking away from my future husband.

Damon noticed the disbelief on my face and said, "I understand if you don't want to get involved. I know it takes a very strong, confident woman to be able to deal with a man who is already involved with someone."

Damon used that reverse psychology shit on me, and I knew that's what the hell he was doing, but I still fell for it.

"Oh, I can handle it just fine. You just better make sure you can handle it and don't fall for me. I do have that effect."

Damon gazed at me as he seductively bit his bottom lip and said, "I like you already."

Damon and I exchanged numbers that day before I went back to the dairy aisle to get another dozen of eggs. He told me I could call him any time of the day because his girl knew better than to touch his phone. When he told me that, I wondered what kind of woman she was to allow that shit. Evidently, she didn't have much of a backbone.

After that day, I finally had a life again outside of work and it was exciting. Even though I was sharing Damon, it was kind of convenient because I didn't have to worry about entertaining him all the time, or spending a large amount of time with him that would distract me from meeting my deadlines at work. It was like having a part time boyfriend and I grew comfortable with that. That comfort didn't last for long. By the way Damon and I got along with each other, and the fun times we had, I knew eventually he would leave his girlfriend and we would be together. That time wasn't coming soon enough and I had begun to expect more from him.

Since we had begun our "relationship", the first big holiday was Thanksgiving. I had agreed this would be the year my family would come to my house for Thanksgiving dinner, so I prepared a huge meal. I knew Damon wouldn't be there for probably the first couple of hours of festivities, but he said he'd for sure be there after he and Kim finished making their rounds to their parent's homes for their gatherings. Yes, the other woman's name was Kim.

As I was finishing up Thanksgiving dinner, guests began arriving, and between the talking and laughing, I kept watching the clock, hoping that Damon would show up earlier than I'd expected. My entire family had already met him and everyone loved him. He was just one of those people you couldn't help but to love. They, of course, didn't know he was already involved with someone, so we were made very uncomfortable when my parents or other relatives would mention marriage to us. We would just try to laugh it off and move on to another subject.

I finished cooking dinner and the hours began to fly by. I continued to watch the clock, trying my best not to call Damon, but I was becoming very irritated. I had to sit at my huge dinner table with my guests, both relatives and friends, who all had their husbands, wives, or significant others sitting next to them, while I had an empty chair sitting next to me. People kept asking me where he was, which upset me even more when I had to lie and say he was held over at work.

My guests began packing up plates to take home and putting on their coats, and Damon still had not shown up or called. The least he could've done was at least texted me to let me know what was going on, but I guess somewhere in the handbook it said being the side-chick didn't warrant even that amount of common courtesy. As I let everyone out one by one, they all told me to tell Damon they said hi and that they hated that he was unable to spend Thanksgiving with us.

It pissed me off that Damon was able to spend so much time with me any other day, but one of the most important days of the year, I didn't hear from or see him. While I stood there alone in my kitchen after everyone left, it took everything out of me to not start throwing plates. I felt like breaking something, but instead, I took a deep breath, turned on some music, took my Ciroc out of the cabinet, and poured a glass. On any normal day, I would've poured a glass of wine, but I needed something a lot stronger at that moment.

As I cleaned the kitchen, I went through the entire bottle of vodka. Before I headed to bed, I looked at the clock and it was already past midnight, which meant Damon had officially went the entire Thanksgiving Day without talking to me. I realized at that moment that I had caught too many feelings for a man that didn't belong to me, and decided it was time for me to take a few steps back. Even though I knew it was the right thing to do, I cried myself to sleep. The alcohol definitely didn't help. I knew I was in love and it was going to take a lot to rid myself of those feelings. That night was the first night I had ever shed a tear over a man, so I guess you could say Damon was my first love. Imagine that.

The next morning, I heard my doorbell. Well, I thought it was morning. I glanced over at my clock sitting on my nightstand and it was two in the afternoon. I slowly lifted my body, and I realized my head was pounding. It became worse each time the person at my door rang the doorbell. I felt like someone was inside my head playing drums. I slowly stood up and said, "I'm coming!" as if the person could hear me. I threw on my robe and glanced in the mirror as I passed by it, noticing that my eyes were puffy from the crying I had done the night before. With every footstep, the throbbing pain in my head became worse and worse.

When I got to the door, I looked through the peephole and smacked my lips. I opened the door and folded my arms.

"Hey, sweetheart. You look like shit. Long night?" Damon said as if he had done nothing wrong.

He stepped into the house as I walked away from him without saying a word, because I felt like if I hadn't, I was gonna slap the shit out of him.

"What's wrong? I know you're not mad about yesterday."

As he continued to talk, I became more and more furious. I went into the bathroom to get some Excedrin out of the medicine cabinet. Next thing I knew he was right behind me.

"Baby, you knew what to expect when we started this thing."

Damon finally had forced me to speak. "This thing? Really Damon? Is that what it is?" I asked as I turned on the faucet.

"You know what I mean. You know I'm with someone and holidays are no guarantee. I have to make sure Kim doesn't suspect anything, and if I go running off in the middle of Thanksgiving dinner, I think that would put up a huge red flag, don't you?"

I took a deep breath and exhaled to keep from exploding. I threw two pills in my mouth, and lowered my head near the faucet to get a drink of water to wash them down. When I raised back up and closed the medicine cabinet, I could see Damon's reflection behind me through the mirror. He didn't look remorseful at all, and I still hadn't heard anything come out of his mouth that was even close to sounding like an apology.

I turned to face him and said, "Damon, what you fail to understand is that it's not even about you not showing up for Thanksgiving dinner. It's about you not even calling or texting to tell me Happy Thanksgiving. I thought I was enough of a factor in your life to at least deserve that."

Damon opened his mouth to speak and I immediately put my hand up and shook my head, letting him know I was not done.

I continued to speak both casually and calmly, never once raising my voice. Not because I didn't want to, but because my throbbing head wouldn't allow for it.

"It's all about being considerate and respectful. You told me you would come by and you never showed up. If you saw that you weren't going to be able to make it, you could've taken a moment out of your day to call and let me know. I told everyone you would be here and they were all looking forward to seeing you, so guess who was left looking stupid! You have been here for over five minutes and you have yet to apologize for your actions! That is completely unacceptable. Yes, we do have an understanding, and part of that understanding is that we respect and be considerate of one another. I do my part and I expect you to do yours."

I tried my best to hold back my tears because I didn't want to show any signs of weakness, but I could feel the tears welling up in my eyes as I stared Damon face to face, eye to eye, as he searched within himself for the words that would fix this. I finally began to see remorse in his eyes, and that's when I allowed one tear to roll down my face. I quickly wiped it, hoping he didn't notice, but I knew he had.

Damon quickly grabbed me. Hugging me tight, he said, "I'm so sorry, Armani. You're right. That was very inconsiderate of me and you deserve better. I promise this will never happen again. I love you."

I couldn't believe what he had just said, and in response, I held my head close to his chest, wiping the residue from my tears that had decided to secretly escape onto his shirt, from my face. Damon reached down and lifted my chin with his finger. I closed my eyes as he kissed me with his soft, full lips.

"Do you love me?" he asked.

Damon and I had never spoke those words to each other and I didn't know if we should've started then. I did feel like I loved him, but our relationship was complicated and I didn't want to make it even more complicated.

"I don't know," I said.

"You don't have to say it, but I know you do. You wouldn't be crying if you didn't."

Damon was right, and just by him knowing that was an advantage to him. He knew it would be hard for me to resist him with the feelings that I had developed. I started off so strong, but at that moment felt so vulnerable. I had let my guard down, which was the last thing I wanted to do. Damon carried me upstairs to my bedroom and made love to me to the point that I never wanted him to leave, but I knew he would. I was beginning to believe there would never be a day that he would stay. He would always have someone to go home to, and the side of my bed that he occupied during his free time would always be empty at night.

After that day, things went back to normal with Damon and me. He spent every free moment he had with me. He even worked in some extra time by telling Kim he had other things to do throughout the day. I became extremely excited around Christmas because Damon promised we would be able to spend part of the day together because he had told Kim he had to go in to work for a few hours that day. I saw that he was making an effort, so I accepted that.

A few days before Christmas, I started coming down with the flu. I couldn't believe I was getting sick right before the first holiday I was going to actually be able to spend with Damon. He was so good to me during that time. I couldn't hold anything down, but he made sure I stayed hydrated. He hated seeing me like that and couldn't stand the fact that he wasn't able to stay with me overnight to make sure I was ok, but he constantly texted me throughout the night to check on me.

By Christmas, I still wasn't doing any better. Damon came over as promised and brought my gift, but I just wasn't up to it. I had already lost ten pounds and was starting to think something more serious was going on with me. Damon was thinking the same thing and became really concerned.

"The flu doesn't last this long, and it gets better after a couple of days. You're not getting any better."

"I know," I said, sounding and feeling weak. I was so happy that Damon kept his word on Christmas, but I was feeling so bad that I wasn't able to express it.

"You want to at least open your . . ."

Before Damon could finish his sentence, I jumped up from the sofa with my hand over my mouth, ran to the bathroom, and knelt over the toilet, letting out the little bit of fluid I had left in me until I began to dry heave. Damon came into the bathroom shortly afterwards with a glass of water. He knelt down beside me and said, "Here, drink this."

I looked up at him, embarrassed, and said, "I'm so sorry."

"Sorry for what?" he asked.

"For messing up our Christmas together," I said as I began to cry.

"Don't cry. It's not your fault," Damon said, as he caressed my back.

He looked at me strangely as I cried and said, "You don't have any tears. Let me see something." He pulled down both of my bottom eyelids and said, "It's completely white."

I managed to stop crying long enough to say, "What does that mean?"

"You're dangerously dehydrated. Come on. You're going to the emergency room."

"For the flu? That's stupid! I'm not going to the hospital on Christmas."

"Don't make me pick you up and put you in the car, Armani."

I saw how serious he was, so I let him help me up off of the bathroom floor. He helped me up the stairs so I could get cleaned up and we headed to the hospital. As soon as we got there, I was taken to triage. After asking me some questions, the triage nurse determined that I was in fact dehydrated. She had me to give her a urine sample, which took almost ten minutes due to the fact I didn't have much left in me. She then quickly got me into one of the beds and hooked me up to an IV to start pumping some liquid into my body, and drew blood to run some tests.

While Damon sat in the chair right next to my bed waiting for the doctor to come in, he kept looking at his watch. I knew he needed to get home soon, but I knew he didn't want to leave me at the hospital either. After an entire hour had passed, the doctor finally came in.

"Hello, Ms. Blair. I'm Dr. Ramsey."

"Hi, Dr. Ramsey."

The doctor looked over at Damon and said, "Hello, Sir. What is your relationship to Ms. Blair?"

Damon looked at me before answering and said, "She's my girlfriend."

Dr. Ramsey looked back at me and said, "Ms. Blair, is it ok for him to be in the room while we talk?"

Becoming nervous, I said, "Yes. That's fine."

"Ok. Well, we did several different tests on your blood, and as you already know, you were extremely dehydrated, but we're correcting that with the fluid we have hooked up to you through your IV," Dr. Ramsey said as he pointed to the bag of fluid hanging from the metal pole.

Damon and I sat there staring at each other, curiously waiting to hear the doctor tell me why I had been so sick.

"Your blood work all came back ok. We found that you are actually suffering from a severe case of hyperemesis gravidarum."

Damon and I both squinted our eyes and frowned, not knowing what in the world the doctor was talking about.

Dr. Ramsey continued. "From the expressions on both of your faces I can tell you don't know what that is. In non-medical terminology it's morning sickness, except you're having it all day, every day."

My eyes grew wide and my mouth dropped open. I glanced over at Damon and he was roughly rubbing his face with the palms of both of his hands in disbelief.

"Congratulations to the both of you! Based on the date you gave us of your last menstrual cycle, you are four weeks pregnant. For extreme cases of morning sickness, there is something I can prescribe for you. It won't completely go away, but will definitely alleviate the symptoms. To give you some relief, it does normally pass after the first few months."

I had heard everything the doctor had said, but I couldn't bring myself to say a word. I didn't know what to say. This was the last thing I expected the doctor to tell me. Damon sat in front of me looking like the world was coming to an end.

"Do either of you have any questions for me or need any referrals to an obstetrician?"

Damon and I both shook our heads.

"Ok, well, good luck to you, and the nurse will be in with your prescription and discharge papers shortly."

After Dr. Ramsey walked out, Damon shook his head and said, "What the fuck, Armani? Did you already know this shit? Did you do this on purpose?"

"What? Do you really think I need to trap someone? Why would I do that? It takes two, love! You knew you were cumming inside of me, and it felt real good to you at the time! You had an option to use a rubber, but you chose not to!"

"That's because I figured you were taking care of it on your end! I trusted you!"

"I was taking the pill, but everyone knows there's still a small chance that something like this could happen. Just maybe it was meant to be."

As I put my clothes back on, I tried to calm Damon down, but he wasn't trying to hear anything I had to say. The nurse finally came with my discharge papers and prescription, and she made sure to congratulate us before we left. The ride home was a long one. Damon wouldn't say a word to me. I wished that I could read his mind because I truly needed to know how he was really feeling.

When we pulled up to my house, I waited for Damon to cut the car off, but it didn't seem as though he was going to. I sat there wondering what was going on and finally said, "Are you going to come in for at least a few minutes?"

He shook his head and said, "Nah."

"Why not?" I asked curiously.

"Armani, I need to tell you something."

I became nervous like I did before Dr. Ramsey told me I was pregnant. "What is it, Damon?"

"Kim isn't my girlfriend. She's my wife, and we have a six year-old daughter."

Before I knew it, I had reached over and slapped Damon. I couldn't believe he had lied to me for this long and I was stupid enough to fall for it.

"How could you have kept something like this from me for so long? You're talking about you trusted me! I trusted you! I would've never become involved with you if I knew you were married! I guess that's why you lied, huh?"

He took a deep breath and rubbed his jaw before saying, "With that being said, I need you to discreetly take care of this."

"So now you're forcing me to have an abortion? Do you think you can really do that?"

"You will if you know what's good for you. Don't let my moments of weakness destroy a family."

"Really? Now you want to be concerned about your "family"? So you just really don't give a fuck about me and my feelings."

"I'm really sorry you have to go through this, but our communication stops here."

I could feel rage within my entire body. It was a feeling that I had never experienced. It was very scary because I felt like if I had a weapon in my hand at that moment, I would've murdered Damon.

"I'm obligated to protect my family and I will do anything necessary to do that," Damon continued.

I had never seen him be so cold. It almost felt like he never cared anything for me, but I just couldn't believe that.

"Ending communication with me will not erase the facts, but I'm happy to oblige, asshole!"

I grabbed my belongings, got out of Damon's car, and slammed the door. Without saying another word, he sped off. I had no idea what to do next. I thought about contacting Kim, letting her know what was going on, but Damon always told me how he had her brainwashed and she would never believe anything negative that anyone had to say about him. I was willing to bet money on that because he was so confident and never worried about me going to tell her anything. With that being said, I knew either he didn't think I would attempt to go to her or she was very naïve and gullible.

I let a couple of weeks go by, waiting to see if I would hear from Damon. After I didn't hear anything, I tried calling him. He had changed his phone number. I was so hurt by what he was allowing me to go through by myself. I didn't want to bring this baby into the world knowing he or she was a product of me fucking a married man. I also didn't want my child to grow up without a father. After I came to accept the fact that my situation wasn't going to change or go away on its own, and I probably would never talk to Damon ever again in life, I found myself on a bitterly cold morning in January, walking past abortion protesters, into an abortion clinic.

Chapter Seven ~ Keith

After tossing and turning all night, I opened my eyes and was hoping what had happened the previous day had all been a dream, but unfortunately, it wasn't. I woke up in my twin-sized bed that I slept in every night during my childhood. I could hear my moms in the kitchen cooking up breakfast, which she always did when I lived with her. I couldn't remember a morning that went by when she didn't cook me a full course breakfast. I wasn't in the best of moods and definitely wasn't feeling work today, but there was no other option. I dragged myself out of bed and stared at the pile of clothes sitting in the corner on the floor. That's when I remembered that I didn't grab any of my dress clothes from Day'ja's house. They were in a different closet in a totally separate room. I didn't have time to stop anywhere to pick anything up, so I would just have to deal with whatever Armani was going to say about my attire for the day. I grabbed a pair of jeans and a white V-neck t shirt from the pile and decided that I'd deal with what I was gonna do about clothes for the next few days after I got off work.

I walked out of my childhood room into the kitchen where I saw my momma slaving over the stove. I pulled out a chair and told her to have a seat while a finished cooking. It was the least I could do for everything she had done for me.

"Don't you have to start getting dressed for work?" she asked, with concern in her voice.

"I still have a couple of hours to get there before the warden starts looking for me."

"Warden?" my momma asked.

"Yeah, she's my new boss."

"She must be pretty tough for you to call her a warden."

As I finished buttering the toast, I grinned and said, "Yeah, she's pretty hard on a brotha'."

Then my momma did what she did best. Started making assumptions, predictions, and basically saying exactly what was on her mind.

"That's probably the exact kind of woman you need in your life! One like me! You need someone to tame you! And that grin on your face that you just had when you were talking about the "warden" tells me she's pretty, too."

"Ma, here you go!"

"I just calls it like I see it.

"Yeah, I know, but she's nowhere near my type."

"You don't even know what your type is!"

Still listening to my mom carry on most of the conversation, I fixed both of our plates and listened. That's all I could do. My momma was the type that when she got in her zone and felt like she knew what she was talking about, there was no shutting her up. I didn't even try. The best thing to do was just nod and say "uh huh".

After having breakfast, I took my shower, got dressed, headed out the door and hoped for the best. I made it to the office about a half hour early since my mom's house was a little closer than when I was coming from Day'ja's. I forgot to factor that into the equation, but with Armani around, it was better to be early than late. When I pulled into the parking lot, it was a lot emptier than it had been the previous day. I guess a half hour made a big difference. One car I did recognize in the parking lot was Armani's white Benz, so I decided to park right next to it, just to get a closer look at what her kind of money could get you. What I hadn't noticed when I pulled into the parking space was that Armani was still inside of her car.

Her driver's side door slowly opened and as she stepped out, she had an unfamiliar expression on her face as talked on her Bluetooth. A smile. She closed her car door and seemed to be waiting on me to get out. As I got out, she continued to watch me with this beautiful smile on her face. I knew the smile was probably because of what the person on the other end of that call was saying, but I made myself believe it was because she saw me. That was my story and I was sticking to it. The complete truth of that smile was behind the eyes. I always believed in the eyes telling all, but I couldn't tell what her eyes were saying behind the large, stylish sunglasses she was wearing.

Armani ended the call with whoever she was talking to and said, "Good Morning, Keith," with the same sweetness in her voice she was giving the person she had been talking to, which I assumed was her man.

There was definitely something different about her. A side of her I had yet to see, but I was just enjoying it while it lasted. I wanted to ask her if her man had finally given her some, but that would've probably changed the entire mood.

I walked towards her and before thinking, I said, "Good Morning, lady."

Armani raised her sunglasses, looked me up and down and said, "Casual today, aren't we? Did I not get the memo? Oh yeah, and my name is Armani. I'm not your lady."

Armani began walking towards the building after I had caused her smile to wither away. She left me standing there looking stupid. I walked quickly to catch up with her so I could apologize for my attire, but as soon as I did, I couldn't open my mouth to speak. When she turned to look at me, I noticed her beautiful hair blowing in the wind. She wasn't wearing those naughty school-teacher glasses that I hated and she actually had on a dress that showed off her beautiful curves. I couldn't help but to look her up and down. She was beyond gorgeous. She rolled her eyes and continued to walk. I watched her from behind for a moment as she took long strides with her long, sexy legs.

When we finally made it to the entrance of the building, I jumped in front of her and opened the door.

She hesitated to walk in, but her pride allowed her to accept my polite gesture. This was one woman I could not figure out for the life of me. Today, she actually seemed like she wanted to be nice to me, but for some reason she was holding back. I couldn't tell if she was a woman scorned, or a woman that just wanted to be a bitch because she felt like it and knew that she could.

When we walked into the department, she didn't say a word. She just walked towards the back to her office. I went into my office and sat my briefcase down, then decided to make another attempt to talk to Armani without getting sidetracked by her beauty. I walked down the hall to her office and knocked on her door that was slightly cracked.

"Yes," Armani said, which I assumed was an invitation to come in.

I walked in and saw Armani standing at her desk in front of her large picture window, preparing for the day.

"Armani, I know you're disappointed in my attire today, and I know how you feel about excuses, so I'm not going to give you any excuses. I had some unexpected things happen yesterday that were completely my fault and I take full responsibility. I would go into detail of what I dealt with after work yesterday, but I'm sure you have plenty to do and really don't give a . . ." I had to pause and remember where I was and who I was talking to before I let something come out of my mouth that I'd regret. " . . . I know you really don't care about my problems, so I'm just going to leave this conversation assuring you that you don't have to worry about me coming into the office like this again. For what it's worth, I did the best with what I had to work with."

Armani walked around her desk and stepped in front of me, leaving only a small amount of space in between us.

She gave me a short smile, then a stern look and said, "I'm sorry about your problems at home, but they're exactly that . . . Problems at home. Leave them there! You knew at the end of the day yesterday that you had work today. Learn to be prepared at all times, Mr. Sanders. It's called being . . . proactive."

Armani then folded her arms and stood there staring at me as if she was daring me to say something back to her. If I didn't really need my job, I would've cursed her ass out, packed up my shit and left, but that wasn't the case. Day'ja had put me out and I needed my job more now than ever. I felt like Armani knew that because she just kept trying me.

Just when I thought she was done, she continued by saying, "And I'm not as disappointed in your choice of dress today as I was yesterday when I realized you had the audacity to leave with your editors when we clearly have plenty to do around here. I hope I haven't led you to feel that comfortable. You leave when I tell you it's ok to leave. You are not an hourly employee. You are salary, therefore, you stay until I no longer need you, even if it's the next morning!"

I took a deep breath, looked her straight in her dark, almond shaped eyes and said, "Understood. I apologize again." I turned to walk away, but as I was walking, I heard my mom's voice in my ear. She always told me that kindness kills, so I turned back around to still find Armani standing there watching me walk out the door with her arms folded, and I said, "You look very nice today, by the way." I watched the hard, tight expression on her face relax to a softer, warmer state.

"Thank you," she said softly.

After turning things around on Armani's crazy ass, I walked around the corner to go to the bathroom and coincidentally ran into Taryn.

Taryn put one hand on her hip and stared me down. "Hey, hey, hey, Keith! Don't you look sexy today! Oops! Am I allowed to say that?"

Taryn definitely knew how to make a situation uncomfortable. I could tell she was the type that didn't care anything about what other people thought. Luckily no one else was around to hear her.

"You know that is inappropriate work behavior. I don't even have to tell you that," I said, trying to be as nice to Taryn as I could. She just wasn't about to be the cause of me losing my job.

Taryn, still smiling, put her hand on her other hip and said, "Is it still inappropriate outside of work?"

I put my hand on my forehead and said, "Taryn, please don't do this right now."

"Ok. I won't right now, but this conversation isn't over."

As Taryn turned to walk away, all I could notice was how perfectly her skintight black leather pants hugged her ass in all the right places. I quickly turned to go into the men's restroom when I realized my dick was ready to make an appearance.

After coming out of the bathroom, I walked past all the ladies, telling them all good morning, trying to avoid eye contact with Taryn. When I finally made it back to my desk, I noticed a piece of paper laying in my chair. I picked it up and the only thing the note said was: **Call me. 773-555-5595.** Apparently, Taryn had snuck into my office before I made it back. I felt like I was stuck between a rock and a hard place. This fine young hottie was basically throwing herself at me, inviting me to take advantage of her, and I had to think twice before accepting the invitation. That's something I never had to do and this was definitely going to be a test.

The rest of the day, I was unable to concentrate because I had other things on my mind that seemed to be a lot more interesting than any of the stories on my desk. Every time I stepped out of my office, it seemed like all eyes were on me. Towards the end of the day, Armani surprisingly stepped into my office. She stood in the middle of the floor until I greeted her, which seemed a little backwards, but with Armani, nothing surprised me.

"Yes, Armani?"

She slowly walked up to my desk and bent down, pressing the palms of her hands against my glass desktop.

"I just wanted to apologize for being so harsh this morning. There's just a high standard for this office that I have to uphold, and if I let one person get away with dressing a certain way, then everyone expects me to do the same for them."

"Yep. No problem," I said as I looked back down acting as if I was busy and she had interrupted me.

"And also, if you feel you've done enough for the day, I just ask that you come to me to make sure there's nothing I need you to do before you leave for the day."

"Okey Dokey," I replied, still without looking up.

Armani slowly stood up as if she were waiting on me to say something else, but there was nothing else for me to say. I was tired to being talked to like shit and I wasn't giving her any more opportunities.

She tapped the desk with her long, manicured nails and said, "Yep, that's all I wanted to let you know. You look busy, so I'll let you finish."

Still looking down at a document that I had already finished reading, I said, "All right. Thanks for stopping by."

Armani walked out and shut the door. It took everything out of me to hold back my laughter. She looked so pathetic walking out and I knew she had to have felt like shit. That was exactly what I was going for.

As quitting time approached and I looked forward to the weekend, I took a chance by walking down to Armani's office to see if it was ok to leave on time today. Her office door was open and she was sitting at her desk, occupied with something on her computer screen. I stood there for a moment without her even noticing I was watching her. I cleared my throat and Armani looked at me like I had startled her.

"Sorry. I didn't mean to interrupt you. Just wanted to come see if you needed me to do anything before I left for the day."

Armani looked at her watch and said, "It's that time already? Time flies when you're having fun, right?" she said, sounding like she was forcing herself to be pleasant towards me. She glanced at a stack of papers, then looked at me and said, "No thanks! I'm good. Enjoy your weekend."

"You mean I don't have to come in to work this weekend?" I asked playfully, trying to break the tension in the room.

"Hey, I'm not that unreasonable!"

That's what you think, I thought to myself, but instead, I laughed and said, "See you Monday morning."

After I packed up, I realized my editors had cleaned their desks and left the office. I looked at my watch and it was definitely that time. I grabbed my briefcase and exited the building. I noticed Reagan still in the parking lot walking to her car, so I yelled, "Have a good weekend, Reagan!"

She turned around and smiled, waving and yelling back, "Same to you!"

Reagan was definitely a mystery, and mysteries always kept me wondering. Taryn had basically already let me know what type of girl she was, and I'd had plenty of them, but Reagan didn't share much and the energy she gave off was a little puzzling. When I got to my car, I heard a horn blow. That's when I noticed Taryn was parked directly in front of me.

She rolled down the window of her black Impala and said, "Hey sexy. Follow me!"

I stood there for a moment and thought about all my options, and possible repercussions of my decisions. It was just something about that smooth chocolate skin and bangin' body that I just couldn't say no to. On top of that, it was the weekend. With my weekends, anything could go. At that moment I was willing to accept whatever consequences I would incur. I nodded and got in my car. We drove for about twenty-five minutes until we reached our destination. I found myself in one of the most lavish parts of the suburbs. Taryn pulled into the driveway of a townhouse and I hesitated before pulling in behind her, not knowing her living situation, and as to whether or not it was ok to park in the driveway. She waved her hand out of her car window, gesturing for me to pull in, so I did.

I waited for her to get out of the car before I moved. After a minute, her car door opened and I saw her shapely legs ease their way out of the car, one by one, until her black stilettos hit the ground. I knew exactly where this was going. I lowered my head, hoping I would suddenly start thinking with the head on my shoulders and stop thinking with the other one that always got me in trouble. Suddenly, I heard a knock on my window. When I glanced up, Taryn was staring me directly in the face, smiling, telling me to come on. I put up my index finger, telling her to give me a second, as if I was in the middle of something. Her smile immediately turned into a frown as if I had insulted her, and she turned around and strutted to the front door of the house, that I assumed was her humble abode. As she unlocked the door, she turned around one last time before opening it and walking in.

Once I was completely sure I was ready to face my weakness, I slowly took my keys out of the ignition, got out, and took my time walking up to the door. I knocked on the storm door as I looked through the glass waiting on Taryn to appear. That never happened.

I took my chances and turned the knob. Taryn had left the door unlocked, letting me know that she knew I couldn't turn down her offer. The only kind of man that could've turned her ass down was a very gay one! I took it upon myself to let myself in. I slowly stepped in onto the hardwood floors leading into the open living area.

"Taryn," I said, waiting for a response. I continued walking, exploring an unfamiliar place. As I walked from room to room, still with no sign of Taryn, I ran into a staircase leading upstairs. I stood at the bottom and yelled Taryn's name one more time. She still didn't answer. I didn't like wandering around other people's houses because I didn't like anyone invading my personal space, but I validated my decision to roam the premises by putting it in my mind that I needed to check on my employee's well-being.

I slowly crept up the stairs. I could then hear music coming from one of the rooms down the hall. I followed the sound, and finally found where the music was coming from. The door was cracked, and for the first time in my life, I was nervous to walk into a room where I would probably find a gorgeous, half-naked woman. I have to say, some of those times I had been disappointed. Some women were experts at looking great with clothes on, but once those clothes came off, everything went south, literally. I was just hoping this wasn't the case.

I stepped to the side of the door and pushed it open with one finger, taking a deep breath.

"You finally decided to come find me?" I heard Taryn say in a seductive voice. "We were getting tired of waiting."

We? I thought to myself. I really became excited, instantly realizing Taryn had set up some type of ménage à trois for us. She must've thought long and hard about this moment. I stepped into the doorway and immediately saw a fully naked Taryn facing me, sitting on the edge of her king-sized bed with her legs extended as far apart as they possibly could've gone. Her perky, voluptuous breasts looked like they were just waiting for me to bury my face in between them. I felt my dick fighting to get out of my slim fit jeans, but I was still looking around for the third party.

Taryn tilted her head back, shaking her tresses off of her shoulders and grinned.

"What are you waiting for? I know you want this. I see how you look at me at the office."

I started walking towards her, biting my bottom lip, still waiting on another beautiful woman to present herself.

"You just knew I wanted you, huh? I love a confident woman, and you definitely are confident."

As I stood directly in front of her, she leaned forward and didn't waste any time unbuckling my belt.

"So where is she?" I asked, as Taryn worked on getting the buckle and zipper undone on my jeans.

Taryn looked up at me with confusion written all over her face and said, "Where is who?"

"You said, "We were tired of waiting", so I assumed . . ."

"Ohhh! You assumed you were getting a threesome!" Taryn giggled. "Definitely not! I don't share on the first date, but I'll see what I can do in the future, depending on if you're all that I expected."

"Is that right?" I said. "So what did you mean by "we"?"

"Me and my kitty," Taryn replied as she licked her fingers and rubbed her pussy.

I fondled Taryn's perfectly round, dark nipples as she aggressively pulled down my jeans and boxers in one tug and exposed my woman pleaser. I was already vain when it came to my piece, but Taryn had made it even worse in a matter of seconds. She gazed at my dick and smiled from ear to ear. It looked like she was putting together a master plan of all the nasty things she could do with it.

"I guess it's to your liking," I said, interrupting her thoughts.

"And more," she whispered, as she began stroking the shaft.

Before she or I could say another word, she had made my entire dick disappear down her throat. I had been with plenty of women, but not one of them had been so talented to be able to do that. I palmed the back of her head as she took it in and out with ease. I stood there, holding my head back and squeezing my eyes tight trying my best to not let this amazing feeling weaken my ability to hold back.

As soon as I felt I was about to have my biggest eruption ever, I pulled away, pushed Taryn back, and lifted both of her legs up over her head. I loved a flexible woman. I stared at her beautiful pink pussy and couldn't wait to taste her juices. I teased her already engorged clit with my tongue, causing her body to shake like it was going into convulsions. I used all my strength to keep her thighs from closing in on my head. I licked her from front to back, taking in all her sweet nectars. Taryn breathed heavily and steadily, even whispering my name quite a few times, letting me know I was properly doing my job.

Coming up for air, I kissed her stomach, and prepared to dive into unfamiliar territory. I stood up and leaned over Taryn, sensually kissing her as she enjoyed the flavor of her own essences on my tongue. My manhood searched for her kitty as our tongues intertwined and our minds got lost in a moment of deep lust. I suddenly felt the warmth and dampness of the inside of her walls and we both let out a loud moan. With each thrust, the headboard sounded like it was going to go straight through the wall. The room became so hot, strands of Taryn's hair stuck against her damp body. With my final, most forceful thrust, Taryn shouted my name as her hips began to gyrate faster and faster. I suddenly felt her insides vibrate against my dick and I couldn't hold back any longer. It felt so good, I wanted to stay inside, but I knew that could present problems that I didn't need. I quickly pulled out as we came together, breathing each other's names.

As we lay there in our juices, Taryn laid her head on my chest. I stared at the ceiling, taking in what had just happened.

After about five minutes of complete silence, Taryn asked, "What are you thinking about?"

Before answering, I tried my best to think of a way to say what I was thinking without unintentionally insulting her.

"I'm just thinking about how wrong this is."

Taryn sat up and looked at me.

"Were you thinking about how wrong this is when you were just fucking the shit out of me?"

I rubbed my face because I didn't know what to say next. This battle had already been lost.

"Honestly, no I didn't." I tried to make up for what I previously said by saying, "You know how when something makes you feel so good, and you know how wrong it is, but it's just sooo gooood?"

"Yeah, believe me, I know," Taryn said, laying her head back on my chest. I don't think about those things though. You only live once, so I'm a firm believer in enjoying every moment and dealing with the repercussions later. Tomorrow is not promised. Live in the moment and have fun. Don't worry about anything else."

If I had ever met a free spirit, Taryn definitely was. It was like she didn't have a care in the world. I tried to lay there and just not think about the fact I had slept with one of my employees, and what would happen if the shit got out. With her being so free spirited, that scared me. What if she went running her mouth to the other girls in the office? What if it got back to Armani? After that horrific thought, I lifted Taryn up off of me, and quickly jumped up and started putting on my clothes.

Taryn sat up and said, "Where you going? I thought maybe we could go hang out tonight."

I quickly thought up a lie and said, "I forgot I need to go home and let my dog out."

"Awww! You have a pooch? Can I ride with you, then we can go to a bar or something?"

Think, think, think Keith! I thought to myself.

"I know you need to get cleaned up, and I do too, so how about I call you later?"

Taryn hesitated and said, "Oh . . . Ok. Let me give you my number."

I strangely looked at Taryn and said, "I already have it."

"You do? Oh yeah. I almost forgot. You are my boss so you would have access to my phone number."

Before I said another word, I was careful about what came out of my mouth next. If she didn't leave the note in my office, then who did?

"Yeah, I do have to have all of you lady's numbers, so I'll dig it out of my briefcase when I get to the house."

Taryn crawled to the edge of the bed with a grin on her face, looking up at me with her big bright eyes. As I was buckling my belt, she puckered up her lips and closed her eyes. I knelt down and gently kissed her forehead. I didn't really want to do that much because I didn't like this uncomfortable situation and definitely didn't want her to feel like we were now a couple.

Taryn opened her eyes, looking puzzled. "Really Keith? Is that really how you feel after what we just did?"

"I really gotta run, Taryn," I said as I flew out of her room, down the hall, down the stairs, and straight out the door.

I had to figure out who in the hell left me that note. I thought of Armani. The number could've been hers. I didn't know hers by heart. I just had it stored in my phone under her name. For me to even think it was her, I had to laugh out loud at myself for having such a thought. Even if she wanted me to call her, her pride wouldn't have allowed her leave me a note. I couldn't even see her ever pursuing a man. She just seemed stuck in her ways and would never change. I couldn't imagine what kind of man her boyfriend had to be to deal with that bitch of a woman.

Before digging the note with the phone number out of my jean's pocket, I pulled out of Taryn's driveway before she decided to come running out trying to convince me to stay. I drove a few blocks down the road, and at the first stoplight I came to, I pulled out the note. I grabbed my cellphone and started dialing. As I was dialing, the cars behind me started honking. I looked up and the light had already turned green, but I didn't budge until I finished taking care of business. By that time the light had turned yellow. I sped through the yellow light and looked through my rearview mirror just so I could laugh at the assholes who were stuck at the red light, screaming obscenities at me. I knew that was a jackass move, but I couldn't stand when people honked at me. That was a sign of disrespect, and I didn't handle that very well.

There was no answer on the other end of the phone, but a voicemail did pick up.

"Hey, you've reached Reagan. Sorry I can't answer right now, but leave a message and I'll call you back as soon as I can."

Chapter Eight ~ Keith

After hearing Reagan on the voicemail of the number I had dialed, I felt some type of way. I didn't know what she would've wanted to talk to me about outside of work. She never showed any real interest in me, and as far as I knew, she was happily married. She seemed like a good girl. Yeah, I had previously had some inappropriate thoughts about her, but they were only thoughts. One thing I refused to do was mess around with a married woman. I knew that was a dangerous zone to be playing in and that wasn't a risk I was willing to take. I definitely wouldn't feel good about breaking up a happy home. I was a whole lot of things, but I did have a heart and was no homewrecker.

As I continued my drive home, which seemed to take an eternity, my cell phone rang. When I looked at the phone sitting on my console, the same number I had just dialed appeared on the screen. I hit ignore, not knowing what I was going to say to Reagan, or how to even approach the situation. I turned up my Drake CD and sped along the dark spiraling road back to my side of town.

I was glad that I hadn't given Taryn my phone number because I knew she would've definitely been calling or texting me by now. Especially after laying the dick on her the way I did. I had to figure out how I wanted to proceed with that situation before having a conversation with her, so that basically only gave me the weekend to figure shit out. Things were just happening so fast I didn't know if I was coming or going. Women always threw themselves at me, but the difference was, I didn't have to face them at work every day. Where the problem lied with that was these women were expected to respect me as their superior, but how would that be possible if I was fucking them afterhours?

When I finally pulled up my mom's crib, I saw Troy walking to his front door looking a lot different from how he had looked the previous day I had seen him. He had on a tan suit, tie, and a nice pair of dress shoes. He had even shaved and gotten a haircut. I blew my horn when I saw him about to walk in the house. He stopped in his tracks and turned around. As I parked along the curb in front of my mom's house, Troy began walking back down the steps of his porch to meet me.

"What's up, Dude?" I said with curiosity in my voice, wondering what the special occasion was."

Troy walked up to me, gave me our ritual handshake, and said, "Man, been out all day . . . Tired than a muthafucka."

"You lookin' mighty clean. What's the occasion?"

"I had a few job interviews today, and after those, went and filled out some more applications."

I was glad to hear Troy was at least trying, but he didn't sound confident at all. That let me know he didn't get any bites.

"That's good, man. You didn't mention to me that you had already been looking. You know I was gonna be lookin' out for you. How'd the interviews go?"

"You already know I know if I can't count on nobody else to look out for me, you will, but the interviews didn't go quite how I would've liked them to go. All I can do is wait and see what happens. I didn't mention the interviews to you because I knew I probably wouldn't catch anything, and I don't have time for nobody feelin' sorry for me."

"What's the problem? Why aren't they going well? Maybe I can help you with going over some interview questions."

"Nah. It ain't nothing like that. It's the fact that I don't have a college degree. Everything goes fine right up until they ask me how much schooling I have. When I tell them I only have a high-school diploma, the interview always goes left. They start hurrying the interview along, just so they can move on to their next prospect. I know I can do the work, but if you don't have college behind you, they won't even give a brotha' a chance."

Troy was finally trying to do something with himself and with him not being able to get a job, I just hoped he didn't lose hope and quit trying. I had already mentioned going back to school to Troy, but even that wouldn't help him right at this moment. For his sake, I was hoping he got at least one call back.

"Well, bruh, hopefully someone will be able to see how intelligent you are and how much potential you have, so that they're able to look past that. Sometimes it feels like my degree is just a piece a paper because I'm still not exactly where I thought I'd be right now."

"Now you know I know the truth to that! We're brothers, remember? Don't downplay that degree. You worked hard for it. You just preferred to mess around with all those bitches, staying out late, partying, instead of focusing on your career. Me, on the other hand, I should've grieved, and listened to you and came back to school. It probably would've been good for me. I needed something to occupy my mind back then because all I did was sit in the house and have pity parties every day. My liver and kidneys probably ain't shit right now from all the bottles I went through during that time."

This was the first time Troy had really opened up to me about what he went through mentally. He kept everything bottled up. I used to always try to call him, but he would avoid my phone calls, so I stopped trying. Every now and then we would talk, but he would never talk about the situation with Tramaine, so I never brought it up. I always figured if and when he wanted to talk about it, or even just vent, he would bring it up. It had taken almost seventeen years, but he was finally starting to come around.

"You can't live in the past. All you can do is make a better future for yourself. It's gonna happen for you. Trust that. But let me get in this house so I can see if moms need me to help out with anything."

Troy had a strange look on his face like he wanted to say something, so I said, "What's up my nig?" I kinda already knew what was on his mind, but I acted as if I didn't.

Troy lowered his eyebrows and said, "What's up with you being at your mom's house?"

I had already come up with what was somewhat of a lie.

"I just moved out of my old place. My lease was up, so I decided to stay here until I found a new place closer to my job."

"Aight. Good luck with that," Troy said.

I told Troy to keep his head up and walked back across the street. I could tell my mom was sitting in the living room because her lamp that she kept on when she sat in there in the evening was lit up behind the white sheer curtains. She must've been looking through the window, watching as Troy and I conversed because before I could knock on the door, she opened it from the other side.

"Worked a late one tonight, huh?" she asked as she held the screen door open for me.

I can't get in the house good before she start asking questions! I thought to myself, but I couldn't bring myself to lie to her. I gave her a hug and said, "Nah, I hung out for a little while after work."

"With that heifa' that got you kicked out of Day'ja's house?"

"No, Ma. I haven't even communicated with that bit . . ." My momma quickly folded her arms and frowned up her face. "That girl," I continued.

"You knew I was about to slap you, right?" my momma said, not joking one bit. "I always told you, don't disrespect a woman by calling her out of her name! You wouldn't like it if somebody called me out of my name, now would you?" she continued.

I was thinking to myself about how many bitches Armani had been in my mind, so I didn't answer my momma's question as fast as she wanted me to.

"You gotta think about it, boy?" she said angrily.

"Naw, Ma! Excuse my language, but you know I'd have to beat somebody's ass if they disrespected you."

She didn't even have to ask that. She knew the answer already. She just wanted to hear me say it.

"Ok, now that we got that clear, what was Troy out there talking about? You need to try and talk some sense into him. I hate seeing him waste away over there, and I hate his momma don't try to encourage him to do anything."

I already knew she was curious what me and Troy's conversation was about, but I wasn't going to bring it up without her asking.

"Actually, he is working on getting a job. He's on the right track, so he'll be ok," I said as I started walking towards my bedroom.

"Where you going?" my mom asked, still wanting to talk more about Troy.

"About to get ready to turn in. I'm getting out tomorrow to try to find me a place."

"You know there's no hurry. You can have as much time as you need. I know you just started this new job and you need to be focusing on that."

She thought she was slick. She knew the longer I stayed with her, the longer she could be in my business, knowing when I was coming and going, and I wasn't trying to have that. It brought me flashbacks of when I lived with her after I first came home after finishing college. That was the longest year of my life. She had to know everything I did, and every person I communicated with every hour of every day.

"I know there's no hurry, and I'm not worried about my job. It's cool. I'm just ready to have my own. . . And I'm kind of big for a twin sized bed now, Ma!" I said holding my lower back and frowning up as if I was in severe pain.

My momma laughed and in the same breath said, "What about the warden at work?"

I wished I hadn't ever mentioned Armani to my mom. Now she was going to continue to ask me about her, and personally, she wasn't at the top of my list of people I wanted to discuss.

"The warden is fine, Ma. Now, good night. I'm tired."

"Mmmhmm. I just bet she's fine," my momma said under her breath, thinking I didn't hear her."

When I finally got from my momma's presence from asking me a million and one questions, I went in my room, shut the door, and undressed down to my boxers. I had rushed out of Taryn's house so fast, my dick was stuck to my thigh from the mix of juices we had both secreted. I grabbed my phone and saw that I had a voicemail, so I decided to check that before I took a hot shower.

"Hi, Keith. This is Reagan. I saw that you called me a little while ago, like I asked you to, and I was just calling you back so we could talk. I know this is a little on the unprofessional side, but I think it's better if we talk outside of work, instead of worrying about a bunch of other people watching. Please call me back when you get a chance. Bye."

I hung up the phone and sat there at the end of my miniature sized bed, debating on whether or not I wanted to call Reagan back. She sounded like she really needed to talk, and I was curious as to what she wanted to talk about, but I had made a big enough mess for the day, so I decided against calling Reagan for the time being. I shut my phone off so I couldn't even be tempted by any phone calls or text messages through the night, took my shower, and went to bed.

I woke up the next morning to my momma screaming my name. I quickly jumped out of the bed and ran into the hallway that led to the front door.

My momma was standing at the door and said, "This is exactly what happens when you play with these women's hearts!"

"What?" I asked, walking briskly to the door to see what my momma was looking at.

Apparently, Day'ja had decided to clean house bright and early and dropped the rest of my belongings off in the middle of my mom's front yard.

"Are you fuckin' kidding me?" I said as I ran back to the bedroom and hurriedly threw on a pair of pants. By the time I got back to the front door, my momma had already went outside in her robe and house shoes and started picking up the mess. I ran out the door so I could hurry up and clean up all of the evidence of me having a dispute with that psycho bitch and getting kicked out. I tried my best to keep my business private, but women always seemed to want to make a scene. It just wasn't part of a woman's genetic makeup to be able to quietly let shit go.

As I started picking up my clothes from all over the yard, I noticed that most of them had been bleached and torn up. My brand new slacks and dress shirts had been torn to shreds, and my True Religion jeans were bleached to the point that I couldn't even play it off like they were supposed to be that way. As I picked up each piece, I became more and more pissed. I was huffing and puffing, and could see my momma looking at me in the corner of my eye as she helped. She could tell how angry I was, so she continued to help take things in the house until we were done, without saying a word.

After we got done, I grabbed my phone and turned it back on, getting ready to call Day'ja, but then decided I wanted to go to her house and talk to her face to face. I got ready to go, and with anger all over my face, told my moms I'd see her later. She knew I was hot tempered and told me to calm down and to not do anything I'd regret. I definitely wasn't about to calm down, and what I was about to do, I wasn't going to regret. That bitch had crossed the line. I thought this shit was over, especially after she had texted me and said she forgave me. I should've known better than that. Women always had to have their revenge one way or another. I was about to make sure Day'ja would never even think to do no shit like this to another muthafucka.

I had road rage all the way to Day'ja's house, darting in and out of lanes like there was no tomorrow. By the time I got there, I was even more heated than I was when I left my mom's house because the shit she had done to my property that I had spent my hard earned money on kept running through my mind. I quickly put my car in park, jumped out, and ran to the door. I beat on the door like I was the police, warning Day'ja upfront of the extent of my anger. I stood there for a minute, and when I didn't get a response, I tried to look through the front picture window to see if I could see her. I didn't see anyone, and I couldn't tell if she was home or not. Even though her car wasn't in the driveway didn't mean she wasn't there. It could've just been parked in the garage, which was where it normally was when she was home.

I tried knocking on the door one more time, trying to be courteous, but after I didn't get an answer after that time, I became extremely irritated. I tried my key that I hadn't given back, but of course the lock didn't turn due to her obviously changing the locks. Although the lock didn't turn, I did notice that the knob turned slightly. I twisted the knob, and the door opened. I didn't know whether or not to go in.

Before stepping completely in, I pushed the door all the way open. I looked to the left into the living room, which I had already gotten a small peak of through the window. I slowly continued through the quiet home, not wanting any surprises. When I got to the doorway of the kitchen, I was confused by what I saw. As I stepped in, I could feel and hear glass crackling beneath my shoes. Almost every cabinet and drawer was open and broken dishes were everywhere. This would concern anyone, but it really concerned me because Day'ja was always a neat freak and I feared something bad might've happened to her. I was pissed at her, but I still cared about her well-being. I was just coming by to put some fear in her heart, but would've never physically hurt her.

Before I jumped to any conclusions by calling the police, I wanted to explore the rest of the house to see what was going on. I ran up the stairs and there was stuff thrown everywhere throughout the hallway. It looked like food had been thrown up against the walls, and the chandelier that Day'ja adored which hung over the stairway had even been broken. I went through every single room of the house and not one of them was left untouched besides the living room. There was still no sign of Day'ja. As I was leaving out of the bedroom that Day'ja and I once shared, I remembered that I hadn't checked the garage to even see if her car was there.

I headed downstairs, walked through the broken glass in the kitchen once more, and opened the door to the attached garage. I did find Day'ja's car. The problem was that the car was running and I could see Day'ja inside through the driver's side window. I quickly ran and opened the car door. Day'ja couldn't have been in the car too long because she was still conscious.

She didn't look like herself at all. Day'ja was always well put together and never let anyone catch her slippin'. Today, it looked like her hair hadn't been combed, and she was wearing an oversized t-shirt that looked even too big for me, a pair of leggings, and flip flops.

She looked at me with tears in her eyes and said, "Why? What's wrong with me? Why couldn't you just be happy with me? I was happy with you."

Day'ja continued to ramble as I reached in to turn the car off and take the keys out of the ignition. After I had the keys safely in my hand, I said, "Come on, baby," with calmness in my voice, forgetting all about what she had done to my clothes.

She just looked at me and kept crying and rambling. I reached down and lifted her up out of the car and carried her into the house all the way upstairs to her bedroom.

As I attempted to lay her down, she grabbed the collar of my shirt with both hands, stared into my eyes and said, "I love you. Please don't go. Whatever I did to make you stray, I'll fix it."

If I could've told Day'ja right at that moment what she had done, I would have. Truth was, she hadn't done anything wrong. As a matter of fact, for a man who was looking for a long-term committed relationship, she had done everything right. I just wasn't at a place in my life where I wanted that. I wasn't a one-woman type of guy. At least not yet.

As I tried to get her to release my collar, she wrapped her legs around me. "Please, just tell me," she said desperately.

"Nothing! You did nothing wrong," I finally said.

"Well then we can just start over," she said, pulling me down on top of her and kissing me.

I could've easily taken advantage of her, but after I had just seen how emotionally unstable she was, I didn't want none of that crazy pussy. I just had to figure out a way to get out of there without leaving her alone. I was afraid that she might've tried something else after I left.

I kissed her on the forehead and said, "I'll be right back. "

I went in the bathroom, remembering I had Day'ja's older sister, Nadia's phone number stored in my phone. We had been pretty cool and she knew how to handle her sister. The girl had lost her mind and I didn't know what else to do. I was just glad that Nadia answered. I didn't go into detail while on the phone with her. I just told her she needed to get over to her sister's house ASAP.

While waiting on Nadia, I went back in the bedroom with Day'ja to try to console her. She seemed calm as long as I was there, but she kept asking me to promise not to leave her. Of course I couldn't do that, so I kept trying to stall and change the subject until Nadia got there. Luckily, Nadia was there to save the day within ten minutes.

When Day'ja heard the door, she had a surprised look on her face, and said, "Who is that? My house is a mess!"

"I'll go get that," I said as I attempted to stand up.

Day'ja grabbed my arm and said, "No, don't answer it! I don't want anyone to see me like this."

I gently yanked my arm from her grip and said, "Let me just go see who it is. I'll be right back." I ran down the stairs to open the door.

As soon as I opened the door, the first thing I saw was the look of worry on Nadia's face. She was only a couple of years older than Day'ja, but she looked out for her like she was her mother. She and Day'ja always talked on the phone at least twice a day. I had never seen two siblings as close as the two of them.

"What's going on, Keith?" Nadia asked, as I let her in.

"Man, your sister is trippin'. I didn't know what else to do."

Nadia folded her arms and said, "What do you mean by "trippin'"?"

I took a deep breath, a little intimidated by Nadia's heavy-set frame.

"I don't know if she told you, but we broke up a few days ago, and she wasn't too happy about it."

Nadia looked extremely confused and said, "No, she hasn't mentioned that, and I've spoken to her every day. You know we talk every single day. Every time I asked her where you were, she said work, or either you had run to the store."

I couldn't believe Day'ja hadn't told Nadia about the split. That was probably the problem. She was holding in all the anger she had towards me and she just snapped. Embarrassingly, I told Nadia about what happened with Day'ja receiving a text message with the nude picture, and in the middle of me telling her, Day'ja began shouting my name from upstairs. Nadia pushed me to the side and headed up the stairs. I leaned up against the wall, and wiped the beads of sweat from my forehead that had come out of nowhere. I heard shouting coming from upstairs and figured I should probably head up there.

When I got upstairs, from where I was, it sounded like Day'ja and Nadia were having an intense conversation. I crept down the hall until I could clearly hear what they were saying.

"I love him, and he does love me. He just doesn't realize it yet. He just needs some time," Day'ja said.

"Haven't we gone through this before, Day'ja? You can't make a man love you, and you can't just let men disrespect you in your own house and beg for them to stay! Shit, he should be begging you to let his ass stay! You are beautiful, successful, smart . . . everything a man would want in a woman. I've told you this before. You can have any man you want. The last man that treated you like this made you have that nervous breakdown. I don't want to see my little sis like that again. Get yo life, girl!"

I could hear Day'ja still sniffling and she finally interrupted by saying, "I've just never met anyone as perfect as him. He just doesn't understand what he has."

Nadia interrupted, "And that's the same bullshit you said about DeShaun after you caught him with that other woman. Might I add, in your bed! If Keith doesn't know what he has by now, he's not going to ever know. You need to just let it go and move on. The family can't deal with any other suicide attempts out of you, and that's exactly where this is going to lead up to if you don't get your head on straight and focus on what's important."

Nadia spoke sternly to her sister, forcing Day'ja to tell her what I hadn't gotten around to telling her.

Hesitantly, Day'ja said, "I was sitting in the garage with the car running and the garage door down when Keith stopped by. He pulled me out before it was too late."

For Day'ja to offer that information to Nadia made me believe she knew she needed help. I couldn't believe what I had just heard. I felt bad for Day'ja, but I also felt relieved that I wasn't the first person that made her lose her fuckin' mind. This one incident made me realize that when you start dealing with a person, you honestly don't know who you're dealing with, what kind of baggage they're carrying, and if they're mentally stable. Some of the most beautiful, confident, successful women could have more problems than a brotha' could ever imagine. I had heard enough, so I crept down the stairs and out the front door. I hoped Day'ja would get the help that she so badly needed.

When I got back home, my mom was sitting on the front porch waiting for me to get back. She stood up when she saw me pulling up. She had the look on her face of a mother that was extremely concerned about her child.

"What happened? Is everything ok?" she asked as soon as I stepped out of the car.

As I walked towards her I said, "Yeah, Ma. Everything's good. She wasn't home, so I just took a drive to cool off. They're just materialistic things. They can be replaced. I just want to be done with it. She got her vengeance, so hopefully now she's satisfied."

I lied because I didn't want my momma putting the blame on me as to why Day'ja was going through what she was going through. Truth was, that girl had issues way before me, but I knew my momma, and she would've never seen it that way. Especially when I knew she and Day'ja had a decent relationship.

I spent the next couple of days shopping, trying to replace everything that Day'ja had damaged. I wasn't even upset about it anymore. I probably would've felt worse if I hadn't gotten to her house in time to save her life.

Chapter Nine ~ Keith

After what I had experienced over the weekend, I had
planned to pretend like I had never called Reagan or
heard the voicemail she left me. I would act normal and
hope that she had changed her mind about whatever she
wanted to talk to me about, and wouldn't bring it up. I didn't
need any extra drama in my life. I guess that was just too much
to ask.

Bright and early, that Monday morning, I walked into the
office on time in a brand new pair of slacks and dress shirt.
When I got in, surprisingly, no one was there yet, including
Armani. I went straight to my desk and sat at my computer to
see if I had any emails about any upcoming deadlines. I saw
that Armani had placed a stack of work in the corner of my
desk. I just looked at it and shook my head. She was right about
one thing. There was no such thing as catching up on work
around here. As soon as I thought I was caught up, she brought
my ass plenty more to work on.

I heard the department door open. I then heard someone
walking through the corridor. I figured it was Armani, so I sat
straight up in my chair to look like I had been there a while and

was already extremely busy. I heard the sound of keys getting closer and closer, then the unexpected happened. Reagan showed up in my doorway. The first thing I noticed was how provocative she was dressed. She was sexy, but still classy. Everything about her was calling out to me, including her beautiful smelling fragrance that filled the air. The vibrant red lipstick she was wearing stood out against her gorgeous caramel skin. This looked like a completely different person from who I had been recently introduced to.

After I finished staring her up and down, hoping she hadn't noticed, I said, "Reagan, I wasn't expecting you."

With a smirk, she said, "Oh really. Then who were you expecting?"

"Well, normally Armani and I walk in around the same time. I looked at my watch and said, "You're a little early."

Reagan smiled, showing all thirty-two of her perfect teeth, and said, "Well, I wanted to make sure I got here early enough to speak with you alone." She swayed her hips from side to side as she walked from the doorway towards my desk.

Me, knowing where this was going, said, "Well, anytime you need to talk to me about anything in private, I'm here, and there's no problem with closing the door. What's the problem? Are you having any issues with your co-workers?"

"Nope, no issues," Reagan said as she walked behind my chair and began caressing my shoulders. She then continued, saying, "You seem tense. I hope I'm not making you nervous."

"You're not," I said, unintentionally enjoying the moment. My eyes began to roll in the back of my head and at that moment, I knew I had to nip shit in the bud.

"Reagan, I thought you came in here to talk about something. What do you need to talk about?"

She squeezed my biceps and bent down so that her lips were probably less than a half inch from touching my ear. I felt her breath as she whispered, "I know you got my message. I was looking forward to your call. What happened?"

As I tried to keep my composure, and search my mind for an answer, I could feel her tongue slide against my earlobe. I had to take a deep breath, and before I could answer, Armani out of nowhere, popped up in the doorway, startling both Reagan and me.

Reagan immediately released her grip and said, "Good Morning, Armani. Keith was just saying he had a crook in his neck, and I was trying to loosen it up for him." Regan looked at me and said, "How does it feel now?"

I could hear the nerves in her voice the entire time, but I had to give it to her. She was quick on her feet.

I twisted my head from side to side and said, "Yes, it actually feels much better. Thanks!"

"Carry on. I just stopped by to say good morning before I went into my office. I have a ton of work, so you probably won't be seeing much of me today," Armani said, not giving any hint as to whether or not she bought our story.

As soon as Armani left and walked around the corner, Reagan took a deep breath. "I'm sorry about that, Keith. Maybe we can talk later in a more private setting."

After that brief, intimate moment with Reagan, I was willing to agree to set something up so we could talk privately. She had awakened my big boy too damn early in the morning. As Reagan walked towards my office door, Taryn came walking in with a folder. I watched her and Reagan stare each other up and down and lightly bump each other as they walked past one another. Taryn had a look on her face like she didn't want anyone to speak to her, so I didn't. She tossed the folder on my desk, giving me no eye contact, and walked right back out, making sure I saw what I was missing by switching so hard, I thought she was gonna throw a hip out of place. I guess she was still upset about me not calling her like I said I would after our session of intimacy. She was behaving very immaturely about the situation, which worried me a little bit. Some women couldn't handle "just sex", and when that was the case, they could be very vindictive.

Taryn and I had one good time together and that was it. She obviously wanted something more out of it. I never took her to be the clingy type. By the way she represented herself, I was sure I wasn't her first one-night stand, and definitely wouldn't be her last. If we didn't work together and there was no chance of me losing my job over her, I would've loved to continue to fuck the shit out of her every now and then, but I wasn't about to take that chance over some pussy that probably had been around the block more than a few times. It wasn't worth it. By the way she was behaving, I knew she wasn't about that life anyway. She was acting as if I was her man and owed her an explanation.

I had been in the office for less than fifteen minutes and had already been visited by three gorgeous women. Something definitely had to give. I always believed that God gave us tests, but at that moment, I felt like he was setting me up for failure. What the hell did he want me to do with this situation? Women were my weakness. They didn't even have to be beautiful. As long as they were able to do something worthwhile for me, it was all good in my book. Beauty was just a bonus.

At the end of the workday, I got ready to pack up and walk out, but Armani had other plans for me. As I closed my office door behind me, preparing to lock it, I heard her voice.

"Keith, I'm glad I caught you before you left. I hope you don't have any plans right now because unfortunately if you do, you're going to need to cancel them."

I took my key out of the door and looked at Armani, who looked like she meant business. I wanted to tell her, fortunate for her, I didn't have any plans, but that wouldn't have gone over too well.

"Actually, I didn't have any plans, so it's cool," I said nonchalantly.

"Good," Armani said with a proud smirk on her face. "I need you to assist me with this project I'm working on. The deadline is coming up, and I could use some of your creative ideas. I could also use a second pair of eyes to look things over. Meet me in my office."

"Ok. I'll be there in a sec," I said as Armani walked with urgency towards her office. I glanced over at the other lady's cubicles. Almost everyone was gone, including Taryn, surprisingly. The only one left was Reagan. I assumed she was waiting on me by the look of frustration on her face. She cut her eyes at me as she straightened up her desk.

"Have a good evening, Reagan," I said as I winked at her, letting her know I didn't forget about our conversation.

"You have a good one, too," she said with a slight grin, as she threw her purse over her shoulder and walked towards the exit.

As I watched her, I smiled, just thinking about all the possibilities. She was very attractive, had a nice body, intelligent, and mature, unlike Taryn. Then the fact that she was very married entered my mind, which quickly brought me back to reality. My fantasy, because I knew that's all it would ever be, came to an end, and I turned the knob to go back into my office so that I could grab a few of my things that I probably would need while I was working with Armani.

The thought of working directly with Armani in her office made me a little nervous, but I thought I had probably survived the worst of her. When I got to Armani's office, her door was open, but she wasn't there. I sat down at her desk, across from her chair. While she wasn't in sight I looked around at everything in her office, trying to get an inkling of who she really was. That was a waste of time. Most normal women personalized their office. Not Armani. Her office looked like she kept everything as it was from the time it first became an office. It was very bland. No nice paintings, decorations, or knickknacks. There were only two personal pictures she had brought from home of her and her fiancé. I hadn't really had time to personalize my office yet, and thought maybe if I did, that would give her motivation to bring more personal things in.

After a few minutes, Armani came walking in.

"Sorry about that. I had to run to the restroom," she said.
"No problem."

Armani looked at me oddly as she walked to the other side of her desk to sit down. When she sat in front of me, she clasped her hands together underneath her chin and gave me a little grin. I looked behind me just to make sure she was looking at me. Surprisingly, I was still the only other person in the room. When I looked back at her, I suddenly realized I hadn't paid attention to her earlier because I had been so focused on Reagan. Armani looked flawless. Her dark hair was pulled back into a sleek ponytail with a side-part. That right there in addition to the dark plum lipstick she was wearing made her look sexy as hell. I knew she was attractive, but had never thought of her as being sexy. I realized then that she was just the type of woman who knew how to easily turn her sexy on and back off again.

Armani interrupted my admiration of her sexiness by saying, "I'm not sitting here staring at you just because I have nothing better to do."

The grin that was once upon her face was now gone.

"Ok, I get that. Sooo, what's wrong?"

"How are we going to work together on this thing and be productive if you're way over there?"

"Oh! I'm sorry. I just see you as a person who likes their space, so I didn't want to invade your personal space."

Armani squinted her eyes at me, and at that moment I knew it wasn't going to be pretty.

"Please don't act as if you know me. We have not been on any type of personal level for you to assume anything about me."

What does this woman want from me? I thought to myself. It seemed like she was always so defensive, making me feel like no matter what I ever said to her, it would always be the wrong thing. I was tired of just saying "ok" all the damn time and letting her feel like she was queen fuckin' bee and the world revolved around her.

Before I knew it I said, "Look, you can take what I said how you want, but we're not gonna get finished with what we need to do if you continue to have a problem with everything that comes out of my mouth. Don't be so defensive all the time. I'm here to help. I'm not against you."

I took a deep breath and waited for Armani to really lose it on me. I looked at her directly in her eyes. She looked astonished, as if I was the first person to speak to her that way.

"Ummm . . . ok . . .," Armani said, as she opened a large manila folder and began pulling papers out. She looked like she was looking for the right words to come back at me with, but couldn't seem to find them.

She cleared her throat and spoke so low I could barely hear her. "You're right. We need to get some work done, so let's do it. You can bring your chair over here, so we can review what I've already done."

As soon as I moved close to Armani, the sweetness of her perfume made me want to kiss her on the beauty mark I noticed on the side of her neck, just once, and then we could go back to being rivals.

Armani caught me gawking at her as she turned towards me, and she tried to not let me see that she was blushing.

"Ok, now let's get to business. I know you've probably heard that the layout of our magazine is being changed because, sorry to be blunt, but the current one sucks, and before you ask, no I didn't come up with it."

Armani opened herself up for it, so I decided to let her see how petty she was being not even two minutes ago.

"Yeah, Armani, you know me very well, because that was going to be my next question."

Armani quickly began to respond by saying, "No, I'm not trying to say I know you . . ."

She stopped speaking and sucked in her sexy lips as soon as she realized what she had gone off on me for just a few minutes prior, was the same thing she had just done.

"Look, Keith. I'm going to say this to you and I'd appreciate if you keep this between us. I know I shouldn't judge anyone, but I did judge you. Looking at you, I see a man that I've seen many times before. You're arrogant and probably used to women falling all over you. I didn't want you coming in here with the belief that you were going to get by easy, thinking I was one of those women."

I was totally shocked at what Armani was saying to me. She was being downright open about what her problem was with me. She had so many notions about me before getting to know me that I didn't stand a chance in hell! The crazy thing was, everything she had said so far was true except the part about me thinking I was going to get by off of my looks. I came into this job expecting to work hard, but Miss Armani obviously didn't feel that way. I let her continue without interrupting.

"I really do want to be more easygoing, but I'm not used to having to manage a man like you. I have to admit, you've done some really good work around here so far, and I appreciate it and expect you to keep it up. I'm going to back off a bit because I do see you're here to be a positive asset to the magazine. This is my baby and I just want to make sure no one comes in here . . . excuse my French . . . fuckin' shit up. I took a chance by hiring a freelance writer, and my boss is watching me, just waiting to prove that I made a bad decision by hiring you. I'll be damned if he proves me wrong. He wanted me to interview more people, and I thought I should have, too, but honestly, I had more important things to do than to continue to interview people who were just going to tell me what I wanted to hear. You understand a little bit now why I've been so hard on you?"

I was kinda feeling where Armani was coming from, but felt she was being a little selfish. She just wanted me to do well so she could get the recognition of choosing a good prospect for the job. She looked like a weight had been lifted off of her shoulders and sat there awaiting my response.

I leaned back in my chair, grinned, and said, "You think I'm a charming dude, huh?"

I had finally gotten a sincere smile out of Armani.

"Is that what you really got out of all I just said to you?"

I laughed and said, "Yeah, but I also got that you assumed that I was an arrogant misogynistic jackass. I never prejudged you," I said, lying through my teeth. I judged her as being a cold-hearted bitch, which she had been up until this point. I continued, "But it's cool. I understand why you've been so harsh from day one. I wouldn't want to be the cause of you losing any of the credibility you've worked so hard to earn, and you won't because I'm here to do a job and I will do it well, so you don't have to worry about that."

Armani, still with a smile on her face, said, "Let's just start over."

When she stood up in front of me, it didn't dawn on me that I should stand too, because I was too focused on her longs legs that looked even longer in the tall black heels and shorter than usual black skirt she was wearing. My mind began wandering, like it too often did, but this time I thought about how tightly Armani could wrap her legs around me.

"Are we going to start over or what?" Armani asked.

I jumped when I heard her voice and hurriedly got up out of my seat. We had made a lot of progress within only a few minutes and I definitely didn't want to regress. She looked up at my 6'2" frame as I stood in front of her. She was only a few inches shorter than me with those five-inch heels on.

She extended her left hand out to me and said, "Hi, Keith. I'm Armani, and it's a pleasure to meet such an intelligent young man who I'm sure will be an asset to *Couture* magazine."

I grabbed Armani's soft, delicate hand and said, "Thank you, Armani. It's very nice to meet such a beautiful, accomplished woman and I know it will be a pleasure working with you." I took her hand up to my lips and kissed the back of it.

She quickly snatched it back, and said, "Ok, let's do this."

I grinned knowing exactly what had just happened between Armani's thighs, as we both sat down and got to work. I had a feeling that only good things would happen from here.

The rest of the week was pretty busy for Armani and me, and of course, since we had a ton of work, the editors ended up having more responsibilities than normal. Armani and I ended up having late nights together every night that week. I didn't know how her boyfriend dealt with it, but if he liked it, I loved it. I hadn't even had a chance to have that conversation with Reagan because work had basically taken over my life. Taryn was still walking around with something stuck up her ass, but I didn't have time to address that either, and honestly didn't give a fuck. She didn't realize her job was in my hands, and if she did try to file sexual harassment, it was her word against mine, and she didn't have any proof that we were ever together outside of work. Shit, I had never even called her.

After a couple of weeks, when the office finally settled down and we all felt like we had time to breathe, the atmosphere became a little more relaxed and there was a little more talking, instead of just hearing the sound of fingertips tapping the keys of keyboards and papers shuffling. I was even able to leave the office in the afternoons right along with the editors. Surprisingly, Armani had begun leaving the office with us, too.

The first time Armani unexpectedly decidedly to leave out with us, I could tell Reagan was a little disappointed. As I was leaving, Reagan was waiting outside for me. I could see Taryn at her car, glaring at the both of us as we stood in front of the building, talking. I kept glancing back and forth from Taryn to Reagan as Reagan and I talked, making sure Taryn wasn't up to no good. I didn't think she wanted to fuck with Reagan anyway. It didn't seem like Reagan played any games.

"So, when do you plan on having time for me?" Reagan asked with a slight attitude.

"You know as well as I know it's been hella busy around here. I had good intentions on calling you quite a few evenings, but Armani and I have been here working pretty late. I know your situation and I didn't want to get you in any trouble at home."

After a minute of focusing primarily on the conversation I was currently having, I realized Taryn was no longer standing outside of her car, but it was still parked.

Reagan looked out into the parking lot to try and see what I was looking at. I think she already knew by the sarcasm in her voice. "Is there something or someone you'd rather be doing? If I'm taking up your time, go ahead and do you."

Reagan kinda caught me off guard, but I definitely didn't need for her to think Taryn and I had anything going on. I didn't know why Taryn would still be sitting there, but I quit worrying about it and continued my conversation.

I didn't know how to respond to Reagan, so I said, "I'm sorry. I was just trying to remember where I parked. Sorry if it came off as being rude."

"Mmmhmm. But anyway, you don't have to worry about calling me at a bad time. Just leave a message if I don't answer."

"Ok. Well, now I know."

Next thing I knew, I saw Armani trying to push the door open to get out of the building with a handful of stuff. I opened the door for her, and Reagan looked down as if Armani wouldn't know who she was. Suddenly, I saw Taryn's Impala speed out of the parking lot, which gave me the indication that she had been sitting there spying on Reagan and me.

"Thanks! I thought everyone was long gone," Armani said, inquisitively looking back and forth at Reagan and me.

Reagan wasn't so quick on her feet this time, so I said, "Nope. Reagan just had some questions on an assignment she's finishing up."

Reagan then decided to jump in and say, "Yeah. I'm going to do some work on it at home this evening, so just wanted to make sure I had all the info I needed because I'm sure Keith doesn't make house calls."

By the dumb look on her face, I could tell Reagan was kicking herself for what she had just allowed to come out of her mouth.

Armani gave me a perplexed look, and said, "Come on y'all. Let's go home."

"Let me help you with some of that," I said as I grabbed some of the items out of Armani's hands.

I knew Armani could tell something wasn't kosher, but she just couldn't put her finger on it. I was hoping Reagan had realized she needed to be more discreet when trying to have conversation with me. She needed to be patient and give me time to get back to her. The three of us walked together, got into our cars, and sped off to enjoy our evening doing whatever our lives consisted of outside of *Couture* magazine.

That evening, I still didn't call Reagan. I didn't even call the next day. Every time I thought about calling, I would find something else I needed to do. To be honest, I wasn't in a hurry to call her. I didn't know what Reagan was expecting to happen, but I was nervous as to what the outcome of this might be. I had finally found an apartment, so I had been busy trying to get everything taken care of with that. On top of that I had to deal with my moms running a guilt trip on me for moving out so soon. She sometimes confused the fuck out of me. She made it very clear that she wanted me to be an independent, responsible black man, but how was I supposed to do that while living with my mother?

When I finally did get around to calling Reagan one weekend, unfortunately she answered.

"Hello," I heard Reagan say after only the first ring.

She didn't even give me a chance to change my mind and hang up. She answered too damn fast.

"Hey there," I replied. "Is this a good time?"

"Yeah, it's fine. How are you?" Reagan said in a soft, sensual tone.

"I'm good. You having a good weekend?"

"It would be better if I could've spent part of it hanging out with you."

"Oh really?" I said, not knowing how else to respond. I knew what "hanging out" consisted of in my book, but she may have meant something different from what I had in mind. I left it at that, hoping she would say something to be more specific.

"That's all you got, huh?" Reagan asked disappointedly.

I decided to just get to the point and asked, "What is it that you would've liked to do?"

"Catch a movie, sit down and have dinner . . . I'm sure we could've agreed on something enjoyable to do."

Just as I had suspected, I was way out of the ballpark from what she meant by "hanging out". Even after getting past that point, I became more curious as to what her status was with her marriage.

"You're not worried about being seen out with another man?" I asked.

Reagan hesitated, and then said, "Chicago is a big city. I'm sure we can find somewhere discreet to have a good time."

"I made it out the hood without being killed. I'm not trying to be killed by no one's husband."

"I wouldn't put you in an unsafe situation. Just trust me. Now can we plan a date? I don't have much longer to talk."

I knew what that meant. Her husband would be home soon. I was already being treated like a side nigga and I didn't know how I felt about that.

"I don't think this is a good idea, Reagan. I've done a lot of things in my life, but never messed with a married woman. I don't think I have it in me."

"But we're not messing around. It's innocent. I just want to have a good time and good conversation. Is anything wrong with that?"

I was silent, thinking of what to say next. I guess I took too long, so she continued.

"I'm not going to force you to do anything you don't want to do, but like I said, it's innocent, and I'm going to make sure you're not in harm's way."

"Ok," I said. How about tomorrow? I'm not doing anything."

"I can make that happen."

I didn't want Reagan to know where I lived just yet, so I told her to meet me at five o'clock at the Wal-Mart a few miles down the road from me.

"Ok, love. See you tomorrow at five," Reagan said, after we plotted our getaway for the next evening.

"Talk to you later."

I didn't know what the hell I was doing. It didn't feel right, but something just wouldn't allow me to say no. I knew it was my dick talking to me, even though Reagan said it would be innocent, but I knew anytime a woman wasn't planning on anything happening, most of the time it still did. Women had a hard time turning down dick just like we did turning down pussy. We were all human and that's just the way it was.

<u>Chapter Ten ~ Armani</u>

I always had a reason for everything that I did, but to be perfectly honest, I didn't have a legit reason as to why I was being such a bitch towards Keith. I was glad that we'd had our talk and was able to clear the air. I had to hand it to him; he had handled me quite well so far.

The next week went better than expected. My work and home life were both going in the right direction. Since Keith and I had made amends, the office's environment was a lot less tense. Since we finally understood each other, I hadn't had to put Keith in his place too many more times, but I was waiting for Keith to put Taryn in her place. I just sat back and watched the interaction between the two of them and noticed she seemed to think she could do whatever she wanted to do. Taryn knew who she could walk over and who she couldn't, and she definitely knew not to play with me. I didn't think she noticed me watching her closely, because otherwise, she wouldn't have been acting the way she was. She hadn't been exactly disrespectful, but whenever Keith told her a certain way to do something, she always seemed to try to act like she had a better way and tried to show him out in front of the rest of the team. Reagan was the one I thought Keith would definitely have some issues with, but I had never seen her smile so much. She normally had a pretty hard exterior. Not as hard as mine, but to the point where she wasn't the type of person that someone would just walk up to and have friendly conversation. I had seen her and Keith being extra friendly towards each other, but it wasn't anything I was concerned about because Reagan was married and she was definitely the loyal type.

I hadn't talked to Keith about Taryn yet. I was just giving him time to handle his business on his own. That was his team and I was trying to keep the peace between the two of us and not step on his toes. I initially didn't think he would work out, but he was definitely stepping up to the plate.

Outside of work, I had other more important things to think about. That is something I thought would never come out of my mouth because work was always my number one priority, but things had definitely changed. Now, don't get me wrong. I still worked hard, because I knew better than anyone that someone could easily come in and take my position. That's exactly how I moved up. The person whose position I took was let go because she wasn't stepping up. I wasn't going to let that happen no matter what else I had going on.

Marcus and I had begun talking more and more about marriage, including what time of the year we were considering to exchange vows. We both agreed that summer or fall would be our seasons of choice. I didn't want to start making any big moves, such as, looking for a dress, renting a hall, and everything else that goes along with planning a wedding because Marcus hadn't officially proposed to me, and in my world, talk was cheap. I was not about to get ahead of myself and possibly come out looking like an idiot in the end. I couldn't see that happening, but you just never knew. Marcus had become so much more considerate, and finally began continuously reminding me of why I fell in love with him in the first place. He made me realize how much he wanted us to work out when he went to his boss and worked something out where he would only work late on Tuesdays, Thursdays, and some Fridays. It may have sounded like a lot, but it was a lot better than not knowing, and not ever being able to make plans with my baby.

I guess Marcus got fed up with it all when I showed up at his job after he had worked four late nights in a row. That happened shortly after the incident when he worked overnight and didn't call to let me know. When I showed up at the news station, I ran through there looking for Marcus like a mad woman. Everyone I asked had no idea where he was. One of his close co-workers, Eric, gave him a call on his cell phone, which I had tried to do, and told him I was there waiting for him. After about a half hour, he showed up with a McDonald's bag.

"I'm sorry, Mani. You should've told me you were stopping by. I would've waited to go get something to eat. I had to get something. I haven't eaten all day!"

I walked up to him and hugged him around his neck. I felt so stupid. My man was trying to make a living for us, not even having enough time in the day to eat, and there I was trippin' over nothing at all.

"No, I'm sorry. I just miss you. I wish we had more time to spend with each other," I said, trying to be as apologetic as possible.

"It's ok, babe, but I know these late nights are getting ridiculous. I'll talk to the boss and see what can be done."

"It won't hurt to try, but you have to do what you have to do. I'll survive, whatever happens."

I gave Marcus a kiss and told him I'd see him later. As I was getting ready to leave, I saw Eric setting up one of the studio cameras and laughing with one of the women who apparently worked in the studio. I hated to interrupt them because he looked like he was working and flirting at the same time. I couldn't blame him. She was a very pretty woman. I knew almost everyone who worked in the studio, but I had never seen her before, and she had suddenly just popped up out of nowhere. As soon as they saw me coming, they stopped laughing.

"Don't mind me! Eric, I just wanted to say thank you for calling Marcus for me. You know I can't be away from my baby too long."

Eric smiled and said, "No problem, Money. You know you're like a sister."

Eric called me "Money" instead of Armani because when Marcus first introduced us, he introduced me as "Mani", which was Marcus' nickname for me. Eric misunderstood him, thinking he said "Money", and had been calling me that ever since. Honestly, I kind of liked it.

I looked over at the woman Eric was talking to, and said, "And who might this be?"

The thin, but shapely woman with the caramel complexion and short, chic haircut opened her mouth to introduce herself, but before she could say anything, Eric said, "Oh, this is one of our programmers, Tamara."

I extended my hand and said, "Nice to meet you, Tamara. I'm Armani, Marcus' fiancé."

Eric strangely looked up at me, trying to figure out when the engagement came about. I looked right back at him, smiling.

Even though Marcus hadn't made it official with a ring yet, I had taken it upon myself to start referring to him as my fiancé.

Tamara shook my hand and said, "Fiancé, huh?" as she tried to quickly glance down at my empty ring finger without me noticing. "Congratulations, and nice to meet you as well!" she continued.

To satisfy her curiosity, I lied and said, "I don't believe in wearing a ring before the actual day."

Shocked to realize that I had noticed her looking at my ring finger, embarrassingly she said, "Oh, I'm sorry! I didn't mean any harm. When someone tells me they're engaged, I automatically look at the finger. I have a thing for beautiful engagement and wedding rings."

To take the attention off of my relationship status and quickly change the subject, I looked at both Eric and Tamara and said, "Sooo, to be only co-workers, you two sure do seem to have a lot of chemistry between you. I saw it from way over there," I said, pointing over to where Marcus and I were standing.

Eric and Tamara looked at each other and both burst out in laughter.

"Nooo, not at all, Tamara said. I'm already spoken for."

"Hey, I'm just saying what I saw," I said as I grabbed her left hand with the empty ring finger, and continued by saying, "And hey, you're not married, so you never know! Let me let you all get back to work," I said, giggling.

"I'm off the clock, so I'll be leaving soon so I can spend some time with my man. I was just chatting it up with my boy before I left," Tamara said.

"Both of you enjoy your night," I said as I walked towards the studio exit.

On the drive back home, I thought about the fact that Marcus had answered his cell phone for Eric, but didn't answer when I called. I almost called him to ask why that was, but I was satisfied just knowing he was going to find a resolution to our problem, and he did just that. That was the last night my man was stuck at work late without warning. If I would've known it was going to be that easy for Marcus to get his boss to work with him on his schedule, I would've asked him to do that a long time ago.

During our early evenings, we spent a lot of time in the city, going to a lot of different events, shows, and concerts. One particular night, Marcus came home with a box. Unfortunately, it wasn't small enough to be a ring box, which I had been hoping for since Marcus still hadn't formally proposed with a ring. It was a pretty big box.

Marcus had already made plans for the evening, and when I asked him what type of attire I should wear, all he told me was to "look beautiful as always." When he came in with the box, I already had on my clothes, which was a black pin skirt, a ruby red, jeweled corset, and my black Peep-toe Red Bottoms. My hair was done in a cute pin-up with a swoop bang, and I even threw on a little make up.

Marcus whistled when he walked in the room and said, "You look . . . There isn't even a word to describe how beautiful you look."

"You are so sweet! Thank you!"

Marcus handed me the box and said, "Here, open this."

"What is it?" I asked curiously.

Marcus eagerly said, "Just open it!"

I sat on the bed with the box, and began opening it, secretly hoping it was a ring in a very large box. When I opened it, it wasn't a ring, but I wasn't disappointed either. Marcus had bought me a gorgeous shimmering champagne colored Michael Kors dress. It was a dress that I had looked at while we were out a couple of weeks before and I didn't buy it because it was over a thousand dollars. I was always the type to spend money on myself and have buyer's remorse and end up taking it right back to the store. What made the dress even more special was the fact that I didn't think Marcus was even paying attention to me when I was looking at it.

"Thank you so much, baby!" I said as I stood up and grabbed his face. "I love you so much," I said as I kissed the love of my life, sucking in his whole bottom lip.

"Damn, girl. Maybe we should just stay home. You got me hot and bothered and only opened the dress! Keep digging, love. You might jump my bones next."

I was so infatuated with the dress, I didn't realize there was anything else left in the box. I pulled out a ton of tissue paper and underneath it all found a box that contained matching shoes. I turned around and looked at Marcus with my arms folded and said, "Wait a minute . . . What did you do, or what do you want?"

Marcus folded his arms, stood with authority and said, "I want your sexy ass to get undressed and put it on while I watch."

Those small moments of control were so sexy and kept me turned on. With that one sentence, Marcus caused me to have to change my panties, and I did exactly what he told me to do. After I was done getting dressed and looked in the mirror, I felt more beautiful than I did before. I just hoped we were going somewhere that was worth me wearing such an expensive garment. After Marcus finished watching me get dressed and getting a blowjob somewhere in the middle, he went and put on one of his best suits. When I looked at him, I felt like the luckiest woman in the world. His cologne lingered through the air making me want to pull him on top of me right at that moment.

"Come on. Let's go before we have to get dressed all over again!" I said.

"Girl, you better control yourself. And y'all women have the audacity to talk about us men!" Marcus said jokingly.

When we got in the car, Marcus still wouldn't tell me where we were going.

"Just relax and enjoy the ride, beautiful. You know, I'm not saying that just to say it. I'm truly a lucky man."

Marcus continued to make me blush, and I blushed even more when we pulled up to valet parking in front of Capital Grille. It was only one of the most upscale restaurants in the city, which I had wanted to go to for years and my baby had finally surprised me. I didn't know what I had done to deserve such a perfect night, but I was enjoying every minute of it.

Upon entering the restaurant, Marcus let the host know he had reservations. The setting was so romantic and we were seated in one of the most secluded, intimate areas. I was glad that I had worn what I did, because if not, I definitely would've felt underdressed. Marcus knew exactly what he was doing. All these years, I hadn't been giving him enough credit at all. The food was as delicious as I had imagined it to be and I was just happy to be spending the greatest evening of my life with my soul mate.

As we sat at the table enjoying our meals we talked and laughed about so many things. We reminisced about the past five years we had been together . . . Our ups, downs, and in betweens, then Marcus became very serious.

As he sat across from me, he stared me directly in the eyes and said, "I'm disappointed in myself because I should've done something special like this for you way before now. You definitely deserve it with everything you've dealt with during these past five years. I know it's been hard, but you've stuck in there with me and helped me learn how to be a good, considerate man to my woman."

Tears began welling up in my eyes as he spoke. I could feel all the love between us. There was no doubt in my mind that this man loved me.

"Marcus, you shouldn't feel disappointed. We all live and learn. I wasn't a pro at relationships when we got together either. We taught each other. I have in no way been the perfect woman."

"You're as close to perfect as it gets."

Those were the most beautiful words anyone had ever said to me and I had never felt so loved. I was at a loss for words. So much at a loss that when the waitress came asking if we were ready for dessert, I couldn't respond.

I saw the waitress walk away and Marcus said, "Bae, are you ok?"

I finally came to and in a breathy tone said, "Yes . . . I just love you so much."

"I love you, too," Marcus said as he stood up, walked around to my side of the table, and knelt to kiss me softly on the lips. When I reopened my eyes, the waitress had placed a plate with a slice of their famous cheesecake in front of me. Written on the plate in strawberry syrup were the words "Will you marry me, Armani?" Shaking uncontrollably, I put both hands up to my mouth in disbelief. I then looked to the side of me where Marcus was now on one knee with a box in his hand. This time it was a small box. He popped it open and it was a platinum ring with a huge solitaire diamond. I didn't even care about the size of the ring. The entire moment in itself was beautiful.

"Mani, this should've been done like this initially. I'm sorry if I ever made you feel less of a woman by not giving you the proposal that you deserve, but I'm hoping it's better late than never."

I still sat in front of Marcus with my hands still up to my mouth and tears streaming down my face. This was exactly why I never wore makeup because when I actually took the time to put it on, it was ruined by something like this. This time it was well worth it.

Marcus gently brought my left hand down from my face, took the ring out of the box and said, "Armani Crisette Atkins, will you please make me the happiest man in the world and be my wife?"

With my right hand I wiped away some of my tears and said, "Yes, baby! Yes!"

Marcus slid the ring on my finger, helped me up, and hugged me tightly. I hadn't even noticed people were standing around watching, video recording, and taking pictures until everyone started clapping. Marcus had made me the happiest woman in the world and no one would ever be able to outdo what he had just done.

Chapter Eleven ~ Keith

I woke up feeling better than I had felt in a long time. I was finally realizing it felt pretty good to live alone and not have to worry about a woman breathing down my neck, always trying to figure out if I was on some sneaky type shit. I could deal with who I wanted to deal with, when I wanted to deal with them. Today, I had chosen to deal with Reagan just to see what she was about. If we did become involved in any type of way, she didn't seem like the type to go crazy on a nigga' like Day'ja did me. I was starting to think maybe I should let women know that I come with a disclosure before getting involved so it wouldn't be too much of a surprise when things didn't go the way they would've liked them to go. Shit happens!

After bumming around the house all morning, I started getting prepared for my meeting. I didn't want to call it a date because I was assuming I wasn't gonna smash. When it came to dates, I always smashed, so I wouldn't be able to determine if it was a date or not until after the fact.

I went in my bathroom and looked in the mirror and saw I was starting to look kinda rough. I took the clippers out and gave myself a fresh cut and lining, and trimmed up my mustache and goatee. As soon as I was done, and began admiring my work, my phone rang. When I saw that it was Reagan, I was hoping she wasn't calling to cancel on me. I had finally convinced myself to do this, so I was going to be pretty upset if plans had changed.

"Hello," I answered, already sounding disappointed.

"Hey! How are you?" Reagan said, sounding excited, which gave me some hope.

"I'm good. What's up with you?"

"Just making sure you haven't changed your mind."

"Of course not. One thing I am is true to my word. When I tell you I'm going to do something, I do it."

Reagan giggled and said, "That's one of the traits I love in a man. That's so sexy."

Just the sound of Reagan's voice was waking up my big man, and I didn't even want him to get his hopes up, so I tried to quickly end our conversation.

"I just treat people how I want to be treated, so if you're cool with this then I'm cool. I'm getting dressed right now, so I'll see you in a little while," I said.

"All right, love. See you soon."

As I was hanging up the phone, I heard another voice in Reagan's background, and it wasn't a pleasant one.

"Who you in here talkin' to?" the deep voiced man asked.

I didn't want to hear anymore, so I quickly hung up. I assumed the person I had heard was Reagan's husband. I couldn't think of any other man that would've wanted to know who she was talking to. As soon as I heard that voice, an image popped in my head of Ving Rhames, and that right there made me a little nervous. I began thinking of ways I could back out, but I had just told Reagan I stood by my word. I was hoping that if Reagan didn't feel confident we wouldn't get caught, she would call it off. She was a smart girl, so I was sure she knew what she was doing . . . At least I hoped so.

When I pulled up in Wal-Mart's parking lot, it was packed, so I tried to park as far out as I could, away from other cars so

I'd be visible to Reagan. I was a few minutes early, but I still looked around for her silver Lexus. She was nowhere in sight. I put in my Miguel CD while I waited, to help relax my mind. I could honestly say this was the first time I ever felt a tad bit nervous about meeting up with a chick.

I had become so absorbed in the music playing, I hadn't realized that Reagan was fifteen minutes late and I wasn't about to continue to wait, because, for one, I waited for no woman, and for two, that couldn't have been a good sign. I started pulling out of my parking space and heard a horn honking. I didn't know where it was coming from, so I slammed on my brakes, making a sudden stop. I looked from left to right and still didn't see anyone or anything until I heard the horn again. This time it came from directly behind me. I looked back and saw Reagan through her windshield, smiling with her thick, perfectly shaped eyebrows raised.

I didn't know if she was going to come to my car, or if she expected me to get out and come to her car to greet her. This was something new to me, so I didn't quite know how things were supposed to go down. We hadn't even discussed who was going to be doing the driving. I just assumed since I was the man, I would. Reagan didn't seem to move, so I got out of my car and headed towards Reagan's driver's side window.

When Reagan saw me coming, she slightly stuck her head out of the car window, still with a grin on her face.

I knelt down to her level and immediately smelled the sweet fragrance that she was wearing, which was flowing from her car into the polluted outside air. When I looked at her, the first thing I noticed was how flawless her sun-kissed skin looked. She had a glow about her I had never seen before. She had even done her hair differently.

After admiring what was in front of me long enough, I said, "We supposedly made plans, but didn't discuss anything beyond this point. We're very bright, huh?" I said jokingly.

Reagan pushed her sleek hair that was parted down the middle, behind her ear and said, "Yeah, I know right? Well, how about I jump in the car with you and leave mine here. Is that cool with you?"

"Fine with me. I don't have to worry about anyone getting mad if they see a gorgeous woman in the car with me, but someone may get upset if they see a fine ass man in your car with you."

"Very funny, but don't quit your day job!" Reagan said as she got out of her car.

She looked me up and down as she glided past me, and said, "And you ain't all that fine, but you all right!"

I smiled, knowing she didn't mean it. When she got to my passenger side door, I saw her going to grab the handle, so I said, "What are you doing?"

"I'm about to get in the car. Isn't that what we just discussed?"

I gently moved Reagan out of the way, and opened the car door for her.

She looked pleasantly surprised and said, "So you're not the jackass that you try to portray."

"You're just full of jokes today. I've never seen this side of you."

After she sat in the car, she said, "Yeah, there's a lot of me you haven't seen yet."

I definitely liked where this was going and hopefully the best was yet to come. When I got in the car, Reagan was already pressing buttons on her phone.

I sat there staring at her for a minute without her even noticing because she was so concerned with whatever was going on in that phone. I decided to interrupt by clearing my throat.

"Oh, I'm sorry, she said still pressing buttons and not looking up. She quickly finished typing whatever message she so urgently needed to send, looked up at me and said, "Ok. I'm done."

By that time, I had pulled out of Wal-Mart's parking lot and started driving aimlessly, not knowing where we were headed.

"Hubby already stalking you?" I asked.

"No! I was texting my oldest to let her know what chores need to be done while I'm gone," she replied defensively.

I didn't want to mess up the mood, so I said, "Just messing with you. I know what the situation is. So how many kids you have?"

"Two girls . . . Fifteen and thirteen."

"Both your husband's?"

"Yeah. We've been together since we were fifteen.

"Fifteen? Wow!"

After letting that marinate for a minute, I was curious about a few things, and when I wanted to know something, I asked.

"So, can I ask you a personal question? You don't have to answer if you really don't want to."

"I think I already know what it is, but go ahead."

Without hesitation, I asked, "So, is he your one and only?"

As I continued to look at the road in front of me, in my peripheral vision I could see Reagan continuously glancing my way before answering. I glanced back at her, and I could tell she was blushing. I think I had embarrassed her.

"I'm sorry. That must not be what you were expecting me to ask."

"Actually, it's exactly what I knew you were going to ask, but for some reason it's still hard to answer, but to answer your question, yes, he's my one and only."

I glanced over at her with a look of disbelief upon my face. I didn't know that women like her still existed. I had officially struck gold, however, I was still a little confused. If after all these years, her husband was still her only, why did she choose to cheat now? Another thought that crossed my mind was that maybe she did this often just for companionship, but never had any plans on fucking me.

I elected to dig further by saying, "So you don't have anything to compare it to, huh?"

Reagan started laughing hysterically and said, "You know, you men are really funny! Always trying to be in competition. Let's get off of this subject and talk about where we're going because to me it looks like you have no idea. Time is of the essence."

Reagan had really thrown me for a loop and made me lose focus of everything except for trying to get some pussy.

"I guess we do need to decide, but it's nice just talking outside of the office getting to know each other, right?" I said.

"Yeah, it is, even though you're only really getting to know me."

"I'll tell you some things about me. Be patient, love. Now where do you want to go? You hungry?"

"Actually, I am. It's been a while since I've been treated out to a nice meal."

I looked at Reagan after she snuck in that "treat" comment. We hadn't discussed who was treating who, but I guess it was on me and I had to pay for what I wanted . . . literally.

"That's what I'm here for," I said like a perfect gentleman would. "I know exactly where to take a queen like yourself."

Reagan had given me serious motivation to wine and dine her, and get her exactly where I wanted her. I turned up the Isley Brothers as I cruised through the city, gently caressing Reagan's thigh. When we finally pulled up to a restaurant that I often visited, Reagan's eyes became big as quarters.

"Are you sure?" she asked.

"What do you mean?"

"I know how expensive this place is. I wouldn't even pay for myself to come here."

"If I didn't have it, I wouldn't have brought you here."

"Ok." she said, biting her bottom lip, trying to hold back her smile.

I got out of the car and by the time I got to the passenger side, Reagan was already closing the door.

"Woman, what did I tell you about that? I don't let women open doors. That's a man's job. Your husband needs to get some tips from me because he obviously isn't giving you the royal treatment."

I offered Reagan my right arm, and as she took it without hesitation, she said, "You better be careful. I just might get spoiled."

After Reagan and I were seated across from each other in the most low-key area of the restaurant, instead of looking through the menu that was in front of her, she gazed at me to the point where I felt uncomfortable for once in my life.

I finally said, "What?"

She shook her head and said, "What are you doing here with me?"

"What do you mean? "

"I mean, do we really know what we're getting ourselves into? Who knows what the future holds?"

Reagan was already starting to think too far ahead. I didn't like to discuss the future with women because if it didn't happen exactly as they wanted it to, it was like their life was over. My intentions weren't to have a serious relationship with Reagan or to mess up anyone's "happy home". I needed Reagan to focus on only today.

"We're just having fun, right? Let's just enjoy now, and deal with the future when it comes. This is only day one."

"You're right. I'm thinking too much. I want you to know that I'm already having an absolutely wonderful time with you."

I was glad that I was able to kill that conversation before it really started. That's where women went wrong. They started giving out pieces of their hearts too soon, and by the time everything is said and done, there's nothing left, so they're just left feeling empty and scorned. While we waited for our meals, we had good conversation and a lot of laughs. I wasn't even gonna lie. I was feelin' Reagan. She was the first woman outside of work who I was able to have an intellectual conversation with, and that was sexy as hell. She knew exactly how to make a man feel good, too. I guess by being married for the last fifteen years, she had an advantage over these women who were off and on with different dudes every other month.

Everything during dinner was perfect until Reagan started asking me a lot of questions about myself. It was all good talking about her, but when it came to me, I had to be sure not to say the wrong thing to throw her off. I knew I was quite a mess and under construction, but she didn't need to know that.

I knew the question and answer session was about to start when Reagan said, "So . . . ," and instead of going ahead saying what she was about to say, she put a piece of steak that was on her fork into her mouth and began slowly chewing as she stared at me.

After she was done chewing, she said, "Tell me why such a fine, as you say, smart, intelligent man as yourself is single."

Before I could answer, Reagan continued, "Oh wait! I may be assuming things, which is never good. You never told me you were single, so are you?"

"Yes, I'm definitely single. I was in a relationship not too long ago, but it didn't work out. To be perfectly honest, I just don't think I'm a "serious relationship" type of guy. It takes some men longer to reach that point in their life where they're ready to settle down. I'm just not there yet, and as you probably already know, most women my age want that full commitment."

Reagan squinted her eyes and raised one of her eyebrows, so I knew she was attempting to dissect what I had just said.

"So, what you're basically saying is you have commitment issues."

"Something like that. I can be committed if I really want to, but I'm just not trying right now. I don't want to enter into a serious relationship and vow to be committed to only her, and disappoint her by not fulfilling my promise. If I come across a woman who I know I want to spend the rest of my life with, then I will be totally committed to her because I wouldn't want to do anything to possibly lose her. In order for that to happen, I have to strongly believe that she is the one."

"I guess that's fair," Reagan said.

Since I had pretty much explained myself, I had decided to get into Reagan's business a little bit. She didn't seem to be shy about what she wanted to know, so I figured why should I?

"Now, can I ask you a question and you be completely honest with me?" I asked Reagan.

"You don't even have to ask me to be honest. I will always be just that. I have nothing to lie about."

"I'm not saying you have anything to lie about. I just want to make sure you don't hold anything back when talking to me."

Reagan folded her arms, sat back in her chair, and said, "Ok. Go ahead."

Why do you choose to spend time with another man when you could be at home with your husband? Are you not happy in your marriage?"

Reagan leaned forward, clasped her hands together like she was about to crack her knuckles, and rested her chin on them. I sat there waiting patiently for her to answer the question, and she wasn't in a hurry. She shrugged her shoulders, and I still waited for more.

"I don't quite know how I feel," Reagan began. "There was once a time in my life that I felt like I couldn't live without Will. Before, I could never imagine my life without him, but lately, it has crossed my mind quite a bit. I just feel like I've missed out on so much by being in this relationship since I was so young. I want to experience other things without having to answer to anyone."

"What do you mean by lately?"

"Maybe I'm being a little misleading by saying "lately". I've been feeling this way for a couple of years now, thinking it would pass, but I feel stronger and stronger about walking away every day. Believe it or not, this is the first time I've ever done this."

I didn't know what to say in reply to what Reagan had just said. I was so used to things being the other way around. I've had several of my boys who were married tell me the same type of shit. I never thought I would hear it come out of a woman's mouth and it felt a little uncomfortable.

"I just feel like I'm slowly falling out of love with my husband," she continued.

"So what are you looking for out of this situation we've begun creating?" I asked curiously.

"I don't quite know. There are a lot of questions that I can't clearly answer at this point because I honestly don't know the answer. I just saw an attractive, intelligent man that I found interesting and wanted to get to know, so I went for it."

"There has to be something you're missing at home. Where's the void that you're looking to fill? If you can at least answer that question, I'll better understand where I fit in the picture and what you're expecting from me. I want to at least be able to let you know upfront if I'll be able to fulfill those expectations. Do you just want to hang out every now and then like we're doing now or is this about sex? Is he not pleasing you sexually?"

I instantly saw Reagan's eyes well up with tears and at that moment knew we should end that conversation there.

"I understand if you don't want to talk about it now. Let's just enjoy tonight, and when you're ready, we can talk."

Reagan, trying to put up a tough façade, tilted her head back to try to hold back her tears and smiled.

"Yes, that's exactly what I want to do . . . Enjoy tonight."

Reagan and I talked some more while we finished our meals and had a little dessert. I was hoping Reagan would be my dessert, but I didn't even get my hopes up. After I saw her about to get emotional on me, I didn't know if I should smash even if I did get the opportunity. From the short time I did know Reagan, I never saw her as being the emotional, sensitive type, but I guess everyone had at least that one thing that could strike a nerve.

After dinner, Reagan and I went to the movies and saw *No Good Deeds* with Idris and Taraji. To my surprise, throughout the entire dinner and movie, I hadn't heard Reagan's cell phone ring, or seen her check it not one time. That made me think maybe things were worse between her and her husband than she led on. Whatever was going on, I was sure it would eventually come out. All I knew was that I was a bachelor and I wasn't making any commitments . . . Especially to a married woman.

After leaving the theater, I drove Reagan back to Wal-Mart to pick up her car so she could head back home to her family, and I could go back to my empty apartment. I pulled up next to Reagan's car, and put my car in park.

"Well, I had a good time. I'm glad you talked me into it. No regrets. How about you?" I asked as Reagan looked out the front windshield.

"I hate the night has come to an end," she said.

"It really doesn't have to. We can go to my place for a little while."

I became excited as Reagan looked at me like she was considering my offer.

"Maybe another day," Reagan said, shooting me down."

"Ok, that's cool," I said trying to not show how disappointed I really was.

As soon as I was about to open my door so that I could let her out, Reagan quickly leaned in, grabbed my chin, and gently kissed me on the lips. It happened so fast I never even closed my eyes. I stared at her while her eyes were closed and our lips became acquainted with each other. Reagan was even more beautiful up close. She slowly released my bearded chin and opened her eyes.

"That was nice," she said, sounding like I had taken her breath away. "I've been wanting to do that all night, but didn't know if it was the right thing to do."

"Well, was it?"

"Definitely."

"Well, good. I do aim to please," I said jokingly.

We laughed together, and after I put that one last smile on her face for the evening, I let her out of my car and gave her one more good night kiss before we said our goodbyes. The night had gone way better than expected, even though I didn't get none. I just didn't want Reagan to do anything she would regret later. I could tell she was definitely a good girl and I actually liked that about her. I didn't know where this was going, but I was willing to be there for her as a friend if that's all she needed.

The next week at the office, Reagan and I tried to act normal, but I guess Taryn's female intuition kicked in and she felt something wasn't right. She didn't have any type of filter and didn't care anything about bringing drama to the workplace. It was probably the way Reagan smiled at me when I walked past, or how often she had suddenly begun coming into my office to "ask me questions". Whatever it was, Taryn caught on to it real fast and called me out on it. She came at me without warning as I walked towards the restroom. I happened to hear brisk footsteps directly behind me, and as I turned around to see who it was, Taryn was walking so fast, she almost ran directly into my chest. She looked stunned, but not as stunned as I probably looked when her ruthless side came at me with full force.

Being extremely blunt, she let me know she definitely knew something was going on with Reagan and me. Before I could explain myself, I was saved by Armani. Sad to say, but by the fury in Taryn's eyes, at that moment, I preferred to explain myself to Armani rather than Taryn. Armani didn't realize how large of a fire she had just extinguished, but I knew it was only temporary, and it would soon re-ignite. I would have to deal with that later. I was just glad that after Armani bailed me out, she asked to see me in her office.

I knew Armani would ask what was going on, and I had planned on continuing on with my lie, but Armani asked even before I was able to speak a word that I not lie about the situation at hand. We had become so much better than that, so I went ahead and told her the truth. I knew she would be disappointed, but there was no point in lying when I already knew Armani pretty much knew the deal. She wasn't a dumb woman.

After that painful conversation, Armani schooled me on my recent work performance, and as she did, I noticed a beautiful ring on her wedding finger. When the words "I'm getting married" left Armani's lips, I wanted to be happy for her, but something inside of me just wouldn't allow it. I still congratulated her, but those were the hardest words that had come out of my mouth in a long time. I never considered myself a hater in any way, shape, or form, but the way I was feeling made me question myself a little bit. I wanted to meet Armani's fiancé just to see what type of man he was. I was curious as to what she perceived as attractive in a man. What I found odd was even with all the hours Armani worked, he never just stopped by the office to see her, and I damn sure hadn't seen any flowers be delivered to her.

As Armani and I got into a little bit of a more personal conversation, I wasn't sure if it was about her or me, but whatever it was about, it caused the temp in the room to rise. I knew that I had worked my magic on her after she began picking up random things to fan with. She was on fire, and just seeing that caused my body temperature to rise. I couldn't allow her to know what effect she was having on me, so when she asked me if I was hot too, I acted normal, making her feel as if it was only her. I was relieved when Armani rushed me out of her office by telling me we needed to get back to work. Armani and I had had several conversations before, but nothing that ever caused that type of sexual tension. I knew anytime a chick could get a man off his game just through conversation, that was one bad ass bitch. Marcus needed to be careful because I knew if I really wanted Armani, I could have her, but at the moment, my mind was focused on the fun I was having with Reagan. I knew our "thing" wouldn't last forever, and that wasn't my desire, but I was going to take advantage of the situation while the opportunity presented itself.

Chapter Twelve ~ Armani

Since finally having a huge rock on my finger, I wasn't modest at all about flaunting it. I didn't even have to tell people I was the future Mrs. Armani Atkins. My ring said it all. The only person that hadn't said anything about it was Keith, but I figured the last thing that a man paid attention on a woman was her finger because it didn't have any curves. Keith seemed like his mind had been elsewhere lately anyway. Anytime I would walk into his office, it was almost like he was in a daze until I snapped my fingers. I didn't know what was on his mind, but he needed to get it together because it was beginning to show in his work big time. His work was still on time, but he was very close to not making deadlines, which made me nervous. His work had also become sloppy. I knew he was better than what he had been turning in to me.

While sitting at my desk, I heard an argument going on near my office door. I quickly got up to go see what was going on.

Before I got to the door, I could hear Taryn say, "I don't know what's going on with you and that bitch, but the shit better stop!"

As soon as I opened my door, I didn't see anyone until I looked to my right and saw Taryn and Keith standing in one of the side hallways, attempting to be discreet. That obviously wasn't working for them. They both looked like they wanted to kill each other.

"What's going on out here? I hear you two out here sounding like an arguing couple, and I know that surely can't be the case because we all know the rule about department relationships," I said folding my arms and waiting for an answer.

While waiting, I was secretly praying that Keith hadn't stooped to that type of ratchetness. Taryn was one of our best editors, but she was still in that young and dumb phase of her life. I had seen her at several of the company's holiday parties and events get sloppy drunk and leave with random men. She wasn't the type of woman I could see Keith going after or even entertaining the thought of being involved with.

Keith and Taryn both looked at each other, trying to communicate with their eyes and facial expressions as to how they were going to explain themselves.

"We're sorry for being so loud. Taryn was just voicing her opinion over a disagreement about something and it got a little out of hand."

Taryn wouldn't even look me in the face. She looked down at the floor and just nodded, agreeing with the lie Keith was telling.

"I hope the disagreement was over something work-related and not personal. If it is personal, I suggest the two of you fix it quickly."

As I turned around to walk back into my office, I said, "Keith, I need to see you."

As I took a seat at my desk, Keith walked in with his hands in his pockets.

"Please close the door behind you."

Keith and I had gotten past the formal stage of our office relationship, but no one else needed to see that side of it. We had actually formed a pretty good friendship.

After Keith closed the door, I quickly stood back up and said, "Keith, are you serious? Please don't tell me you have something going on with that girl!"

"It's not like that," Keith casually responded, as if what had just happened was normal.

"What do you mean it's not like that? Then what is it like?"

He opened his mouth to speak, and I felt the need to interrupt by saying, "And please don't lie to me."

Keith took a deep breath and rubbed his palms together. That's when I knew what it was.

"We had a slight indiscretion, and now she's a little upset because I didn't allow it to go any further."

My heart sank because I had come to think so much more of Keith.

"Sooo, not boss to employee, but friend to friend, you hit and quit?"

I could tell how uncomfortable Keith was having that conversation with me, but I needed to know exactly what was going on, even though at that moment I wished I hadn't overheard them arguing in the hallway because I no longer wanted to know about Keith and Taryn's affair. It made me have visual thoughts that made me feel some type of way.

There was still something that wasn't making much sense, so I asked, "So what "Bitch" was Taryn talking about?"

"Huh?" Keith said, looking confused, when I knew that he really wasn't. Since he wanted to play that game, I gladly refreshed his memory.

"When the two of you were standing in the hallway just now, I heard Taryn say, "I don't know what's going on with you and that bitch, but the shit better stop.""

Suddenly, Keith had an epiphany.

"Oh yeah. She thinks I have something going on with my ex, so now she thinks that's the reason why I didn't continue a relationship with her, when the truth of the matter is, after we had already did what we did, I realized how wrong it was because I was her boss. I knew if anyone found out, I could potentially lose my job."

Keith's answer sounded legit and I could only go by what he told me, so I accepted that.

"Keith, you're great at your job. I really can't afford to let you go, and it's really not my place to tell you who you can be with, but you have to be smart, because if my superiors found out about this, it would be out of my power to keep you here. Taryn is reckless. I had already noticed the tension between the two of you a while back, but I just thought it was workplace drama. You don't want to allow her to make you lose what you've worked so hard for."

"I realize all of that, and I apologize for putting you in an uncomfortable position."

I could tell Keith believed that Taryn would soon forget about what happened and move on, but I was a woman, and I knew better. I knew I had to figure out a way to take care of the problem and that's what I would be working on until it was resolved. As for now, Keith and I needed to talk about other things.

"Have a seat. I needed to talk to you anyway."

"Uh oh. What'd I do now?" Keith asked with a smile on his face.

As I sat down, I laughed and said, "It's not horrible, but I want to catch it before it gets that way. You're cutting it very close with your deadlines, and on top of that, your work hasn't been as great as it had been previously. Is it the Taryn situation that's had you spaced out lately?"

"Nah. I've just had a lot going on. I recently moved to a new place and I've been dating someone, so I admit I haven't been putting enough time into my work, but starting right now, you don't have to worry about that."

"Ok! Good!" I said. As I pushed my hair out of my face, I saw Keith's eyes follow my hand until I put it down on my desk.

"Something wrong?" I asked.

Keith brought his eyes back to my face and said, "I was just admiring that beautiful rock on your finger. So, what does it mean?" he asked, looking more serious than I had ever seen him look.

"I guess I'm getting married."

"Really? Wow. Congratulations."

Even though Keith told me congratulations, for some reason it just didn't seem sincere.

"Thank you. Are you just now noticing I was wearing a ring? I've been wearing it for at least a couple of weeks now."

"I hadn't noticed, but I wish the best for you and your guy."

"Marcus," I corrected him.

"What?"

"Marcus. That's my fiancé's name."

"Oh. Yeah, right . . . Marcus."

Since I had briefly spoken on my relationship status, I felt it was ok for me to be a little nosey and ask about the woman Keith had been dating.

"How long have you been dating your friend, if you don't mind me asking?"

"Not at all. Just a couple of weeks. Nothing serious. Just having a good time for now."

"Oh, a fresh romance. I remember how that feels. Everything about it makes you feel good."

I got lost in my thoughts and said, "He always compliments you, and every time he does, your heart flutters. Every text and phone call gets you excited, you can't wait to get off work to see him because he always has a surprise for you . . ."

I thought to myself, *I wish that feeling of newness never faded.*

Keith interrupted my thoughts and asked, "Are we talking about you or my relationship?"

"Oh, I'm sorry! I'm speaking in general. The beginning is always the best."

"But if a man is doing his job right, his woman should always feel that way, no matter how long you've been together."

Hearing those words come out of Keith's mouth and watching his sexy lips as they moved, I quickly lost focus. Before realizing what was going on, I grabbed a sheet of paper from my desk, folded it a few times and began fanning myself. That wasn't working, so then I picked up a magazine and began fanning with that.

"It's hot in here. You're not hot?" I asked Keith.

"Nope, I'm fine," Keith replied, with a smirk on his face.

I then realized that the heat I was feeling was generating from within the inside of my body and not at all coming from the temperature in the room.

"Ok, well, we both need to get to work, so I'll talk to you later," I said, politely telling Keith it was time for him to go.

"Ok. See you later," Keith said as he stood up and walked towards the door.

I watched him, as his beautiful physique would not allow my attention to focus on anything else.

When he opened my door, he turned around and said, "You want me to leave this open so you can get some air circulating up in here?"

"No, that's ok. I don't need any distractions."

As soon as Keith shut the door, I took a deep breath and slouched in my chair.

Chapter Thirteen ~ Armani

Another late night working, and that's all it seemed like I did lately. I wasn't a stranger to working my life away, but Keith, on the other hand, was new to it. He was learning very quickly that there really wasn't any other choice in our line of work. We either got it done or start looking for a new job. That wasn't an option for me, and the way Keith put up with me during the first few weeks of working with me, I assumed that wasn't an option for him either. Anyone else would've walked out on me without a second thought. Keith stuck with me and I was actually happy that he had.

As I was going over some of our proofs of the final draft that were getting ready for print, Keith walked in with dinner. Time had escaped us and it was already 10pm. We still had a lot to do, which meant we would probably be in the office for a few more hours, so Keith had offered to go pick us both up something to eat. When I saw him walk through the door with a handful, I quickly got up from my desk to take a few things off his hands.

"What did you do? Order everything on the menu?" I asked, as I grabbed the drink carrier out of one of his hands.

Grinning, he said, "Nah. You didn't exactly tell me what you wanted, so I just got you a few different options."

"Thanks! You are so thoughtful."

I sat down and as I rummaged through each bag, I felt like I was being watched. When I looked up, my assumption had been correct. Keith was sitting across from me, watching me with a sly look on his face.

"What?" I asked.

"Nothing. I'm just enjoying the view. I love just looking at you."

Keith shocked me with those words. He had never said anything out of the way to me, and I didn't know if I considered what he'd just said as being out of the way, but it definitely gave me a feeling I was unable to describe.

I cleared my throat and quickly looked away from Keith as I settled on grilled chicken that I pulled out of one of the bags that Keith had brought in. The room was so quiet that it became uncomfortable.

"Aren't you gonna eat?" I asked after I finished chewing a piece of chicken.

"I don't want to get full off of any of that before I have what I really want."

I looked at Keith with a puzzled look on my face because I was beyond confused.

"You bought all of this food, and none of it is what you want?" I asked inquisitively.

"What I want, money can't buy. My taste buds are very particular about what they want, and I have this craving I need to satisfy."

Keith stood up, and as hard as I tried, I couldn't take my eyes off of him. I watched him as he walked towards me. He turned my chair until I was facing him and knelt down on one knee. My heart began pumping insanely, and in my mind I was asking Keith what he was doing, but of course, that wasn't helping one bit. One by one he lifted my feet and unbuckled my strappy heels. He removed both of them and carefully placed them out of the way. He took one foot into his large hands and gently massaged it. Just from his touch, he sent a tingling sensation throughout my entire body. I was thanking God that my feet were freshly pedicured, while I should've been thinking about the fact that I was happily engaged and trying to put a stop to what was happening. As soon as I tried to focus on what was the right thing to do, I felt Keith's soft lips as he gently sucked my toes. I felt my eyes as they rolled to the back of my head and felt my lips parted as I inhaled deeply. As all thoughts that were non-factors at that moment left my mind and all I could focus on was the pleasure that was currently fulfilling every need of my mind, body, and soul, Keith made his way up to my stomach, pulling my neatly tucked blouse out of my skirt. He slowly slid both hands behind my back, unsnapping by bra. He made my spine quiver as his smooth hands made themselves visible once again. He then slipped them underneath my bra, massaging my erect nipples. He carefully placed kisses across my stomach as if he was methodically telling me what he wanted, by doing so.

"You want me to stop?" Keith whispered.

"No," I whispered back, with my eyes closed, and as soon as I replied, his hands found their way underneath my skirt as they searched for my black lace panties. When they found them, I lifted my ass just enough for Keith to pull them down without struggle. He stood up and grabbed both of my hands, pulling me up out of my chair. He looked at me with passion in his eyes and turned me around to unzip my skirt. As my skirt fell to the floor, he spun me around and licked his lips as he stared at me.

"Take off your blouse," he demanded. "I want to see all of you."

He was in control of this situation and he knew it. It actually turned me on even more. He watched as I was submissive to his demand, removing my blouse, and then the bra that was already half removed.

"Wow, you're perfect," he said as he motioned for me to come closer.

I got so close that I could've sworn I heard his heart pounding through his chest. I knew if I could hear his, he could definitely hear mine.

He looked down at me and said, "Unwrap the gift that I know you've been waiting for."

I sucked in my bottom lip, and as I began loosening his belt, he grabbed my ass, squeezing it as if he never wanted to let go. His pants fell to the ground and I had almost finished unwrapping my gift. I looked up at him, and he kissed me on my forehead, gesturing for me finish. When I unleashed his juicy dick from underneath his boxers, it curved with its head standing straight up like a snake looking for its prey.

Keith took my arms and wrapped them around his neck and carried me over to the huge picture window in my office. He pressed my warm body up against the cool glass. While keeping one arm tightly wrapped around me, he reached down with his other hand and rubbed his dick back and forth across my pussy until he was ready for me to feel what I had been waiting for. As he slowly eased his way inside of me, we exhaled together. With each thrust after that, the heat between us became hotter and hotter like we were creating a fire. My entire body jerked each time he hit my G-spot. It felt like someone was behind me, literally pushing my body into his.

"Baby, please don't make me cum yet!" I pleaded.

Keith, of course, didn't listen. My begging just turned him on even more. He was high off of me and began thrusting harder and faster. Just as we were both about to climax . . .

"Armani!" I heard a familiar voice say, but it wasn't Keith's.

I jumped straight up in a cold sweat to find Marcus sitting up in bed, right beside me.

"You ok?" he asked, sounding worried.

Still breathing heavily and moving my hair that was damp from sweat out of my face, I said, "Yes, I'm fine."

"You don't seem fine. Did you have a nightmare? You were jerking all over the bed. I thought you were having a seizure for a minute!"

"I guess I did have a nightmare. Sorry for waking you," I said as I rolled over, repositioned my pillow and tried to go back to sleep.

Marcus wrapped his arm around me and kissed me on the back of my neck.

"I love you, bae. Sweet dreams this time!"

"Love you, too," I replied.

As I tried my best to go to sleep, every time I closed my eyes, I saw Keith's face. I kept wondering why I would have such a dream. Yeah, I thought Keith was attractive, but I would've never thought of having any type of sexual relationship with him. So many lustful thoughts began clouding my mind. I even began wondering how accurate my dream was when it came to Keith's body up underneath those clothes. My thoughts didn't allow me to doze back off before my alarm was going off to get ready for work. I reached over to shut it off and took a deep breath. Marcus didn't move. The dead weight of his muscular arm was holding me down, so I wiggled a little bit to wake him.

When I finally got him to move, I said, "You must be exhausted! You didn't even hear my alarm go off."

"Yeah, I am a little tired. A lot has been going on at work. By the way, I'll be working a little later than normal tonight. Not too late, though."

"But it's Wednesday!" I pouted. "Wednesday evenings are supposed to belong to us!"

"I know, sweetheart. I'm sorry. If there was a way out, you know I'd make that happen, but I have no other choice. You know I'll make it up to you."

With my lips still poked out, I said, "I know babe. Do what you have to do."

Then Marcus tried to turn things around so he wouldn't feel so guilty by saying, "I haven't been the only one having to spend late nights at work lately. If I didn't know any better, I would think you have yourself a little sidepiece," he said, laughing, knowing there was absolutely no truth to that.

"Yeah, ok! You just don't be out too late!" I said and jumped out of bed to begin getting ready for another long day at work. I figured I'd get a lot done since I knew Marcus wouldn't be home early. There was no need for me to try and rush home.

When I got to the office, Keith had already made it in. I had caught on to his routine. When he felt like he was going to try to leave work at a reasonable time, he tried to get started early with his day. This must've been one of those days. When I walked past his office, his door was open, but I knocked on it anyway to get his attention as he took a sip of his coffee.

"Good morning, Armani," he said sounding like he was happy to see me.

Maybe he had the same dream I had last night, I thought to myself.

I attempted to clear my mind of vulgar thoughts and said, "Morning!" with just as much enthusiasm as Keith had in his voice.

"You must've had a good night!" Keith said, grinning from ear to ear.

"You just don't know how good of a night we had," I mumbled under my breath, hoping he didn't hear me.

"Oh wow! Marcus must've put it on you last night."

"I prefer that we not discuss my sex life," I said politely.

"Oh. Ok. I completely get it! Glad you had a good time!"

"Thanks!" I said as I laughed. "You planning on a short day today?" I asked, just because I wanted to be nosey.

"Yeah, I'm hoping for it. I should never make promises with this work schedule, but I kinda promised my friend I'd try my best to get off early so we can do something nice."

"Oh. Ok. Well, I hope it works out for you. Let me get to work. There's lots to be done," I said and rushed out of Keith's office. Although I was happy for Keith and his "friend", I seemed to feel strange when he brought her up in conversation. The rest of the day, I basically stayed closed up in my office, trying to convince myself that I didn't have any type of unprofessional feelings for my subordinate. I went over in my head a million and one reasons why I couldn't possibly have feelings for Keith, and a billion reasons as to why I probably had the dream, countering any conclusion that pointed to me having some type of sexual feelings or desires towards him. Each time he came into my office for something, when he left, I would have to start the process all over again, so just imagine how productive my day was after he walked in and out of my office at least fifteen times during the eight hours he was there! One thing I did realize was that he really liked the chick he was dating. He made it a priority to make sure he got more than enough work done to make sure he made it out of work early, just as he had promised her. He seemed to have his life in order, so I needed to get it together and focus, and that was exactly what I was going to do.

Chapter Fourteen ~ Keith

Since Reagan and I weren't able to have any overnight rendezvous', I had planned something special for her just so we could get away from the world for a few hours and enjoy each other's company. We had been out quite a few times, but hadn't been sexually involved. I can be honest and say that in the beginning that's what I was primarily interested in, but Reagan was a cool girl and I didn't want to push it on her. She wasn't that type of chick. She was different from others, and even though she was married, and I didn't get to see her as often as I would have if she was all mine, I hadn't even been fuckin' with other women. I was in a drought and was going through severe withdrawal, but Day'ja definitely taught me a lesson to be careful where I stuck my dick. Although I didn't want to pressure Reagan, in the back of my mind, I was hoping that what I had planned for her in the little bit of time that we had together would get me what I felt like I deserved. The cookies.

I made sure that by the end of the work day, I had completed so much work that Armani would be left speechless.

Surprisingly, she stayed to herself most of the day, which wasn't much like her. Every time I went into her office she seemed tense, but I figured she was just in one of her moods, so I made sure I watched everything I said before the old Armani resurfaced. I didn't need to give her any reason to try to keep me afterhours. This might've been the last opportunity I had to show Reagan that I deserved what she had to offer.

Before leaving the office, I stopped in and told Armani I'd see her the following morning. She was sitting at her desk wearing those ugly ass glasses that I hated, and had about ten neatly stacked journals sitting in front of her.

"Late night tonight?" I asked.

She looked up as if I startled her and quickly removed her glasses.

She took a deep breath and said, "Yeah, unfortunately. I don't have any plans like yourself, so what better way to spend my evening other than working?"

Armani looked like she needed someone or something to lift her spirits, so doing what I do best, I worked my magic. One thing I was always good with was words.

With a smile I said, "I'm sure a beautiful woman as yourself can find something to do in this big city."

Armani giggled and said, "Sorry brotha', your charm does not work on me, but I have an idea! Maybe I can be the third wheel on your date."

My smile quickly disappeared and I began stuttering as I tried to produce the correct response in my head. It wasn't coming to me quick enough.

Armani finally attempted to take me out of my misery and said, "It was a joke! I'm not pathetic. I do have a man . . . a fiancé in fact . . . who just had no choice but to put work before me today."

I was glad that she said the third wheel thing was a joke, but she didn't make the conversation any more comfortable by making me feel bad for her like I was the one who left her hanging.

"Well, I'm sure he's working on trying to make sure your wedding day is the best day of your life. You'll have plenty of other nights to spend with him. Trust me when I say he knows what he has and he hates having to be at work tonight just as much as you hate that he has to be there."

Armani pooched her lips and grinned before saying, "You're right. Quit wasting time in here and go have a good time."

As I was leaving the office, for some reason I still felt like I owed Armani something, but wasn't sure what it was. I felt like I needed permission from her to do what I was about to do. I suppressed every thought of Armani from my mind when I walked out of the building, and pulled out my cell phone to call Reagan to make sure she was on her way to the parking garage where we had agreed to meet. She must've been just as excited about our evening as I was because I hadn't even seen her leave the office.

"Hey, babe! You on your way?" Reagan said as soon as she answered.

"Yep, just leaving the office. Sorry I'm running a few minutes behind schedule. Armani needed me to take care of something before I left."

"Sure she did. You know she just tries you to see what you'll tolerate from her."

I didn't know where Reagan was coming from with this, but she sounded like she had some type of beef with Armani.

"Well, sweetie, I don't really have a choice but to tolerate whatever she dishes out. She's gotten a whole lot better since I first started at the job. We now have an understanding."

Reagan was silent for a moment and then said, "Understanding, huh? Just be careful and don't get too close."

There goes that unnecessary cattiness, I thought to myself and decided it was time to deaden that conversation.

"I hear ya! I'm pulling out of the parking lot now. I'll see you in about five minutes."

"Ok, love."

As I hung up the phone, I shook my head in disbelief at the way Reagan was talking about Armani. She never seemed to have a problem with her before, and nothing had changed. At least not that I had noticed. It seemed like her feelings had shifted from Taryn's crazy ass to Armani. Don't get me wrong, Reagan still couldn't stand Taryn, and I was sure Taryn felt the same, but they stayed in their lanes. Taryn would still give Reagan and me dirty looks, but so far, she hadn't run to anyone else with her assumptions. We wouldn't have anything to worry about in about a week because Taryn was being transferred to the office way on the South Side of Chicago. I kinda believed that Armani had something to do with that due to the fact that this came about only a couple of days after I told her about Taryn and me. Until Taryn was officially gone, Reagan and I would still make sure that we were very careful with how we interacted with one another in the office to avoid any interoffice drama.

I darted through traffic trying to get to Reagan as quickly as possible. Time was of the essence and I was determined to make every minute count. When I finally made it to the parking garage, I circled around each level until I finally found Reagan leaning against the hood of her car, smiling as I pulled up in front of her. I got out of the car and as soon as I did, she came walking towards me with her arms spread wide and bright red lips puckered.

I grabbed her, hugging her tightly. Next thing I knew, her tongue was down my throat.

"Oooh! I see somebody missed me!" I said, flattering myself.

"You know I did! Question is, did you miss me?" she replied.

"Can't you tell?" I said, looking down at the bulge in my pants.

Reagan's eyes followed mine, and she said with arrogance, "I guess you did."

I opened the car door for her so we could head to our destination, which she had no clue about. The whole way there, she asked a million questions, trying to figure out what I had planned. From the corner of my eye, I kept noticing that Reagan's phone kept ringing and she kept pressing "ignore".

"Everything ok on the home front?" I asked.

"Yeah. Everything's fine."

Reagan had gotten to the point where every time I asked her anything about home, her answer was always the same. Everything was always fine. I felt clueless as to where she and her husband stood. I really didn't care, but I just wanted to make sure there wouldn't be any issues that would involve me.

When we finally arrived at our safe haven for the evening, I looked over at Reagan and she twisted up her mouth.

"Is something wrong?" I asked.

"So you got us a room?" she asked, sounding unimpressed.

At that moment I felt pretty disrespected and unappreciated, but I wasn't going to let her know that because I knew it would've just started an argument that I wasn't trying to have. I needed to run some quick game on her and get her on board. I had spent what I already felt like was too much for the best suite the Sybaris had for only a few hours, but I had to come correct, and for her to downplay it really made me feel some type of way.

"Baby, you know I think more of you than just getting you some room. I got us the Chalet suite . . . Pool, hot tub, the works. I thought we could just relax and talk without having to look over our shoulders every few minutes. This is just about me and you. I thought it was special, but if you're not feeling it, I'll understand, and we can do whatever you want to do. This isn't about sex. We don't have to do anything but chill. I just enjoy your company."

Well, part of what I said was true. I exaggerated a little bit, but it worked.

"Keith, I'm sorry. I didn't mean to make you feel like I don't appreciate this. The first thing that popped in my head was that you were just trying to have sex with me, but I do know that's not the case. I need to just relax and enjoy."

Feeling accomplished, I said, "Ok, then! Wait here while I run in and get the key."

I gave Reagan a peck on the lips before I got out of the car to go into the office, just to reassure her everything would be ok and she was definitely doing the right thing. Well, I thought so.

When I walked in, I waited on a couple to finish up who were in front of me at the counter picking up their key, and ordering a few extra things for their room. They looked like they had been together for quite some time and were quite in love by the way the woman interlocked her arm inside of his and kept kissing him on his neck. They also seemed to be very familiar with the girl at the front desk.

"I made sure I saved your usual suite. I know how special it is to the both of you," the redhead with green eyes said to the couple from behind the desk. "Everything is just how you like it, and remember, if you need anything, don't hesitate to call us.

"Thank you, Kara!" they both said as she handed the man their key.

When they turned facing me, the gorgeous woman with the fly ass haircut and perfect body smiled, and said, "Hello!"

"Hi. How you doin'?" I replied.

"Good. Thanks!"

I looked at her husband and briefly nodded and smiled before squinting my eyes trying to recall where I had seen him before.

"Hey, man. Do I know you from somewhere?"

He looked me up and down like I was small and said, "Nah, I don't think so, but are you staying here this evening?"

Hesitantly I said, "Yeah."

"Enjoy your night! Kara will take care of you if you need anything! She always takes good care of us.

I watched as the couple walked out of the office, still thinking, *Where in the world do I know that cat from?* He was probably someone I had just seen on the street, but he didn't have to look at me like I had done something to disgust him. I had to admit, he was one lucky man, though. I didn't normally like when women chopped off all of their hair, but that woman's face was so beautiful, she didn't need any hair distracting from her beauty. Just then, I remembered I had a beautiful woman sitting in the car waiting for me and it was time for me to get this party started. I got my key from Kara and headed back to the car to show my prized possession for the evening how I wined and dined the ladies.

When I got back in the car, Reagan put her finger up to her lips, gesturing for me to be quiet as she talked to someone on her cell phone.

"Baby, you know my job can sometimes get hectic and this is one of those times. Everything on my desk has to get done tonight," Reagan said to the person on the other end as she tried to avoid eye contact with me.

As I turned the car on, I turned the radio down so that, who I assumed to be Reagan's husband, didn't hear music playing in the background. While she continued to talk as if I wasn't in the car, I drove to our suite. Enough time had already been wasted.

I tried to block out Reagan's conversation, but it was pretty difficult to do since I couldn't even turn on the radio. I pulled into the garage of our suite, turned off the car, and waited for Reagan to finish her conversation. I pulled out my cell phone and began checking my call log to see if I had missed any calls. By this point, I was getting irritated listening to Reagan talk about husband and wife stuff as if everything in her life was perfect.

"I'll be home as soon as I can. I miss you too, love."

At that moment, I got out of the car and slammed the door. I walked into our suite and looked around at everything I had set up just for Reagan, wondering if she was even worth it. Maybe this was all a mistake. The setting was perfect for two lovers. Upon first walking in, there was a table with a vase that contained a dozen red, long stemmed roses, a bottle of champagne, and two glasses. In the bedroom, bright red rose petals were carefully placed in the shape of a heart on top of the white bedding, and a bottle of stimulating massage oil sat on the nightstand next to the bed.

I sat in the massage recliner and leaned all the way back as I waited for Reagan. I finally heard the door open, but I didn't move. I felt she had been extremely rude continuing a conversation with her husband, knowing our time was already limited.

"Oh my God! You did all this for me?" I heard Reagan say from downstairs.

When she finally got up the stairs and came into the bedroom, her face lit up even more as her beautiful smile spread across her face. I remained leaned back in the recliner with my feet up and hands behind my head without a single trace of a smile on my face. She ran over to me and leaned over trying to kiss me, but I politely turned my head.

She stood straight up and said, "What's wrong? Did I do something?"

I looked up at her and said, "I did all this for you and you want to spend your time on the phone with your husband."

"Do you hear yourself? You know the situation. I have to make my story as believable as possible. I don't have room for error. If I would've rushed off of the phone with him, he would've known something."

I really wasn't in the mood to argue with Reagan. I just wanted to let her know how I felt so that it didn't happen again. I could've been with any other woman at that moment and I chose to spend it with her, so I expected her to realize that and respect my time as I much as I respected hers. Even though the mood had been thrown off a little bit, I still wanted what I wanted, so I set aside my pride and apologized. We could have this conversation at a later time.

"I know, and I'm sorry, baby," I said as I grabbed her and pulled her on top of me in the recliner.

She wrapped her arms around me, pressed her lips up against mine for a brief moment and said, "I'm sorry, too. Thank you for this. It's all very thoughtful."

I grabbed the back of her neck and brought her lips back close to mine. I parted her lips with my tongue and kissed her passionately. She turned me on even more by rubbing the back of my head as she sucked in my bottom lip. We both breathed heavily and I could tell we were both ready for what was about to happen. I lifted her up and held on to her succulent thighs as I stood up from the chair. We continued to kiss without coming up for air as I carried her over to the bed and laid her down. I stood over her, admiring her fully dressed body before I uncovered the beauty that I knew existed underneath.

"Are you ready for this?" I asked before going any further.

She smiled and whispered, "Yes."

I slowly began removing each piece of her clothing until I made it down to her pink and black lace thong and matching bra. Just as I had expected, she was flawless. I knelt down and kissed the inside of both of her thighs, then her stomach. She smelled so sweet. I could feel her shaking. I didn't know if it was from nerves or if she was just that turned on by me. I gave her time to calm down as I undressed. She watched as I revealed my entire body to her. I got the same reaction from her that I got from every woman the first time they got a glimpse of what I had hiding beneath my pants. I could tell she tried to keep from staring, but she couldn't help herself.

I put both hands on her hips and slipped my fingers underneath the delicate fabric of her thong, gently pulling them down and over her feet. She suddenly sat up and pulled herself to the edge of the bed. She grabbed the back of my thighs, pulling me as close as possible, and before I knew it, she had performed a disappearing act on my dick. I could feel all eight inches in the back of her throat and couldn't help but to wonder if she had lied to me about only ever being with her husband. I couldn't get caught up in those thoughts, though, because the shit felt good as hell. I grabbed her hair, pulling it tight as her head bobbed back and forth.

"Oooh baby," I said right before I was about to cum. I wasn't done with her ass, so I pushed her back onto the bed, pushed her legs over her head and licked her wet pussy with the entire width of my tongue. I stuck two fingers in, as far as they could go, searching for her G-spot, as I slowly licked her clit. I could tell when I found it, by the way she lifted her hips and gyrated on my hand. She moaned loudly, which turned me on even more. I was always turned on by the reactions I got from women, and this was definitely no different. I began sucking her clit and that's when she let go, screamed, and released all of her orgasmic fluids for me to taste.

I removed my fingers from her pussy and sucked them as her body shook intensely. I got up and grabbed my pants off the floor. I reached in my pocket for my wallet and pulled out a rubber. Reagan laid there watching with an expressionless look on her face as I put it on. As I laid on top of her, she wrapped her legs around my waist, and my dick slid right in. We embraced each other and moaned in unison. With every stroke I went deeper and deeper, and she moaned louder and louder. I held out as long as I could before exploding, and when I did, it was well worth it.

As I rolled over from on top of Reagan, I laid flat on my back taking a deep breath. Reagan was completely silent. I looked over at her and she was staring at herself in the mirror on the ceiling.

"You ok, baby?" I asked, hoping she wasn't already having regrets.

In a breathy tone she spoke slowly, sounding unsure of what she wanted to say.

"Did you plan for this to happen?"

"No, of course not! I just wanted to show you a good time. I told you that nothing had to happen, and that's what I meant. It just happened. What made you think that?"

"You were prepared," she responded.

"What do you mean?" I asked, really not knowing what she meant by that.

"You had condoms."

I laughed, not trying to make her feel silly, but I just couldn't believe she had just said that.

She sat up and became very serious. "What's so funny?"

"Trust me, I'm not laughing because of the situation. I'm laughing because you're showing how long you've really been out of the game. Every man who's not in a committed relationship has at least one rubber in his wallet. It's better to be safe than sorry. What if we had both gotten all hot and bothered like we did and I didn't have protection? Then we would've been sitting here looking stupid, right?"

"So you make it a habit of sleeping with random women?"

"Is that all you got from what I said? All I'm saying is that I'm single, and I just don't want to get caught off guard."

Reagan quickly jumped up out of the bed and walked towards the bathroom. As she walked into the bathroom, right before she slammed the door she said, "I can't be sleeping around with someone who's out in these streets screwing everything with a pussy. I think this may have been a mistake."

I threw a pillow over my face and shook my head. There I had gone and pissed off another woman. What I didn't understand was how Reagan could possibly get mad at me if I did sleep with other women! Her ass was married! I was hoping she didn't think we were going to be in a secret relationship and I was supposed to be faithful to her. From the conversation I heard her and her husband have, they sounded like they were in love with no marital issues, so I didn't understand what she needed me for anyway. Again, the complex mind of a woman was about to get the best of me.

I heard the shower start and thought I'd sneak in with Reagan to soften the mood. I turned the knob, and I guess she wanted to be alone because she had locked the door. While she was in the shower, I decided to go take a swim to get some more of my money's worth since it seemed as though the rest of the evening had gone south. I still planned on taking Reagan to dinner, so I was hoping she could get her mind right while she was in the shower.

From the lower level, I saw Reagan through the glass window in the bedroom, come out of the bathroom. I saw her looking around for me and when she spotted me in the pool, she tried to act like she was looking around for her clothes. I jumped out of the pool, dried off, and went back upstairs so that I could take my shower and try to see where Reagan's mind was. When I walked in the room, I grabbed Reagan, who had already finished putting on most of her clothes, and wrapped my arms around her. She did surprisingly reciprocate, but she looked away from me.

"You want to have a glass of champagne before I get in the shower?" I asked Reagan, not wanting to let it go to waste.

"No, thanks. Go ahead. I'll be waiting."

She sounded so disappointed. I had never slept with a woman and left her seemingly depressed. This was different for me and I didn't quite know how to handle the situation. I couldn't think of any way that I could've handled the situation differently that would've ended with a positive response, except for not sleeping with her at all. I was even a gentleman by asking her if she was ready. Maybe she was right. Maybe it was a mistake. This was like a lose-lose situation and I didn't know if we would be able to come back from this.

After I took my shower, we left the suite without even putting the hot tub to good use. As I pulled out of the garage, I asked her where she wanted to eat and she declined my offer.

"Look, I'm trying to show you a good time. I told you I would and I try to keep my word. I don't know what I did wrong, but whatever it is, I do apologize."

Reagan exhaled and said, "You didn't do anything wrong. Maybe it was me who wasn't prepared for what happened. I told you I've never done this before and I guess I didn't really know what to expect, or how I would feel afterwards."

"I think that's part of the problem. We both don't know what we're doing or what to expect from this. I thought you were just looking for companionship and maybe sex sooner or later, but the way you were talking in the room, sounds like you want more. I just don't see how I can do any more than that with you being married. Earlier, you sure sounded to me like the two of you were in marital bliss."

I had just given Reagan the cue to speak on the status of her marriage, and of course, she avoided it like she always did.

"I just think I need to let all of this marinate and go from there, but as for dinner, not tonight. Please believe me when I say I appreciate everything you did for me today. My mind is just a little cloudy right now."

"Ok," I said, not having any other words.

I turned the radio up to drown out the uncomfortable silence the entire way to the parking garage where we had left Reagan's Lexus. We said our goodbyes with a friendly hug and a peck on the lips, and I had no idea what the days ahead would bring.

<u>Chapter Fifteen ~ Armani</u>

I sat at work as long as I could listening to nothing except for the sound of my nails tapping the keys of my keyboard and my stomach growling, which became louder and louder each time. I would've rather been spending my evening with my baby, Marcus, but I understood that he had a job to do, just like I did. I tried to stay focused on what I was working on, but I just felt the need to be outside of the office. I didn't feel like I was being as productive as I was capable of being due to my lack of focus, so I decided to just pack up and leave for the evening.

As I was walking out, Ben jumped up from the front desk to walk with me.

"I didn't expect for you to be leaving for at least another hour or so," Ben said, letting me know just how much of a life it seemed I didn't have, and how predictable I had become once again.

As he opened the door to the fresh, outside air, I said, "Yeah, well I decided tonight wasn't a night to be sitting in the office all evening. I thought I'd get out and enjoy the evening breeze while I could. It's such a beautiful night."

"It's a nice night to ride out to the beach with that man of yours," Ben said.

"Yeah, it would be. Unfortunately, he's working."

"So he works late nights, too, huh? How do the two of you find time for each other with such demanding jobs?" Ben asked, patiently awaiting an answer.

I sighed as I searched my normally deep intellect for an answer, but there was no answer that would've satisfied Ben's curiosity.

Ben stopped me in my tracks and stared at me, waiting for me to say something.

"Well?" he asked.

"We tend to find time for each other. Actually, we get to spend more time together than we used to. He was able to cut his hours down some."

"You know, Armani, you can talk to me. I don't like being in people's business, but I've been working around here for a while now, and I must say I've seen you happier. It seems like part of you is empty. Are you truly happy?"

My mind went to a dark place for a moment because I knew I shouldn't have had to hesitate with the answer to that simple question. It should've been an immediate "yes", but I honestly didn't know. I knew at times I felt extremely happy, but then, as Ben was saying, I sometimes felt like I was missing something in my life, but couldn't figure out what it was. The thing was, I couldn't think of anything else I could've possibly needed.

As we approached my car, I said, "I sometimes feel like I could be happier, but I don't know what could make me any happier than I am. I have the world!"

Ben put his hands on my shoulders, looked me straight in the eyes and said, "Sometimes your true happiness is right in front of your face. Don't put all of your eggs in one basket. You should never have to find time for the love of your life. It should never be lost."

Ben was a very wise man and made a lot of sense, but I couldn't help but to think he was hitting on me. I guess he could tell by the expression on my face what was going through my mind at that moment, so he quickly cleared things up.

As he quickly removed his hands from my shoulders, while laughing hysterically, he said, "I'm so sorry! I hope you didn't get the wrong idea. I was just giving you some words of wisdom I thought you should hear. I hope you didn't think . . ."

Even though that was what I thought, I played it off and said, "Oh no! I knew exactly what you meant. I appreciate those words and I will definitely take heed to everything you said. You always somehow know exactly what to say. Some woman, whenever you get ready to settle down with just one, will be lucky to have you!" I teased.

Ben laughed and said, "Yeah, someday, but probably not soon. I'm having too much fun right now, but when I do, I'm going to definitely make sure I'm truly happy."

I got Ben's point loud and clear and after our conversation felt like I might've needed to do a little soul searching.

"Have a good night, Ben. Thanks for the talk."

"Anytime, baby girl," he affectionately said.

As I sped off, I turned up my Elle Varner CD and cruised down the freeway until I decided on a destination. There was a restaurant Marcus and I had frequented pretty often in the past, but hadn't been there in quite a while. I was in the mood for a steak cooked to perfection and I knew Theo's Steakhouse wouldn't let me down. It felt strange to go there alone, but tonight was going to be about me. It had been a long time since I had been somewhere nice, or done something for myself without having Marcus around. Today I would test out the waters.

As I pulled up to the restaurant, I felt even sillier because the parking lot was full of cars, meaning it was packed inside. The fact that it was packed wasn't what made me feel silly. The fact that the restaurant was probably full of loving couples and happy families was what made me feel like I might've felt a little out of place walking in there all alone. I decided not to worry about the fact that I may look like a lonely ass bitch. In reality I was a hungry ass bitch and wanted a good ass steak.

As soon as I walked in the door, I looked around because I just knew I would have to wait, seeing all the traffic in the parking lot. Surprisingly, everyone else had already been seated, so the hostess immediately approached me, asking how many people I needed seating for.

"Oh, it's just me," I said, feeling like I had just lost all pride.

The petite waitress whose fake lashes made her look like she was going to fly away at any given moment, squinted her eyes and wrinkled her forehead, which I could barely see due to her lace front covering most of it. I didn't know if she had never seen anyone come in there and eat alone, or if she thought she knew me from somewhere.

She finally said, "I'm sorry."

"Excuse me?" I asked.

"I'm sorry you're alone. Follow me and I'll be happy to seat you, or would you like to sit in the bar area?"

After her comment, I decided to sit at one of the booths in the bar because I felt like I needed a few drinks. The closer I was to the bar, the better.

As the hostess, who seemed to be in her early to mid-twenties, seated me, she said, "Your hair is gorgeous! What kind is it?"

I giggled, and being the bitch I knew I could sometimes be, I said, "Mine," with a straight face.

Expectedly, she rolled her eyes, and with her back turned as she walked away, she said, "Yeah, ok. Your waitress will be right with you."

After she got a few feet away, I heard her mumble, "Enjoy your lonely meal . . . bitch."

This was not starting out good. I had never had such bad service in my life. This was supposed to be a classy restaurant and they had one of Chicago's most ratchet women working for them. I had a mouth full for her, but I couldn't stoop to her level. My elevator definitely didn't go down to that floor. I was a businesswoman and couldn't afford to find myself locked up in a jail cell.

As I looked through the menu, my waitress, Mandy, who didn't come with all the extra facial and hair accessories as my "hostess" did, stopped by and asked what I wanted to drink. She was so much more pleasant and tolerable, which helped to bring my adrenaline rush down from my prior experience I had just had. A margarita with a shot of Patròn was my choice of drink for the evening.

After ordering my steak dinner, I slowly sipped my potent drink. The more I sipped, the more I thought about my conversation with Ben. Each time I let his words cross my mind, they made more and more sense, but I would then try to convince myself that they weren't worth dwelling on by thinking, *Who in the hell is Ben and what does he really know about love and happiness?* I then realized I had a slight buzz when my thoughts began turning into songs playing in my head. I began hearing Marvin Gaye's "Love and Happiness". For a brief moment, I thought it was playing in the restaurant, but it was all in my head.

As I began to take another sip, as soon as my lips touched the straw, I heard a familiar voice speaking with the ignorant hostess at the door. I tried to focus my attention beyond the music that was playing in my head, on top of all the chitter-chatter and music playing in the restaurant.

"Would you like to sit at the bar, Sir?" she politely asked.

"No, I'm ordering to go," the familiar voice said.

"Oh, ok, you can follow me so the bartender can take your order."

The hostess walked around the corner showing off her crooked smile. I could tell she had seen something she liked, and a few feet behind her I saw what that something was. Keith walked into the bar area looking straight ahead, not paying attention to anything else. He looked stressed, and I thought I was the only person who could make him look that way.

As Keith was about to sit on one of the barstools, I yelled his name from my booth on the other side of the bar. He looked around, trying to find where my voice was coming from.

"Over here," I said as I waved my hand and smiled.

Keith finally spotted me, smiling and putting his index finger up, letting me know he was on his way over. The hostess looked my way and her smile completely disappeared from her face. I saw Keith turn to her and say something. I couldn't tell what it was, but he pointed my way, so I assumed he told her he was going to come over to my table. Not wanting to come near me, she handed him his menu and walked in the opposite direction, out of the bar.

When Keith made it over to my booth, he stood there and said, "Hey! Surprised to see you here."

"Yeah, last minute decision," I said, not sure if it would've been appropriate for me to stand and give Keith a hug, which is what it looked like he was waiting for.

After he didn't see me budge, he sat down across from me, and immediately opened up his menu. Seemingly trying to avoid eye contact, Keith continued to look through the menu as he said, "So, did you get a lot of work done this evening? I know I sometimes focus better when it's nice and quiet."

I didn't get as much as I would've liked to get done because surprisingly, I couldn't focus much. It seemed a little too quiet and my stomach started yelling at me!"

We laughed together, and as I took a sip of my margarita, he looked at me in shock.

"What?" I asked.

"I just had no idea that you drink."

"I don't think telling you that I sometimes get "turned up" would be an appropriate discussion to be having in the office," I said, giggling like a young school girl.

"And are you tipsy?"

"What? Nooo!" I said, knowing it was a lie, but I didn't need Keith knowing how low my tolerance was for alcohol. Who knows? He might've tried to take advantage of me. From Keith's response, I had the feeling he knew I was lying anyway.

"Yeah. Ok. I guess that's your story and you're sticking to it," he replied, exposing that sexy ass smile that was even sexier when I was under the influence.

I had to get it together and quick. Luckily the waitress came by the table and asked Keith if he was ready to order his to go meal. While she was there, I asked for a glass of water to help dilute what I had already drank.

"I think I'll dine in since I now have someone to enjoy my meal with," Keith said to the waitress, Mandy.

"Ok, that's no problem," she said smiling at the both of us. "Would you like something to drink?"

He was about to grab the drink menu, then looked at me.

"I think I'll have what's she's having," he said.

"Ok. A margarita with a shot of Patrón coming right up! I'll be right back to take your order."

After the waitress told Keith what drink he had just ordered, he looked at me in shock again.

"No wonder you're feeling good!"

"Very funny! Anyway, I just thought about something. What happened to your date? Shouldn't you be out having dinner with her?"

Keith's entire expression changed and even though I was a little tipsy, I could tell something wasn't right. He went back to looking at the menu, acting as if he was trying to decide what he was going to eat, while I believed he already knew what he was going to order.

Without looking up, he said, "My date was cool. Something came up that she had to tend to, so we had to cut it short."

As soon as he finished feeding me that bold-faced lie, he looked up from the menu and closed it.

"I'm so sorry. That has to suck. I know how much you were looking forward to spending the evening with her."

"Yep, things happen," Keith said, looking relieved when the waitress came back to bring his drink and take his order.

As he took a sip of his drink, I sat back and folded my arms. I wanted Keith to know that I knew he wasn't being completely honest, so I turned up my lips and waited to see if he was going to go into more detail about what REALLY happened.

After he finished his taste test and nodded his head in approval, he looked up at me, and said, "Something wrong?"

I leaned my body in closer to the table and said in a low tone, "I don't think I believe you."

I was unable to read into Keith's visible mix of emotions, as he frowned in disgust, but at the same time laughed as if I sounded ridiculous.

"What reason do I have to lie to you about my love life? To be honest, I've probably told you more than I should have. This should be a professional relationship that we have, right?"

I sat straight up in the cushioned booth, not expecting Keith to get so defensive. I definitely thought we had gotten a little past the professional part of our relationship and thought we both considered ourselves to be on the level of friends. I didn't quite know how to take his reaction, but I decided I would back off of that conversation. The silence at the table created an awkward vibe that I didn't enjoy at all. I tried looking out the window, aimlessly staring at people as they walked to and from their cars. Keith took out his phone and began quickly sliding his thumbs across the screen.

All of a sudden, all silence was broken when I heard a voice from my past . . . a voice which made my stomach turn, say, "Armani!"

I reluctantly turned away from the window and looked up at the beautiful face that I remembered so well, but hated so much. The smile that once gave me butterflies, now absolutely repulsed me.

"Hey Damon," I said with absolutely no enthusiasm in my voice.

Still smiling, he said, "Well can I at least get a hug?" he asked, motioning for me to get up.

Noticing that Damon wasn't showing any type of respect for my male dinner companion, as he didn't know the relationship between Keith and me, I looked over at Keith, who was looking back and forth at Damon and me. I could tell he didn't know what to think of the situation.

When Damon noticed my attention was with Keith, he faced Keith and said, "Man, I'm so sorry. No disrespect, but I just had to stop by and at least speak to this beautiful lady." He glanced back over at me and continued by saying, "You were beautiful back then, but even more beautiful now. Lucky man you are. Are you going to introduce us, Armani?"

Before I could say anything, Keith stood up, extended his hand, and said, "I'm Keith, and Armani and I are . . ."

"Engaged!" I interrupted.

As Keith and Damon shook hands, they both looked at me with stunned looks on their faces.

"Wow! Congratulations," he said as he looked down at my ring finger.

"Thanks," Keith said with a question mark across his entire face. Then he did the unexpected. I didn't know if he was trying to get me back for prying in his business, but if so, he was being very petty.

"So, how do you know my fiancé? I don't remember her ever talking about a Damon."

Damon looked at me grinning and said, "You mind if I sit?"

Before I could answer, he slid in the booth right next to me, pushing me over so that he was sitting directly in front of Keith.

"Well, Armani and I met some years back at the grocery store. Like I said, she was beautiful then and I couldn't resist getting her number. Thing is though, I was a playboy back then. I'm a changed man now," he said with emphasis, looking over at me, winking. He continued, "That was back when Armani didn't mind sharing. I was married, but it didn't bother her. She was content with getting all of my time I'd have left over after spending the majority of the time with my family.

As he spoke, he looked Keith directly in the eyes. Keith was quiet the entire time Damon spoke, but his eyes squinted more and more with every word that came out of Damon's mouth. He then began to crack his knuckles. I sat there in shame, not knowing how to end this nightmare. I couldn't quite understand why Damon would do this after all these years. He had hurt me enough back then, and now wanted me to feel the pain all over again.

"I can't even lie to you. I enjoyed Armani. She knows how to make a man happy, but I'm sure you already know that! I almost even fell in love with her. I don't know what might've happened if she hadn't tried to trap me by getting pregnant."

Damon laughed as if the entire incident was a joke. He looked over at me with that evil grin still across his face and said, "You never know, Armani. I might've eventually left her for you, but I guess we'll never know."

I looked down at Damon's ring finger and he didn't have a wedding ring on. There wasn't even a tan mark on that finger, which told me he hadn't worn one in quite some time. That led me to believe that he was no longer married and probably miserable, and kicking himself for doing me the way he did. At that moment he hated seeing me with another man, so wanted me to be just as miserable as he was.

Before Damon could further damage my character, the waitress came over with Keith's and my dinner.

"Oh, I didn't realize there was another guest sitting here. Would you like to order something, Sir?" the waitress asked Damon.

As soon as he was about to answer, Keith said, "No. He was just about to leave."

"Actually, I ordered to go, but I was enjoying conversing with the two of you, so I think I'll . . ."

Keith slammed his fists on the table and balled them up. He leaned in close enough so that Damon heard him clearly and said, "You will not continue to sit here and disrespect both me and my lady. It's time for you to go."

Keith used a deep, intimidating voice I had never heard him use before.

It was enough to make Damon say, "Yeah, I do have a couple more stops to make and it's getting late." Damon slid out of the booth, and said, "Congrats again," as he headed over towards the bar to pick up his order.

"Okaaay . . ." the waitress said, wondering what had just happened. "Is everything ok?"

"Yes, everything's fine now," I said, feeling embarrassed.

"Well, enjoy your meals and let me know if you need anything."

As she walked away, Keith said, "Are you serious? Is that the type of man you allow in your life? I see you have interesting taste in men. I hope your REAL fiancé is nothing like him."

Not able to look Keith in the eye, I played with my food with my fork and said, "No, he's nothing like that asshole. When I met him, I was vulnerable. All I did was work and just felt like I needed a man in my life at that time."

"A married one, though? I could never see you as being the type of woman to share a man."

"I didn't know he was married. He did tell me he had a girlfriend, which wasn't much better, but if I would've known upfront that he was married, I would've never become involved."

I knew the next question that Keith asked was coming, and when he asked, it felt like a knife stabbed me in my heart.

"So, about the pregnancy . . . Was that true?"

It took a while, but after so many years, I managed to push that memory to the back of my mind, and never thought about it. I knew that wasn't good and I should've talked about it back then with someone, but I was so embarrassed and humiliated, I couldn't. I cried every day for weeks after the abortion, feeling like I had made the biggest mistake of my life.

"Yes, it's true."

"So what happened? You have a baby I don't know about?"

I looked at Keith with sadness in my eyes, quickly wiping a tear before it fell, and said, "Damon walked away from me when I told him. I was so hurt, and I knew I couldn't go through it alone, so I . . ."

"I'm sorry for asking. You don't have to talk about it anymore."

"It actually feels good letting it out. It has been over five years and I've never talked to anyone about it. I guess I finally met the person that it was meant for me to share that dark part of my life with," I said with a small grin.

"Well, I'm glad I could be that special person," Keith said smiling back at me.

Keith and I made light of the situation and didn't have any more conversations about our past or current love lives. We talked about our childhoods, friends, and family while we enjoyed our delicious dinner and a few more drinks. We continued to laugh and talk even after the waitress brought over our check.

I reached into my purse and pulled out my debit card so that I could pay for my portion.

As I was about to lay it on the table, Keith shook his head, put cash on the table, and said, "I got you."

"No, you've done enough. I can pay for my own," I said, feeling flattered, but he didn't owe me anything.

"You can treat next time," Keith said, winking.

After that, I gave in and let him pay. One thing I learned about Keith that night was that he definitely knew how to treat a woman. It was a very emotional night, but at least I could say it definitely ended on a good note.

Chapter Sixteen ~ Armani

Completely drained from the mix of emotions the night before, I sat at my desk, barely able to focus on anything. I kept thinking about how Keith had stood up for me with the Damon situation. He could've just stepped back and continued to let Damon ridicule me, but he didn't. He did what a true friend would do, and at the end of the night, my respect for Keith had progressed to an entirely new level. I thought about how Marcus might've handled the situation if he had been there, and to be honest, I really didn't know. Marcus was the nonchalant type who usually brushed things off, especially if it didn't directly pertain to him. Even though I was his woman, he would've considered Damon and my situation to be part of my past, which was before him, which in turn didn't affect him in any way.

As I sat at my desk with work in front of me, but glaring at my computer screen, my desk phone rang, awakening me from my trance.

"*Couture* . . . Armani speaking," I said, greeting the person on the other end.

"Hey, babe," Marcus said.

"Hey!" I said, surprised to hear from him. He rarely ever called while I was at work, and when he did, he'd just call my cell phone.

"I have a little free time today and thought we could meet for lunch. How does that sound?"

I opened my mouth to accept Marcus' offer, but then looked at the stack of work sitting on my desk that I had been staring at for the past hour.

I exhaled and said, "That sounds great, baby. I would love to, but . . ."

"Great! Where do you want to meet? Anywhere you want!"

Marcus sounded so excited and I felt so guilty for having to let him down, but I had to get my mind right and quit slacking.

"I was going to say, I would love to, but I have way to much work in front of me right now. Rain check?" I asked, hoping Marcus wasn't too disappointed.

"Wow. You trying to get me back for having to work last night?"

I couldn't believe Marcus was treating this as if it were a game of retaliation. I had already come to terms with the fact that when duty calls, there's nothing that can be done about it, except answer it.

"Of course not! I really have a lot of work I have to get done in a short period of time, and by the time I leave, meet with you, and get back, I would have lost at least two hours. I'm sorry, but you know I'll make it up to you."

With displeasure in his voice, Marcus accepted my rejection. When I hung up the phone, I felt awful. It was rare that I turned down an opportunity to spend extra time with Marcus, but I had to prioritize today, and unfortunately going out to lunch with my boo wasn't at the top of my list of priorities. I got up from my desk and closed my door to prevent any unintentional distractions while I attempted to do some work.

After a couple of hours of nonstop reading, typing, and talking to myself, I heard a lot of noise coming from the other

side of my door. I saved the work that I was working on and
went to see what was going on. When I entered the front office,
I was shocked to see Marcus standing there with a dozen
rainbow colored roses in one hand, and a bag in the other,
conversing with the ladies.

I folded my arms and shook my head.

"I told you I had to see you," Marcus said with his
irresistible smile.

One of the older ladies, Carmen, said, "That is so sweet! You
have you a good one, Armani! About time we got to meet the
special man in your life."

Then out of nowhere, Reagan said, "Yeah, I was beginning
to think there wasn't one."

The entire room became uncomfortably quiet. I squinted
my eyes at her, trying to formulate in my mind what to say to
her that wouldn't sound too harsh in front of everyone else, but
would surely get my point across. She should've considered
herself a lucky lady when just at that moment Keith walked out
of his office.

"Are y'all out here having a party without me?

I smiled at Keith and said, "Of course not!" I walked over to
Marcus, grabbed my roses, wrapped my arm around his and
said, "My fiancé just thought he'd come by to bring me these
beautiful roses. I don't think the two of you have met. Keith,
this is my fiancé, Marcus. Marcus, this is my Senior Editor,
Keith."

I watched as Marcus and Keith stared each other down, as if
they were sizing each other up. They each hesitated in bringing
forth their hands to shake. I didn't say a word. I just continued
to closely observe their reactions towards one another, trying
to read their actions and thoughts.

"Nice to finally meet you," Keith said with one eyebrow
raised. "Congratulations on your engagement. You're marrying
a very special woman."

Sarcastically, Marcus said, "Yes, I already know that. We've
been together for quite some time now and she does

something to remind me just how special she is on a daily basis."

As Keith and Marcus spoke, they were still tightly gripping each other's hands, and continuously shaking them. This introduction seemed to be getting more and more intense, so I decided to intervene while things were still civil.

"Ok! Marcus, let's go into my office. No sense in you just dropping off flowers and leaving!"

Marcus finally released Keith's hand and said, "Sounds good. Since you were too busy to come out for lunch, I brought lunch to you," he said, as he held up the bag in his hand.

"You're so thoughtful," I said, and gave Marcus a peck on the lips.

"Since there's no party going on out here, you two have a nice lunch," Keith said as he walked back into his office and shut the door.

I looked at Marcus and he shrugged his shoulders. I led him into my office and closed the door after him. I felt something was just not right, but couldn't put my finger on it. I didn't even know what questions to ask Marcus in order to get to the bottom of what had just happened.

"You have a nice office," Marcus said as he looked around with his hands in his pockets.

I had completely forgotten that after all these years, Marcus had never been to my office, which made me wonder why today?

"Thanks. So why were you so determined to see me in the middle of the day today?"

"Well, I didn't get to see you last night. I assumed you would've been home by the time I got there last night, but you weren't. You didn't even wake me when you got there. What time did you get home, anyway?"

So I had finally figured it out. Marcus was bothered by the fact that I was out late the night before and he didn't know how to react or what to think. I was up and out before he had even awakened this morning, so he didn't get a chance to talk to me face to face so that he could have the opportunity to attempt to read my expressions like he was trying to do right now. He came to see me with way too much on his mind and as soon as he saw that I worked with a very attractive man, he felt some type of way about it. I thought about telling a little white lie by saying that I got home earlier than I really did, but unfortunately, I didn't know what time he had gotten home. I didn't want to catch myself up by saying that I got home before he did. I also didn't know if he woke up and glanced at the clock when I crept into the room and slid into bed. This may have just been a trick question to see if I was going to be honest. Truth was that Keith and I were enjoying each other's company so much that we honestly lost track of time.

"I got in around two," I said as I opened the bag of food that was getting cold. I was no longer really hungry, but I was avoiding eye contact with Marcus.

"Two, huh?" Marcus said, sounding pissed. "Where did you go?"

"Theo's."

I grabbed my food out of the bag and briefly looked up at Marcus.

"Theo's? They're not open that late, are they?"

"Yeah, actually they are. The bar is open 'til two. I left right before they closed."

"Who'd you go with?"

I was finally fed up with all the questions and said, "Are you serious right now? I went alone, since you were unable to spend time with me."

"Don't try to turn this around on me. It's just very hard for me to believe you were at Theo's all alone 'til two in the morning."

At that point, I was determined to look at Marcus straight in his eyes because what I was about to say was about to come from my soul. I walked directly in front of him, folded my arms, and said, "If you were so concerned about where I was, why didn't you call and check on me?"

"I didn't want you to feel like I didn't trust you."

"What, like right now?" I said, probably loud enough for everyone in the next room to hear. I quickly realized I needed to bring down my tone, and put my hand over my mouth.

"I'm sorry for upsetting you. This isn't what I came here for."

Marcus walked behind me and wrapped his arms around my waist. He gently kissed me on my neck and whispered "sorry" in my ear. He then pulled my snug skirt up over my waist and bent me over my desk. I slammed both palms down on the glass and breathed heavily as my entire body began to heat up. I heard the sound of Marcus unzipping his pants, and all I could think about was if I had locked the door. No one normally walked in when my door was closed, but there was always a first time for everything. Marcus slid my panties down, and at that point, I couldn't worry about the door.

He slowly entered my palace of pleasure. As I sighed, he leaned over me and again began whispering in my ear.

He started with just saying, "I love you."

After that, he began going back to the conversation we had just left alone. With each question he asked, the thrusts began to get harder and harder. If I didn't answer loud enough or fast enough, he went deeper and deeper.

"You giving away my pussy?"

"Nooo."

"What? I can't hear you."

"No, baby," I said louder, but trying not to be too loud.

"I don't know if I believe you. Is he as good as me?"

"There is no one," I responded, trying to breathe and talk at the same time.

There was a sudden knock at the door. Marcus quickly pulled out and I stood up trying to hurry and pull myself together. I began panicking because I hadn't checked to see whether or not the door was locked. Just my luck, this would've probably been the one time someone just walked in without knocking.

"Armani," Keith said from the other side of the door. "I don't mean to disturb your lunch, but I have something that needs to be signed by you so I can . . ."

I realized the door was, in fact, unlocked when I opened it as Keith was talking. "What were you saying?" I asked.

Keith, trying on the sly to see what was really going on, said, "I was just saying, sorry for interrupting. I need you to sign this so I can get it out in the mail. The postman is waiting. It needs to go out ASAP."

I grabbed the document out of Keith's hand and skimmed over it as I walked over to my desk to sign it. After I finished signing it, I turned around to find Keith so close behind me that our abdomens managed to touch.

"Here you go," I said.

"Thanks," Keith said, grabbing the paper from me. He then put his nose in the air and said, "What did the two of you have for lunch? It smells like something I've eaten before."

"Just some chicken from Po Boy's," I quickly said, glancing over at Marcus.

"Nope, that's definitely not what I smell," Keith said.

"Well, that's what it is!" I said nervously.

"You know what? I haven't been there in a long time, and I normally get their fish, so maybe that's why I don't recognize that delicious aroma. I'll have to try the chicken. Anyway, sorry again for the interruption and enjoy the rest of your lunch."

Keith walked out and I was so pissed at him for making sexual connotations regarding my food and the aroma in my office. I was just hoping Marcus didn't pick up on it. He was already feeling like I was guilty of something. I definitely didn't need him thinking something was going on between Keith and me.

"Is he interested in you?" Marcus asked as soon as Keith walked out the door.

"No! Why do you ask?"

"Just the way he looks at you. Seems like something is there."

"To be honest, we can barely stand each other. He is so damn arrogant it's disgusting!"

I tried my hardest to downplay my friendship with Keith. Marcus wouldn't have wanted to hear how cool Keith and I had become. The less he knew, the better. Everything between us was completely innocent anyway, so there was really nothing to tell.

"Just making sure. You would tell me if he came incorrect in anyway, wouldn't you?"

"Of course I would."

Marcus got up and gave me a hug and a kiss on the forehead. "Well, we didn't get to have lunch, but dessert was great until it was interrupted," he said laughing as he squeezed me tighter.

"Yes, it was! At least I have something to eat for later. Thanks for thinking of me."

"I always think of you. Don't ever think anything different."

I walked Marcus to the front to walk him out. I guessed Keith had gone back into his office and shut the door, which was a relief. Keith and Marcus had seen enough of each other for one day.

As I walked back into my office, I smelled exactly what Keith had smelled when he came into my office, and it wasn't chicken. Sex was all throughout the air. I shut my door back so it didn't go out into the hallway, and I opened the windows in the office to air it out a bit. I put my gorgeous roses in some water, and when I felt the room was kosher, I opened the door and went on my mission.

First, I went to the restroom to get cleaned up as much as I could. I then went to Keith's office and knocked on the door.

"Come in."

I cracked the door open and peaked my head in. Keith was on the phone, but he quickly told the person to hold, which made me assume it was a personal call.

"Oh, is your visitor gone?" he sarcastically asked.

"Yes, Marcus is gone. Can I see you for a minute when you get a chance?"

"Sure. I'll be there in a minute."

As I turned around to go back to my office, Reagan stared me down with a pen hanging from her mouth. I didn't know what her deal was, but I stared right back at her, reminding her with my eyes who the boss was. She might've reported directly to Keith, but her job was ultimately in my hands. I had gotten rid of Taryn, and I could've definitely gotten rid of her, too. She continued to stare until we were no longer in plain view of one another.

While I sat at my desk twiddling my thumbs, impatiently waiting on Keith to enter, I tried to get my thoughts together. Finally, after waiting about fifteen minutes, Keith finally walked in with a smile gleaming across his face.

"Hey. Sorry it took so long. You want me to close this?" he asked, holding on to the doorknob.

"Yes, please."

After shutting the door, he asked, "What's wrong? You look so serious . . . Like you did when we first met. That's not a good look."

"Have a seat," I said, still keeping a straight, serious face. He sat across from me, and began to look serious.

"What's up?" he asked.

"You tell me what's up."

"I got a lot going on right now. All the editors have been working extremely hard. I'm very impressed. All deadlines are being made, which is another plus.

As Keith continued to ramble about everything I didn't care about at that moment, I stared at him with a blank look on my face and he finally noticed how uninterested I was.

"You ok, Armani?"

"Yes, I'm fine, but you're not going to be if you don't tell me what is really up."

"What are you talking about? Quit beating around the bush and tell me what's on your mind, love.

The word "love" rolling off of Keith's tongue was so tantalizing that I almost forgot what I was talking about, which was probably his intention.

I looked at him, shook my head and said, "Please don't do that."

Keith grinned and bit his bottom lip like this was all a joke.

"Come on. Let's be professional now. Remember, we are at work."

"But it doesn't sound like you're trying to have a work-related conversation," Keith said.

He was right, but he wasn't just about to sit there and flirt with me and act like everything was ok. Especially not when I was trying to get some very critical information out of him.

"It's not, but I have to know, because the vibe was just off when Marcus was here. Do you have an issue with him?"

"How can I have an issue with someone I don't even know?"

One thing came out of Keith's mouth, but his facial expression said the complete opposite.

"Well, he thinks you have a thing for me."

Keith laughed and said, "What kind of thing? You mean attracted to you?"

"Yeah, what's so funny about that?" I asked, feeling offended by his laughter.

"What's funny is that your fiancé thinks that men aren't going to be attracted to you. You're a beautiful woman. Who wouldn't be attracted to you? That doesn't mean I have to want you in an inappropriate way."

"Ok. That's fair . . . And thanks for the compliment. I just felt like there was some type of animosity between the two of you."

"Not at all, sweetheart. Did you tell him we're just coworkers who happen to be friends?"

"Ummm, not entirely. I kinda told him that we can't stand each other for the most part."

"Let me get this straight. So you have to tell your man that we don't get along so that his insecure ass can feel ok about us working together?"

Feeling offended again, I felt the need to defend Marcus by saying, "He's not insecure. I just don't want him to feel like he has anything to worry about. You would do the same if your woman felt like we had something going on."

"I get it. You're probably right, but don't worry, there's no beef. At least not on my end."

"All righty then," I said, not fully satisfied with our conversation, but what else was I to do? As Keith got ready to stand up, I thought about something else that was bothering me.

"Oh, yeah, and what's up with your employee?"

Keith curiously asked, "Which one?"

"Reagan."

"Nothing that I know of."

"Oh, she hasn't been acting strange towards you?"

"Not at all. What did she do to you?"

"She just keeps giving me these looks like I did something to her. Maybe she's just having a bad day."

"You need me to talk to her?" Keith asked.

"No, it's cool. I will if it continues."

"Ok. See you later."

As Keith walked towards the door I said, "Thanks for stopping what you were doing to come and talk, and thanks again for dinner last night. I had a good time."

"Me too," Keith said, pulling the door closed behind him.

"Oh, Keith . . ."

Keith turned back around and said, "Yeah?"

"The remark you made about the smell of our food was so unnecessary and very unprofessional."

Looking confused, Keith said, "Oh, sorry. I wasn't trying to be at all. I just know when I smell something I'd like to try. Sorry if you took it the wrong way," he said, grinning.

"Goodbye, Keith," I said, shaking my head. Before heading out the door once more, he winked and shut the door behind him. All I could think about was how he got on my damn nerves, but I couldn't even get mad at him.

Chapter Seventeen ~ Armani

When I got home later on that evening, Marcus' car was surprisingly parked in the driveway. I wasn't expecting him to be home 'til late, especially since he had left work during the day to make up for the time we missed the day before.

When I walked in, I heard Marcus' voice coming from upstairs. I slipped off my heels and slowly crept up the stairs, trying to surprise him with my presence.

"Sorry I left you hanging earlier. I had some things to take care of," I heard Marcus say as I got closer to my bedroom.

"I know I owe you. You know I'm good for it," Marcus laughed.

When I entered the room, he was facing the window in only a pair of boxers, staring into the outside darkness where the full moon lit up the sky, as he continued talking to the person on the other end. He laughed like I had never heard him laugh before, which made me wonder who he could've been talking to, so I decided not to announce my presence just so I could hear a little bit more of his conversation.

Marcus must've sensed my presence because before I could hear another word, he quickly turned away from the window as if I had startled him, but at the same time, calmly said, "Hey, baby! I didn't even hear you come in."

Without saying a word, I walked over to the bed and sat my purse down. The look on his face was full of uneasiness as he still held the phone up to his ear.

"I'm gonna have to talk to you later," he said.

After hanging up the phone, he laid it on his nightstand and walked over to me, wrapping me up in his arms as he tried to pretend that he wasn't nervous about something.

I tensed up as he held me, letting him know that I wasn't feeling him like that.

He released me and said, "What's wrong?"

Before getting down to the bottom of what I really wanted to know, I beat around the bush a little bit, just so I could see him sweat some more. Something wasn't right. I felt it.

"Nothing. It was just a long day. I'm just a little tired. How was the rest of your day?"

"It was great after I got to see you!"

"How sweet you are," I said, with a phony smile.

"You need me to do anything? You hungry?"

"No, I just got around to eating the lunch that you brought me a little while ago. You're home early tonight."

"Yeah, I finished up a little early today."

"Your schedule has been a little unpredictable lately. Any changes going on at the job that maybe I should know about?"

"Nope," he answered, being elusive in not offering any further information and avoiding looking me in the eye.

Since he didn't want to offer up anything else and wanted to act as if he wasn't having an intimate conversation when I walked in, I decided to remind him.

"So, who were you talking to when I came in?"

"Eric," he answered without hesitation. "We were talking about some funny shit going on around the office."

"So, why do you owe him?"

"Because he covered for me when I left earlier to come see you."

Marcus was coming with his answers to my questions pretty fast, which meant one of two things. He was either telling the truth, or I had given him too much time to get his story together in his head. I continued to search for questions to ask to try to catch him up. I wasn't giving up that easily.

"I heard you say you had to take care of some things. Why couldn't you just tell him you left to go to lunch with me? That is your boy, right?"

"Yeah, he is, but I didn't want to give him the impression that it's ok to fool around during work hours, my boy or not. People like to throw that kind of stuff back in your face."

"I guess you're right," I said, feeling almost fully satisfied with his explanation, but that wasn't the end of my question and answer session with Marcus.

Before I could begin my next set of questions, I began taking off my work clothes so that I could get comfortable. I saw the alleviation in Marcus' entire demeanor as he propped up his pillow before laying back with one arm behind his head and skimming through channels with the remote in his other hand.

"How'd you like meeting my co-workers today? They're all pretty cool, huh?"

Marcus acted as if he was tuned into whatever he had found on TV to watch.

"Hey!" I said, obviously irritated.

"What's up, baby?"

"You mean to tell me you didn't hear me?"

"No, I didn't. Sorry. I'm in another world. What'd you say?"

"I was asking how you liked my co-workers, since it was your first time meeting them all."

"Oh. They seem like a cool group of ladies . . . and gentleman."

There was my chance to get down to it, so I went for it. I laid next to Marcus and rubbed my fingers across his bare chest, and said, "Speaking of gentleman, there seemed to be some friction between you and Keith. Is there a reason behind that?"

"There's no friction. I just reacted the way any man would react towards a man who spends almost just as much time around his woman as he does. I was just trying to feel him out and see what he was all about. I needed to see if he had any other ulterior motives. Did he say something?" Marcus asked, seemingly wanting to have something against Keith.

"No. He didn't say much at all. Like I told you, I'm not too fond of him, and I'm sure he probably feels the same."

"Ok. Well just let me know if he ever says anything out of the way. You know I'll handle that."

As flattering as it was to see that Marcus felt the need to defend me, I also knew that he had never acted this way as long as we had been together. Something had gotten into him. Maybe he really did feel like Keith was a threat. I would, of course, never know, because as a man, Marcus would never admit to it. I decided to leave Marcus alone for the time being. I had gotten all of the information out of him that I was going to get for now, so I laid my head on Marcus' chest and eventually dozed off.

Chapter Eighteen ~ Keith

During my unplanned dinner with Armani, I incidentally learned a lot more about her than she probably wished for me to know. She had been through some things, which were probably the cause of her hardened outer core that I had to work so hard to break through. If I had known the things about her relationship prior to the one with her fiancé, I might've understood and excused her previous behavior, but how would I have possibly known? Damon was an asshole and if Armani and I had been in an intimate relationship, I would've probably whooped his ass up and down that bar. Fuck probably! Without a doubt I would've whooped his ass! Without her even being my woman, I wanted to hurt him.

Listening to Damon dog Armani out to me made me think about some of the things I've done to women, and made me ask myself what made me so different from him? My mom always asked me how I would feel if a man treated her like I treat women and I heard where she was coming from, but it never really clicked until that night out with Armani. It disgusted me to listen to Damon and witness the painful expression on

Armani's face. I had never seen her display any sign of weakness until that night and I couldn't let her go out like that.

As all of that was happening, I didn't even have time to think about how my, what was supposed to be "perfect" evening with Reagan went way left from the beginning to end. The next morning, when Reagan and I crossed each other's paths for the first time, I was reminded of everything that happened the previous day. It was probably the most uncomfortable feeling I had ever felt in my life. Everything with this picture was all wrong. She was married, we worked together, and just last night we had fucked.

I didn't know how Reagan was feeling on the inside, but on the outside, she looked just as uncomfortable as I felt. We greeted each other with a good morning and went our separate ways. My mind was once again thrown off from what was going on between Reagan and me when Armani's fiancé came to the office to bring her lunch.

When I walked out of my office to see what all the commotion was, I first noticed Armani standing there with the biggest smile on her face. I then looked at the dude who was standing there with roses. When he looked me in the face, he tried to quickly turn away after he had realized what I was still trying to figure out. Before Armani introduced us, I was hoping he was just the floral shop delivery guy, because, if he was messing around with one of the ladies in the office, they were getting played. The pieces of the puzzle finally came together when Armani introduced me to the dude, who ended up being her fiancé. I didn't know how to quite handle the situation, so without words and with all body language, I let him know that I knew exactly who he was and that I could destroy what he had going on in a matter of seconds if I really wanted to.

This was the same guy I had seen in the office at the Sybaris the night before. What made me remember him so well was the beautiful woman he was with, and that woman was not Armani. I remembered looking at him the night before, trying to figure out where I knew him from, and at that very moment, I realized it was from Armani's pictures in her office. From the short conversation he and I had the night before, he made it very clear that it was not his first time there with that same woman. I felt bad for Armani because she definitely didn't deserve what Marcus was doing to her, but I didn't feel it was my place to tell her what I knew.

I shook hands with the bastard, but from the grip that I had on him, he knew that I didn't like the situation at all. What made me almost snap and tell it all was when this negro had the nerve to try and get sarcastic with me after I tried to tell him how good of a woman he had, even with knowing what I knew. He was treading in black waters and needed to be careful of what he said to me, or even how he looked at me. Two days in a row, I had been in situations involving Armani and her men and I didn't understand why. I had enough drama in my own life. I didn't need to be a part of anyone else's.

To keep from saying another word, I excused myself from the awkward situation, went into my office, and regained my composure. I had a debate within myself as to whether or not to say something to Armani. I didn't want to, but because we had become not only co-workers, but also friends, I kinda felt obligated to share the information with her. I then thought about the fact that Armani was also talking about how we needed to keep the office environment professional and to leave our personal lives at home, so that right there led me to make my final decision. I would keep it to myself.

While sitting at my desk, I incessantly tapped a pen against my glass desktop, unable to focus on anything except for the fact that I felt like I was failing Armani as a friend. I'd never been the snitching type and I didn't plan to start at this point in my life either. I kept going over several different scenarios in my head as to how this whole thing could play out if I did or if I didn't say anything. Time was ticking away and I couldn't get any work done. In addition to trying to make the right decision, the thought that Marcus and Armani could've possibly been alone in her office at that very moment, crept through my mind. I was wondering what they were talking about, was he touching her, kissing her, telling her more lies? I never cared much about her relationship before, but knowing that she was being treated the way she was bugged the hell out of me.

I grabbed a document off of my desk that needed to be signed by Armani and decided to run it to her. I knew it could've waited, but I didn't want to wait. Something had come over me at that moment. I felt obsessed with torturing Marcus with the information I had because he deserved to suffer.

When I walked out of my office, me and Reagan's eyes met, and when she saw that I was going in the direction of Armani's office, a stack of papers mysteriously fell off of her desk and flew all over the place. All of the other women just looked down at the mess and continued to work. Although I knew that she had deliberately dropped the papers, I couldn't leave Reagan sitting there looking stupid, even though I really wanted to. She was being childish in the way she was trying to get my attention. I was giving her some time and space to figure out what she was really looking for. Obviously she didn't like where things were headed.

I walked over and knelt down beside Reagan, helping her pick up the mess she had intentionally made.

Without looking at me, she whispered, "We need to talk."

"Later. I can't deal with this here," I said sternly, letting her know that I wasn't happy about the way she was going about things. I didn't know what kind of game she was playing, but I didn't want to participate.

I stood up and slammed the papers on Reagan's desk. As I was walking away, I noticed Taryn scrutinizing every piece of me. I'd had enough of the madness. I just wanted to have a normal work day. I already had too much other shit on my mind that I shouldn't have been concerned with. Since Taryn wanted to play that game, I decided to call her ass out.

"Is there something I can help you with, Taryn?"

Apparently she wasn't expecting me to address her. Her face immediately straightened up when she noticed that everyone's eyes were on her. She loved attention so much, she should've enjoyed the spotlight. Obviously that wasn't the type of attention she liked. She only liked it when she put the attention on herself so that she would be fully prepared for her moment of "fame".

"Nope, I'm good," she said, trying to sound calm and collected.

"Good," I said. I looked around at everyone else and said, "Everyone else good?"

A few of them nodded their heads. I took one last glance at both Reagan and Taryn. They acted as if they were suddenly focused on their work. I felt like I had made a statement and could finally move on to my mission.

Armani's door was closed, just as I had suspected, so I knocked. I had heard voices from the other side before I knocked, but at that moment it became very quiet, so I started talking from the other side of the door. I was now extremely curious as to what was going on on the other side of that door. As soon as Armani finally opened her door, I knew exactly what had been going on. I smelled the sweet aroma of Armani. At that moment, I felt a bit of envy come over me. I had never felt that before, and it took a moment for me to realize what it was. It didn't feel good. I couldn't leave without letting them both know that I knew exactly what I had just interrupted. I was even more focused on making Marcus feel like something was, or potentially could be going on with me and his fiancé. Once I felt like my mission was accomplished, I left, hoping I had left Armani wetter than she already was before I walked in, and Marcus sweating more that he already was.

I went and sat back at my desk, still not feeling like getting into any work. I rubbed my face with the palms of both of my hands and suddenly thought about Troy. I hadn't talked to my brother in a while and knew I should check on him. My moms hadn't even mentioned him lately. I picked up the phone, dialed him up, and let the phone ring so many time that I was just about to hang up when someone answered.

"Hello."

"Hey, bruh!" What's up with you, boy?"

"Keith?"

"Yeah, Man. What's up?"

"Nothin' much. Same ole, same ole," Troy said, not sounding too happy to hear from me.

"You ok? You sound like something got you down. Your moms ok?"

"Yeah. Everything's good. I saw this phone number and I thought maybe it was somebody calling with a job offer."

"Oh. I'm calling from work. We all have 1-800 numbers here."

"Yeah, well it got me all excited and shit."

"Still no bites, huh?"

"Nothin' at all, bruh. I guess I waited too long to try to get out into the workforce."

"Or maybe you're just trying to get jobs that you need more education for. You should really try going back to school and getting your degree. It's not too late. For now, just get a job to help out your mom. You don't have any kids to support, so right now, a little something is better than nothing. You gotta crawl before you walk."

"I hear you, but I ain't trying to go out there and flip no burgers. I know I'm better than that."

Troy said he heard me, but he really wasn't trying to hear nothing I was talking about. We both knew he was better than flipping burgers, and that's not what I was trying to convince him to do. I was just trying to tell him not to be so picky right now, and to work his way up to what his potential really was. I really felt bad for him. He didn't sound good at all. I knew I was going to have to make my way by there soon and hang out with him, and try to talk some sense into him. I wasn't sure what he had on his résumé, but it couldn't have been much of anything. He hadn't done anything résumé worthy that I knew of.

"I know, man," I said, trying to sound like I was reasoning with him. I didn't want to discourage him while I was trying to be an encouragement. "I've still been keeping my eyes and ears open for you."

I heard a knock at my door and closed my eyes to say a quick prayer that it was not Reagan or Taryn on the other side of the door.

"Come in," I said as I took a deep breath.

I almost forgot I was on the phone until Troy said, "You need to call me back?"

Armani walked in and I said, "Nah, hold on a second."

I put Troy on hold so I could see what it was that Armani needed. I couldn't help but to think about the fact that she and Marcus had just fucked in her office and I could smell the scent of his cologne all over her as soon as she stepped into the room. I thought about the fact that his lips were all over her when those same lips had just met the lips of the woman's pussy I had seen him with the night before, and poor Armani had no idea.

"Oh, is your visitor gone?" I asked.

"Yes, Marcus is gone. Can I see you for a minute when you get a chance?" she asked, sounding as if I had offended her in some way. *Here we go . . .* I thought to myself.

I told Armani I'd be there in a minute and resumed my conversation with my boy. I told him I'd be that way in a few days. My moms was getting new floors installed and needed me to come help her move some furniture around. He offered to come over and help, too. I told him that was cool. I knew that would give me the opportunity I needed to let him know I wouldn't tell him anything wrong and I had his best interest at heart. I loved Troy like he was my blood brother. He was the only real friend I really had who was always loyal. I felt like I owed him and I was going to do my best to help him out. I just wished he had more background behind him, but he didn't, so I would work with what I already knew of him. He was a good guy who just had some fucked up shit happen during the time in his life when he was supposed to shine.

After hanging up from with Troy, I sat there wrecking my brain, thinking of places that may be hiring, or even just a start up plan for Troy. I was so into my thoughts, I forgot all about

Armani requesting to see me, so I jumped up and headed over to her office. Her door was already cracked. Before making my appearance I put on my million-dollar smile to act as if none of the day's events had any effect on me. During the entire time I was in her office, Armani tried her hardest to figure out what was going on between Marcus and me. I used my magic of soothing her soul with several terms of endearment to throw her off track and reassured her that there was no type of animosity towards the "love of her life".

The only thing I had left to do was address Reagan about cutting her eyes at Armani. She obviously didn't know who she was fooling with, but Armani was ready to show her, so I had to put a stop to it before it went too far. Other than Armani being suspicious about the interaction between Marcus and me, the only thing that came out of our conversation was me learning that Marcus was a very insecure man and felt as though I was a threat. He just didn't know, I wasn't trying to take his woman. I just didn't appreciate the way he was doing her, but from my own experience, I had learned that everything done in the dark always came to light.

Chapter Nineteen ~ Keith

Today was one day I couldn't wait to come to an end. I didn't think I had ever had so many different emotions going through me at once. For once, I felt like I wasn't in control. I wasn't in control of Armani's situation or Troy's situation, but I felt like I should've been able to determine both outcomes some kind of way. It was, somehow, a painful experience to watch these two individuals go through the things they were going through. Even though Armani really didn't have a clue that she was going through anything, just me knowing the pain she would endure if she found out made me feel sympathetic towards her. I couldn't figure out for the life of me what I was feeling for Armani, and why. Yes, I thought she was interesting and attractive, but I could've never thought of her as being that woman who I cared about intensely and wanted to be with. I couldn't help but to wonder if God was punishing me for every woman I had wronged in my life by allowing me to go through watching a friend of mine get disrespected by a man.

I really didn't feel like dealing with anything else, so instead of leaving with everyone else at the end of the day, I stayed in my office with the door closed until all the traffic cleared the building. Shortly after everyone was gone, besides Armani and me, I got a text message from Reagan. She wanted to meet with me, but this time was different. She didn't want to meet at any random spot. She wanted to come to my house. I had a slight problem with that. I still didn't feel comfortable telling her where I lived. For one, I didn't know if she might turn into a psycho bitch one of these days and come around my peaceful abode acting a fool. For two, she had a husband who one day may have just decided to follow his wife to her side dude's house. I just didn't feel like any piece of ass was worth my peace, or even possibly, my life.

Instead of texting Reagan back, I called her because we needed to talk about her office behavior. Between her throwing shit on the floor and looking at Armani like she wanted to fuck her up, Reagan was on her way to losing her job and I really didn't want to see that happen.

"Hey, bae," Reagan said as soon as she answered the phone, only letting it ring a half of a ring.

"What's going on with you?" I asked.

"Just thinking about you. I really would like to see you in person. It would be nice for me to at least be able to know where you live."

"Do I know where you live?" I asked, not trying to be an asshole, but after it came out, I realized how much of an asshole I sounded like.

Reagan got quiet, and I could tell she didn't know what to say.

"I'm just messin' with you," I said playfully.

She giggled, but it didn't convince me that she believed that I was only joking. I had to be straight up with her and tell her how I felt about it.

"So what's up with tomorrow after work? We can relax and talk in the comfort of your own home," Reagan said.

I knew women were extremely sensitive creatures, so I tried to be as gentle as I could with my words. I took a deep breath and said, "I like you a lot and we really need to discuss some things, but right now I don't think that my place is the best place."

"Why not? Wait, don't tell me. You have a woman living with you, right?"

Before I could get a word in edgewise, Reagan had concocted this entire story about why she couldn't come to my house and began having a conversation with herself.

"You could've just told me," she continued. "I don't know why you wasted both of our time. I knew there was a reason you had rubbers outside of that bullshit ass story you told me about you being single and had to be prepared "just in case"! Bullshit!"

I repeated Reagan's name over and over again, trying to get her to shut up and listen, but it was like she had gone deaf. I was trying to keep my voice at a minimum because Armani was right in her office and I didn't want her to overhear me. I got a little louder, saying, "Reagan!"

Still no response. She continued to ramble.

I put my phone's mic as close to my mouth as possible and shouted, "Reagan!"

All of a sudden, there was complete silence on the line.

"Are you listening now?" I said, lowering my tone again.

"Yes, but . . ."

"Shhh. Just listen . . . Please."

"Ok," she replied.

"I don't have anyone living with me. I'm single, just like I told you. I have no reason to lie to you, baby girl. You're married. Why would I hide it from you if I were in a relationship? Think about it. That shit doesn't even make sense, now does it?"

Reagan didn't respond, so I said, "Ok, you can speak now."

"Are you sure you're done?"

"Yes, I've said my peace."

"So, since you say you're not in a relationship and you don't have a live-in, then what's the secret? Why can't I come to your house?"

"To be honest, this is a dangerous situation we're in and I don't feel comfortable with you coming to my house. I just think it's safer for the both of us that you don't even know where I live. You may slip up one day, not paying attention, and your husband end up following you to my house. That wouldn't be cool."

"I promise that won't happen. I'm very careful."

"Reagan, you cannot promise me that."

"Just think about it, ok?" Reagan said.

I hesitated, but the least I could do was sleep on it, or say I was going to sleep on it just so I didn't have to hear any more about it right now.

"Ok. I'll sleep on it and let you know tomorrow. Wherever we end up meeting, we have to have a serious talk. Today's behavior was not cool."

"I don't know what you're talking about, but ok," Reagan said nonchalantly. "Where are you anyway?"

"Still at the office."

"Oh . . . Is she there?"

I knew exactly who Reagan was talking about, but I still asked, "Who?"

"Don't play dumb with me. You know who. Your bff."

"You said you didn't know what I was talking about, but this is the behavior I'm talking about right there. It has to stop, but we'll talk more about it tomorrow. I'm about to get out of here, and I'm sure you've almost made it home to your family, so I'll talk to you."

"Whatever," Reagan said.

Without saying another word, I hung up, threw my phone on the desk, and rested my face in the palms of my hands. What a day! A good drink was definitely in order.

When I walked into Armani's office to tell her goodnight, she looked like she'd had the same kind of day that I'd had.

"I'm gone. See you tomorrow," I said, while chucking her a deuce.

Although she looked like she wasn't in the mood to joke around, she still pooched up her lips, chucked a deuce right back at me and said, "Holla!"

"Really?" I said, as we both started laughing.

"The best way to end the day is with a good laugh," she said.

"You're right about that. Drive home safely, sweetheart, and don't hang around here too late."

"You too, and I'll be ok. Ben always looks out for me," Armani replied.

"Mmmhmm. You better be careful. Marcus may not like that very much."

Armani rolled her eyes and said, "Goodbye, Keith. Have a good night."

I didn't want to leave on a sour note, so I said, "You know I'm just messing with you. Calm down."

Armani took to heart everything I said about Marcus, which showed just how much she loved his punk ass. Most women these days wouldn't defend their dude if he wasn't around. They'd just laugh it off. He didn't know how good he had it, and how good of a woman he had.

While walking out, I happened to see Ben sitting at the security desk looking down at his phone, texting away.

"Goodnight, Man," I said.

Ben was so deep into whatever conversation he was having that he hadn't even noticed me walking past.

"All right now, Keith. Have a good one," Ben said when he finally realized I was on my way out the door.

Ben started standing up and looked like he had something else to say. I kept walking until he said, "Wait a minute."

He came close and put his arm on my shoulder. I didn't know what this was all about, but it seemed like whatever Ben had to say, he didn't want anyone else to hear it.

"Armani still in there?" he asked, sounding concerned.

"Yeah. I told her don't be here too late. Is something wrong?"

"It really ain't none of my business, but I just think for a beautiful, young woman, she spends way too much time closed up in that office. Especially for her to be engaged and all that nonsense. That man don't know how easy it would be for another good man to sweep her off her feet and she wouldn't think twice about him. The only memory she'd have of him would be all those lonely nights that she had to sit here and do work so that she didn't have to think about how miserable she really was."

I looked at Ben, patted him on the back and said, "Smart man. My sentiments exactly, except, I don't think Armani is miserable."

Ben nodded and smiled, seeming as if he wanted to say something else, but before he could, I said, "You have a good night, and please make sure she gets out of here at a decent hour."

"I'll try, but you know how stubborn she is."

"I sure do," I said as I laughed and walked out the door.

The entire drive home, I thought about everything Ben had said to me. He made me wonder if the real reason Armani spent so much time in the office was because she was, in fact, miserable. She seemed like she was happy and in love, which led me to wonder if it was possible for a person to be happy and in love, but still be miserable at the same time. I always had a belief that anything that could be either a verb or a noun was already too complicated. From that one fact, amongst other things, I always knew that love was a complicated thing. That was why I had never been in love. I avoided it at all costs.

I had been so distracted by my thoughts that when I pulled into my complex, I couldn't even remember driving home. I grabbed my briefcase out the back seat. I had planned on staying in and getting some work done from home since I hadn't gotten much done during the course of the workday. As I headed towards the entrance of my building, I heard a car door slam and immediately afterwards, I could hear the sound of brisk footsteps behind me. Without looking back, I assumed it was one of my neighbors who was trying to catch the door before it shut and locked behind me.

Once I got to the door and unlocked it, I turned around and was unpleasantly surprised by who stood directly in front of me.

"Man, what you do, follow me?" I said aggressively.

"Not that I'm proud of it, but yeah, I did. I didn't know how else to discreetly handle this complex situation," Marcus' punk ass said, looking pitiful as hell.

He looked like he hadn't slept a wink the night before. I was laughing on the inside because he was probably worried all night the night before and today's entire work day that I would tell Armani what I knew. I had to admit, as a man, this was exactly the type of shit we didn't think about when making certain choices that could possibly affect our "comfortable situations."

"What you want? I can't think of any reason right now why a man would be following another man home. That's some crazy shit!"

Marcus looked around like he was worried about someone seeing us and said, "Can we step inside?"

I folded my arms and said, "So you think I should let a complete stranger into my home?"

"Look, I'm not going to beg you, but I do need to talk to you, man to man, if you don't mind."

I held the door open, gesturing for Marcus to go in. He stood there and waited for me to lead the way to my 3rd floor apartment. As we walked up the stairs, Marcus tried explaining himself, making sure that I knew this wasn't something he would normally do. I didn't say anything the entire way up. I just enjoyed listening to him try to justify following me home.

When we got to my apartment, I suddenly felt like I was making a mistake by talking to Marcus at all without Armani being around. I kinda felt like I was betraying her, but I had to see what he was on.

I put the key in my door and turned the knob, but before I opened it, I said, "Before I let you into my personal space, I want to make something very clear. This is my domain, so respect it and respect me."

"Man, I'm not here to start no trouble with you. I'm just think we need to talk and make sure the both of us are on the same page."

"Aight," I said, as I pushed the door open. "Come on in."

Marcus looked around and said, "You got a pretty nice place here. You live with someone or got your own, personal interior decorator?"

I looked at him, slowly shaking my head. "You already asking too many questions. You didn't come over here to compliment me on my décor. Stay out of my business and have a seat."

Marcus hesitantly sat on my zebra print chaise, which was, by the way, chosen by my personal interior decorator, but I preferred for Marcus to wonder if I had a woman and who that woman was. It would've satisfied me even more to know if he had any suspicions whatsoever that "Mani" had ever sat in that very same seat he was sitting in right at that moment. I walked over to my bar area and grabbed a glass. "You want a drink?"

"No thanks."

I grabbed my bottle of Effen Vodka and walked towards Marcus so we could talk face to face.

"Ok, so what you wanna talk about?"

Marcus cleared his throat and began by saying, "Mani never spoke of you much, so I can only go by as much as she has told me regarding the type of work relationship the two of you have."

I interrupted, "And what has she told you?"

"I'll speak on that momentarily, but I say that to say I'm not sure how obligated you feel to tell her what you saw a couple of nights ago."

I poured my Vodka, and threw it back right before repeating myself. "Ok, and back to my question. What has she told you about us?"

"Is there something I should know about the two of you?"

"She's your fiancé, so I'm sure you know everything that she feels you should know."

I could tell Marcus was getting pissed off. His eyes began to squint and his eyebrows began to rise. That let me know I had his mind wandering, which was exactly what I wanted. He deserved to feel how it felt to wonder what his woman had been doing behind his back. At that moment, he felt the need to defend his relationship with Armani.

"Mani and I have a great relationship and we understand each other, meaning, she tells me everything. I have no reason to believe she has lied to me about anything and from what I hear, she can't stand your ass."

"Oh, is that what you hear? Ok," I said.

"Ok what?" Marcus asked curiously.

"Nothing. Just, ok. You just said she tells you everything and the two of you have an understanding. So, does that understanding consist of her having to tell you everything, but that same rule not applying to you?"

"You're a man, Keith. You won't admit it, but you know what the deal is. As a matter of fact, you've probably been in this very same position. I just wanted to come here to make it clear that I love Mani to death and I would do anything for her. I needed to make sure I didn't have to worry about things that didn't need to be revealed coming out at an inconvenient time."

Marcus was full of shit. He wanted his cake and eat it too, and he was willing to do whatever was necessary to make sure his great situation remained intact. He would tell me anything just to make sure I didn't open my mouth to Armani. This guy had it made. He had not one, but two beautiful women in his life, and both seemed to love his dirty drawers.

I responded to Marcus' pathetic declaration of love for Armani by saying, "So, you just said you would do anything for her, so my question is, are you willing to leave the other woman alone?"

Marcus' phone started ringing and as he quickly glanced at the screen and hit "ignore", he said, "I already have."

By the way he got rid of that call, I could tell he'd had a lot of practice at it and it was part of his normal routine.

"I realized how wrong I was the moment Mani introduced me to you. In that very moment, I realized how quickly I could've lost her forever and how much it would've hurt me."

Hurt him? Is he serious? I thought. By this time, I'd had more than just a few drinks, and I continued to pour them. The more I drank, the more he sounded like an arrogant bitch ass nigga.

Marcus' phone rang again, and he made the exact same motion as the first time.

"So, is that Armani or the side hoe?"

"Let's not name call," Marcus said.

"So you're defending the hoe, too? You know what, let's just cut to the chase so you can get the fuck out of my house. What do you want to hear me say? What? Do you want me to say, "Hey man, you're a dude? I get it?" I'm not about to say that."

"That's not what I want you to say," Marcus said, slightly raising his voice.

I stood up and said, "Wait a minute. You better calm down. I told you about respecting my domain." I was hot as hell. The Vodka started seeping through my pores. On a regular day, I would only have a drink or two, but listening to this bitch, two wasn't enough.

"All right, Man. My badd. Sit down."

I stood there staring at him like I wanted to beat his ass at that very moment.

"Please," he said. "Let's just finish our conversation so I can get out of your way."

I sat back down and said, "Ok, so if that's not what you want me to say, then what do you want? Why are you in my house sitting on my chaise?"

"I just want to know that I don't have to worry about this ever coming out. That's it, bruh."

I rubbed my chin, and said, "And what if I say you don't have to worry about it? What do I get out of the deal for allowing you to keep your good, faithful, honest, respectable, classy, successful, drop dead gorgeous woman?"

I realized how desperate Marcus was when he stood up and pulled out his wallet. He grabbed the money out of it and started throwing hundred dollar bills on my coffee table.

"How much is it going to take?" he asked.

Is this nigga serious? I said to myself.

"You don't have enough money to pay me off, but luckily, I don't need your money! You must've planned this because who in the hell carries around that kind of cash anymore? Oh, I forgot. You might have to pay for the Sybaris in cash in the spur of the moment so that there's no paper trace, right?" I laughed.

Frustration was all over Marcus' face, and I completely understood. I didn't like to deal with my damn self when I'd had too much to drink, so I could just imagine how he was feeling, but he brought everything on himself.

Marcus looked at his watch and said, "Can we please just settle this? You see I'm willing to do almost anything."

"I think I might need a job with you the way you throw away money. What do you do anyway?"

Marcus hesitated before he said, "I'm the Program Director over at ABC, but for some strange reason I don't think you and I would work well together."

That's all he had to say in order for the light bulb to go off in my head. If he wanted me to keep his little secret quiet, I for damn sure was going to get something worthwhile out of the deal. From what it sounded like, Marcus had some pull. This was my opportunity to help Troy get his life back on track.

"So, if I knew someone who was in need of a job, you would be able to help?"

"Well, they would have to be qualified."

I looked at Marcus directly in the eyes and said, "So you wouldn't be willing to train the person?"

Marcus began to stutter. He was feeling the pressure. He knew this was the solution to his problem, but he didn't know what type of person to expect.

"W-w-well, as long as he or she is trainable . . ."

"And I'm not talking some low-paying entry-level position."

"Y-yeah, I can make sure they get a position with decent pay."

"And a chance to move up just like anyone else."

"Of course."

I stood up and extended my hand out to Marcus. He quickly stood up and we shook hands. "You got yourself a deal. His name is Troy Tolliver. He's a good guy. A lot like me. Give me your number and we'll be in touch," I said, satisfied with my accomplishment.

Marcus gave me one of his business cards and said, "I'm glad we could come up with a resolution, even though it was harder than I thought it would be."

I didn't know what that was supposed to mean, but I needed to get him out of my house while there was still a little bit of peace in the atmosphere.

"Now get your money off my table and get out," I said.

Marcus laughed as he picked his money up off the table. He thought I was playin', but I was so serious. I should've made him leave it as my tip for having to listen to his sorry ass. I walked him to the door and as he was walking out, I thought of one last thing I wanted to leave him with.

As soon as he got out into the hallway, I said, "Hey. I just thought about something. I know you can't really believe that Armani can't stand me."

Marcus put his hands in his pockets and said, "Why do you say that?"

"Because if you believed that, you wouldn't even be here right now. If she couldn't stand me, do you think she would believe me over you if I told her you were cheating on her? If she really couldn't stand me, you wouldn't have any worries because it would be my word against yours, and she loves you and hates me, right?"

Marcus stood there for a second with a dumbfounded look on his face. He slowly turned around and started walking away.

"I'll be talking to you and Troy soon," he said as he headed down the stairs."

I slammed the door and laughed out loud like a crazy man as I plopped down on the sofa. My evening didn't go quite as planned, but I felt like I had accomplished one thing. I had helped out my brother from another mother. I couldn't wait to tell him, but I was going to wait until I went to my mom's house in a couple of days since he had said he'd come over to help out anyway. I had to tell him this in person. I wanted to see the smile on his face that had been missing for so many years.

I did get to do one thing I had planned on doing when I got home, and that was to have a much-needed drink to relax my mind. Marcus killed the vibe a little bit, but at the end of the day, everything seemed to work out in my favor. I glanced at my empty glass sitting on the table, and next to it, the newly opened bottle of Vodka, which was now empty. Just from the thought that I had finished the entire bottle, all of my thoughts vacated my mind and everything went black as I passed the fuck out.

<u>Chapter Twenty ~ Armani</u>

I only stayed at work for a few extra hours after Keith left. I probably would've stayed longer, but I couldn't concentrate on any work because Ben kept peeking in on me every fifteen minutes, wanting to start up a conversation. I finally gave up and started packing up for the evening. I knew that I needed to stop at the grocery store to pick up a few things anyway.

On my way to the store, I tried calling Marcus, even though I knew he was probably still at work, but I had a 50/50 chance on him answering. I was normally always on the losing end. The phone rang one time, and just as I had predicted, it jumped straight to voicemail. Before the beep, signaling me to leave a message, I listened to Marcus' sexy voice, wishing that when I got home, he would be there waiting for me.

"Hey, bae. I just wanted to let you know I was thinking about you. I'm on my way to the store, then home. I hope to see you before I go to bed. Love you."

As I hung up, I pulled into the crowded parking lot. I had to look at the time, thinking I was confused about what time it was. It was a quarter after eight, but you would've thought it was the middle of the day by the way the crowd was looking. I pulled into a parking space next to a woman who was loading up her car. She had a cart full groceries, and as soon as I closed my car door and started to walk away, the woman's buggy started rolling away, without her even noticing. She was too busy putting one of her bags in the backseat.

In my heels, I felt like a fool chasing this woman's buggy through the parking lot. I finally grabbed a hold of it, bracing myself so I wouldn't tip over as I tried to stop. As I stood there trying to catch my breath, I heard the click of someone else's heels coming up behind me.

"Girl, thank you so much! You were gone after that buggy! I appreciate you, baby!" the younger looking older woman said.

She could've passed for being in her forties, but I could tell she was probably in her fifties, but took very good care of herself all the years of her life. She had a beautiful bronzed skin tone and a head full of soft, bouncy blonde curls. She was a petite woman with a better shape than myself. In her case, fifty was definitely the new thirty.

Still catching the rest of my breath, I said, "No problem at all!"

"I remember when I used to be able to run in those heels like that! Now I can barely stand walking in them, but I'll never give them up!" she said as she let out the cutest little laugh I had ever heard.

"Well, I guess I better finish getting this junk in the car so I can get home. You know us old folks have curfews!"

"You're not old! It's all about how you feel, and you look like a beautiful, young, vibrant woman to me!"

"Girl, you're describing yourself," the woman said, as she stared me up and down. She began trying to load up everything once again. I couldn't leave her to do it alone.

"Let me help you with those."

"You are such a sweetheart! I never had any daughters, but if I did, I'd want her to be just like you! What's your name, honey?"

"Armani."

"Beautiful name, too. As a matter of fact, I own a few pieces by Armani."

"Oh really?" I said, sounding enthralled.

"Naw, girl! I wish!" she said, laughing again.

The woman had the most beautiful spirit I had ever gotten to know. When I finished helping her put her groceries in the car, she gave me a big hug and a kiss on the cheek.

"You take care, baby, and make sure that man takes care of you, too!"

I looked at her with a confused look on my face wondering how she knew I had a man.

"The ring, child! I'm very observant. You learn to be that way by the time you reach my age. Plus, I was trying to see if you were available. I would've set you up with my son," she said, winking, as she got in the car and closed the door.

I smiled and began walking towards the entrance of the store. The woman, who remained nameless, because I somehow forgot to ask her name, had made my day. I truly enjoyed her for the few minutes I had the pleasure of talking to her. It made me think about how sometimes the smallest things could make a big difference in a person's day. There I was sitting there feeling sorry for myself because I had to go home to an empty house. I was ashamed of myself. I had to learn to be more appreciative of the beautiful life I had, and the wonderful people in it.

When I got home that evening, more joy was brought to my day to find that my baby had decided to surprise me by being home when I got there. He told me that when I called and left a message on his voicemail, he was on his way home at that time, but didn't want to ruin the surprise. Marcus was so thoughtful sometimes. I didn't think there was any better fit for me.

It was so nice to spend an evening just sitting back relaxing, chatting it up with the man I loved. We hadn't talked much about a wedding date since Marcus proposed, but he seemed to be pressing the issue this particular evening.

"So, when do you want to make this official?" he asked as he laid next me, gently caressing my arm.

I looked at him and jokingly said, "Official? I thought we were official."

He kissed me on the forehead and said, "You know what I mean. I'm ready to get it on paper. I'm prepared to sign my life away!"

"So extreme! Is marrying me going to be that bad?"

"Of course not. You know I'm messing with you. I just want to see "Mrs. Armani Atkins" written on paper!

"Let me get a sheet of paper. I can do that for you now," I giggled.

Marcus let out a short laugh and then seemed to become serious. "You know what I mean. Once I get married, that's it because I don't believe in divorce. I'm just ready to make it final so that I'll know you'll belong to me forever."

"Awww. You are so sweet. I'm just messing with you. I've been ready, but I just didn't want to seem like one of those women that pressure their man into rushing into marriage just because we're engaged."

"Well, let's do it," he replied.

"Ok! Well, we both agreed on a Spring or Fall wedding, so how about next Spring? That'll give us at least six months to plan and get everything organized."

"I was thinking more like next month," Marcus said.

"Seriously?" I said, with mixed emotions going on in my mind. I was ready to get married, but I just didn't feel like a month would give me enough time to put together the wedding I'd always dreamt of having.

"You don't want to?" Marcus asked with concern in his voice.

I looked down at my hand and began playing with my engagement ring. Marcus put his hand on top of mine. I looked up at him, and after analyzing my response in my head before saying it out loud, and I simply said, "Ok."

Chapter Twenty-One ~ Armani

Keith sat across from me at my desk rambling on and on about a project the big boss wanted him to work on. What he wanted him to do was way above his salary cap, but Keith was ambitious and he wanted to enhance his skills and move up in his career with the magazine. I was proud of him for being able to make such a good impression on the higher ups so soon. Although I was happy for him, I was unable to show much enthusiasm because I had so much on my mind. I tried to fake it by continuously smiling and nodding, but it wasn't long before Keith realized something wasn't right.

"Armani? You ok?"

Trying to act normal, I said, "Yeah. I'm fine. Why'd you ask?"

"You just look like you're not here . . . Like something is on your mind."

"Nope! Just listening to you. I'm so happy for you! So, was dealing with me early on worth it?"

Keith laughed and said, "More than worth it, but you weren't that bad."

"Hmmm . . . I guess I'm going to need to work on my initiation technique. It doesn't look like you'll be hanging around this department for long. I have to be good and ready for the next recruit."

Keith looked directly into my eyes and said, "I like it right where I am. I don't plan on going anywhere anytime soon. How about you?"

I felt like that was my cue to go ahead and let Keith in on what was diverting my attention elsewhere.

"I love it where I am, and the position I'm in. I may be forced to relocate sooner or later due to Marcus' job. He has to move around if management asks him to, so with us getting married soon, some things may change sooner than I'd like them to. Hopefully he's able to just stay where he is."

I could tell Keith had some questions going on his mind and he was trying to decide what he wanted to ask first.

After a brief silence, Keith said, "Well, you still have a while before the wedding, so there's no point in even thinking that far ahead."

"Well, I don't have that long."

Keith, looking even more confused than before, said, "Y'all haven't even set a date, right? I've never been engaged or married, but I'm sure there's at least a year of planning to do after setting the date."

I didn't know why I was shying away from telling Keith the truth, but I couldn't find any reason why I needed to lie to him. As far as I knew, he was in a happy relationship, and so was I. We were only friends.

"Actually, we're getting married October 10th."

"Oh, you got plenty of time!" Keith said, for some reason sounding like he had a sigh of relief. "That's a whole year from now."

"Actually, a month from now."

Keith leaned back in his chair and began rubbing the hairs on his chin. "Ohhh. You mean this October."

"Yeah."

"Ok, ok. That's cool."

I could tell Keith didn't know what to say next, and I surely didn't.

"You should be excited . . . Are you excited?"

Truth was, I wasn't sure if I was excited or not. I definitely wanted to marry Marcus, but I wasn't expecting it to be happening so soon. It now seemed surreal, when before, it just seemed like something that would happen, but I didn't want to believe it until it actually happened.

Trying to sound confident in my decision to get married sooner than expected, I said, "Of course I'm excited!" I then continued with hesitation, saying, "I just didn't know how you would feel about it." My heart skipped a beat as soon as I let those seemingly harmless words leave my lips.

Keith sat back up in his chair and immediately began asking questions that I honestly didn't know the answers to.

"What do you mean by that? Should I feel a certain way, and why is how I feel even a factor?"

I had just made myself look like a complete idiot and I didn't take well to that at all. One thing I couldn't stand was when people made me look stupid. That was exactly why I had problems opening up to people, because any time I had done that in the past, people saw that as me being weak and vulnerable. That eventually resulted in the people who I opened up to, taking advantage of me. Keith took this as an opportunity to try and make it seem like I was coming on to him, and make me feel rejected, so I had to make it very clear that that was not the case.

"Honey, you are not a factor. I was simply just trying to say I didn't know how you would feel about being responsible for my workload, in addition to your own while I was off enjoying my lovely honeymoon." I ended by rolling my eyes to let Keith know that I was highly irritated and didn't appreciate him making any presumptions as to what my intentions were with my statement.

Keith stood up and said, "I guess that's my cue to leave, because we're obviously having a huge case of miscommunication right now. I'll go to my office and we can try this again later once we've both cleared our minds and are in a better place mentally. It's still early. I'm gonna go get a cup of coffee. Want some?"

I sighed and pushed my bangs back off my forehead with both hands, and painfully said, "No, thank you."

Even after attempting to go off on Keith, I still felt foolish. I didn't know what I was thinking to give Keith any indication that I possibly had any feelings for him outside of the friendship we'd managed to form. I slouched in my chair, wishing I could've rewound the situation and not said anything at all, but it was too late. I couldn't sit there and cry over spilled milk. To take my mind off of that situation, I decided to take out a notepad and begin writing a list of things to do before my big day. It would be here before I knew it, so I really didn't have time to be worrying about what Keith thought of me. He was irrelevant, and what he thought was even more irrelevant.

Chapter Twenty-Two ~ Keith

After somehow upsetting Armani, I went back to my office confused about what had just happened. I just couldn't figure out for the life of me why Marcus would be in such a hurry to marry Armani all of a sudden. The thought of Marcus really changing and trying to be faithful crossed my mind, but I wouldn't allow that thought to marinate long enough in my mind to actually believe it. The woman I saw him with was definitely no random one night stand. I could tell he'd had a relationship with her for a long time and just wasn't about to give that up that easily. Even if he was willing to give it up, I knew for a fact that the other woman wouldn't let him throw her away like that. I knew women well enough to know at least that much.

I wondered what Marcus had up his sleeve. All the drama he had, he'd brought upon himself and it was so unnecessary, which brought me to the point of thinking about my drama and how it was also unnecessary. Under normal circumstances, I would've waited 'til afterhours to talk to Reagan, but I needed to terminate our situation ASAP, so I peeked out of my office and told Reagan I needed to see her for a moment. Taryn cut her eyes at me. I could tell that Taryn was capable of some evil wrongdoing and I wasn't dumb enough to not know that I really needed to keep an eye on her up until it was time for her to move on to her next journey. I knew she was already pissed about being transferred, so I had to be prepared in case she decided to cause some trouble for me before she left.

I asked Reagan to close the door behind her. She sat across from my seat and I saw the sun from the big picture window beaming directly in her face, so before I began with my spill, I closed the blinds.

"Thank you," Reagan said as I walked back towards my chair to have a seat.

I stared at Reagan's gorgeous face and took a deep breath. All I could think about was that evening at the Sybaris. None of the negative thoughts crossed my mind . . . Only the thoughts of me loving on her body, and her, loving on mine. I couldn't lie and say I didn't want more of those evenings. If she hadn't been married, there wouldn't be any issues between the two of us.

"What'd you need to see me about?" Reagan asked, interrupting my thoughts.

"As you probably already know, it's not work-related."

"I didn't know that. I assumed it was, since I know how you like to keep it strictly professional."

"Can you lower your voice, please?"

"Oh, I'm sorry. I wouldn't want Armani to hear us," Reagan replied sarcastically, rolling her eyes.

"You know what. Actually, part of this conversation is going to be work-related. I've been meaning to have this conversation with you anyway because I would hate to see you lose your job over something really petty."

I had captured all of Reagan's attention at that point, and she said, "Lose my job? What do you mean?"

"Exactly what I said. I don't think you realize that Armani is my boss, as well as your boss. She's in charge of all of us, so whatever decisions she makes, neither of us can do anything about it, so when you're looking at her crazy and talking to her with an attitude, keep that in mind."

Reagan leaned back in her seat and folded her arms. I assumed she heard me loud and clear when the expression of arrogance left her face and became a look of defeat and humility. I looked at her, raising my eyebrows to make sure we were on the same page.

"Ok. I get it," she finally replied.

"All right. On to the next order of business, which was what I was initially calling you in here for." I lowered my voice, trying to be sure that no one else could hear me. "You know, I've really had a really good time with you up to this point. You're an amazing individual, but like I said before, I think you want more out of me than I can give you without feeling like a fool."

"What do you mean by that?"

"For one, you want me to be faithful to you, and that's not going to happen. And for two, you expect me not to be upset when your husband interrupts our limited time together. Thirdly, this is just wrong. There is no way I can justify this, and believe me, I've tried thinking of ways that it could be justified, but we both know that this is beyond wrong. You have given me no reason to believe your husband deserves to be treated the way you're treating him."

Reagan knew where this was going, so she immediately began trying to quickly turn things around.

"You just don't know our entire background. There are things I don't wish to share with you right now, but things are about to change a whole lot very soon. Please, just let me handle a few things before you make the decision to cut ties with me."

I began shaking my head and said, "Reagan, I can't make a decision based on just you telling me things are going to change. That's very vague information towards a very real situation. I need more to go on, sweetie."

Reagan bit her bottom lip and began twiddling her thumbs.

"Just say what's on your mind. No judgment here."

Reagan looked away from me and said, "He's been cheating on me for years and I've been accepting it. Not only that, he beats on me every time I try to confront him about it. It's time for me to finally let him go and that's what I'm about to do."

I intriguingly listened to Reagan. I immediately tried to recall a time when Reagan ever came to work and looked like she had been beaten, and I couldn't. She was either very good at hiding it, or she was lying. The cheating part could've easily been true, and by the way tears were welling up in Reagan's eyes, I was lead to believe she was being one hundred percent honest with me. This information that she was giving me explained why Reagan seemed to have her guards up most of the time, as if someone was out to get her. I felt bad for her. No woman deserved for a man to put his hands on her unless she was a deadly threat, which I couldn't see her being.

"Look. This is what we'll do. We'll continue to see each other until you get your shit together, but in the meantime, you cannot feel any type of way about me possibly seeing other people. Not saying that I will, but just in case."

She procrastinated on agreeing to my terms, but she did, and in turn, a smile managed to come across her face.

Reagan stood up and leaned over my desk just enough to allow her soft lips to come in contact with mine.

After the unexpected kiss, Reagan grinned once more, saying, "I got this, Babe. Just be patient."

She turned to walk away, and I was taken aback by the way her snug skirt hugged her body, showing off her small waistline and round ass. I sucked in my bottom lip and shook my head as she headed towards the door. She grabbed the handle and before I was able to sufficiently contain myself, she quickly turned around. I tried to quickly look at the computer screen to act as though I wasn't admiring the badness that was walking away from me.

"Do you think it's wise for me to walk out of here empty-handed?" she asked.

My mind was somewhere else at that moment, so I had to playback her question in my head.

"Hello?" she said, trying to make sure she had my attention.

"You're probably right." I grabbed some work out of my drawer that I had been meaning to give her anyway, but since I had been trying to avoid contact with her the past couple days, I had just been holding on to it.

"Here you go."

Reagan looked at me strangely as she grabbed the stack, and said, "Are you ok?"

"Yeah, I'm good," I said as I subconsciously thought about how many positions I could put her in right there in my office.

"Ok," she said, doubtfully, and resumed heading out the door.

I pushed my chair away from the desk and looked down. My man had been standing at attention the entire time Reagan had been in the room. I hadn't quite mastered self-control, especially around a beautiful woman.

After finally cooling down and getting my mind right, I began to get some work done. I wanted to get as much work done as possible so that I could go into the weekend without worrying about what was going to be waiting on me Monday morning. I had already planned to stay after hours so I could start working on some preliminary pieces for my big project. I would sometimes cut down my workload by working at home during my free time. I knew I wouldn't have any time unaccounted for this weekend because Troy and I would be helping out my mom, and I'd probably be trying to get with Marcus so he and Troy could work out everything. Maybe then I could even get some more information behind the urgency in this wedding.

The day went by fairly quickly. In fact, it went by so fast that it was a quarter after seven, and I hadn't even realized everyone had gone home for the day. I was so caught up in getting ahead on my work and doing some research to get a head start on what my big boss had so much confidence in me conquering, that I hadn't been at all aware of my surroundings.

I continued to work while my juices were flowing. The thing about being in the writing field was that you had to take advantage of the opportunity when your thoughts were running wild or you could possibly miss out on something exceptionally ingenious.

My thoughts were suddenly distracted when, from the other side of the door, I heard the doorknob to my office turn. My fingers immediately stopped typing and remained stagnant on the last keys pressed while I stared at the door as it slowly opened.

I suddenly saw Armani's head peak in from the other side of the door.

"Hey! I thought you were gone," I said, hoping that she was in a better mood than she had been in earlier.

"I thought the same about you, but I saw the light underneath your door as I was walking by, so thought I'd double check. What you working on?" she asked while walking towards my desk.

"Just trying to get a head start on this big project."

"You must be excited about it to be here this late!" she said, reminding me in a subtle way that is wasn't often that I stayed after hours. Especially as late as it was.

"I am, and I've been having a lot of great ideas, but of course I'd like the master to look at what I have so far just to see if I'm going in the right direction with it."

Looking puzzled, Armani said, "Master?"

"Yeah! You! You're the pro! Compared to you, I'm an amateur."

Armani tried to hide the fact that I had made her blush, but I could tell she was by the warmth showing in her cheeks.

"I wouldn't say all that, but I can definitely take a look at what you have so far," she said, surprisingly trying to be modest. "You can wait for me in my office. I have to run something down the hall."

After Armani left my office to run her errand, I grabbed my flash drive and folder and walked over to Armani's office.

When I walked in, I could smell her beautiful aroma flowing through the room as if she was there. I carried a chair around to the side of the desk where Armani sat and placed it right next to her chair so that it would be easier for us to review everything together.

As I sat waiting for Armani to return, I noticed that she had written on a notepad several names of bridal boutiques in the area. On her computer screen, she also had up the website of a very extravagant banquet hall. I was surprised that Armani would be taking care of personal business on company time. She just wasn't that type, but I guess she only had a little bit of time to get a whole lot done.

When I heard Armani walk in, I immediately took my attention away from the computer screen. I didn't want to seem like I was being nosey.

"Sorry I took so long. I got a call on my way back that I had to take."

"Marcus checking in on his baby, huh?" I said, just trying to see what type of reaction I'd get out of it.

She tried to keep a straight face, so I really couldn't read her expression to see how she really felt about the call. She said, "Yeah, just trying to see around what time I'd be heading home. Not that it matters anyway."

As she moved her chair a few inches away from mine so that she could sit down, and hurriedly tried to get all of her wedding material out of sight, I asked, "Why doesn't it matter?"

She took a deep breath and said, "Because he's obligated to work late every Friday anyway. He probably won't be home 'til around two in the morning."

In my mind, I was thinking how he was probably just making sure Armani was still at work to be sure that there would be no chance of him running into her. I also thought about how perfectly Marcus had his life set up for his convenience. Friday evenings was his time to spend with his side chick, while Armani sat at home thinking he was working hard. He was working hard all right. Just not in the way she thought he was.

Suddenly, I heard Armani say, "What does that mean?"

I had no idea what Armani was talking about.

"What does what mean?"

"You shaking your head."

Oh shit! I thought. While I was thinking about how much of an asshole Marcus was, I must've outwardly expressed my thoughts.

"Oh, I was just thinking about how I would feel if I had to let my woman be home alone at those hours due to my work schedule. That has to suck for him."

"Yeah. He really hates it, but what can he do?"

I didn't say another word about it because I didn't want to accidentally say too much. Armani asked to see my progress, so I handed her my flash drive to insert into her computer, and we began comparing ideas.

Chapter Twenty-Three ~ Armani

While I sat in my office, I knew that Keith hadn't left for the day yet, solely due to the fact he hadn't come by my office to tell me goodnight. It didn't matter whether he was upset with me or not, he never left without saying something. I knew I had been an unreasonable bitch earlier, so while sitting at my desk, I was devising a plan on how I was going to approach him. Instead of just going to him and apologizing about how I reacted to his little comment, I lied and said I saw the light from up underneath the door just to give me a reason to stop by his office. I was surprised that he acted as if nothing had transpired between us.

Upon returning back to my office after inviting Keith to meet me there, I noticed how close Keith had placed his chair next to mine. The two were so close that if I hadn't moved mine, I might as well had sat on his lap. I then looked at my computer screen and everything else sprawled across my desk. I had completely forgotten that I'd decided to take a break in between work and browse a little bit for wedding ideas. I talked to Keith to try and keep his attention focused on me while I got rid of any reminder of our argument from earlier.

Once Keith and I finally got on the same page regarding what things were a necessity for the project and what things he could throw out, it was smooth sailing. We worked great as a team. We both had a lot of great ideas, and I realized just how talented and knowledgeable Keith was. I already knew he was, but he was so committed to this project that he was letting everything that he had in him come out.

I put my hand over my mouth and let out a huge yawn.

"You ready to call it a night?" Keith asked.

I was having such a good time. It was a long time since I'd found fun in work. Keith and I were able to joke and laugh together and still get the job done.

"No, not yet," I said, knowing I didn't have anything better to do on a Friday night. "But I know it's Friday, so if you have something you need to do, I understand."

"Nope, I'm cool, but I am hungry."

Right at that moment, my stomach let out a thundering growl. I put my hand to my stomach and embarrassingly said, "Oh my God! I'm so sorry."

Keith smiled and I could tell he was trying to hold back his laughter so I didn't become more embarrassed than I already was.

"Don't be sorry. I was just about to ask if you were hungry too, but I guess your stomach already spoke for you!"

I laughed at myself, and said, "Yes, I guess I do need to eat something if we'll be here a while longer."

"Ok. Order whatever you want," he said and handed me his card to pay.

I shook my head at Keith and said, "No, it's my turn to treat, remember? You paid the bill at Theo's and saved my pride in the same night."

"Woman, if you don't take this card. This is not the norm for me. I'm normally the one being wined and dined, so you better take advantage of my generosity."

As I snatched his card out of his hand and picked up the phone to order Chinese, I cut my eyes at Keith and said, "Mmmhmm, I just bet the ladies wine and dine you."

While we waited for the food to arrive, Keith and I took a little break from work and began talking a little about what was going on in our personal lives. I actually provoked the conversation because I hadn't heard Keith say anything about his lady friend lately and I was curious as to how that was going.

"So, how are you and your female companion doing?" I asked.

I could tell Keith wasn't expecting me to ask about her by the expression on his face.

"We're cool. Still learning a lot about each other. We'll see what happens."

Keith ended it right there. Straight and to the point, which led me to believe he really didn't want to discuss her at that moment, so I left it alone.

Before our conversation could go any further, the office phone rang and we both looked at our watches and then at each other. The office phone never rang after hours while I was there.

"Whatever it is can wait 'til tomorrow," I said.

"Who would be calling this time of night, anyway?"

"Probably the wrong number," I replied as the ringing ceased.

"What if it was Marcus?" Keith asked, raising his eyebrows.

"It wouldn't be him. He always calls my cell phone. Perhaps it was for you," I said, reciprocating the sarcasm.

"Whoever wants to talk to me knows to call my cell phone, too."

Keith began digging around in his pockets. I assumed he was searching for his cell phone.

"Oh well," he said, as he stopped looking.

"What's wrong?"

"I was looking for my phone. I guess I left it in my office. "

"You wanna go get it?"

"Nah, it's ok. You're not supposed to make yourself available all the time," he said.

Keith was so smooth, and he knew it. The arrogance that I once saw was now just a whole lot of charm and swag. That's what I figured drew the ladies to him, in addition to his good looks.

The office phone began ringing again.

"I probably should get this just in case it's some type of emergency," I said.

I hit the button for the speakerphone and in my most professional voice, said, "*Couture.* How can I help you?"

"Hello?" A woman's voice said, sounding like she was crying and in trouble.

I looked at Keith and he raised up in his seat.

"Hello, Ma'am? Do you need help?" I said, moving my face closer to the speaker to make sure she could hear me clearly.

Clearing her voice, she slowly spoke, "Is Keith Sanders there?"

Keith jumped up with urgency and snatched the handset off of the receiver and put it to his ear.

"Ma! What's wrong?" Keith said, now standing, with worry all over his face. "Are you safe?"

There was a brief pause. I sat there feeling helpless, not knowing what to do or say. I could feel Keith's pain. My heart was probably pounding just as hard as his.

Keith took a deep breath. "As long as you are safe. Now stop crying and tell me what's wrong. I can't understand you."

Keith suddenly put his hand on his head and started breathing uncontrollably. A large vein began bulging down the middle of his forehead, and tears began to fill his eyes.

"What?!?!" he yelled. Nooo!"

Keith dropped the phone and dropped to his knees. He began pounding the floor with his fists. I immediately got up and tried to console him. I didn't know what had happened, but I knew it had to have been tragic for him to lose it like that. I knelt down in front Keith and wrapped my arms around his neck.

"Whatever it is, it's going to be ok. I'm here. Whatever you need."

"Nooo!" Keith continued to say, while crying uncontrollably.

I hated to see a man cry, and seeing him cry made me cry. Keith and I rocked back and forth on the floor. I held his neck and rubbed the back of his head. His face was buried in my cleavage and I could feel his tears running down the middle of my chest. I gently kissed his forehead as I continued to reassure him that everything would be ok. I looked over and saw the phone on the floor, remembering that Keith's mom was on the line. Without letting go of Keith, I stretched my arm out to reach for the phone. I put it to my ear, not expecting his mom to still be there.

"Hello."

"Is he ok?" his mom asked.

"I'll make sure he is and I'll have him to call you back."

"Please make sure you keep an eye on him. He was his one and only real friend. He was like a brother."

"Don't worry. He's in good hands."

"Thank you, sweetie," Keith's mom said, before hanging up.

I could hear the pain in her voice. Obviously, something had happened to one of Keith's close friends, so I knew he needed me to be there for him at that moment, and I owed him at least that much. I wrapped both arms back around Keith's neck, and his breathing began to calm. He lifted his head out of my cleavage and looked me in my eyes. Next thing I knew, his lips were pressed up against mine. Both of our eyes were still open, and our lips didn't move at first. It seemed as though we were both questioning what we were doing and what the next move should be.

Keith closed his eyes and gently parted my lips with his tongue. I received him by opening my mouth and allowing him in. He grabbed both of my thighs and wrapped them around his waist. He then stood up lifting me up off the floor as I tightly held his neck. He carried me over to my sofa and laid me on my back. Standing over me, he looked at me for confirmation that what was about to happen was ok. I knew morally it wasn't ok, but I wanted it to happen. It felt right and I didn't want to stop it. He then sat next to me and began kissing my neck as he unbuttoned my blouse. The affection that he was showing me made me feel so good that I held him like I never wanted to let him go. Keith, then carefully lifted my abdomen, just enough so that he had enough room for his hands to slide underneath me to unsnap my bra.

I felt my breasts reveal themselves from underneath my bra, and Keith immediately took advantage of the moment, partaking in both a handful and mouthful. I didn't resist. I felt my eyes roll to the back of my head, and Keith was turning me on so much that my clit began to throb. I felt like maybe I should've been the one to stop this because I knew Keith was vulnerable due to the news he had just received. I kinda felt like one of those men who took advantage of women when they were clearly drunk. Marcus crossed my mind for a second, but that thought quickly dissipated when I felt Keith's tongue between my second pair of lips. It was such an amazing feeling. When any part of him touched me, it was electrifying. I felt like I was in heaven. I didn't know if this was a dream like the last time, but if it was, I didn't want to wake up until the very end. Reality of what was really happening didn't set in until I felt every inch of Keith inside of me.

I exhaled and moaned loudly with the initial plunge. Keith slowly put his index finger to my lips to remind me where we were. Every thrust afterwards seemed longer and harder, and it became harder and harder for me to be discreet. I could feel my nails digging into Keith's back, but nothing was phasing him. We both had blocked everything else out. No one else in the world existed at the moment, except for the two of us. That is, until the door opened and we heard someone else in the room talking.

"Y'all must really be into your work! You know I normally don't just walk in, but I thought . . ."

Ben's mouth opened so wide, I thought I could see what he'd had for lunch.

"I thought you might want your dinner, but I see you skipped to dessert. No pun intended."

Keith and I remained motionless, butt naked on the couch, not sure how to react. I was so embarrassed, but upset at the same time that Ben had interrupted the best sex I'd had in years, and I'd had some pretty awesome sex! Ben Walked over to my desk and sat our food down, and proceeded to walk out.

"Ben . . ."

Without looking at me, Ben put his hand up and said, "No explanation necessary. Now, carry on." As he walked out the door he shook his head, giggling to himself.

Keith, still on top of me, looked at me with disappointment in his face.

"I'm so sorry. This shouldn't have happened."

My guards immediately went back up. I didn't want to be the only one feeling like this was a great thing. I didn't want him to know I enjoyed it as much as I had since he was already having regrets.

I said, "It's ok. We just have to make sure it doesn't happen again."

Keith got up from on top of me, lifted my legs so he could sit down, and I rested my legs on his lap. He caressed my legs as he stared at the wall. I knew he was in deep thought.

"You want to talk about it?"

Keith looked at me and said, "I'm sorry. I was in a daze. It's like it's happening all over again. I wish this all was a dream."

"What happened?"

Keith took a deep breath. "My friend . . . No. . . He was more than a friend. My brother decided to take his own life tonight." Keith leaned back, put his hands over his face, and shook his head. "I can't believe this shit."

Keith was deeply hurting. I sat up, kissed him on the cheek and laid my head on his shoulder. He became quiet, and I let him take his time. I knew how it was to lose someone close. I had lost my older sister, Chanel, to breast cancer ten years ago.

She was only twenty-nine years old. It was so hard, and I didn't want to talk to anyone about it. She was my best friend. I talked about it when I was ready, and even to this day, I only talked about her when I felt like it.

I decided to share my memories of my sister with Keith so he didn't have to talk about what he was going through. He didn't say anything as I shared some of our special memories that I'd always kept to myself. I did get a laugh out of him when I told him her name was Chanel, and my mom had named us after the brand she was wearing on the day she went into labor with us, and how I was so happy she hadn't been wearing something like Gucci or Prada!

After I'd broken the ice, Keith finally began talking. He told me his "brother's" name was Troy and they had been friends since kids. He was feeling even more awful about the situation because he knew Troy was depressed about not being able to get a job, and Keith had found an opportunity for him, but wanted to wait to surprise him when he was supposed to see him the very next day. He felt like he could've prevented this by giving Troy the good news before today.

I tried to stress to him that it wasn't his fault and not to beat himself up about it, but I knew, due to the circumstances, it was going to be hard for Keith to get over this and not blame himself. I felt bad because in those types of situations, you just don't know what to say to a person, and with me once being on the same side where Keith was right now, I knew that sometimes saying nothing was the best thing.

After we talked a bit and got dressed, we put our work away and tried to prepare ourselves to face Ben. Keith told me to take the food home that we didn't get to eat.

"What about you?"

"I'm not hungry," he said.

"You have to eat," I said. "You'll be hungry later." I opened the bags and divided up the food to make sure he had plenty to eat. I knew he didn't have an appetite, but I was hoping once he got home, he at least tried to eat something.

On the way out, we stopped in Keith's office to get his cell phone. He looked at it and had over thirty missed calls. Most of them being from his mom. She had called the office because he wasn't answering his cell. I hoped she was doing ok. She sounded like such a nice woman. She and Keith probably needed each other right then.

Keith and I looked at each other and took a deep breath before walking past the security desk. Trying not to look at Ben, I said, "Ok, Ben, have a good night." Keith and I kept walking."

"Wait a minute," Ben said as he got up out of his seat. He stood in front of both of us and said, "Now y'all know you don't have to worry about me saying anything to anybody. I've been waiting on this day, and I knew it would happen soon."

I looked at Ben with a confused look on my face, and I guess he realized that hadn't come out quite right.

He laughed and quickly corrected himself. "Not walking in on the two of you, but you two seeing what I saw in the both of you. I've been wanting the two of you to give each other a chance. You both remember the conversations I had with the both of you, right?"

In unison, Keith and I nodded our heads and said, "Yeah," in a perplexed tone, as we both briefly thought back on the conversations we'd had with Ben, and it still didn't add up for me.

"Well, we're not a couple, so don't get too excited. It was just something that happened . . .," I said.

Keith interjected and said, "And you never know. Anything is possible."

Ben gave me a slight smirk. I rolled my eyes at Keith for leading Ben to believe that the there was any chance that he and I would ever be a couple. I had a fiancé at home who I loved past death, and I'd made a mistake that I couldn't dwell on.

As we walked out to the parking lot, I said, "Keith, why'd you do that?"

"Do what?"

"Make it seem like we'd one day miraculously be a couple?"

"I was just messing with him. You know Ben jokes around a lot. He wasn't serious, and he knows I wasn't serious."

"Ok," I said with doubt. "Are you going to go to your mom's tonight?"

"No, not tonight. I'm not ready. Troy lives right across the street from my mom."

"I think she needs you."

"Believe me. She's a very strong woman. She'll be ok, and I know she'd appreciate your thoughts."

Keith walked me to my car and before I got in, I reached my hand out like an idiot to shake his hand. I never knew saying goodnight could ever be so awkward.

He looked at me like I was crazy, then said, "Come here, girl," grabbing and kissing me on the forehead. "Thank you for being there for me tonight. I can't think of any other person I would've rather been in the presence of at a time like this. Thank you."

"Anytime. Call me if you need me," I said as I got in my car. As Keith closed my car door, I said, "Goodnight."

I sped off and watched Keith in my rearview mirror as he stood there watching me until I exited the brightly lit parking lot.

Chapter Twenty-Four ~ Keith

I laid in the bed thinking about my brother and how I could've prevented this from happening. I wished I could just go back one day. That's all I needed was one day. I knew that I would continue to blame myself for Troy's death for the rest of my life. It was already eating me up inside. Throughout the entire night, each time I managed to doze off, I was awakened by a vision of Troy's face and him asking me to help him. I tried to stay strong and make myself believe this wasn't my fault, but it was. I was experiencing the exact same thing Troy went through when he blamed himself for Tramaine's death. I now knew exactly how he felt. I had shared with Armani the reason why I felt like I could've prevented this, leaving out the part about the job offer for Troy coming from Marcus. I decided not to tell anyone else. That information would've probably made it harder on everyone else, not to mention, everyone would have probably hated me for it. I hated myself. I knew it was going to be extremely hard the next day facing my mother, and especially Troy's mother. She lost the only thing she had left. Her boys were her life and now they were both gone.

Since I couldn't sleep, I turned on the legendary Tupac, and started doing some cleaning around the house. I thought that would at least keep my mind occupied for the moment. That was the first time I had ever wished I was in a committed relationship. I enjoyed my single life, but being in a relationship with someone you could call your best friend had its pros, too. One of those major pros was during times like this, I would have someone to call on that I knew would be there for me. I appreciated Armani for giving me her shoulder to cry on. The bad thing about that was I couldn't bring her home so she could hold me through the night and continue to comfort me and let me know everything would be ok.

I also couldn't help but to wonder how things would now be between us since we'd been intimate. I felt bad because I didn't want the reason behind us having sex to be a result of pity on her part. It just so happened that we were together when I got the news about Troy, and if we hadn't been, Armani and I would've never had sex. I would have to deal with whatever repercussions that might've come about later. I had worse things going on.

When I finished cleaning to the point that there was not a speck of dirt or dust on anything in my apartment, I grabbed my cell phone and sat at the kitchen table. I went through my call log and saw that in addition to my mom's million and one calls, Reagan had also called a few times, but she didn't leave any messages. I realized why she hadn't left any voice messages when I looked at my texts. She had been blowing me up the entire evening while I was working with Armani. She began by sending very sexual texts, letting me know just how much she wanted me and needed to see me. After receiving no response from me, I guess she got angry because I could sense her frustration more and more in all the later messages.

I looked at the time and it was just a few minutes past seven in the morning. I wondered if it was too early to text Reagan on a Saturday morning, but I was sure after all the texts she had been sending me throughout the night, she was probably keeping her phone very close, waiting on me to respond. Well, if she was smart that's what she should've been doing, and I considered her to be a smart girl, so I texted her back.

"So sorry. A lot happened last night. Call me when you can."

Short and simple, and before I could lay my phone back down, it rang.

"Hello."

"Hey! You ok?" Reagan asked.

"Not really . . . Not at all."

"Oh no! What's wrong?"

"My brother passed away last night." I chose not to go into details over the phone with Reagan because I wasn't really sure if I even wanted to tell her the circumstances behind his death.

"I'm so sorry," she said in a low, solemn tone.

I was hoping she left it alone right there, but of course that was too much to ask.

"Was he sick?" she asked.

"No. It was very unexpected."

"Well, do you and your family need anything? I'm free today. You want me to come by?"

"No, I'm good. I'm going to go by my mom's house in a couple of hours."

"I'll go with you!"

Reagan was way too determined to see me and I didn't know whether I should've taken it as her really being concerned with what I was going through, or was this all for her own satisfaction.

"I don't know if that will be a good idea. Only close friends and family should probably be with each other right now."

"Well, I'm considered your close friend, right? I just want to be there for you."

Reagan was very persistent. I had just thought about how I didn't have a woman to be there for me to help me through this, and here Reagan was, trying to be the support system I was wishing I had. I didn't know if it was the greatest of ideas since neither my mom nor Troy's mom knew Reagan, but I felt like I needed her right then.

"Ok," I said, and before I knew it, I'd given her my address to meet me at my house. After I gave it to her, I closed my eyes and shook my head, hoping I hadn't made the worst mistake of my life.

My doorbell rang at ten sharp. Reagan was right on time and I was a little nervous. Not just about bringing Reagan around on a day like today, but also about bringing her around my mom for the first time. I knew my mom could be very blunt in saying exactly what was on her mind. I buzzed Reagan in and gave her a minute to get up the steps to my floor before I opened the door. To my surprise, she was already standing on the other side of the door by the time I opened it. She looked at me with a sympathetic face and immediately stretched her arms open wide to give me a hug. I snatched her up, bringing her inside, and spun her around. It felt so good to hug someone.

After I put her back down on the floor, I gave her a kiss and thanked her for offering to come with me.

"You know it's no problem at all. I know you're hurting and I want to do whatever I can to make this easier for you. You need to be around people who love and care about you, and I'm definitely one of those people. "

I squinted my right eye a little bit, trying to pretend I didn't hear her just tell me she loved me. I hoped Reagan wasn't prematurely getting herself in too deep with this situation.

"You're right. I do need real friends and family right now," I said, completely avoiding the "L" word.

On the way to my mom's, I thought maybe I should've warned my mom I'd be bringing Reagan along, but it was too late now. We were on our way.

"Is there a store on the way to your mom's house?" Reagan asked.

"Yeah, why? You need something?"

"I just want to pick up a cake, pie, or something. I just hate to go empty-handed."

Reagan was so thoughtful. I was really appreciating her entire display of generosity, but I needed her to know that she was already doing enough.

"You don't need to do that. I just appreciate you being here."

Reagan grabbed my arm and said, "Please! I want to do this."

I took a deep breath and said, "Ok."

I stopped at the nearest grocery store and Reagan got out and said she'd be right back. While I was sitting there listening to Miguel on the radio, my phone rang. I figured it was probably my mom because I hadn't talked to her yet. I picked up the phone through my car's Bluetooth and heard the sweetest voice.

"Hey honey, how are you?"

It was Armani checking on me. I was definitely surprised to hear from her.

"Hey! I'm doing ok, considering."

"Yeah, that's understandable. You sound much better, but I know it's going to be a process."

"Yes, it definitely will be. Thanks for . . ."

Without warning, Reagan jumped back in the car.

"Got it!" she said, smiling and holding up a bag.

"I'm sorry. I didn't hear you," Armani said.

Reagan and I both looked towards the dashboard where Armani's voice was coming from.

"Keith, are you there?"

"Yeah, I'm here. Ummm, I was just saying, thanks for being there."

I looked over at Reagan and she was still staring at the dash with a look of disbelief. I wanted to just completely end the conversation with Armani, but didn't want to seem like I was being rude. However, on the other hand, I kinda felt like I was being rude to Reagan. I could've quickly taken Armani off the Bluetooth, but I didn't want Reagan to feel like I had any reason to hide anything from her. Beads of sweat began to form on my forehead as I prayed that Armani didn't mention our sexual encounter the night before. I didn't think that she would because her main concern at that moment was how I was dealing with Troy's death, but you could never be completely sure what might come out of a woman's mouth.

"It was my pleasure. I'm glad I was able to be a shoulder for you to cry on. Did you call your mom back? I'm worried about her, too. She sounded really distraught."

"No, but I'm on my way to her house as we speak."

"Good! Let me know if you need anything. You know I'm here."

"Ok. Thanks again, Armani."

"Bye, love," she said before I ended the call.

I cleared my throat and looked at Reagan out of the corner of my eye. She was looking straight ahead, and I could see her eyes blinking one hundred times a minutes. I could hear her tapping her nails on the door. This couldn't be good.

Hesitantly, I asked, "You good?"

"Yep. I'm fantastic," she said, tight-lipped.

"Sooo, what kind of cake did you get?"

"A strawberry shortcake. Something I thought everyone should be able to enjoy."

I nodded as I watched the road and said, "Yeah, that should be fine."

It became too quiet for my liking, so I turned up the radio a bit. Immediately afterwards I heard Reagan say something.

"What was that?" I asked.

Reagan repeated herself with frustration in her voice, saying, "I said, is Armani going to be there, too?"

"No, she isn't. What makes you ask that?"

"It sounds like she's pretty close to your family by the way she spoke of your mother."

"Here you go assuming things. She doesn't even know my mom. We just happened to be at the office together when my mom called with the bad news."

"Ok, Keith. Sorry for assuming," Reagan replied.

Nothing else was said for the remainder of the ride to my mom's house.

When I parked in front of the house, Reagan looked around and then looked at me.

"What? Is something wrong?"

"This is where you grew up?"

"Sure is. I know it doesn't look like the best of neighborhoods, but it's where I called home for many years. Don't worry. Everyone's very friendly."

"I'm not worried. I guess I just expected you to have grown up with a silver spoon in your mouth. This experience has really given me a new perception of you."

Experience? I thought to myself. Reagan acted as if joining me to my mom's house was a field trip to the hood. I felt a little insulted, but I was going to let that slide. It was a sensitive time for me. Maybe I had just taken what she said the wrong way.

I got out of the car and before going to let Reagan out on the other side, I glanced across the street at Troy's house. There were a few cars parked outside, and the front door was open. I imagined Troy standing outside on the porch, where I would normally see him. I just couldn't imagine not seeing him there anymore. Everything at that moment became so real. I opened Reagan's door and she got out glancing around some more, still seeming to "admire" my hood. We got all the way to the front door without my mom opening it, which was odd. Normally she would be in the living room and could see everything through the window. I reached in my pocket and took out my key to let us in. When we walked in, I could smell the aroma of pancakes and bacon.

"Ma," I said standing in the hallway, waiting on her to greet us.

"Maybe she's in the bathroom," Reagan said.

Yeah, maybe . . ."

Right at that moment, I could hear my mom coming from around the corner, saying, "Hey, baby! I was just finishing up my morning prayer." When she realized I wasn't alone, the diminutive smile that she did have turned into a complete expression of disappointment.

There was nothing I could do at that point except to introduce Reagan. I wished I could've pressed rewind and never brought her with me, but unfortunately life isn't that simple. If it was, most of the world would be pressing rewind on a daily basis and none of us would ever get anywhere.

I first gave my mom a hug and said, "Ma, this is my friend Reagan. Reagan, this is my mom."

My mom folded her arms after hugging me. Reagan looked a little uncomfortable, but tried to make the best out of the situation.

Reagan presented her Colgate smile and said, "It's a pleasure finally getting to meet you, but I just wish it was under better circumstances, Ms. Atkins. So sorry for your loss."

Uh oh . . . I thought to myself.

Reagan reached out her hand to shake my mom's.

My mom unfolded her arms and held out a firm arm to shake Reagan's hand.

"First off, I'm Ms. Banks. Sunshine is what most call me, but you can call me Ms. Banks. And finally get me meet me, huh? How long have you been around?"

Still smiling, overlooking my mom's unusual unpleasant demeanor, Reagan said, "Well, we met when your gentleman of a son began working for the magazine. We just started hanging out about a month ago."

My mom looked Reagan up and down and said, "Hanging out, huh? Ok, well, nice to meet you and thanks for your condolences."

My mom walked towards the kitchen and said, "Keith have you eaten? I wasn't expecting you, but I still have some food left over."

I followed her to the kitchen, with Reagan not too far behind. "Why weren't you expecting me? I was supposed to come help move your furniture today, anyway."

"Too much going on. I cancelled the floors for now."

I could see my mom tearing up and she then turned her back to us. I walked over, turned her around and gave her a hug. Reagan then walked up to us and put her arms around both of us as if we were a big happy family.

"Again, I'm so sorry for the loss of your son, Ms. Banks. I couldn't imagine."

Moms freed herself from the both of us, with her tears drying up quickly, and said, "My son? You've known Keith for this long and don't know that he's the only child?"

Reagan stepped back and gave me a perplexed look.

"Ma, that's my fault. I just told her my brother passed. She didn't know that we weren't blood brothers, and just really good friends."

"I'm so sorry!" Reagan said as she looked at me with a stern look.

"That's ok. I'm sorry for jumping to conclusions. I'm just overprotective of my baby boy. My only baby!"

"Don't worry. He's in good hands," Reagan said, and gave me a kiss on the jaw.

"Very good, then," my mom said.

I could tell she still wasn't feeling Reagan, but she was trying her best to not say what was really on her mind. I was sure I'd hear about it later.

"Now, what do you have in that bag you're carrying around?" my mom asked.

"Oh! I forgot all about it! I wanted to bring something over. I know during a time like this there'll be a lot of guests to come and go, so I picked up a strawberry shortcake."

"How thoughtful. Let me put that in the refrigerator. We can take that to Troy's real mom's house after while," my mom said as she took the cake and put it away.

Reagan looked at me and smiled, feeling better about how this was going.

Reagan and I devoured the rest of Mom's breakfast that she had left over. She said she was only cooking for herself, but she always made enough for me, even if she wasn't expecting me, just in case. She thought I wasn't on to her, but she had been my mom too long for me not to know her the way I did. That was my mom though. Always looking out for others, especially her baby boy.

We stayed at my mom's the entire morning, sharing some of the memories we had of Troy with Reagan. Reagan kept a bright smile on her face the entire time. I was kinda glad she did come. Everything seemed to be working out after my momma started warming up to her. We put off going across the street to Troy's house as long as we could. Both, my mom and I, knew we were procrastinating, but we were probably the closest people to Troy, next to his mom.

Before we left to head over, Reagan grabbed the cake out of the refrigerator. When we walked outside, I noticed there were a lot more cars outside Troy's mom's house than there were when we first got there. I paused and took a deep breath. My mom looked at me and rubbed my back to calm me down.

"It's ok, son. It's going to be all right."

She grabbed my hand and walked side by side with me. Reagan looked down and saw that my mom and I were having a moment, and she insisted on being a part of that moment by grabbing my other hand and walking on the other side of me. When we finally got across the street and walked up to the front door, before we could knock, one of Keith's aunts let us in. My mom immediately walked in looking for Troy's mom.

"So good to see you, Keith," Troy's Aunt Joslyn said, as she snatched me out of Reagan's tight grip, and gave me a big hug and kiss right smack dab on the mouth. I knew it was coming. That was just how Aunt Joslyn was. She didn't mean any harm. She just didn't have any problem expressing her emotions in whatever way she felt, and she didn't see anything wrong with it. I'd had many of kisses on the mouth from her throughout my life and I never minded it because she was fine as hell. I used to joke with Troy all the time about her, telling him he would someday be calling me "Uncle".

As soon as Aunt Joslyn released me, I got ready to introduce her to Reagan, but to my surprise, all I saw was the back of

Reagan walking through the crowd of people towards the kitchen.

"I'll be right back, Auntie," I said, as I followed Reagan.

When I got into the kitchen, Reagan was already sitting down next to my mom. My mom was sitting at the table holding Momma Tolliver's hand, trying to console her. It hurt so much to see Troy's mom like this. It reminded me of the day Troy and I came home from college after Tramaine died. She was torn to pieces. I walked over and knelt down to give my second mother a hug, and she began to cry even harder. I continued to hold her and didn't let go. Next thing I knew I felt someone massaging my shoulders. I looked up and saw Reagan standing over me.

"It's going to be ok guys. Troy is in a better place and he wouldn't want you all crying. He would want you to be celebrating his life and the wonderful times you had together."

Mama Tolliver quickly freed herself from my clutch and looked up at Reagan. In the most stern voice I had ever heard her use, even when she was upset with her boys, she said, "Who are you?!?!?" putting extreme force on each word.

Before I could try to cool her down, Reagan began to speak again, and I began to sweat bullets. I knew she was only trying to help, but what she didn't understand was she didn't know my people like that, so in this type of situation, she just needed to sit down, look pretty, and not say anything unless she was being spoken to.

"I'm Reagan, Keith's good friend. I brought the strawberry shortcake over."

I had never heard anyone sound so proud about bringing a damn cake to someone's house after losing a loved one.

Mama Tolliver stood up, pounded her fists on the wooden kitchen table, and said, "I don't care about no goddamned cake! Can you bring my son back since you're so good at bringing stuff?"

The entire house got quiet. Reagan jumped back in shock and covered her mouth. My mom immediately jumped up to mediate the situation.

She grabbed Mama Tolliver and hugged her. I heard her speaking softly in her ear, saying, "She didn't mean any harm. She thought she was saying the right thing. We know there's really no right thing to say right now. Come on. Let's go talk."

My mom cut her eyes at me as she gave Momma Tolliver some tissue to wipe her eyes, and walked her out towards the den. I shook my head and looked at Reagan. She just shrugged her shoulders. In the midst of everything that had happened, she had the nerve to stand there and ask me who the woman that kissed me on the mouth was.

"Are we really going to do this right here?"

"I just asked a question. You would ask me, too, if some man came up to me and did that while you were standing there."

I was so frustrated that I said, "No, I wouldn't, because I really don't care who you kiss or who kisses you. You're not my wife . . . Not even my woman!"

My mom just happened to be standing in the doorway and I had no idea. Reagan began breathing rapidly and looked at me like she was ready to kill me.

My mom stepped in and said, "Well, I just laid Sylvia down. She needs some rest. I'm going to stay over here and entertain the guests for her, so the two of you can leave."

"Ma, I'm going to stay here with you. I need to be around my people."

She immediately gave me that look that she would give when she meant what she said and said what she meant, so I knew it was time to go.

The ride home was nothing enjoyable. I really cared about Reagan and was willing to see how this whole thing played out, but she wasn't making it easy. As I drove, she sat in the passenger seat with her arms folded and would every so often peek over at me. By the time I would look back at her, she would turn her head to act as if she wasn't looking. We definitely needed to clarify some things, but I didn't know how to begin the conversation, which I knew would end in an argument. I ended up not having to start the conversation because Reagan decided to.

"I'm sorry," she said solemnly. I didn't mean to make this an uncomfortably dramatic day for you. I know how much your friend meant to you and I'm extremely sorry for making it so that you couldn't spend as much time as you would've liked to with all the people who cared for Troy as much as you did."

"Thanks for the apology. I appreciate that," I said. I should've known it wasn't going to end there, though.

"But, I will not apologize for asking who that woman was!" Reagan said, as she turned her entire body towards me in her seat, and rolled her neck as she spoke.

"She was just Troy's aunt, which is like my aunt."

"Well, I feel it's very inappropriate for her to be kissing her "nephew" like that! Anyone who didn't know any better would've thought she was a cougar and you had given Stella her groove back!"

"I can't apologize for anyone else's actions, but I'm sorry you feel that way. That's just how Aunt Joslyn is, and always has been."

I decided to change the subject and put Reagan on the spot. "So how is your situation going?"

I glanced at her and she looked at me and rolled her gorgeous, cat-like eyes.

"Everything is going just as planned. I'm taking care of my business on my end to make sure I end up with what I want. I just hope you're doing the same. I know you're dealing with this right now, so let's just focus on that. I want to be here for you. Anything you need, you can depend on me."

Right at that moment, while stopped at a red light, Reagan unbuckled her seatbelt, reached over and unzipped my pants, and began putting her mouth to work. There was nothing she could've told me at that moment that I wouldn't have believed. She had proven herself to be the real MVP.

Chapter Twenty-Five ~ Armani

A couple of weeks had gone by and Keith and I hadn't talked about our little indiscretion. I was giving him some time to try and cope with the death of his brother, and felt a couple of weeks was sufficient enough time to allow for him to finally be ready to have that talk. We both knew things like that just didn't happen if there wasn't something deep down inside the both of us that had somehow escaped. Since Keith wasn't going to bring it up, and continued to go on about his normal routine as if nothing had happened between us, I arranged a meeting for the two of us in a discreet location. There was a lounge about 10 miles south of the office where I knew we would be able to have a private booth so that we could talk without any distractions.

When I pulled into the parking lot, I noticed there weren't too many cars, which was a very good sign. I was glad Keith had actually been able to find time to meet with me. It seemed like he'd had so much on his plate lately, or just pretended to so that he could avoid talking to me about that particular situation. I asked the hostess for the most private booth they had available, which happened to be located all the way in the back near the fire exits. The atmosphere was sexy, with the lights being very dim, which was what I was looking for. I didn't need anyone going back telling Marcus they had seen me out on a romantic rendezvous with another man just two weeks away from the happiest day of my life. Especially with that other man being Keith.

I sat at the booth, waiting on Keith for about twenty minutes. I ordered a drink and decided if he hadn't arrived by the time I finished it, I was leaving. I purposely sipped my vodka and cranberry slowly, hoping Keith would walk in any minute. As soon as I stopped paying attention, Keith slid into the seat across from me.

"Waiting on someone?" he asked, looking more delicious than I'd ever seen him look.

I tried to act as if I was upset with him for being so late, but I was distracted by the muscles bulging through his white tee.

Once I kinda regained my composure, I said, "You could've called or something and said you were running late."

"I'm sorry. I got caught up in the gym, and I know you didn't want me to show up smelling like a funk pot, so I had to go home and shower."

"You're right about that," I said, laughing, forgetting I was even upset.

"So, what do I owe the pleasure of you setting up a private meeting for the two of us?"

I had completely thought this evening through, and rehearsed several times everything that I was going to say to Keith, and it all seemed so simple in my head, but my stomach began turning and I didn't know if I still wanted to have the conversation at all. I knew I needed to because my conscience had been kicking my ass since the incident. I had never cheated on Marcus before and I felt horrible about it, but at the same time, I didn't know if I would've changed a thing. I just needed to talk everything out hoping I would feel better.

"Well, you do realize the wedding is only two weeks away."

"Yeah. What? Are you getting cold feet?"

"No . . .," I hesitated. "I just feel like we need to talk about our incident."

"What about it? We're both grown, consenting adults, and we did what we did. I know you love Marcus, and I've grown pretty close to the woman in my life. Especially the past couple of weeks. She has been there for me in ways no other woman has been before."

I sat there staring into Keith's eyes, listening to the words that were coming out of his mouth, and it seemed like with every word, I felt a pain that became worse and worse. It was like that evening meant nothing to him at all. I didn't know what I expected, but definitely not that, so I had to reciprocate with my defense mechanism.

"You are exactly right! I'm so glad we're on the same page. I just wanted to make sure we got it out in the air and spoke on it so it didn't seem to pose any type of issue with any misunderstandings later on."

"I feel you. No misunderstandings here," Keith replied.

He was just way too nonchalant for me. I didn't get it. He normally seemed to be so gentle with me and my feelings, but I couldn't assume he knew what my feelings were without me coming out saying it. Hell, I didn't know what my feeling were.

"I'm glad we met up, though. There's something I wanted to talk to you about," Keith said.

At that moment, the waitress came over and asked Keith if he needed anything, and asked if I'd like another drink.

"Yeah. I'm probably going to need a drink. Let me get a Long Island . . . please."

I replied to the waitress, saying, "No, I think I've had enough."

Before the waitress walked off, Keith interjected and said, "Please bring her another of whatever she had."

"I said I didn't want anything else!"

The waitress stood there, confused, looking back and forth at the both of us.

"Shhh," he said, putting his finger to his lips. "I believe you may need this, too."

Keith had me worried. What in the hell did he need to talk to me about?

"Ok . . . I guess."

The waitress nodded, smiled and said she'd be right back with those.

I leaned in closer to the table and said, "What is it, Keith? Please don't tell me you're leaving."

That's was the first thing that came to mind, which gave me anxiety from even thinking about finding someone else to replace Keith.

"Nooo, that's not it. I have it too good where I am. You're stuck with me," he laughed.

We had a quick laugh together and I said, "Please don't scare me like that! It took me long enough to get to like you!"

"You liked me all along. You just didn't realize it!"

"Oh, is that what you think?" I said, smiling and blushing like a little teenage schoolgirl.

Keith's tone suddenly got serious as he said, "That's what I know," and raised his eyebrows.

The truth was, I did like Keith all along, but he was wrong about one thing. I was well aware of it. I just didn't want him to know!

The waitress came back with our drinks and I said, "Just in time for the real news! Since I know you're not leaving, I don't think anything else could be worse than that right now."

Keith leaned back in his seat and took a deep breath. He looked regretful before even saying anything. My expression changed to a look of worry. *Maybe it could be worse,* I thought.

"I don't know if it's the right thing for me to share this with you, but with the position you're in, I think it's only fair that you know because you're going to find out either way, and I prefer if it comes from me."

Preparing myself, I took a sip of my drink and said, "Ok. Spill it."

He shook his head, looking as if he were trying to put his thoughts in place. "Reagan and I are dating. She's the woman I've been involved with all this time and it's getting pretty serious, so I felt it was time."

I felt like someone had just kicked me in the chest and punctured my heart. I had never felt anything like it before. The pain was intense.

"W-w-what? All this time and you never said anything?"

"I couldn't find the right time."

"Maybe before I fucked you?!?!" I exclaimed, but at the same time trying to remain restrained.

"Armani, you know that just happened. Our emotions were all over the place."

"Well, you know it's against company policy for the two of you to work together."

"Armani, are you serious? I thought we were speaking as friends. I didn't know you had your boss hat on right now."

"I don't need to have my boss hat on to also know that this is morally wrong! She's married, Keith! How in the hell are you in a serious relationship with a married woman?!?! Not only that, you're jeopardizing my job, and this isn't the first time you've done this!"

"So you would've preferred if I would've just kept it a secret until you found out from someone else, huh? I guess if I would have done that, Reagan and I could've held on to our jobs a little bit longer."

I knew I was being a bitch and Keith thought he was doing the right thing, but I was hurt, and I wanted him to hurt, too.

"I guess so! The worst part about this is you knew why that bitch was being so disrespectful to me and you still failed to mention to me as to why!"

"I spoke with you about it. I made sure I nipped it in the bud for you!"

"For me? Was it really for me, or to make sure she kept her job?"

Keith just sat there shaking his head at me.

"You know what? I think I'm done here." I flagged down the waitress to pay my portion of the bill and left Keith sitting right where he was.

On my way home, I thought of all the times Reagan had given me dirty looks, or said something sarcastic to me. Obviously, she had to have felt like I was threat and that Keith felt some type of way about me. One thing I couldn't stand was an insecure bitch, and she was obviously one of them. I couldn't sit there long enough with Keith to ask the hundred and one questions that were going through my mind without getting angrier and angrier. I did the best thing I could've done, and that was to get up and walk away.

When I got home, I still needed to calm my nerves, so I went into the liquor cabinet to find something stronger than I'd had at the lounge that could help ease my mind. Maybe I was overreacting, or maybe I wasn't, but one thing for sure was that I wouldn't know until my mind was clear. My Marcus must've felt that something wasn't right with me because he came home early and as soon as he walked in the door, he gave me what felt like the most comforting hug I'd ever had. As he held me, I went to kiss his neck and noticed something unfamiliar.

"Why do I smell perfume on your neck?" I spoke softly in his ear.

Marcus caressed my back and said, "You know Tammy who works with us, right?"

"Tammy?" I said, trying to recall who he was talking about.

He then reminded me by saying, "Tamara."

"Oh yeah, I said. The woman who looked like she had something going on with Eric."

Marcus looked at me strangely and said, "Yeah, but she and Eric definitely don't have anything going on."

"How do you know what goes on in their personal lives? You're not with them 24/7."

Marcus lifted me up off the floor and carried me to the bed. "You always like a good scandal, don't you?" he said.

"You know it!" I said, as I spread my legs so he could lay in between them.

I kissed him on the lips and he said, "You been drinking?"

"Don't change the subject," I said. "You still haven't explained why Miss Tammy's perfume is all over your neck."

He kissed me back and said, "We had a surprise birthday party for her in the office today and she gave everyone a hug. Now, why do you smell like Tequila?"

"I had a drink when I got home. It was long day," I said. I didn't lie.

"So you're good and ready, huh?" Marcus said as he pulled off my pants. He always knew what Tequila did to me. I was ready for him to do whatever he wanted to do to me.

"You want me?" he asked, seductively.

"Yes," I whispered.

"You need me?" he asked.

"More than you even know," I said, being very honest. I needed Marcus to take away everything that was troubling me. I wished I had a refresh button that would renew everything that was on my mind and put me in a place of serenity.

After making love to the man who would be my husband in two weeks, I laid in the bed next to him as he wrapped his arms around me, thinking about how I had reacted to Keith when he was only trying to confide in a friend. I felt bad and decided to make it my business the next day to give him the most sincere apology I could. I might've let my emotions interfere a little too much, forgetting about the fact that I was in a happily committed relationship and Keith, indeed had his own life.

<u>Chapter Twenty-Six ~ Keith</u>

During the entire course of the preparation for Troy's funeral, Reagan had my back. She constantly called and made sure I was ok, and to check to see if the family needed anything. She wasn't the only person that had been calling. Marcus had been blowing up my phone and I kept letting it go to voicemail. His calls were a constant reminder that I could've prevented Troy's death with one simple phone call. I planned on telling Marcus that the deal was off, and he didn't have to worry about me saying anything to Armani about his infidelity. I knew that's what he was worried out, but I just couldn't talk to him yet.

A few days after Momma Tolliver snapped off on Reagan, she called to apologize. I knew she was very stressed and emotional due to her losing the only son she had left, in addition to the fact there was no life insurance policy. She'd had one on Troy, however, she transferred it into Troy's name, putting the responsibility of paying it on him, and unfortunately he ended up letting it lapse. Even with that being said, Reagan shouldn't have opened her mouth. I still let Momma Tolliver know that there was no need to apologize and

Reagan and I both knew what she was going through. My mom, on the other hand, still wasn't convinced that Reagan was a good fit for me.

She called me later that evening after she had made Reagan and me leave Momma Tolliver's house.

"What do you see in her?" she asked, sounding like she was confident that my answer wouldn't be good enough.

I didn't even want to answer her question because I felt like I was too old to be answering to my mother about who I dated. However, I knew if I didn't answer her, she wasn't going to let it go.

"First off, she's a beautiful woman."

"What about the inside, Keith? That woman's insides ain't no good."

"I wasn't finished. That was only one of her great qualities."

"Ok. I'm waiting," she said.

I shook my head and took a deep breath before I began again.

"She's very caring, respectful, and one of my best employees."

My mom paused a second before saying, "You done now?"

"Yes, I am, but I have a question for you. Why do you think she's no good?"

"She's crazy! I know a crazy woman when I see one. Look at her eyes. They do some crazy stuff. I call them the "crazy eyes". I can tell just by looking into those eyes that she's very deceitful and she'll do anything to get what she wants. If you try to leave her alone, you're going to have a fatal attraction on your hands."

My mom said she knew a crazy woman when she saw one, but all I could think about was the fact that she didn't know Day'ja was crazy, and still didn't know because I never told her how I found Day'ja the day I went to her house after she destroyed all my shit.

"I think you have Reagan all wrong. She's a sweetheart, and nowhere near deceitful. She honest with me and I'm honest with her."

"Ok. Looks like I'm not gonna win this one. This is something I'll just have to let you find out for yourself. "

After hanging up the phone from with my know it all mother, I thought about what she said about Reagan's eyes. I definitely didn't see what she saw, but my mom wasn't the only one not happy to learn about me and Reagan's relationship status. Getting it off of my chest and telling Armani about Reagan and I during our little meeting she had put together for us sounded like a good idea at the time, but it went way worse than I thought it would. It might've gone better if Armani and I hadn't had sex. We both had mixed emotions about that, but Armani was getting hit by it hard and I could tell. As a man, I was able to keep emotions to a minimum when it came to sex. I knew I had some feelings for Armani, but I knew how to handle mine. Armani tried to suppress her feelings while we had our talk that evening, but the more she tried, the angrier she became. I shouldn't have been surprised, but I was because of the fact she was engaged to be married in only a couple of weeks.

I chose to not even tell Reagan about me telling Armani about us. I already knew Reagan disliked Armani, and I didn't want to add fuel to the fire. I definitely didn't want her to begin to feel too comfortable with showing affection towards me in the workplace just because Armani knew about us when I didn't even know how Armani was going to handle the situation. Reagan and I had gotten a lot closer during the past couple of weeks. So close, I would find myself forgetting she was married and when I had to bring myself back to reality, I'd have to pump my brakes. She was still very secretive about what was going on in her marriage. Anytime I'd ask about it, she'd say she was still working on getting everything in place for her to be able to leave him. I didn't know what to think, but I knew I couldn't let things go on the way they were for much longer.

The morning after my meeting with Armani, as soon as I walked in the department's door, Armani was standing there waiting for me.

"Good morning, Keith. Can you come with me?"

I didn't want to, but what choice did I have? I followed behind her, watching her ass move from side to side and her calf muscles flex with each step she took. She stopped at the door to her office, gesturing for me to go in. After I walked in, she shut the door and immediately wrapped her arms around me, giving me a hug. I stood there clueless, but slowly wrapped my arms around her.

"I wanted to catch you before anyone else got here. I am so sorry," she said with sincerity in her voice. "I understand how hard it was for you to tell me about you and Reagan, and I should've been a friend and respected the fact that you did tell me at all. You didn't have to."

She gave me an unexpected peck on the lips. I wrinkled up my face, feeling even more dumbfounded.

"Now that's the last one of those you'll get," she said, laughing softly, almost sounding like she wanted to cry.

I then reciprocated with an apology.

"I'm sorry I put you in an uncomfortable situation. I should've never become involved with her, but I did, and now a relationship exists that I just can't end."

Armani replied, "I know you can't control who you love."

I frowned and said, "Love? Who said anything about love?"

"I just assumed since you said it had become serious that you were in love with her."

"Nah. I wouldn't say all that. Yes, I like her a lot, but I can't put all my feelings into this and she's still with her husband. I'm not even going to let myself get in a position to be hurt. That's what a lot of women do with men who have ulterior motives that the woman doesn't know about, and then when it all comes out, she ends up hurt."

"I see," Armani said. "Well I just didn't want there to be any hard feelings and wanted you to know I'm still here for you as a friend. I know I acted out of character last night and knew I needed to fix it immediately."

Out of character? Definitely not! I thought to myself. Acting like a bitch was part of Armani's character. She just had learned to temporarily disguise it when we were together, for the most part.

"Thanks for that," I said, "but I was partially at fault. I'm just glad we can still be friends."

I gave Armani another hug, and started off giving her a peck on the lips, but somehow slipped my tongue into her mouth. Next thing I knew, we were lost in a deep, passionate kiss. I don't know how long it lasted, but the only thing that stopped us was a knock at the door.

Before I released her to answer the door, I said, "Your last kiss wasn't good enough. I saved the best for last."

Armani grinned, and went to open the door. To both of our surprise, it was Reagan.

Reagan looked right past Armani like she wasn't standing there and said, "Keith, your mom is here."

"Good morning to you, Reagan," Armani said, attempting to sound sincere, when she was really being sarcastic.

"Good morning, Armani," she replied, as she briskly turned away, whipping her hair in Armani's face.

"See. You gotta fix that."

"I will," I said, disappointed that Reagan was acting up again. "I'm glad that we did have this talk."

"Me too," Armani said, still smiling as I turned away from her to go meet with my mom.

I already knew what this surprise visit was about, but after the last conversation, or should I say, debate that we had, I wasn't sure when I'd see or talk to her again. My moms could be very stubborn and set in her ways when she wanted to be, and this was one of those times. I couldn't remember the last time we had let weeks go by without speaking to each other. As a matter of fact, I didn't think we had ever gone more than two days without talking.

When I walked into the front office, I didn't see anyone. That's when I thought to walk into my office. Reagan had let both, herself and my mom into my office. She was standing next to my mom, looking as if she was trying to hold a conversation with her, and the expression on my mom's face told me she was uninterested in anything Reagan had to say. I was just glad that Taryn had already left quietly to move on to her new office. That would've been someone else my mother would've felt the need to address with me because knowing Taryn, she would've taken that as the perfect opportunity to make it known that we'd had relations. I definitely didn't need my moms thinking that I was the office man-whore. As soon as my mother saw me, she acted as if Reagan wasn't saying anything and she ran up to me, giving me a hug and a kiss on the cheek. I hugged her back and kissed her on the forehead.

"Happy birthday, baby!" she said, handing me the gift bag she had been holding on to.

"Birthday?" Reagan said, sounding disappointed as she folded her arms.

My mom glanced at her and said, "Yes! It's my baby's birthday! I thought you would for sure know that. Everyone who cares about my son knows when his birthday is!" After she finished coming for Reagan, she looked at me with her beautiful smile as if she hadn't just scowled at poor Reagan.

I looked at her, not sure if I even deserved a gift from her. I felt bad for allowing my pride to get in the way of me calling my mom to at least check on her within the past couple of weeks.

"Boy, what's wrong? Why you look so surprised?"

"I just wasn't expecting this. Thank you!"

"Remember, no matter what we go through, that will never change the way I feel about you! I love you more than anything on this earth and that will never change! You're my . . . what they say? Day one!"

I laughed and gave my moms another hug. As I held my mom tight, I saw Armani walking into the room. I turned my mom around to introduce her to the woman she knew as "the warden". Unbeknownst to me, she actually knew her as more than that.

"Mom, this is . . ."

Before I could finish my introduction, a huge smile came over my mom's face.

"Armani, right?" my mom said and rushed over to give Armani a hug.

"Yes! How are you?" Armani said as she hugged my mom back, as if she had known her for years.

I stood there with my hands in my pockets, not sure what was going on. I glanced at Reagan and she still stood there silent, but glaring at me as if I'd been deceitful to her. What she didn't know was I was just as confused as she was. I shrugged my shoulders, letting her know I had no idea what was going on.

I cleared my throat as a reminder to my mom and Armani that I was still standing there. They both looked at me simultaneously, with their faces glowing and their beautiful smiles gleaming. They held each other's hands like mother and daughter. I realized I was looking at two of the most amazingly beautiful women I had ever seen in my life, and they were standing right in front of me. A feeling came over me that I had never felt before. It was a feeling of extreme gratification.

Before I could even ask how they knew each other, my mom said, "Keith, this is the one!"

I didn't want to believe my moms was saying what I thought she was saying, so I tried clarifying it by saying, "Yes, Ma. This is my boss I told you about."

"No! I mean she's the one for you!"

At that moment, Reagan ran out of my office, slamming the door. I started to run after her, but my mom had come here for my birthday and I wasn't about to let the drama of a married woman who could be here for me one day and gone the next come in the middle of a special moment between me and my mom.

"All righty then," Armani said, and proceeded to change the subject. "Well, let me tell you how I met this special woman who just happens to be your mom!"

Armani and my mom together told me about how they'd met one evening in the grocery store parking lot. I laughed as my mom described Armani as Superwoman, chasing down her grocery cart in the middle of the parking lot. I could just imagine the entire scene. It was just crazy to me how fond my mom was of a complete stranger. She knew basically nothing about Armani, except that she had helped her one night, but already seemed to love her.

"Now, how did I not know it was your birthday, Keith?"

My mom interjected and said, "He has never been into birthdays. He doesn't make a big deal out of them like some of us do!" she said, looking up at me, grinning.

"I see, because he definitely never once mentioned it. I'm going to have to pick you up a little something," Armani said.

"Don't worry about it. Like my mom said, birthdays aren't a big deal to me."

"Well they should be, especially with you being a Black man living in America. Each birthday is a blessing!"

"Amen! My sentiments exactly!" my mom agreed. "See, this is the type of woman you need! You need this woman!"

I could tell Armani started feeling a little uncomfortable.

"Ma. Stop it. Armani is getting married in a couple of weeks."

"She's not married now, is she?"

"Please, Ma! Come on! She's happy."

Armani interjected and said, "Leave your mom alone! It's quite flattering. Thank you Ms. . . . . I do apologize. I never asked you your name."

"That's ok, sweetie. Angie Banks. You can call me Ms. Angie, or Sunshine, like my friends do.

My mom sure had a way of stirring things up for me, but at the same time, it was hard for me to be mad at her.

"Ok, Keith. I think I've said enough today. I hope you like your gift," my mom said as she got ready to leave.

"Thanks again. Love you."

"Love you, too, baby, and nice seeing you again, Armani!"

"Nice to see you too, Ms. Angie," Armani replied as my mom was walking out the door."

My mom turned around as if she had forgotten something and said, "You know what? I don't like that. Call me Ma!"

"Ma!" I exclaimed, as my mom giggled. She was just messing with me now. "I'll be back. Let me walk Miss Sunshine out!" I walked my mom out to her car and stood in the parking lot until she drove off to make sure she didn't start up any more fires that I'd later have to extinguish.

When I walked back in, I noticed Reagan was sitting at her desk, and wouldn't even look at me. I looked around for Armani and didn't see her. I thought that maybe she was still in my office, so I peeked in, and still no sign of her. As I walked towards her office, I looked back and caught Reagan watching me. She quickly turned back around and pretended to work. When I got to Armani's office, her door was open. I still knocked and heard her tell me to come in.

"Hey. I just wanted to apologize for my mom's behavior. She lets it be known what she is thinking at all times!"

"It's ok. She's a sweetheart. I see where you get your charm from."

I smiled and said, "Well, I'm glad she didn't offend you."

"Not at all. We're good!"

"Yes, we are," I said winking at her as I walked out of her office.

Chapter Twenty-Seven ~ Keith

After work that evening, I wasn't surprised to get a call from Reagan asking if she could come by to talk. I agreed to see her because I knew how my mom must've made her feel, and she definitely didn't deserve that. I wanted to put my all into Reagan, but I couldn't, knowing she wasn't mine. I would've probably checked my mom if that had been the case, but how could I possibly defend someone against my mom when they belonged to someone else? My mom would always be my mom. During that period of time, Regan and I were basically sexual companions.

When I opened the door for Reagan, she had an expression on her face like she had just lost her best friend.

"Come in, sweetie," I said in a comforting voice.

She didn't say a word, so I tried to break the ice by giving her a hug.

When I let her go, I looked at her and saw tears streaming down her eyes. I knew my mom made her feel unimportant, but I didn't realize she was so hurt by it.

"What's wrong, baby?" I asked.

At that moment, her sadness erupted into anger. I mean, she went from zero to a hundred real quick! My mom's words "crazy eyes" went through my mind when I looked at her.

"What the fuck do you mean what's wrong with me?!?! Why does your mom hate me and love her? Armani can't have you! We love each other and we will be together so you can tell Armani and your mommy that!"

Reagan grabbed one of my basketball trophies off of my mantle and threw it at the wall, missing my head by a millimeter. I ran and grabbed her, holding her arms down at her sides.

"Calm down, Reagan! I don't want, Armani! She's happy and I'm happy!"

I could still feel Reagan shaking as I held her.

"Are you ok?"

"Yes," she said in a whisper.

"So, can I let you go without you throwing anything else at me?"

"Yes."

I slowly released Reagan from my tight grasp. She hugged me and said, "I'm so sorry. I know it's not your fault. Please forgive me."

"We all can lose it at times. I know you have a lot going on and today didn't make things any better. I've been honest with you. There's nothing going on between Armani and me. You don't have to worry about that, love."

I could tell Reagan was embarrassed about the way she had reacted. I wanted her to know I wasn't holding any grudges, so I asked her to stay and watch a movie with me. Surprisingly, she declined.

"Will is waiting for me to get back. I told him I was stopping by the store to pick up a few things."

That was exactly why I couldn't bring myself to love Reagan the way that I would've liked to. The situation just wouldn't allow my heart to open all the way up to her. I had never opened my heart up for any woman, but whenever I would decide to, I didn't want it to be damaged. I knew Reagan was there for me as much as she could've possibly been, but I needed her to be available whenever I asked.

Before Reagan left, she apologized a hundred more times. I forgave her and wanted to move past it, but I couldn't lie. I couldn't help but to wonder if what my mom had said about her had some truth to it. When it came to my life, I didn't like to listen to my mom, but the majority of the time she ended up being right. It was possible that she might've been right about Reagan, but she was completely wrong about Armani being the one for me.

After Reagan was gone, I went into my bedroom to get my phone. I had learned to hide it while she was around because she had a habit of questioning every call and text that I would get while she was in my presence. I knew that could be a very bad sign, especially in the beginning stages of a relationship. However, with Reagan, the pros outweighed the cons, and I knew no one was perfect.

When I grabbed my phone from underneath my mattress, it was lighting up. Marcus had just left me a message. He had called five times within the past half hour.

"Hey, Keith. This is Marcus. I was just calling to see what was up with your boy who needed the job. I've been trying to get at you for a couple of weeks now. I was trying to avoid having to leave a message, but I need to know what's up. Call me when you get a chance."

I could hear worry all in Marcus' voice. I was concerned with Armani marrying someone who was treating her the way he was, but one thing my moms taught me was that everyone is put in your life for a reason, and no matter what it is, good or bad, everything happened for a reason. I couldn't help but to think maybe I was placed in Marcus' life to help him realize what he had so that he could change his ways before he took that final step with Armani. Again, no one is perfect and maybe Marcus did deserve a second chance. As a man, I knew sometimes we did fuck up. It was a part of life's lessons. I decided to call Marcus back to ease his anxiety.

The phone rang a few times and right before I hung up, I heard a voice on the other end say, "Marcus Atkins."

"Hello?" I said, almost feeling unprepared for the conversation.

"Hello? Keith?" Marcus said.

"Yeah, it's me."

"You're a hard man to reach. Maybe I should've left you a message from jump."

"Yeah, I've been dealing with some things. I've been meaning to call you. I just wasn't ready for this conversation yet."

"So, you're going to go through with messing up what Mani and I have, huh? I know I made a mistake. I admit that, but it's over."

"That's not what I was going to say. I know that we all make mistakes, and as hard as it is for me not to tell Armani what you've been doing, I feel like you just might deserve another chance. It's not my place to tell her in the first place."

The other end of the line was silent for a moment. Marcus finally replied, "So, when do I get to meet the newest member of our station?"

"Unfortunately, Troy passed away a couple of weeks ago, so our agreement is null and void, but I'll keep my end of the agreement because you were willing to help out my brother."

"I'm so sorry to hear that," Marcus said, trying to act as if he cared, when I knew he only cared about himself. "What happened?" he asked.

"I don't care to get into that. I'm just going to end our conversation with saying you better treat Armani like she is the best thing that ever happened to you, because she is."

I hung up the phone and took a deep breath. I was just hoping the decision I made to keep everything quiet was for the best.

A minute later, my phone rang again. Without even looking to see who it was, I knew it was Marcus. He just couldn't be satisfied with me being done with everything.

"There's nothing else to talk about!" I said after answering the phone.

"Hello? You ok?" my momma asked.

Stuttering, I said, "Oh! Yeah, Ma. I'm good."

"Yeah, ok. I was just calling to tell you I put a couple of steaks and baked potatoes in the oven if you want to come by and have a birthday dinner. That's if you're not too busy."

"Ok. Sounds good. Give me about a half hour."

"Perfect. Dinner should be ready by then."

I could tell in my mom's voice that she didn't believe that everything was ok, so I might as well had prepared myself for the third degree. I should've known she was going to cook me dinner. She cooked dinner for me every birthday for as long as I could remember. Even when I was off at school, she would let me know what she cooked just to celebrate in my honor, even though I wasn't there to eat it.

On the ride to my mom's house, I kept thinking about how Reagan had spazzed out on me. I had never seen her act like that before and it was scary, even for me. I didn't know where that anger came from, but it felt like something that came from the depths of hell. I just kept in mind that once Will was out of the picture, I could get to know Reagan better, seeing every side of her. I knew Reagan, but not as well as I needed to know her. I wanted to know as much I could about her.

When I got to my mom's house, she was setting the table. I began helping her, not saying much because of so much being on my mind.

As she carefully put the plates down on the table, she said, "You know I know when something's wrong with my one and only child, right?"

I took a deep breath as I began placing the silverware. "Yeah, I know, but Ma, I really don't . . ."

"I know you don't want to talk about it, but I really feel that you need to. Worry causes health issues, and I don't need you getting sick over some mess you don't have no business worrying about. Now what is it? Get it off your chest."

Something in my mind kept telling me to just keep it to myself, but I really didn't know if I was doing the right thing. I just needed to hear someone else's views on the situation with Marcus and Armani, and who would be the best person with experience other than my momma?

"Can we at least sit down first?" I said.

"Ok," my momma said, as she filled our plates.

She sat down and blessed the food. As soon as she finished, she said, "Ok. Go ahead. What has my baby boy so upset?"

"I wouldn't say I'm upset. It's really hard to explain how I feel."

I began telling my mom about how I had seen Armani's fiancé at the Sybaris with another woman, and that we had come to an agreement for me not to tell Armani. My mom remained expressionless as she ate and I told her everything, leaving out the part about me and Armani's session of intimacy. She was really listening for once and not interrupting. I knew this conversation was going to be hard because of me having to bring up the part about the agreement being that Marcus had to give Troy a job, and how he would've still been here if I would've told him just one day sooner instead of trying to surprise him.

When I got to that part, I completely broke down. My mom quickly got up out of her chair and stood in front of me grabbing my face like she used to when I did something wrong as a kid.

"Listen! You did nothing wrong. Troy committing suicide is not your fault. You cannot carry that weight! It'll kill you!"

My mom cried as she tried to convince me of what she was saying. She knelt down and wrapped her arms around my neck. "Please let this go, baby! If you don't it will eat you alive. Ok?"

"I'll try, Ma."

"No! You have to. Promise me. And if you need to go to counseling, I'll go with you. Whatever you need, you know I'm here."

"Ok. I promise."

My mom walked away and came back with Kleenex for the both of us. I actually felt a little better by letting things out.

As my mom sat back in her chair, she wiped her eyes, which were now red and puffy. I hated seeing my momma cry and I knew she felt the same way about me. I knew we weren't done yet, though.

"Now, about Armani and her fiancé . . . Are you really going to let her marry the wrong man?"

"But how do you know he's the wrong man? Maybe he's just a man who made a mistake. People can change, right?"

"Yes, people can change, but they aren't even married yet and he's already bored with her. She has a beautiful spirit. I saw it the first time I met her and began praying that you found someone just like her, not knowing you worked with her every day. I know he's not the right man for her because you are."

"I'm not, Ma. You already know what type of man I am. You know how I've treated women."

"Yes, women, but not that woman. She brings out a different type of man in you. I saw it from just the few minutes I was around the two of you. She'll bring out the best in you."

"Well we don't have that type of relationship. She's happy where she is and I'm happy. That's it."

"Happy with who? Raggedy Ann?"

"Reagan, Ma."

"Let me ask you this. Why is it you feel like you're good enough of a man for Raggedy Ann, but not Armani? What am I missing?"

I looked down at my plate, knowing exactly why I felt the way I did, but hesitated on telling my mom. She sat back in her chair, folded her arms, and waited.

"Armani is ready for a committed relationship. I'm not sure that I am."

"This is still not making sense, Keith! So you mean to tell me . . .," my mom looked up in the air trying to remember Reagan's name, and continued, "Reagan isn't ready for a committed relationship, because she sure seems serious to me! Come on with it, son!"

I took a deep breath and leaned forward putting my elbows on the table.

"I don't feel obligated to be committed to her because . . ." I stopped and shook my head because I couldn't believe what I was about to say.

"Because what?" my momma asked impatiently.

"Because she's married," I mumbled.

My momma jumped up and said, "She's what?!?!? Keith! You know better! Why are you even entertaining this?"

"Calm down, Ma! They're in the middle of splitting!"

"Oh, is that what she's telling you? You're smarter than that! I already told you she's crazy, and crazy women have even crazier men! You don't know what's really going on over there. For all you know, everything could be perfect, but she just wants to have herself a man on the side, just like a . . . Oh Lord forgive me! I have no right calling that bitch a hoe!"

My mom never really cursed, but when she did, she was highly pissed. Now I knew that Reagan definitely didn't have a chance at getting in good with moms.

"Ma, I really have a good feeling that Reagan is telling the truth about her situation. I really do like her, so please just find it in your heart to show her some respect. If not for her, please do it for me. If I'm making a mistake, I'm man enough to accept my mistakes and learn from them. I appreciate you listening and being here, but I'm a grown man. The same goes for Armani. She's a grown woman, and if her marrying Marcus is a mistake, she'll find out in due time and learn from her mistake. I just can't be the one to break up something that just might be ordained by God."

My mom sat down in front of me with her hands clasped underneath her chin. I could tell she was disappointed in me and didn't have the words to explain just how disappointed she was.

"Ok. You're right. We all have to learn from our mistakes. Just be careful. You're treading dangerous waters and I just don't want to see you get hurt."

"Understood."

Moms and I finished dinner and tried talking about other things. I tried my best to bring a smile to her face. She would smile for a moment, but not the big, beautiful, genuine smile I was used to seeing. It was forced, but I knew I couldn't ask for much more. At least not today.

Chapter Twenty-Eight ~ Armani

It was exactly one week before I would become Mrs. Armani Atkins and tonight was my bachelorette dinner, then after-party. I left all the planning up to my three friends, LaDonna, Tara, and Tamia, who were with me when Marcus and I first met. It would be a nice reunion for us since we didn't get to see each other often. We all had our own busy lives now with successful careers and families. Well, Tara and Tamia were married with children, but LaDonna was the one who ended up with a baby and a baby daddy, however, she still had a very successful career as a celebrity make-up artist. I remembered the days when we all worked for *Couture*, doing totally different things for the magazine. I was the only one that was still there. The other three ladies branched off to do independent work, which I didn't blame them for. LaDonna made so much more money being an independent celebrity make-up artist than she did doing make up for photo shoots when working for *Couture*.

"Mani! Your ride is here to pick you up," Marcus yelled from downstairs as I was finishing up my hair.

I looked out my bedroom window and saw a limo waiting out front. My girls told me someone would be here to pick me up, but I had never imagined it would be a limo. I got even more excited as to what my evening would consist of. It had been a long time since I'd had fun with just the girls and I was definitely looking forward to it.

"Ok. I'll be down in a ..."

Marcus walked in as I was screaming down to him.

"Damn, you look gorgeous, woman! You sure I can't go with you? You might need a bodyguard to keep all the dogs off of you."

I smiled and said, "Thank you, but I'll be just fine!"

I looked in the mirror and finalized my look with Ombre lips to match my wine colored mini bodycon dress. I could truly say I was feeling myself, and just knowing this day had come had caused reality to truly start to set in.

"Ok, baby! I'll see you later!" I said as I grabbed my phone and keys, and carefully walked down the stairs in my five-inch heels.

Marcus followed behind and said, "Ok, love. Have a good time, and don't have too much fun without me."

I looked at Marcus up and down and said, "You're looking pretty debonair. You got plans of your own?" I asked curiously. I had just noticed how good he was looking and smelling.

"Me and some of the guys from work may go out and have a few drinks. That's all."

"Oh ... Ok ..."

"Is that ok with you?"

"It's fine. I just hadn't heard you mention anything about it 'til now."

"It was a last minute thing. I didn't want to be sitting here alone all night since I don't have to work."

Oh, like the many of nights I've sat home alone? I thought to myself. Something didn't sit right with me, but this was my night to have fun and I wasn't about to let it be ruined by wondering what Marcus had up his sleeve.

I gave Marcus a soft kiss on the lips, trying not to mess up my lipstick. "Don't wait up," I said, as I winked and strutted out the door.

I had no idea where my dinner was being held. I just looked out the window as the limo driver drove me to the secret destination. Wherever we were going seemed like it was taking forever to get there. Tamia called while I was on the way, making sure the limo had picked me up and that we were en route.

"We're on the way, and I would tell you how far away we are, but as you know, I have no idea where I'm going, so I'll see you when I see you!" I said sarcastically right before hanging up on her. I giggled to myself and became excited all over again after talking to my longtime friend.

The limo finally pulled up in front of Charisma, which was one of the most popular restaurants in the area. The girls had already outdone themselves and the night had just begun. The limo driver got out and opened my door.

"A hostess by the name of Bridgette should be at the desk waiting for you," the driver said.

"Ok. Thank you," I said politely and smiled.

The driver nodded and walked back around to get back into the limo.

As I began walking into the restaurant, I could've sworn I heard someone call my name. I looked back and saw Keith waving and walking towards me. I stood within the crowd of people waiting for Keith to catch up.

Keith finally caught up and said, "I thought that was you! Wow, you look amazing!"

I blushed and said, "Thank you. You look quite suave yourself."

"Well, I do what I can do," Keith said, playfully popping his collar. "What's the special occasion?" he asked.

"My bachelorette dinner and party."

"Oh, ok. Well let me walk you inside," Keith said as he offered his right arm, and I accepted.

As we walked in, I asked, "What are you doing here?"

"Just here to have a nice dinner with my mom and Reagan. I'm hoping this will help them to get to know each other a little better, so that they can at least be able to tolerate each other."

Keith had already told me that his mom wasn't fond of his situation with Reagan, but what mother would be? I completely understood her concern, and I wasn't even a mother. I also understood Keith's side. He just wanted to make his own mistakes, and for his mother to not say a word. I tried to explain to him that his mother was his mother and was only concerned with his safety.

When we got to the front desk, I saw a hostess standing there whose nametag said "Bridgette". She greeted us and I told her who I was.

"Ok. Right this way!"

Keith looked at me and said, "Oh, do I have the pleasure of escorting the guest of honor to her destination?"

"I guess so!" I said.

We continued to follow Bridgette, and when I assumed we had arrived, she opened the double doors to the room and I saw all of my friends and relatives. I was so surprised! I was only expecting a few close friends, and my mom and dad at most.

I put both of my hands up to my face and began crying like a big baby. I turned to Keith and buried my head in his chest.

"Mission accomplished ladies and gentlemen! You got her to cry! I didn't think she knew how!" Keith jokingly said to the crowd of people who were strangers to him.

Next thing I knew, I heard a familiar voice and someone grabbing my arm.

"Ok. I can take it from here," Marcus said, pulling me away from Keith.

As Marcus tried to get me away from Keith as quickly as possible, I said, "Wait a minute! Can I at least introduce him to my people?"

Marcus released my arm and rolled his eyes. I didn't know what had gotten into Marcus, but I was starting to believe he was definitely threatened by Keith's presence.

"Keith, come with me so I can introduce you to some of the most important people in my life."

Keith looked at his Movado and said, "I'm sorry, I have to head back to the front. My mom and Reagan will be here any minute."

"Ok. One second." I turned around to the crowd and said, "Hey everyone! This is my co-worker, Keith! Keith, these are my peeps!"

"Hey Keith," everyone said in unison.

"Nice to meet everyone!" Keith said as he waved goodbye.

I was wishing Keith could stay and really get to know the people I loved.

After Keith left, I approached Marcus and said, "What was up with that?"

"With what?"

"You reacting the way you did with Keith."

"People would've thought he was your fiancé and not me. You stroll in here with him on your arm. How do you think that looked?"

I thought about it, and Marcus did have a point. "You're right. I'm woman enough to admit I wouldn't have liked that if the shoe was on the other foot. I apologize."

"Don't worry about it. Enjoy tonight. I love you," Marcus said and kissed me on the lips.

"Love you, too."

I ran over to my momma and daddy and gave them both big hugs. They lived out of state, so it was rare that I would see them. I definitely wasn't planning on seeing them tonight due to the fact they were going to have to fly in next weekend for the wedding. While conversing with my family, my girls managed to pull me to the side asking about Keith.

"So, when were you going to introduce me to your friend, girl? You know I need a good man," LaDonna said.

"Yes! If I was single, I would've been all over that! He is sexy as hell. How do you work with him every day and concentrate at the same time?" Tamia asked.

I tried to act nonchalant by saying, "Are y'all serious?"

Tara was just sitting back in the cut as she always did, not saying a word.

"Tara, did you see anything special about Keith? These ladies act like he's Omari Hardwick or somebody!"

"That negro is fine as fuck and has more swag than any man I've seen in a long time! I wouldn't be surprised if you gave him some once or twice," Tara replied.

One thing about Tara was that she was cool as a cucumber, but when somebody asked for her opinion, she was quick to let you know how she really felt.

"See, now if Tara said it, it has to be true. So how was it?" LaDonna asked.

"Come on now! Y'all know me better than that. I'm as loyal as they come."

"Yeah, she's right y'all. She don't have it in her to do that. Especially with a man like Keith. After you have something like that, there's probably no going back to anything else, period!" Tamia said.

I felt a little offended by Tamia's comment. She acted as if I couldn't pull a man like Keith, but I knew the truth. Of course, I couldn't admit the truth to them, but thinking about it made me smile on the inside.

LaDonna cleared her throat letting us know Marcus was on his way over.

"Hey ladies. What's going on over here?"

"Nothing. Just catching up!" I quickly said, not giving the girls a chance to say a word. All I needed was for them to say the wrong thing, and that would've been anything with the mention of Keith's name.

"So, now I know why you were looking and smelling all good before I left the house! You had me worried for a minute." I said, teasing with Marcus, but telling the truth.

"Baby, you don't have anything to worry about. You're all the woman I need. No one else could possibly compare."

"Get a room!" LaDonna said.

Tamia added, "Yes, please save the vows for the wedding!"

We all had a good time at the dinner. We laughed, ate, and laughed some more. I didn't want the night to end. At the end of dinner when everyone got ready to leave, Marcus gave me a kiss and told me he'd see me later.

"Where are you going?"

"Did you really think men were allowed at the party? Dinner only babes! Now the men have to go!" Tamia said before Marcus could answer.

"Ohhh! Ok, baby. See you later!"

The last to get ready to leave were my parents. They had a rental car and were staying at an Extended Stay hotel not far from my house. I told them they could stay with me, but they refused. They were the private type and liked their own space. I got it honestly. As my parents and I, and the other girls left the room, I saw Keith still sitting at a table with Ms. Angie and Reagan, so I decided to stop and say hello. Everyone else followed.

As soon as Ms. Angie looked up and saw me heading her way, a big smile came across her face and she immediately stood up.

With my tall heels on, I towered over her even more than I did before.

"Hey, Ms. Angie!" I said as I knelt down to give her a hug.

"Hey, baby doll!" she said. "Good seeing you."

I looked at Reagan and said, "Hey, lady!"

"Hey," she replied with the fakest smile I'd ever seen.

I wasn't about to let her mess up my natural high, so I continued doing what I came over to do.

"Ms. Angie, these are my parents, William and Evelyn Blair. Mom and Dad, this is my friend, Keith's mom, Angie Banks.

"Nice to meet you both. You have a beautiful daughter, inside and out. You should be proud," Ms. Angie said as she shook both of my parent's hands.

My mom said, "Thank you, and it's our pleasure! Now, we didn't really get to meet Keith up close and personal."

Keith quickly stood up and shook hands with my dad, and took my mom's hand and kissed it. "Nice meeting you both. Armani is really a great person, like my mom said."

My mom looked at Ms. Angie and said, "What a gentleman you've raised."

"I did the best I could on my own."

"You did a great job," my dad said. "I like y'all. I can tell you're good people."

My girls were quiet. I looked back at them and they were sitting at an empty booth analyzing the situation. I could tell when they were gossiping because that's what we used to do together quite often, and they were definitely gossiping at that moment.

Right before I was able to say, "Let's go," my mom said, "And who is that young lady? Your daughter?"

I could tell Ms. Angie struggled as she tried to keep her smile from turning to a frown, but she did. "No, this is a friend of Keith's. Her name is Raggedy . . ."

Keith quickly interjected and said, "Reagan."

I could not believe Ms. Angie was really about to call that poor girl Raggedy Ann. Keith had told me it was bad, but I was sure it had gotten better. I guess I assumed wrong.

"Nice to meet you, too, Reagan," my mom said. Surprisingly, Reagan also stood up and shook both of my parent's hands.

"Well, we're sorry for interrupting your meals, but I really wanted my parents to meet you guys."

I suddenly heard the clearing of throats behind me, coming from the booth where my girls were sitting.

"Oh, how can I forget y'all? I said, giggling. The three stooges stood up and I introduced them to Keith and his mom. They were more interested in meeting Keith, and they made that quite evident. They couldn't have appeared thirstier than they did. Keith kissed all of their hands and they all acted as if they were going to faint.

"Ok! Party time!" I had to get my parents out of there before my mom asked anymore questions to make everyone uncomfortable. Just when I thought I had succeeded, she stopped walking and started up again.

"Will I be seeing you all at the wedding?" she asked.

Ms. Angie said, "Well I haven't gotten a formal invitation."

"Now, Ms. Angie, I invited Keith, so you know you're invited," I assured her.

"Ok, then I'll be there, Evelyn!"

"Ok, see you then, Angie."

After finally getting my parents out the door, the girls and I jumped in the limo so that the driver could take us to our next destination. It didn't surprise me one bit when we pulled up in front of a strip club. The girls had reserved a VIP section for us where we had the sexiest male strippers to ourselves for the entire night. I was never really a strip club type of girl, but once the girls got enough drinks in me, I was lobbying for lap dances all night long. The last thing I remembered was dancing on stage with the finest strippers I had ever seen, then being carried out to the limo by two of them that I tried to take home with me. I don't think I had ever had so much fun in my life. It was definitely a night to remember.

Chapter Twenty-Nine ~ Keith

As I got ready for Armani's wedding, I had a weird sensation in the pit of my stomach. It felt like a sense of nervousness. A feeling that I would imagine I'd have on my own wedding day. I assumed it was just probably something I had eaten that hadn't quite agreed with me. I was just hoping I would begin to feel better before the wedding.

This entire week, Armani was extremely excited, which showed me how in love she was with Marcus. I allowed myself to finally become genuinely happy for her. I felt like I had done everything I could to help the situation by letting Marcus know what a great girl he had. He should've already known that, but I felt like I had really gotten through to him and he was ready to change for her. Even if I did tell Armani what I saw, it would've been my word against his, and I already knew who she would've believed. Considering how Marcus had worked so hard to make sure I didn't say anything to Armani, I got the assumption that he believed Armani would've believed me over him. I didn't feel that was the case at all. I would've been left looking like a liar and a snitch. On top of that, at the end of the day, I would have lost a great friend. It wasn't worth it.

"Knock-knock," I heard Reagan say as she opened the bathroom door while I stood in the mirror shaving.

"Hey, Babe. How was your nap?"

"It was great. We had a long night last night," she said, winking at me.

Last night was the first full night Reagan and I had spent together and I couldn't even lie. Reagan knew how to treat a man. I had asked her to be my date to Armani's wedding and she accepted, of course. She told me that she told Will that she had to go out of town on business for a couple of days, just so that we'd have plenty of time to spend together. The night before, I took her out for a nice dinner before going downtown to listen to some live Neo-Soul music. I had heard through a few people that Vivian Green and Raheem DeVaughn were in town, so I found some last minute tickets. Reagan smiled the entire night. I could tell that Will didn't do special things for her like that, and she let me know just how much she appreciated it once we got back to my place. We had the best sex we'd had since we had been seeing each other. She was so wild and aggressive. So different from the very first time we'd had sex, but I loved it. She made me smile the rest of the night.

"Yeah, it was a long, beautiful night," I replied. "I see you got the itis after breakfast."

Reagan came closer to me, standing on her tiptoes to give me a kiss. "Yes, I did! Thanks for cooking breakfast for me. At home, I'm normally the one slaving over the stove," she said.

"Well, you already know, I got you. You wouldn't have to worry about a thing if you belonged to me."

Reagan began blushing and brushed her hair back behind her ear with her hand. She looked so sexy wearing my oversized wife-beater, which reminded me that she had never brought in her clothes from out the car.

"As soon as I'm done shaving, I'll get your bag out of the car for you."

"You're such a sweetheart. Thank you," Reagan said, as she proceeded to walk over to the toilet, pulled the wife-beater up over her waist, sat down, and commenced to piss.

Reagan's comfort level around me had skyrocketed. This was something I wasn't used to, but I didn't want to make her feel uncomfortable, so I pretended that what was happening, really wasn't happening. Even when I lived with women, they never just walked in the bathroom and started pissing while I was in there.

After I finished shaving, I grabbed Reagan's keys and went out to the car to grab her bag. I opened her trunk and there were around five or six bags that looked like luggage, so I went back inside and said, "Woman, you look like you're living out of your car. Which bag is the one with your clothes?"

She smiled and said, "All of them!"

"You sure did pack a lot of clothes for just a couple of nights. How in the world did you get away with that?"

"I have my ways!"

I ran back outside, making two trips, lugging in Reagan's bags.

When I was done, she started rummaging through her luggage and asked, "What color are you wearing?"

I pulled out a suit that I had hanging up in the closet, especially for the wedding. Armani had told me her wedding colors were powder blue, mint green, and cream, so I happened to have a beige suit, which just so happened to be Armani, and a blue dress shirt and black tie I'd put together.

"That's nice!" Reagan said. "Now, which one of these bags did I put the blue dress in?"

I gave Reagan a puzzled look as she continued unzipping bags, going through each one. I finally had to ask, "Did you pack a dress in every color?"

"Yeah ... Well, almost every color. I didn't pack a black dress. I just refused to wear black to a wedding, so if that would've been your color of choice, you would have had to do something about that."

"Hmmm . . ."

"Here it is!" Reagan said, holding up a light blue, elegant dress. "I'm glad I went with this blue instead of the royal blue. This one will match you perfectly."

I wanted to someday be in a real relationship with Reagan, but for some reason, she was kinda freaking me out. Maybe because I wasn't expecting this out of her, but who packs every color? Where do they do that at? She could've just called and asked me what color I was wearing. It would've saved her a whole lot of time she spent packing.

"You're going to look even more beautiful than you already are," I said, trying to make light of the situation. Knowing me, I was probably overreacting. I didn't realize it before, but I began to notice something about myself. Anytime something seemed even close to being a committed relationship, I ran, or tried to look for all of the flaws in that person. I would sabotage it in one way or another. I wasn't scared of many things, but commitment was one of them.

After we both got dressed and walked out looking like we were on our way to prom, we headed to the banquet hall where Armani's wedding and reception was being held. It was a beautiful, warm, sunny day outside. Picture perfect for an outdoor wedding. Armani had chosen the most beautiful day of the year to get married.

As I drove, bobbing my head to the music, Reagan said, "Do you think Armani is going to mind me being at her wedding?"

Here she goes again thinking Armani has something against her, I thought.

"Reagan, Armani is marrying her life partner today. This is what is going to be the happiest day of her life. I'm sure you being at the wedding will be the furthest thing from her mind. Like I've tried to stress to you, Armani has absolutely nothing against you."

"Well good, because if she invites you to any other events in the future, she should get used to seeing me on your arm."

I stopped at a red light just in time to look at her and say, "What are you talking about?"

"I told Will it's over between us. I packed most of my clothes and left. I'm all yours, baby! Surprise!" Reagan said, grinning from ear to ear.

I had so many questions running rampant through my mind, but couldn't quite gather my thoughts. As soon as I was getting ready to form a sentence that I was hoping would come out comprehendible, I heard cars behind me honking their horns. I still didn't budge.

"The light is green, baby," Reagan said.

I released the brake and slowly stepped on the gas as cars went around me, flying past.

"So, what did he say?" I finally managed to say.

"He was very angry. He even started crying and begging for me to stay. I told him it wouldn't be fair to him or me if I stayed because I'm in love with someone else and I deserve to be happy. I made sure I told him that he hadn't done anything to make me fall out of love. Shit happens."

Shit just wasn't making sense to me. What did she mean he hadn't done anything? I was pretty sure I wasn't hearing things when she specifically told me he had been cheating on her for years, and even beat her.

"What about the cheating and the beatings?"

I glanced over at Reagan as I drove and it seemed like she was trying to get her thoughts together.

"Well, that's been happening for so long and I've been dealing with it for all this time. I honestly don't feel I can use that as a legit reason for leaving. Loving you is legit."

"What about your girls? You just left them there?"

"I told them as soon as we make arrangements for them, I'll be back to get them. They're ok with their dad for now. He'd never hurt them."

Apparently, Reagan and I had a lot to talk about. I never told her I was ready to be a stepdad, or have teenage girls living with me. I had just pulled up to the banquet hall, so we would have to put this conversation on pause for now.

Before getting out of the car, I said, "We'll continue this later. Once again, we have a lot to talk about."

I walked over to the passenger side door to let Reagan out, and by the expression on her face, I could tell she knew that I wasn't particularly feeling what she had planned out without discussing any of it with me. I offered my arm to her, hoping my reaction hadn't upset her too much. As we walked past the parked cars, I saw my mom's car parked right in front. She was always early for everything.

As we walked, we began to see fountains and finally came across the bridge that I assumed Armani would be walking across to get to her groom, Marcus. We saw hundreds of white chairs for the guests. Many people had already arrived, some sitting and some standing around talking amongst each other.

We both looked around. I used my hand as a visor above my eyes to shield them from the bright sun.

"Do you see my mom?"

Reagan began squinting and said, "There she is," as she pointed towards the front seating area where I saw my mom's golden hair glistening in the sunlight.

We walked over to where my mom was sitting and startled her when I said, "Well, hey beautiful!"

When she noticed it was me, she smiled and stood up to give me a hug.

"Hey handsome! I saved you a seat!" She then noticed I had company and said, "Thankfully there's two seats here. I didn't know you were bringing a guest."

I became worried, but then my mom did the most unexpected thing. She said, "You look lovely, Reagan. Come here and give me a hug."

Reagan smiled and said, "You look lovely, as always," and hugged my mom without hesitation.

It was crazy how my mom was all of a sudden taking to Reagan, when at that moment, I was the one having mixed emotions about what was going on between us. As I sat there, between my mom and Reagan, I kept looking at the time, getting more and more anxious by the minute. My stomach was

in knots and started growling uncontrollably. Loud enough that
my mom and Reagan both heard.

"You ok, son?" my mom asked.

"Yeah, I'm cool. My stomach has just been bothering me all
day."

"Nerves, huh?" she said.

"I think it's just something I ate."

She whispered, "You know, our bodies always have a way of
speaking to us. Sometimes we need to listen."

It wasn't the time or place for this conversation, and I could
tell Reagan was being nosey, trying to ear hustle, so I decided
to excuse myself for a minute.

"I'll be back."

I walked around the venue, taking in all the peacefulness
within the entire scenery. I decided to walk inside to get a peak
of the room where the reception would be held. I got a clear
view of everything through the crystal clear glass. Powder blue,
mint green, and cream, exactly how Armani wanted it. After
admiring all the décor, I searched for the restroom, and
unintentionally walked right into the room where Armani and
her bridesmaids were completing their final touches.

"Oops! I'm so sorry!" I said as I backed out of the room and
shut the door.

As I walked away, I thought about the picture perfect vision
of Armani I had just seen on the other side of that door, when
all of a sudden, I heard her call my name. With my hands in my
pockets, I stopped and turned around. I saw a halo around
Armani's entire silhouette. She looked like an angel coming
towards me. I walked towards her as she came closer and
closer.

Once we were in arm's distance of one another, I took both
of her hands into mine, shook my head and said, "You are
stunning."

"Thank you," she said, as she smiled, but her hands shook
nervously.

"You ok, love?"

"Yeah, just some pre-wedding jitters, but I'm fine. I know I'm marrying my soul-mate. He loves me unconditionally, and I know that's hard to do. No one could love me the way he does, and I'm so deeply in love with him."

I didn't know why, but it seemed as though Armani was either trying to convince me that she was doing the right thing, or wanted confirmation from me that she was.

"You're going to make a wonderful wife and I'm sure Marcus knows just what he has," I said.

Armani held her head back trying to hold back her tears.

"Please don't mess up your make-up. I don't want to be the blame for that!"

Armani laughed and gave me hug. Before I knew it I whispered in her ear, "I love you, girl."

There was a short silence as we stood there holding each other. She then said, "I love you, too."

At that moment, one of her bridesmaids came out of nowhere and said, "Armani, come on! We only have about twenty minutes left."

Armani released me and I caught her arm and let my fingers run down its length until our hands briefly met, and then parted. She blew me a kiss and headed back towards her dressing room.

I finally found the men's restroom. I just needed a place to get my thoughts and emotions together. I walked in and went into one of the first stalls that I saw. I stood there and took a deep breath. I could smell the scent of Armani all over my suit. I felt like I had just given my angel permission to leave me and to go and take care of someone who didn't know her true value. I had to trust my instincts that I was still doing the right thing. While I stood there trying to remove the doubt from my mind and remain optimistic, I heard mumbling outside the restroom door. I then heard the door open and the voices continued as they came inside. The odd thing was that I heard a man and woman's voice.

"Check the stalls," the woman whispered.

I didn't know why I was doing it at the moment, but I quietly placed my feet on top of the toilet. I could hear the man and woman's feet as they moved throughout the large restroom, trying to be sure no one was inside.

"Lock the door," she demanded.

"What is up with you? It's my wedding day. I don't have time for your temper tantrums today."

"How can you not understand how I feel, Marcus?!?! I can't do this. I cannot sit out there and watch you marry another woman when I know you don't love her. You love me! Why are you doing this?"

"Tammy, like I've told you, nothing between me and you is going to change. I just have so much time invested in her. She'll lose it if I left now, but who knows what the future will hold. You know I'm madly in love with you. I'll continue to shower you with any and everything you want."

"Prove it," Tammy said.

"What?"

"I said prove it! Fuck me right here on your wedding day."

I couldn't believe what I was hearing. Marcus still hadn't learned. He was still playing Armani for a fool after almost getting caught up. This dude just didn't care.

"You want this dick right now, huh?"

"Yes, baby. Let me take it out for you."

Next thing I heard was a bunch of moaning. I slowly got down from the toilet and cracked open the stall door. I couldn't believe what I was hearing until I actually saw it with my own eyes. What I saw made me feel the pain that Armani would've felt if she had seen what I was looking at. The same woman I saw Marcus with at the Sybaris was sitting up on the counter, and Marcus was fucking the shit out of her without a bit of shame. I took my cell phone out of my pocket and hit record. I couldn't let Armani go out like this.

I waited a few minutes after they left to come from out of the stall and get back to Reagan and my mom. I knew they were probably wondering where I was. When I got back to my seat, they were both looking concerned.

"Is everything ok, bae?" Reagan asked, grabbing my hand to hold.

"Yeah, everything is good."

My mom looked at me with worry on her face. "I hope what I said didn't get you upset. Just do what's in your heart. Don't let me persuade you to do something you don't want to do. I'm sure you'll do the right thing," she said.

I sat there holding on tightly to my phone, not sure what I was going to do with the evidence I had just created. Just then, I heard music begin to play, and Marcus and his best man walked out and got into position. Once they were in position, Stevie Wonder's "You and I" began to play, and the wedding party began walking out, beginning with Armani's mom who was escorted down the aisle by one of the gentlemen I'd seen at Armani's bachelorette dinner.

I couldn't keep my eyes off Marcus. I couldn't believe he could just stand there like he hadn't just fucked another woman in the men's bathroom. I was just looking for a hint of remorse come across his face, as if that would've changed the way I felt about him at that moment. He kept looking out in the crowd with this silly ass grin on his face, and when I finally pinpointed where he was looking, I just shook my head. He kept smiling at the other woman, who was sitting across the aisle from us, and she was smiling right back at him. He then took his index finger and swiped it underneath his nose, winking as his whore. I looked around at everyone who was there to share this "special" moment with Armani and Marcus, trying to see if anyone else was taking notice of what was going on. Everyone, except for me, was fixated on, and taking pictures of the beautiful wedding party coming down the aisle; clueless as to what was going on right in front of their faces.

I took my handkerchief and wiped my face as beads of sweat began to form on my forehead. I wasn't hot from the temperature outside, but from the anger that was bubbling up inside of me. As angry as I was becoming, I tried my best to keep my cool. The entire wedding party had taken their places, and I knew Armani would soon reveal herself as soon as I heard K-Ci and JoJo's "This Very Moment" start playing. Everyone stood up, getting their cameras ready. We soon saw Armani walking over the bridge, with her dad next to her. She looked absolutely gorgeous. I stood there smiling as if she was coming to meet with me. I felt myself tear up, so, hoping no one would notice, I tilted my head back just enough to still make it look like a natural motion, and blinked a few times.

My mom looked up at me smiling and said, "She's so beautiful."

"She is," I said.

Reagan grabbed my hand, and said, "Oh my God! That dress is gorgeous."

Everything Reagan did and said was now getting underneath my skin. That comment right there bothered me because instead of complimenting Armani, she preferred to comment on Armani's dress. Reagan was truly showing me her true colors and I honestly didn't know if she was the right one for me. I wasn't going to make that decision, however, until we had our long talk.

Armani's radiant smile captured everyone's attention as she came closer and closer. My mom snapped a picture as she walked past us. I caught her eye and she winked, but as soon as she saw Reagan next to me, her entire expression changed.

My mom saw what had just happened and said, "You look beautiful, sweetie!"

Armani's smile reappeared as she blew a kiss to my mom.

Armani's dad released her to Marcus, and sat down in the front row next to Armani's mom. The music stopped, and the pastor began to speak. Armani and Marcus were lost in each other's eyes. I looked over at Marcus' side chick, and she looked like she was ready to explode. As I said before, she was also a very attractive woman. I just wondered why she chose to settle on a man who was already taken.

Marcus and Armani affirmed their vows to one another, and just hearing Marcus say his made me sick to my stomach. He had already broken his vows a million times over. I knew Armani truly meant hers because she kept getting choked up as she spoke every other word. Tears were streaming down her face. Marcus shed not one tear. I didn't understand how he could marry someone as beautiful as Armani and not get emotional as soon as seeing her walk across that bridge.

"If anyone has any just cause as to why these two should not be married, please speak now or forever hold your peace," the pastor said, as the wedding was coming to its conclusion.

Everyone remained quiet with smiles upon their faces. I saw my mom give me the side eye, but didn't say a word. Side chick cleared her throat, drawing attention to herself for a short moment.

"Ok. Well, I now pronounce. . ."

Something in me would not allow me to sit there and just do nothing. Before I knew it, I was standing and all eyes were on me.

"I have something to say." My mom stepped out of my way as I walked into the aisle.

"Ok, son. We're waiting," the pastor said.

I looked around and saw that everyone's face was expressing a different emotion towards me. Reagan was shaking her head with tears streaming down her face. Marcus' face was full of rage. Armani looked confused, yet, still beautiful as ever. My mom's face was the deciding factor for me to proceed. She smiled at me and nodded.

I began, "Since no one who knows exactly what's going on wants to be honest, I guess I will have to be the one."

"I know what's going on! You think you're just gonna take my wife from me?" a deep, angry voice said from behind.

Before I could turn around completely, I heard a shot being fired, and Reagan screamed, "Will! No!"

I saw a tall, muscle-bound man standing there with a gun in his hand pointed right at me, looking like he was ready to fire it again. I looked down on the ground, and there lay my mother.

She had jumped in front of the bullet to protect me. I tried to quickly get down to the ground with my mom, who wasn't moving, but as soon as I did, Will made it very clear that he was in control.

"Don't move!" Will shouted at me.

"Ok, man. Calm down," I said, as I stood straight up and put my hands up in the air, extremely worried about my mom's condition. I felt helpless. Everyone else in the crowd remained quiet and did not move.

"Look what you've done, Will!" Reagan shouted.

"No, look what you've done! All these years, I've been dealing with you messing around on me with both women and other men. What is this? Number ten? Eleven? I've treated you so good, regardless of everything you've done to me, and you still can't do right. After all I've been through with you, you had to expect for me to snap sooner or later!"

I stood there, still not moving, watching Will wave his gun around as he spoke to Reagan. I kept glancing down at my mom, wanting to so badly to pick her up and carry her out of there.

"I'm sorry!" Reagan said, "But this isn't the answer. We can get help. We'll go to counseling. I know you're a good man, and I have the problem. We'll fix it," she said with tears in her eyes, as she slowly walked towards her husband.

I stood there watching, as I saw Ben, who was also attending the wedding, slowly coming up behind Will. When he was only a foot away from Will, Reagan looked at him, causing Will to realize someone was sneaking up on him. When he attempted to turn around, Ben quickly tackled him. The gun flew out of Will's hand as he hit the ground. Ben rolled him over on his stomach, handcuffed him, and began reading him his rights. I quickly fell down to my knees, and my mom was unresponsive.

"Ma! Wake up! Please wake up! Somebody call an ambulance!"

<u>Chapter Thirty ~ Armani</u>

I stood in shock, remaining in the exact same spot where I had just said my vows to the love of my life, as everyone scrambled in panic, looking for a safe exit. I watched as the owners of the venue tried to safely evacuate the area in an organized manner. I saw Ms. Angie on the ground, lifeless and bleeding. Tears streamed down my face. Keith was knelt down beside her, shouting for her not to leave him. I saw my mom and dad by Keith's side, calling for help. Reagan sat in her seat, with her face in her hands, looking helpless. I saw Ben in the distance, walking the handcuffed gunman, who happened to be Reagan's husband, to his squad car. I felt like I was watching a horror film. Both, the pastor and my groom had left me at the altar. I looked around for Marcus, and when I finally pinpointed his location, he was hugging and consoling his co-worker, Tamara, who looked to be crying.

I slowly left the altar, looking back and forth at Keith and Marcus, deciding in which direction to go. I didn't have to think very hard about it. When I made it over to Keith, he had his mom's head propped up on his lap, gently rubbing her head as his tears fell from his face onto hers. It didn't look good. I held Keith, trying to calm him down as we waited on the ambulance.

"Who could do something like this, at a wedding of all places? I just don't understand!" my mom said.

At that moment, Reagan got up and walked off without saying a word. We then heard sirens, and the ambulance and three squad cars came speeding through the grass as we waved to signal to them where we were. The EMT's worked extremely quickly getting Ms. Angie onto a stretcher and into the ambulance. I heard them say that her pulse was very faint, which worried me. Keith tried to jump in with his mom, and the EMT shook his head, saying the police needed to speak with all the witnesses.

"I need to go with her! She needs me!" Keith shouted.

I pleaded with the EMT and said, "This is her only child. The only person she has. Please let him go."

The EMT looked at Keith and took a deep breath. "Ok, Sir, but you have to calm down. We're going to do everything we can to try to help your mom."

After the ambulance pulled off, two cops then came over to question us. My mom and dad didn't have specific details. All they were able to tell the cops was a madman came through and shot Ms. Angie. As I told the entire story to the cops, my parents looked at me in astonishment. The cops asked where Reagan was so they could get a statement from her, but she was nowhere in sight. My mom asked them if we were safe and they assured my mom that the gunman was acting alone, and Ben had already apprehended the suspect and taken him in.

After the cops left, I gave my mom and dad a hug. I couldn't even imagine what Keith was going through. Minutes later, Marcus came strutting over as my parents and I were discussing what had just happened. I looked in the direction of where I had last seen Marcus standing with Tamara, and saw her nowhere in sight.

"See, that's why you have to be careful of the type of people you befriend and invite to nice events. Some people just aren't used to nice things," Marcus said.

I looked at him and said, "Are you serious right now? Do you understand that Keith's mom was just shot and may not make it? You're more concerned with where Keith came from rather than the condition of his mom! And why in the hell were you over there consoling your co-worker and not me? The person you were supposed to be marrying today!"

Marcus grabbed my hands and said, "I'm sorry, baby. I didn't mean anything by it. I just wanted your day to be special, and yes, I'm a little upset that it wasn't as perfect as I'd imagined it. And about Tammy, she was freaked out because she said a bullet flew right past her head. I saw you were ok, so I went to see what was going on with her. You know I love you and I'm going to always make sure you're good first and foremost."

I sarcastically giggled and said, "A bullet flew past her head, huh? There was only one shot and it hit Ms. Angie, so what imaginary bullet flew past Miss Tammy's head?"

"Baby, I'm just telling you what she told me. I'm sorry for making you feel insignificant, but you know that's definitely not the case."

My mom interrupted and said, "Come on. Let's all go. We are all understandably emotional. It has been a long day full of all kinds of emotions. Let's all just go home and pray for Angie."

"You're right, Ma. Let's go."

As we began walking, I almost stepped on a cell phone that was on the ground. I knelt down to pick it up and the only person with a phone case as ugly as that was Keith. I took it with me so I could give it to him when I saw him.

Before I got in the car with Marcus, my parents asked if I wanted them to come by the house.

"No, I'll be fine, but thanks. I just really want to get some rest. Today has truly been an emotional roller coaster, and I'm still not married."

"Well, call me if you need anything. You know where I am," my mom said.

My mom blew me a kiss before they pulled off and headed back to their hotel.

The ride home was quiet. Because of everything that happened, I had forgotten all about Keith standing up to say something at the wedding before Will fired that shot. I was curious as to what in the world he possibly had to say.

"Marcus," I said.

"Yeah, babe."

"What do you think Keith was going to say when he stood up at the wedding? It seems to me he obviously thought he had a good reason for us not to be married."

"I know for a fact he didn't have a good reason. What I believe is your "friend" has a thing for you and wants you for himself. He'll say or do anything to get you." Marcus glanced over at me and said, "Even if he has to lie. When a man sees something he wants, he's willing to do anything to get it."

"Maybe you're right," I said.

I honestly couldn't believe Keith would've waited until my wedding day to profess his love for me. He had plenty of opportunities to tell me if he had those kinds of feelings for me. I knew for a fact that he had deep feelings for Reagan, so what Marcus was saying was not logical at all.

After we finally got home, I wanted to call Keith, but I had his cell phone, and I wasn't sure which hospital they had gone to, so for now, I would just wait to see if he'd call. My phone was blowing up with calls and texts from my girls making sure I was ok. I didn't feel like talking, but I did text them to let them know I was fine and I'd talk to them later. After the excitement, everyone ran out of there so fast, I didn't see anyone before they left, but I couldn't blame them. I took my wedding dress off and hung it back up in the same place it had been hanging before I had put it on today. I took a long, hot shower, and at the same time, had a long, hard cry as I prayed for every situation that was going on around me. I knew that everything happened for a reason, but I needed so badly for God to reveal to me why these things were happening. I prayed for revelation and clarity. I felt like my mind had been clouded and I had been blinded for a very long time. I was realizing that since I had been with Marcus, my life was consistently only involving him and work. I needed balance. Things needed to change. I needed to sometimes spend time with my friends and family. I had been abandoning some very important people in my life, and this past week, I realized how much I had missed them.

I wished all the time that Marcus would desire to hang out with my friends and their significant others, or go out of town with me to visit my parents, but he just never seemed to mesh well with my people. He always seemed to feel out of place the few times we were all together. I secretly wished he was like Keith when it came to family. Even though it was only him and his mom, they were so tight knit. Even when it came to friendships, they were good, loyal people. I saw how easily they connected with my parents, and it immediately touched my heart. Both of Marcus' parents had passed away years before I met him, so I had no idea of what type of people they were. He never said much about them, except for they weren't very close. That's why I tried to bring him in and make him feel comfortable, showing him how it felt to have a close knit family, but all he seemed to do was cause me to be more like him . . . Distant. Marcus was a good man, and I was going to continue to pray for him to be the man God meant for him to be.

After spending an hour in the shower, I threw on my robe, and went halfway down the stairs where I saw Marcus sitting in the front of the TV, texting on his phone.

"You getting a lot of text messages from friends, too?" I asked, causing Marcus to jump and quickly put his phone away.

He turned around and said, "Yeah. I was just texting back and forth with Eric about what was going on."

"Ok, well I'm about to lay down and try to get some rest."

"Ok. I'll be up there soon."

I went back to the bedroom and walked past my dresser, glancing at Keith's phone sitting there. I got in the bed and turned the TV on, but I continuously looked over at my dresser. Keith's phone was calling me. I didn't know why I was so curious to see what was in it, or what it would matter to me in the first place. I guess I was just being a woman and wanted to be nosey. I jumped up out of the bed, ran and grabbed his phone, and jumped back in bed. I went straight to his text messages and saw a million messages back and forth between him and Reagan. I only read a few of them, but from what I read, he was such a gentleman with her. He was giving her time to get her complicated situation resolved, but she seemed like she was wanting and demanding a lot more from him than he was ready to give her until she left Will.

All the other messages were from me and his mom. It looked as though Keith was actually being loyal to a married woman, which was very bizarre to me. I knew for a fact he was definitely a lady's man.

I saw his gallery, but was a little scared to look. I didn't need to see any nude pictures of Reagan, which I was sure there would probably be at least a few of, so I put the phone down on my nightstand. I tried watching TV again, aimlessly flicking through the channels. I still wasn't satisfied. I had to see what else was in that phone. I grabbed it off of my nightstand and clicked on the gallery, closing my eyes at the same time, afraid of what I might see. I then slowly opened them back up, hoping I didn't open them to a surprise.

What should not have been much of a surprise to me, because he loved himself so much, was the number of selfies Keith had! I did see a recent video that he had recorded. From the still image, it looked like a sexual video of him and a woman. It was too small to really see, so I hit play. Apparently, the volume on Keith's phone was as high as it possibly could've gone because the moaning in that video must've echoed throughout the entire house. I kept pressing the volume button trying to hurry and turn it down before Marcus heard, but I suddenly stopped trying when I paid close attention to the screen and realized the man and woman was not Keith and Reagan, or any other woman, but was actually Marcus and Tamara.

I sat there watching Marcus fuck another woman while wearing his wedding tux. All I could think about was how much Marcus had to have hated me to do me like that.

Marcus came walking in the room and said, "What are you in here doing? Watching porn without me?"

With a straight face, still staring at the phone's screen, I said, "I guess you can call it that. Not very good porn, but it's porn."

Marcus frowned up his face and snatched the phone from me saying, "What is that?"

As he looked at it, I said in a very calm voice, "It's my revelation that I just asked God for. Why did you stay, Marcus? Why did you even ask me to marry you?"

Marcus stood there looking pitiful. He looked as if he was the one who was hurt.

When coming up with what he felt were the best words to say to me, he cleared his throat and said, "This is the longest real relationship I've ever been in, and I truly do love you, so I felt marrying you was the right thing to do. I knew if I did try to leave, you would be devastated. I know how weak you can be in stressful situations, and I didn't want you to go through the misery of not having me by your side. That's how I fell for Tammy. She's such a strong woman. So different from you, but right now with all that is happening, I realize that I only want you, and not her."

I got up out of the bed, snatched Keith's phone from Marcus, and began getting dressed.

"Where you going?" he asked, as if he had said or done nothing wrong.

"I'm going to be with people who care about me as much as I care about them. Make sure you and all of your shit is out of my house when I get back. Whatever is still here when I get back will be destroyed."

"Where am I supposed to go?"

"I really don't care where you go, but I do hope you were at least cheating with someone who has their own house! Go stay with Tammy, since that's who you like to fuck in bathrooms on your wedding day! Hell, you're probably paying for her to live somewhere, so go get what's yours!"

I ran down the stairs straight out the front door, got in my car, and sped off. What was strange was that I wasn't angry or sad. I felt relieved. Relieved that I hadn't made the mistake of marrying someone that never really loved me. I just wished I had found out sooner so I hadn't wasted so much time with a man who wasn't worthy of me. This experience gave truth to the saying that everyone and everything in your life is either a lesson or a blessing, and Marcus had definitely been a lesson. It was now time for me to find my blessing.

Chapter Thirty-One ~ Keith

As I remained right next to my momma's bedside, I just kept hearing her tell me how I was treading dangerous waters, and even how Reagan may have been lying to me about how bad her marriage was. She ended up being right once again. Reagan wasn't the one being cheated on, like she had told me. She acted so innocent, as if she was the victim, when she had done this several times, and not with only other men! With women, too! It all made me wonder if anything she had told me was the truth. For once in life, I was the one who got played. I fell for Reagan's game, big time! Even though I hadn't listened to my mom, she still loved me enough to take a bullet for me. I loved my momma more than life itself and I just prayed that God would let me keep her here with me. She was all I had left. She was all I really ever had and I didn't know what I would do if I lost her. The doctors had already performed surgery to remove the bullet that was lodged in her chest. She still hadn't awakened and the doctor said they had done everything they possibly could, but couldn't make any promises about which way this might go. Basically, all we could do was wait.

This was the last thing I would've thought could happen due to my poor choices. I wanted Will and Reagan to rot in hell. They deserved each other. If I hadn't been here caring for my mom, I would've probably gone to wherever will was being held and killed his ass. Then I would've hunted Reagan down and killed her ass, too. I wished at that moment that I could've just gone back in time and ignored all of Reagan's advances. All of this could've been avoided. I had a habit of thinking about what ifs when what I needed to do was deal with what I was being confronted with right at that moment. I needed to pray for my mom's healing. I took my mom's hand into mine and kissed it.

"Please, God, don't take her away from me. Please!" I continued to hold my mom's hand, and put my head face down on the hospital bed, not knowing what else I could do. I felt helpless once again.

I heard keys and a knock on the door, and I turned around to see who it was. It was Armani, looking very different from when I had seen her a few hours earlier, but still beautiful.

I was so happy to see a familiar face coming to support me. I stood up and gave her a hug.

"Thanks for coming. I was going to call you, but I lost my cell phone somewhere and there's no phone in this room."

Armani reached into her purse and said, "Here you go," as she handed me my phone. "I found it in the grass after you left."

"Thank you."

"How's she doing?" she said as she walked over to the other side of the bed and began gently rubbing her hand through my mom's blonde tresses.

"She hasn't woken up at all. She went through surgery to have the bullet removed from her chest, but now it's just a waiting game."

Armani pulled a chair close to my mom's bed and caressed her arm as she spoke softly to her. "Miss Angie, I know you can hear me. You have your baby boy sitting here worried about you, but I know you're just resting. I knew how strong you were from the first time I met you. That's what intrigued me about you. Just get your rest for now, and get your words ready for Keith, because I know you have more than a few of them, all in love."

Armani looked up and smiled at me. "She's not going anywhere," she said.

"How are you so sure?" I asked her.

"Because she has to stay here and take care of you, silly!"

Armani made me laugh, and actually gave me some hope. The doctor had almost made me lose faith that my mom could make it through this, when my mom always told me that God always had the final say.

"So, I was thinking about something once I got home," Armani said.

"What's that?"

"What was it you were going to say when you stood up at the wedding?"

I knew Armani would ask that question sooner or later, but I was hoping it would be later. I no longer wanted to tell her about Marcus after everything else that had happened. I practically ruined her entire wedding, and I definitely didn't want to add salt to the wound. I looked at her as she looked at me for the truth, but unfortunately I couldn't give her that at that moment, if ever. I was already hurting. I didn't want her to hurt, too.

"It was nothing. I think I might've felt a little bothered that you were about to marry Marcus. A little jealous, I guess."

"So, you mean to tell me you thought you had feelings for me for a moment, and was going to profess it to me in the middle of my wedding?"

I looked down and said, "Yes."

"Liar!" Armani said. "You can't even look me in my eyes."

"Can we just leave it alone? Trust me when I say it wasn't important."

"Can I tell you something?" Armani asked.

I sat there without saying a word, wondering what it was she possibly needed to tell me. It sounded like even if I said no, she couldn't tell me something, she was going to tell me anyway.

"Well, can I?" she asked.

"Go right ahead."

"Well, I didn't want to snoop, but something just kept telling me to look, so I kinda went through your phone, and I saw the video."

My heart skipped a beat and my eyes got big as quarters. I sat back in my seat and said, "Oh shit. Are you ok?"

"Yes, surprisingly I'm fine. I asked God for a revelation and he gave it to me."

"I'm so sorry. I didn't mean for you to find out like that."

"But God did, and he makes no mistakes, so don't be sorry. So, is that what you were going to say at the wedding?"

"Not quite."

Armani looked confused and said, "Then what was it?"

Since Armani had already seen the video, there was no point in me trying to keep the rest a secret. I began telling her how I'd seen Marcus and Tammy at the Sybaris a while back, but didn't feel it was my place to say anything. I could tell she became a little disappointed in me when I told her about the agreement Marcus and I made, but the disappointment she had in him trumped everything. I told her I truly felt he was going to make a change after I had caught him up, and if I didn't sincerely feel that way and felt it was a necessity to tell her, I would have before it got this far.

"So, where is he now?" I asked Armani.

"He better be at my house packing his shit. I told him to be gone by the time I get back."

Marcus had messed up with Armani and there was absolutely nothing he could do to fix it. I didn't break the news to Armani, but God still made sure she received the memo.

An uncomfortable silence came over the room, and with that, Armani and I kept glancing at each other, but kept avoiding eye contact at the same time. Suddenly, Armani walked over and sat on my lap.

"Can I tell you something else?" she asked.

"Oh boy. What now?"

"Nothing bad. I just want to be honest with you, and hopefully you'll be honest with me," Armani said as she ran her fingertips across the top of my head.

"I don't want to be anything but honest with you," I replied.

"Good. Well, I just want you to know, that day when we were intimate, I felt a very strong connection to you, and whatever bond we formed that day, it seems to be unbreakable."

One of my mom's machines began beeping. "Hold that thought," I said as I ran to get the nurse. I ran back in with the nurse, and Armani was standing over my mom talking to her. The nurse began pressing buttons and the beeping stopped.

"Is everything ok?" Armani asked the nurse.

"Yes! Actually, things are looking up. Her blood pressure is stabilizing. Are you two in here talking to her?"

Armani and I looked at each other and starting smiling.

"You can say that," I said.

"There's not medical proof that people in this state can hear what's going on around them, but I tend to believe they can, so keep talking," the nurse said. She told us to let her know if we needed anything else, and left us to continue our conversation. I sat back down, and Armani sat back on my lap.

"I think your mom is enjoying listening in on our conversation," Armani said.

"I'm sure she is. Now, what were you saying?"

"I was basically trying to say I have feelings for you that I have been trying to deny, but I can no longer deny them. I feel like I've known you and your mom for years, and the two of you already feel like family to me."

After Armani finished expressing to me how she felt, I said, "What would you say if I said I've been feeling the same way, but had too much pride to tell you because I saw how in love you were with Marcus, and I didn't want to be left looking like a fool?"

Armani turned up her lips and said, "I don't believe it."

"It's the truth. I've been secretly in love with you."

"You love me?" Armani asked.

"No. I'm in love with you."

I gently caressed Armani's face and gazed into her eyes. I gave her a peck on the lips and said, "Let's give it a try."

Armani reached in and kissed me again. "I'm in love with you, too," she said before gently kissing me on the forehead.

"I told you she was the one. Did I have to almost die for you to realize that?"

Armani and I jumped up out of the chair and looked at my mom who was laying there with her eyes barely open, still trying to smile.

"Thank God you're ok, Ma!" I said kissing her on the cheek.

"You didn't think you were getting rid of me that easily, did you?" she said in a weak, but adamant voice. She looked over at Armani, and said, "I heard you. You knew all the time I'd be ok. My son needs you to help him to be able to have the kind of optimism and faith that you have. Thank God for you."

"No. Thank God for the both of you," Armani said, as she knelt down and hugged my momma's neck.

From the time Armani and I first met, 'til now, we had both noticeably become two very different people. We brought out the best in each other and didn't even realize it. We always had the qualities that we were able to bring out of each other, but no one else who had entered our lives over the years had ever been able to bring them out. That's how you know when you've met your soul-mate. They help you to become a better person . . . that person you are meant to be, and they are truly your better half. God has molded someone just for you, and the only person who can get in the way of you ending up with that person, is you. I knew for a fact that the next chapter of our lives would be full of genuine love and happiness.

The End

Office Affairs
By
Qiana Rae

www.ingramcontent.com/pod-product-compliance
Lightning Source LLC
Chambersburg PA
CBHW030026180626
46810CB00001B/231